ROYAL DESTINY

The Playboy Prince

and

The Name of the Game

Sign of Seven Trilogy
Blood Brothers • *The Hollow* • *The Pagan Stone*

Bride Quartet
Vision in White • *Bed of Roses* • *Savor the Moment* • *Happy Ever After*

The Inn Boonsboro Trilogy
The Next Always • *The Last Boyfriend* • *The Perfect Hope*

The Cousins O'Dwyer Trilogy
Dark Witch • *Shadow Spell* • *Blood Magick*

The Guardians Trilogy
Stars of Fortune • *Bay of Sighs* • *Island of Glass*

The Chronicles of The One
Year One • *Of Blood and Bone* • *The Rise of Magicks*

The Dragon Heart Legacy
The Awakening • *The Becoming* • *The Choice*

The Lost Bride Trilogy
Inheritance

EBOOKS BY NORA ROBERTS

Cordina's Royal Family
Affaire Royale • *Command Performance* • *The Playboy Prince* • *Cordina's Crown Jewel*

The Donovan Legacy
Captivated • *Entranced* • *Charmed* • *Enchanted*

The O'Hurleys
The Last Honest Woman • *Dance to the Piper* • *Skin Deep* • *Without a Trace*

Night Tales
Night Shift • *Night Shadow* • *Nightshade* • *Night Smoke* • *Night Shield*

ROYAL DESTINY

The Playboy Prince

and

The Name of the Game

TWO NOVELS IN ONE

NORA ROBERTS

St. Martin's Paperbacks

Published in the United States by St. Martin's Paperbacks, an imprint of St. Martin's Publishing Group.

ROYAL DESTINY: THE PLAYBOY PRINCE copyright © 1987 by Nora Roberts and THE NAME OF THE GAME copyright © 1988 by Nora Roberts.

For information, address St. Martin's Publishing Group, 120 Broadway, New York, NY 10271.

www.stmartins.com

ISBN: 978-1-250-32233-3

Our books may be purchased in bulk for promotional, educational, or business use. Please contact your local bookseller or the Macmillan Corporate and Premium Sales Department at 1-800-221-7945, ext. 5442, or by email at MacmillanSpecialMarkets@macmillan.com.

Printed in the United States of America

St. Martin's Paperbacks edition / August 2024

10 9 8 7 6 5 4 3 2

The Playboy Prince

For Tara Bell,
with hope that her wishes come true

CHAPTER 1

The stallion plunged over the crest of the hill, digging hard into the earth and kicking up dust. At the peak, he reared, powerful forelegs pawing the air. For an instant, horse and rider were silhouetted against the bright afternoon sky. One looked as dangerous as the other.

Even as hooves touched earth, the rider's knees pressed to the stallion's side and sent them both recklessly racing down the sheer incline. The track there was smooth, but hardly gentle with a wall of rock on one side and a drop into space on the other. They took it at full speed and gloried in it.

Only a madman rode with such arrogant disregard for life and limb. Only a madman, or a dreamer.

"*Avant*, Dracula." The command was low and challenging as was the laughter that followed. The tone was one of a man who considered fear a banquet and speed the wine.

Birds, startled by the thunderous pounding of hooves on dirt, flew from the trees and bushes on the cliff above to wheel screaming into the sky. Their noise was soon lost in the distance. When the path veered to the left, the stallion took it without a pause. The edge of the road gave way to cliffs that spilled sharply for seventy feet to the white rocks and blue sea. Pebbles danced off the dirt to shower soundlessly into the empty spaces.

The rider glanced down but didn't slow. He never even considered it.

From that height, there was no scent of the sea. Even the sound of waves crashing was indistinct, like thunder far off and still harmless. But from that height, the sea held a danger and mystique all of its own. Every year she claimed her tribute in the lives of men. The rider understood this, accepted this, for so it had been since the beginning of time. So it would continue to be. At times like this he put himself in the hands of fate and backed his bet with his own skill.

The stallion needed no whip, no spur to drive him faster. As always, his master's excitement and confidence were enough. They tore down the twisting path until the sea roared in their ears and the cry of gulls could at last be heard.

To the onlooker, it might seem the horseman was fleeing from devils or racing to a lover. But anyone seeing his face would know it was neither.

If there was a gleam in the dark eyes, it wasn't one of fear or anticipation. It was challenge. For the moment, and the moment only. Speed whipped the man's dark hair as freely as the horse's dark mane.

The stallion was fifteen hands of coal-black energy, wide at the chest, powerful at the neck. The horse's hide glistened with sweat, but his breathing was strong and even. Astride him, the rider sat erect, his tanned, narrow face glowing. His mouth, full and sculpted, was curved in a smile that spoke of both recklessness and pleasure.

As the path leveled, the stallion's stride lengthened. Here, they passed whitewashed cottages where clothes flapped on lines in the sea breeze. Flowers crowded for space in tidy lawns and windows were opened and unscreened. The sun, still high in the sky after noon, flashed its brilliant light. Without slackening, without needing his master's light hands on the reins to guide him, the stallion sprinted for a hedge as high as a man's waist.

Together, they soared over it.

In the distance were the stables. As there were danger and deadly attraction in the cliffs behind, so were there peace and order to the scene ahead. Red and white, and tidy as the lawns surrounding them, the buildings added another touch of charm to a landscape of cliffs and greenery. Fences crisscrossed to form paddocks where horses were being exercised with far less drama than Dracula.

One of the grooms stopped circling a young mare on a lead when he heard the stallion's approach. Crazy as a loon, he thought—but not without grudging respect. This horse and this rider, merged together in a blare of speed, were a common sight. Even so, two grooms waited at attention for the stallion to slow to a halt.

"Your Highness."

His Highness, Prince Bennett of Cordina slid off Dracula's back with a laugh that echoed the recklessness. "I'll cool him down, Pipit."

The old groom with the slight limp stepped forward. His weathered face was passive, but he passed his gaze over both prince and stallion, checking for any sign of harm. "Your pardon, sir, but a message came down from the palace while you were out. Prince Armand wishes to see you."

Not without regret, Bennett handed the reins to the waiting groom. Part of the pleasure of the ride was the hour he normally spent walking and brushing down the stallion. If his father had sent for him, he had no choice but to forgo pleasure for duty.

"Walk him thoroughly, Pipit. We've had a long run."

"Yes, sir," said the groom who'd spent three-quarters of his life with horses. Among his duties had been seating Bennett

on his first pony. At sixty, with one leg game from a fall, Pipit
remembered the energy of youth. And the passion. He patted
Dracula's neck and found it damp. "I'll see to it myself, Your
Highness."

"Do that, Pipit." But Bennett loitered long enough to loosen
the cinches. "Thanks."

"No thanks necessary, sir." With a quiet grunt, Pipit hefted
the saddle from the stallion's back. "Isn't another man here who
has the nerve to deal with the devil," he murmured in French
as the horse began to dance in place. In moments, Dracula settled again.

"And there isn't another man I'd trust with my best. An extra scoop of grain wouldn't hurt him this evening."

Pipit took the compliment as no less than his due. "As you
say, sir."

Still restless, Bennett turned to walk from the stables. He
could have used the extra hour to cool himself down as well.
Riding fast, riding reckless, satisfied only part of his thirst. He
needed the movement, the speed, but most of all, he needed
the freedom.

For nearly three months he'd been tied firmly to the palace
and protocol, the pomp and procedure. As second in line to
Cordina's throne, his duties were sometimes less public than
his brother Alexander's, but rarely less arduous. Duties, obligations, had been a part of his life since birth, and were normally taken as a matter of course. Bennett couldn't explain to
himself, much less anyone else, why sometime during the last
year he'd begun to fret and chafe against them.

Gabriella saw it. Bennett thought perhaps his sister even understood it. She, too, had always had a thirst for freedom and
privacy. She'd gained a portion of that two years before when
Alexander had married Eve, and the weight of responsibility
had shifted.

Still she never shirked, Bennett thought as he passed through the palace's garden doors. If she was needed, she was there. She still gave six months of every year to the Aid for Handicapped Children while keeping her marriage vital and raising her children.

Bennett dug his hands into his pockets as he climbed the stairs that would take him to his father's office. What was wrong with him? What had happened in the last few months that made him want to slip quietly out of the palace some night and run? Anywhere.

He couldn't shake off the mood, but he managed to tame it as he knocked on his father's door.

"Entrez."

The prince wasn't behind his desk as Bennett had expected, but was seated beside a tea tray at the window. Across from him was a woman who rose to her feet at Bennett's entrance.

As a man who appreciated women of any age, of any form, he took an easy survey before turning to his father. "I'm sorry to interrupt. I was told you wished to see me."

"Yes." Armand merely sipped his tea. "Some time ago. Prince Bennett, I would like to introduce Lady Hannah Rothchild."

"Your Highness." Her gaze swept down as she curtsied.

"A pleasure, Lady Hannah." Bennett took her hand, summing her up in seconds. Attractive in a quiet way. He preferred less subtlety in women. British from her accent. He had an affection for the French. Slim and neat. Invariably, the more voluptuous caught his eye. "Welcome to Cordina."

"Thank you, Your Highness." Her voice was indeed British, cultured and quiet. He met her gaze briefly so that he saw her eyes were a deep and glowing shade of green. "Yours is a beautiful country."

"Please, sit, my dear." Armand gestured her back to her chair before he lifted another cup to pour. "Bennett."

Hannah, with her hands folded in her lap, noticed Bennett's

quick look of dislike at the teapot. But he sat and accepted the cup.

"Lady Hannah's mother was a distant cousin of yours," Armand began. "Eve became acquainted with her when she and your brother visited England recently. At Eve's invitation, Lady Hannah has agreed to stay with us as Eve's companion."

Bennett could only hope he wouldn't be expected to escort the lady. She was pretty enough, though she dressed like a nun in a gray, high-collared dress that came a discreet two inches below her knees. The color did nothing for her pale, British complexion. Her eyes saved her face from being plain, but with her dark blond hair pulled back so severely from her face, she put him in mind of the old Victorian companions or governesses. Dull. But he remembered his manners and treated her to an easy, companionable smile.

"I hope you enjoy your stay as much as we'll enjoy having you."

Hannah gave him a solemn look in return. She wondered if he was aware, and thought he was, of how dashing he looked in casual riding clothes. "I'm sure I'll enjoy it immensely, sir. I'm flattered the Princess Eve invited me to stay with her while she awaits the birth of her second child. I hope to give her the companionship and help she needs."

Though his mind was on other matters, Armand offered a plate of frosted cookies. "Lady Hannah has been very generous to give us her time. She's quite a scholar and is currently working on a series of essays."

Figures, Bennett thought, and sipped at the hated tea. "Fascinating."

The smallest of smiles touched Hannah's lips. "Do you read Yeats, sir?"

Bennett shifted in his chair and wished himself back to his stables. "Not extensively."

"My books should be here by the end of the week. Please

feel free to borrow anything you like." She rose again, keeping her hands folded. "If you would excuse me, Your Highness, I'd like to see to the rest of my unpacking."

"Of course." Armand rose to lead her to the door. "We'll see you at dinner. Be sure to ring if you require anything."

"Thank you, sir." She curtsied, then turned to extend the courtesy to Bennett. "Good afternoon, Your Highness."

"*Bonjour*, Lady Hannah." Bennett waited for the door to close behind her before dropping onto the arm of his chair. "Well, she should bore Eve to tears within a week." Ignoring the tea, he took a handful of the small iced cookies. "What could Eve have been thinking of?"

"Eve became very fond of Hannah during her two weeks in England." Armand walked to a scrolled cabinet and, to Bennett's relief, took out a decanter. "Hannah is a well-bred young woman of excellent family. Her father is a highly respected member of the British Parliament." The brandy was deep and rich. Armand poured it sparingly.

"That's all well and good, but—" Bennett stopped abruptly as he reached for the snifter. "Oh good God, Father, you're not thinking of trying for a match here? She's hardly my type."

Armand's firm mouth softened with a smile. "I think I know that well enough. I can assure you Lady Hannah was not brought here to tempt you."

"She could hardly do that in any case." Bennett swirled the brandy, then sipped. "Yeats?"

"There are some who believe literature extends beyond equestrian handbooks." Armand drew out a cigarette. There was a knot of tension at the base of his neck. He forced it to concentrate there rather than allowing it to spread.

"I prefer the useful rather than poetry about unrequited love or the beauty of a raindrop." When that made him feel small and ungracious, Bennett relented. "But in any case, I'll do whatever I can to make Eve's new friend welcome."

"I never doubted it."

His conscience soothed, Bennett moved on to more important matters. "The Arabian mare should foal by Christmas. I'm betting it's a colt. Dracula will breed strong sons. I have three horses that should be ready to show in the spring, and another I think should be taken to the Olympic trials. I'd like to arrange that within the next few weeks so that the riders will have more time to work with the horse."

Armand gave an absent nod and continued to swirl his brandy. Bennett felt the familiar push of impatience rising and fought it down. He was well aware that the stables weren't high on his father's list of priorities. How could they be with internal affairs, foreign affairs, and the very tricky politics within the Council of the Crown?

Yet, didn't there have to be something more? The horses not only gave pleasure, but added a certain prestige when the Royal House of Cordina possessed one of the finest stables in Europe. For himself, it was what he considered his only true contribution to his family and country.

He'd worked for the stables as hard and as menially as any groom or stable boy. Over the years, he'd studied everything he could about breeding. To his delight, he'd found within himself a natural skill that had added spark to his education. Within a short time, Bennett had turned a good stable into one of the best. In another decade, he was confident it would have no equal.

There were times when Bennett needed to discuss his horses and his ambitions with someone other than a stable hand or another breeder. Still, he understood, and always had, that that person would rarely be his father.

"I take it this isn't the time to discuss it." Bennett took another small sip of brandy and waited for his father to reveal whatever weighed on his mind.

"I'm sorry, Bennett, I'm afraid it isn't." The father felt

regret. The prince could not. "Your schedule this next week. Can you tell me about it?"

"Not really." The restlessness was back. Rising, Bennett began to pace from one window to another. How close the sea seemed and yet how far away. He wished for a moment that he was on a ship again, a hundred miles from any land, with a storm brewing on the horizon. "I know that I have to go into Le Havre at the end of the week. The *Indépendance* is coming in. There's a meeting with the Farmers' Cooperative and a couple of luncheons. Cassell fills me in each morning. If it's important I can have him type up the highlights for you. I'm sure I'm cutting at least one ribbon."

"Feeling closed in, Bennett?"

With a shrug, Bennett tossed off the last of his brandy. Then the easy smile returned. Life, after all, was too short to complain about. "It's the ribbons that do it. The rest, at least, seems worthwhile."

"Our people look to us for more than governing."

Bennett turned from the window. Behind him the sun was high and bright. Whatever he might sometimes wish in his secret heart, the royalty he'd been born with cloaked him. "I know, Papa. The problem is I don't have Alexander's patience, Brie's serenity or your control."

"You might need them all soon." Armand set his glass down and faced his son. "Deboque will be released from prison in two days."

* * *

Deboque. Even the name caused fury to churn in Bennett's stomach. François Deboque. The man by whose orders his sister had been kidnapped. The man who had planned assassination attempts on both his father and his brother.

Deboque.

Bennett pressed a finger to the scar just below his left shoulder. He'd taken a bullet there, and the trigger had been pulled by Deboque's lover. For Deboque. By Deboque.

The bomb planted just over two years before in the Paris Embassy had been meant for his father. Instead it had killed Seward, a loyal assistant, leaving a woman widowed and three children fatherless. That, too, had been Deboque's doing.

And in all the years, nearly ten now since Gabriella's kidnapping, no one had proved Deboque's involvement in the kidnapping, the conspiracies or the murders. The best investigators in Europe, including Bennett's brother-in-law, had been brought in, but none of them had proved that Deboque had pulled the strings.

Now, within days, he would be free.

There was no doubt in Bennett's mind that Deboque would continue to seek revenge. The Royal Family was his enemy if for no other reason than he'd been held in a Cordinian prison for over a decade. Neither was there any doubt that during that decade, he'd continued to deal in drugs, weapons and women.

No doubt, and no proof.

Guards would be added. Security would be tightened. Interpol would continue its work, as would the International Security System. But both Interpol and the ISS had been trying to nail Deboque with murder and conspiracy to murder for years. Until he was gotten under control and the strings to his organization severed, Cordina and the rest of Europe were vulnerable.

Hands in pockets, Bennett strode out to the garden. At least they'd dined *en famille* that evening. It had relieved some strain, even though little could be said in front of Eve's new friend. He doubted if anyone that quiet and prim would have picked up on any tension around the table. She had answered when spoken to and nursed one glass of wine throughout the meal.

He would have wished her back to England a dozen times if he hadn't seen how good she actually was for Eve. His sister-in-law was three months pregnant with her second child and didn't need the additional strain of talk of Deboque. Two years before she'd nearly been killed protecting Alexander. If Lady Hannah could keep Eve's mind off Deboque, even for a few hours a day, it would be worth the inconvenience of having her in the palace.

He needed to talk with Reeve. Bennett drove his balled fists into his pockets. Reeve MacGee was more than his sister's husband. As head of security, he would have some answers. And Bennett certainly had the questions—dozens of them. More was being done than the placing of extra guards. Bennett refused to go through the next weeks blindly while others worked to protect him and his family.

Swearing softly, he looked up at the sky. The moon was cloudless and half full. Another time, with the scents of the garden wafting around him, he would have itched for a woman to watch the sky with. Now, filled with frustration, he preferred the solitude.

When he heard the dogs bark, his body stiffened. He'd thought himself alone; he'd even been sure of it. In any case, his aging hounds never barked at family or familiar servants. Half-hoping for a confrontation, Bennett moved quietly toward the sound.

He heard her laugh and the sound surprised him. It wasn't quiet and prim, but rich and delighted. As he watched, Hannah leaned down to stroke the dogs, which pressed against her legs.

"There now, what a lovely pair you are." Smiling she bent farther still to nuzzle. The moonlight slanted over her face and throat.

Instantly, Bennett's eyes narrowed. She hardly looked plain and subdued at the moment. The moonlight accented the hollows and contours of her face, enriching the soft English skin and deepening the already deep green eyes. He would have sworn that he saw both strength and passion there. And he was a man who recognized both in a woman. Her laughter floated out again, as rich as sunlight, as sultry as fog.

"No, you mustn't jump," she cautioned the dogs as they circled her. "You'll have mud all over me and how would I explain that?"

"It's usually best not to explain at all."

She snapped her head up as Bennett spoke. He saw surprise, or thought he did, but it passed quickly. When she straightened, she was the calm, unremarkable Lady Hannah again. He chalked up the passion he'd thought he'd seen to a trick of the light.

"Good evening, Your Highness." Hannah took only a moment to curse herself for being caught unaware.

"I didn't know anyone else was in the garden."

"Nor did I." And she should have. "I beg your pardon."

"Don't." He smiled to put her at ease. "I've always felt the gardens aren't enjoyed nearly enough. Couldn't you sleep?"

"No, sir. I'm always restless when I travel." The dogs had deserted her for Bennett. She stood beside the flowering jasmine and watched him stroke them with strong, capable hands. She was well aware that numerous ladies had enjoyed the same easy touch. "I'd seen the gardens from my window and thought I might walk awhile." In truth, it had been their scent, exotic and alluring, that had urged her to loiter after she'd noted the layout of the space.

"I prefer them at night myself. Things often look different at night," he continued, studying her again. "Don't you think?"

"Naturally." She linked her hands together just below the waist. He was marvelous to look at, sun or moon. When he'd strode into his father's office that afternoon she'd thought that riding clothes suited him best. The dogs came back to press their noses against her joined hands.

"They like you."

"I've always been fond of animals." She unlinked her hands to stroke. He noticed for the first time that her hands were delicate, long and slender like her body. "What are their names?"

"Boris and Natasha."

"Suitable names for Russian wolfhounds."

"They were given to me as puppies. I named them after characters in an American cartoon show. Spies."

Her hands hesitated only a heartbeat. "Spies, Your Highness?"

"Inept Russian spies who were forever after a moose and squirrel."

He thought he saw it again, the flash of humor that lent something special to her face. "I see. I've never been to America."

"No?" He moved closer, but saw nothing but a young woman with good bones and a quiet manner. "It's a fascinating country. Cordina's become closely linked with it since two members of the Royal Family have married Americans."

"A fact that disappointed a number of hopeful Europeans, I'm sure." Hannah relaxed enough for a cautious smile. "I met Princess Gabriella several years ago. She's a beautiful woman."

"Yes, she is. You know, I've been to England several times. It's strange we never met."

Hannah allowed the smile to linger. "But we did, Your Highness."

"Boris, sit," Bennett commanded as the dog lifted a paw toward Hannah's dress. "Are you sure?"

"Quite sure, sir. Then you'd hardly be expected to remember. It was several years ago at a charity ball hosted by the Prince of Wales. The Queen Mother introduced you to me and my cousin Lady Sara. I believe you and Sara became . . . friendly."

"Sara?" His mind backtracked and zeroed in. His memory, always good, was faultless when it came to women. "Yes, of course." Though he remembered Hannah only as a vague shadow beside her glamorous and bold cousin. "How is Sara?"

"Very well, sir." If there was sarcasm, it was well coated with manners. "Happily married for the second time. Shall I send her your regards?"

"If you like." He dipped his hands into his pockets again as he continued to study her. "You were wearing blue, a pale blue that was nearly white."

Hannah lifted her brow. She didn't have to be told that he'd barely noticed her. The fact that he hadn't, yet still remembered the color of her gown gave her a moment's pause. A memory like that could be useful—or dangerous.

"You flatter me, Your Highness."

"I make it a policy not to forget a woman."

"Yes, I can believe that."

"My reputation precedes me." The frown was there, then gone, to be replaced by a careless smile. "Does it concern you to be alone in the garden, in the moonlight with—"

"The Royal Rake?" Hannah finished.

"You do read," Bennett murmured.

"Incessantly. And no, Your Highness, I'm quite comfortable, thank you."

He opened his mouth, then laughed and shut it again. "Lady Hannah, I've rarely been put so neatly in my place."

So he was quick—another point she'd have to remember. "I beg your pardon, sir. That certainly wasn't my intention."

"The hell it wasn't, and well done." He took her hand and found it cool and steady. Perhaps she would prove to be a great deal less dull than he'd anticipated. "I should beg your pardon for baiting you, but I won't since you obviously hold your own so well. I'm beginning to see why Eve wanted you here."

Hannah had learned long ago to block off any form of guilt. She did so now. "I became very fond of her in a short time and was delighted with the opportunity to stay in Cordina for a few months. I confess, I've already fallen in love with little Princess Marissa."

"Barely a year old and she's already ruling the palace." Bennett's eyes softened as he thought of his brother's first child. "Maybe it's because she looks like Eve."

Hannah withdrew her hand from his. She'd heard the rumors that Bennett had been half in love, or possibly more than half in love, with his brother's wife. It didn't take even so talented an observer as she to hear the affection in his voice. She told herself to file it away. It may or may not have its uses later.

"If you'll excuse me, sir, I should go back to my room."

"It's still early." He found himself reluctant to let her go. It was unexpected that she would be easy to talk to, or that he would find himself needing to talk to her.

"I'm in the habit of retiring early."

"I'll walk you back."

"Please don't trouble. I know the way. Good night, Your Highness." She merged quickly with the shadows while the dogs whined a bit and thumped their tails against his legs.

What was there about her? Bennett wondered as he bent to soothe his pets. At first glance she seemed almost bland enough to fade into the wallpaper, and yet . . . He didn't know. But as he walked back toward the palace with the dogs at his heels, he resolved to find out. If nothing else, probing a bit beneath Lady Hannah's quiet breeding would keep his mind off Deboque.

Hannah didn't wait to see if he followed her, but walked quickly through the garden doors. She'd been born with the talent to move quietly, so unobtrusively she could easily be missed in a group of three people. It was a talent she'd honed to a skill and which served her well.

She moved up the stairs without a sound, never looking back. If you had to check whether you were being followed, you were already in trouble. Once inside her own room, she locked the door and slipped out of her practical pumps. Because the woman she professed to be would never leave her clothing scattered, Hannah picked them up, and with only a brief look of distaste, placed them neatly in her closet.

Checking only to see that her curtains were drawn, she peeled off the unflattering cocktail dress.

Although she thought it deserved its day in the garbage, she carefully hung it on a padded hanger.

She stood now, a slimly curved woman with milk-pale skin and long legs in a skimpy lace-edged teddy. Drawing the confining pins from her hair, she let it fall heavily to her waist with a sigh of pure pleasure.

Anyone who knew Lady Hannah Rothchild would have been stunned by the transformation, so complete, so ingrained was the role she'd played for nearly ten years.

Lady Hannah had a passion for silk and Breton lace, but confined it to nightwear and lingerie. Linens and tweeds were more fitting to the image she'd worked hard to create.

Lady Hannah enjoyed reading a pot-boiling thriller in a steamy bubble bath, but she kept a copy of Chaucer on her nightstand and if asked, could quote and discuss a handful of obscure passages.

It wasn't a matter of split personality, but necessity. If she'd given it any deep thought, Hannah would have been able to state that she was comfortable with both of her selves. In fact, more often than not she thoroughly liked the plain, polite and marginally pretty Hannah. Otherwise, she could never have tolerated the sensible shoes for extended periods.

But there was another part to Lady Hannah Rothchild, only

daughter of Lord Rothchild, granddaughter of the Earl of Fenton. That part was not quiet and unassuming, but shrewd and sometimes reckless. More, that part had a taste for danger and a mind that absorbed and stored the most minor detail.

Combined, those parts of Lady Hannah Rothchild equaled an excellent and highly skilled agent.

Ignoring her robe, Hannah opened her top drawer and drew out a long, locked box. Inside was a strand of pearls handed down from her great-grandmother with matching earrings her father had had reset for her twenty-first birthday. In the drawers of the box were several other pieces of jewelry befitting a young woman of her class.

Hannah pulled a notebook out of the false bottom and taking it to the rosewood writing desk, began to write her daily report. She hadn't gone into the garden merely to smell the roses, though she had lingered too long because of them. Now she had the complete layout and no longer had to rely on the information fed her. She took the time to draw a sketch of the palace, including the doors and windows most easily accessible. By the following day, or the day after at most, she would have a schedule of the guards.

It had taken her little time to form a friendship with Eve. Securing an invitation to the palace in Cordina had been as easy as asking for one. Eve missed her sister and the familiarity of her own country. She'd needed a friend, one she could talk to, one who would share her delight in her daughter.

Hannah had obliged.

She felt the quick trickle of guilt again and ignored it. A job was a job, she reminded herself. She couldn't let the fondness she felt for Eve interfere with a goal she'd begun to work toward two years ago.

With a shake of her head, she made her first notes on Bennett. He wasn't completely what she'd expected, Hannah thought now. Oh, he was as charming and as attractive as his dossier had said, but he'd given the dull Lady Hannah his time and attention.

An egotistical womanizer, Hannah reminded herself. That had been her own conclusion after doing her research on him. Perhaps he was a bit bored and entertained thoughts of distracting himself with a vulnerable and accessible woman.

Narrowing her eyes, Hannah looked back on the way he had smiled at her. A man of his looks, position and experience knew how to use that smile or a soft word to enchant a woman of any age and any class. The fact that he'd done so, with astonishing regularity, was well documented. Perhaps he would try to add another jewel to his crown by seducing her.

She remembered the way he'd looked in the moonlight, the way his eyes had warmed when she'd bantered back with him. His hand had been firm and hard when it had taken hers—the hand of a man who did more than wave regally to his people.

With a shake of her head, she brought herself up short. It wouldn't do to consider a dalliance with Bennett for enjoyment, but for its usefulness. Thoughtfully, she tapped her pencil on the pad. No, a romance with Bennett would only lead to complications, no matter how advantageous it might be in the long run. She'd keep her eyes down and her hands folded.

Carefully, Hannah hid the notebook again and replaced the false bottom. The box was locked, but left in full sight if anyone searched her dresser.

She was in, she told herself with a growing sense of anticipation as she looked around the room.

When Deboque walked out of prison in two days' time, he'd be very pleased.

CHAPTER 2

O h, Hannah, I'm so glad you agreed to visit awhile." With her arm hooked with her new friend's, Eve strolled behind the backdrop at the theater. Her body remained slender during the early months of her pregnancy, but her dress was cleverly cut to conceal even the slight weight gain. "Alex doesn't find it as necessary to pamper me to death now that you're here. He finds you so sensible."

"I am sensible."

Eve's low chuckle flowed into her easy Texas drawl. "I know, that's the beauty of it, but you're not always telling me to sit down and put my feet up."

"Men sometimes look at pregnancy and childbirth as a traumatic disease rather than a fact of life."

"That's it exactly." Delighted with Hannah's dry wit, Eve drew her into her office. With Gabriella so often in America and her own sister visiting only rarely, Eve had indeed yearned for another woman to relax with. "Alex keeps expecting me to faint or get overly emotional. I never felt better in my life, except perhaps when I was carrying Marissa."

Tossing back her fall of dark hair, Eve perched on the edge of her desk. Here, at least, she could still claim some measure of the privacy she'd given up when she'd married a prince.

Though she never regretted the sacrifice, she always enjoyed stealing a bit of her own back.

"If you hadn't come, I'd have had to fight him tooth and nail to continue working. He only agreed because he felt you'd keep a close eye on me when he's busy."

"Then I won't disappoint him." Hannah took quick stock of the office. No window, no outside access. With a smile, she chose a chair. "You know, Eve, I really admire you. The Fine Arts Center always had a good reputation but since you took over here, this theater has become one of the most important in Europe."

"It's what I've always wanted." Eve looked down at the diamond-encrusted band on her finger. Even after two years it sometimes astonished her to find it there. "You know, Hannah, some mornings I'm almost afraid to wake up; I think that I'll find out it was all a dream. Then I look at Alex and Marissa and think, they're mine. Really mine." Her eyes clouded a moment with both fear and determination. "I won't let anything or anyone hurt them."

"No one will." Eve's thoughts were on Deboque, Hannah surmised. The princess was bound by duty to keep some fears to herself. "Now, not to pamper, but I think we could both use some tea, then you can show me what sort of job I can do around here."

Eve brought herself back with an effort. Nightmares of Deboque, a man she'd never seen, continued to plague her. "Tea's a wonderful idea, but I didn't bring you to the Center to work. I just thought you'd like to see it."

"Eve, you of all people should understand that I need something to do or I'll be bored to death."

"But I'd hoped this could be a vacation for you."

The guilt shimmered a bit. "Some people aren't meant for vacations."

"All right then. Why don't you watch rehearsals with me for an hour or two and give me an honest opinion?"

"I'd love to."

"Great. I'm worried about the opening. We only have a couple of weeks left and I've had nothing but trouble with this playwright."

"Oh, who is it?"

Eve rose and took a deep breath. "Me."

* * *

Hannah drank her tea and stayed in the background. It didn't take long for her to see that Eve was respected not only as the wife of the heir, but for her knowledge of theater. She noted too that guards, unobtrusive but in force, were always close at hand. When the princess was in the theater, every entrance was blocked, every interior door was double guarded. Hannah was also aware that a special unit of security checked the Center daily for explosives.

While seated mid-theater with Eve, Hannah watched the rehearsal. She'd always had an affection and respect for actors, as she understood the effort and skill that went into characterization. Now, while lines were cued and staging set, she matched the members of the troupe with the information she already had compiled on each of them.

They were certainly talented, Hannah thought as she found herself drawn into the rhythm and emotion of Eve's play. The sets were still incomplete, but the players needed no more than Eve's words and their own skill to make a statement. Each one of the actors had a reputation in theater and a complete security check.

But it had been an actor—Russ Talbot—who'd nearly carried out Deboque's revenge two years before. Hannah couldn't forget that it was a strong possibility that someone other than herself had been planted. Deboque was known for covering his bets.

"She's wonderful, isn't she?"

Drawn back, Hannah looked over at Eve. "I beg your pardon?"

"Chantel O'Hurley. She's exquisite." Shifting in her chair, Eve leaned on the seat back in front of her. "She rarely makes a stage performance, so we're lucky to have her. I'm sure you've seen her films in England."

"Yes." Hannah gave her full attention to the curvy blonde center stage.

Chantel O'Hurley. Hannah paused to recollect everything she'd read in the actress's file. Twenty-six. American film star. Residence, Beverly Hills. Daughter of Frances and Margaret O'Hurley, traveling entertainers. Sisters, Abigail and Madelaine. Brother, Trace.

Hannah frowned and continued to watch. She had full background information on the entire O'Hurley family, except the brother. There her sources had closed tight. In any case, Chantel O'Hurley was a talented actress with an impressive list of screen credits and no known affiliation with any political group. Nonetheless, Hannah would keep an eye on her.

"She's found the heart of it," Eve murmured. "I'd finished the play and was trying to work up the courage to produce it, when I saw her in her last film. I knew immediately she'd be the perfect Julia." On a long breath Eve leaned back again in an unprincesslike slouch. "I can't believe she's here, reciting my lines. There isn't an emotion that voice can't pull out."

"I'm sure she's honored to be performing in a play written and produced by Princess Eve of Cordina."

On a half laugh, Eve shook her head. "If the play had been lousy, I could have been Empress of Europe and Chantel wouldn't have accepted the part. That's what I'm hanging on to."

"A member of the Royal Family doesn't write lousy plays."

At the sound of the voice behind her, Eve was springing up and reaching out. "Alexander! What are you doing here?"

"I, too, have an interest in the Center." He kissed the hand he held before turning to Hannah. "Please, sit, I didn't mean to disturb you."

"No." Eve sighed and glanced back at the stage where rehearsals continued. "You meant to check up on me."

It was, of course, the truth, but Alexander only shrugged. In the dim light, Hannah saw his gaze sweep over his wife's head to the guards placed at several strategic points. "You forget, *ma mie*, that I am still president of the Center. In addition to that, my wife's play is in rehearsal. I have a small interest there as well."

"And you came to be certain I wasn't staying on my feet." Over the frustration came the tug of love. Eve rose to her toes to kiss him. "Thank you. Hannah, tell His Highness I've been taking care of myself in the four hours and forty minutes since he last saw me."

"Your Highness," Hannah began dutifully, "the princess has been taking excellent care of herself."

A smile softened his features, but he continued to stand protectively near his wife. "Thank you, Hannah. I'm sure the credit goes to you."

With a low laugh, Eve tucked her hand through Alexander's arm. "Hannah, you can see that I wasn't joking when I said that Alex thinks I need a keeper. If you hadn't come I have no doubt he'd have hired a two-hundred-pound wrestler with tattoos."

"I'm glad I could save you from that." What was this? Hannah wondered. A tug of envy? Ridiculous as it seemed to her, she recognized the emotion as she studied Alexander and Eve. So much in love, she thought. The power of it all but cast an aura around them. Did they realize, could they realize, how rare a thing they'd found?

"Now that I've interrupted," Alexander was saying, "I was hoping to convince you to join me for my luncheon with the American senator."

"The Yankee from Maine."

With a smile, Alexander stroked her cheek. "My dear, it continues to fascinate me how your country divides itself into sections. But yes, the Yankee from Maine. We should be finished by three and be back at the palace when Marissa wakes from her nap."

"But you had a meeting this afternoon."

"I canceled it." He brought her hand to his lips. "I wanted to spend some time with my family."

The glow of pleasure all but lit up the theater. "Give me five minutes to get my things. Hannah, you'll join us?"

"If it wouldn't inconvenience you, I'd really like to stay and watch the rest of the rehearsal." Her mind was already shooting ahead. Alone, she could take a casual tour of the complex. If there were vulnerabilities, she'd find them.

"Of course, stay as long as you like." Eve bent down to kiss her cheek. "We'll have a car wait for you at the stage door. Five minutes," she repeated to Alexander before she dashed off.

"What do you think of the play?" Alexander asked Hannah as he took the seat beside her.

"I'm hardly an expert on the theater, Your Highness."

"In private, please call me Alexander."

"Thank you," she murmured, aware that this gave her an intimacy rewarded to few. "There's an intensity, an immediacy in the dialogue that makes one care deeply about the characters. I don't know the end, but I find myself hoping Julia wins even while I'm afraid she won't."

"Eve would like to hear that. The play—and other things—have her very tense right now."

"You're worried about her." In a gesture that was pure instinct, Hannah placed a hand on his. "She's very strong."

"I know that, better than most." But he'd never been able to block off the memory of how her body had stiffened, then gone limp in his arms when a bullet had struck her. "I haven't told you before how very grateful I am that you came to be with her. She needs friendship. I changed her life, selfishly perhaps because I couldn't live mine without her. Whatever can be done to give her a sense of normalcy, a sense of peace, I'll do. You understand the obligations of royalty. The limitations. Even the risk."

"Yes, I do." Hannah left her hand on his another moment before removing it. "And I understand a happy woman when I see one."

When he turned to her then, Hannah saw the strong resemblance to his father. The lean, almost scholarly face, the aristocratic lines, the mouth that was held firm. "Thank you, Hannah. I think perhaps you'll be good for all of us."

"I hope so." She looked back at the stage, at the players, at the roles. "I do hope so."

* * *

Alone, Hannah watched for another half hour. Yes, the play was good, she decided, even gripping, but she had other games to play.

The guards remained, but with no royalty present they were more for the purpose of keeping others out than monitoring those already in. Lady Hannah was already established as the princess's confidante and companion. Trusted by Prince Armand himself, she wasn't followed when she rose and slipped through a side door.

There was a miniature camera concealed in a lipstick case in her handbag, but she didn't use it now. Her training had taught her to rely on her powers of observation first, her equipment second.

A building the size of the sprawling Center wasn't easily secured. Hannah found herself giving Reeve MacGee a nod of respect as she walked through. Heat sensors as well as hidden cameras. But the sensors were activated only when the Center was closed.

Security passes were required at the door for members of the cast and crew. On the night of a performance, however, entrance could be gained for the price of a ticket. Deboque would step from behind bars in a day's time.

As she walked, leaving one corridor for the next, Hannah drew a blueprint in her mind. She'd studied the layout of the Center on paper before, but preferred to walk in it, to focus on it, to touch the walls and floor.

Too many blind corners, she thought. Too many small rooms used for storage. Too many places to hide. Even with Reeve's expertise, the building could be vulnerable with the right plan of attack. But then, Hannah believed any building could be.

She turned into Wardrobe, pretending a casual interest in the costumes. Did the guard at the door know everyone by sight? How easy would it be to replace one of the technicians? A photo was affixed to the pass, but makeup and hairpieces could take care of that. How often had she, or another like her, gained access to a place by faked credentials or a clever disguise?

Once inside, a man could disappear easily. If a man on the security panel could be bribed or replaced, so much the better.

Yes, she'd put that scenario in her report and let her superiors chew on it awhile. She'd add to that the fact that no one had checked her bag. A small plastic explosive could be easily carried and easily planted.

She walked from Wardrobe into a rehearsal hall walled with mirrors. With a little shock, she stared at her reflection on all sides. Then, as she had in the garden, she let out a low, easy laugh.

Oh, Hannah, she thought, how miserably dull you are. Turning to the side, she shook her head. No, maroon did nothing for her, and the high-necked jacket with its bulky belt only made her look unattractively thin. The skirt came well below the knee to hide her legs. She'd braided her hair today, tightly, then had circled the braid at the base of her neck.

Being a part of herself, it was the best cover she could have conceived. She'd been too skinny as a child, with unmanageable hair, and knees that were forever scraped. Her facial bones had been prominent even then, but in the young girl's face had seemed too sharp, too angular.

Then when the other girls had begun to bloom and curve, Hannah's body had remained stubbornly straight. She'd been bright and athletic and cheerful. Boys had patted her on the back and called her a good sport, but they hadn't been interested in taking her to any dances.

She'd learned to ride, swim, shoot skeet and to put an arrow in a bull's-eye from a hundred paces, but she hadn't dated.

She'd learned to speak Russian and French and enough Cantonese to surprise even her father, but she'd gone alone to her own graduation ball.

When she turned twenty, her body changed, but Hannah hid the late blossoming under dull clothes. She'd already chosen her path in life. Beauty turned heads and in her field it was always best to go unnoticed.

Now, she looked at the results in the wall of mirrors and was satisfied. No man would desire her. It was human nature to look at the physical shell and draw emotion from that long before you dipped beneath to the intellect or soul. No woman would envy her. Dull was safe, after all.

No one would suspect a plain, bookish woman of excellent breeding and quiet social manners of deception or violence. Only a select few were aware that the woman beneath was capable of both.

For a reason she couldn't name, that thought made her turn away from her reflection. Deception had been with her all of her adult life, and yet she couldn't quite dismiss the twinges of guilt she felt whenever Eve looked at her as a friend.

It was a job, Hannah reminded herself. No emotional attachments, no emotional involvements were permitted. That was the first and most important rule of the game. She couldn't afford to allow herself to like Eve, to even think of her as anything but a political symbol. If she did, everything she'd worked for could be lost.

The envy had to go as well, Hannah reminded herself. It was a dangerous lapse to let herself look at the love between the prince and Eve and wish something similar for herself. There was no room for love in her profession. There were only goals, commitments and risks.

There would be no prince for her, royal or otherwise.

But before she could prevent it, her thoughts turned to Bennett and the way he'd smiled at her in the moonlight.

Idiot, she told herself and began tightening a few loose pins. He was the last person she should think about in a personal way. If for no other reason, there was his dossier and the astonishing list of women who'd been part of his life already.

Use him, certainly, her mind went on. But don't think about him as anything but a means to an end. Romantic fantasies had ended for her at sixteen. Ten years later, in the middle of her most important job, was hardly the time to begin to weave them again. She would do well to remember that the stiff-lipped, proper Lady Hannah would never see His Royal Highness Prince Bennett de Cordina in a romantic light.

But the woman within dreamed and for a moment strained against the confines she'd built herself.

Hannah turned to look back at the mirrors when she heard the footsteps.

Immediately alert, she cast her eyes down and walked from the room.

"Ah, there you are."

At Bennett's voice, Hannah gave an inward curse, but curtsied. "Your Highness."

"Taking the grand tour?" He walked closer, wondering why she looked as plain as a maiden aunt and continued to intrigue him.

"Yes, sir. I hope it's all right."

"Of course." He took her hand, willing her to look directly at him. There was something about her eyes. . . . Or perhaps it was her voice, that cool, always composed British tone. "I had some business in town. Alexander suggested I swing by when I'd finished to see if you were ready to go back."

"That's very kind of you." And oh, how she would have preferred a silent, anonymous driver who'd have given her the opportunity to assimilate her report on the drive back.

"I was here." He felt the restlessness layer over him as she drew her hand back to her side. "If you'd like to see more, I'd be happy to take you around the rest of the Center."

Hannah weighed the pros and cons in a matter of seconds. Another quick look might add something, but she'd already gone through the main theater twice, once with Eve and once alone. It might begin to look odd if she went through again with Bennett.

"No, thank you. It is a fascinating place. I've never seen a theater from this side."

"Eve's territory. I confess I prefer front row center myself." He took Hannah's arm and began to lead her down the hall.

"If you hang around her for any length of time, she finds something for you to do. With me, it's usually moving boxes. Heavy boxes."

With a laugh, Hannah slanted him a look. "That's one of the best uses a woman can find for a man."

"I can see why Eve took to you." He'd come simply to do his sister-in-law a favor, but now found himself glad. Outward appearance aside, Lady Hannah was anything but dull. For perhaps the first time in his life, Bennett was beginning to look beneath the physical. "Have you seen much of Cordina yet, Hannah?"

She noticed he'd dropped her title, but decided to let it pass. "Only snatches so far, sir. Once I'm a bit more familiar with Eve's routine, I plan to explore a bit. I've heard your museum has some excellent exhibits. The building itself is reported to be a fine example of post-Renaissance architecture."

He wasn't interested in exhibits, but in her. "Do you like the water?"

"Of course. Sea air is very beneficial for the constitution."

With a half laugh, Bennett paused at the top of the stairs. "But do you like it?"

He had a strange talent for looking at a woman as though he were seeing her for the first time. And looking as though it mattered. Despite her training, Hannah felt her pulse rate accelerate. "Yes. My grandmother has a place near Cornwall. I spent several summers there as a girl."

He wondered what she would look like with her hair down and the sea wind teasing it. Would she laugh as he had heard her laugh in the garden? Would he see that light flash in her eyes again? Then he realized it didn't matter how she looked. He went on impulse, knowing he might regret it.

"I have to go into Le Havre in a couple of days. The drive runs along the coast. Come with me."

If he'd asked her to step into the storage room and neck, she would have been no less surprised. Surprise turned quickly to caution and caution to calculation. But beneath it all was the simple pleasure that he wanted her company. It was the pleasure that worried her.

"It's kind of you to ask, Your Highness, but Eve may have plans."

"Then we'll check with her first." He wanted her to go. He found himself already looking forward to spending a few hours with her away from the palace. Perhaps it was for the challenge of it, the challenge of picking away at that prim, proper exterior and finding what, if anything, lay beneath. Whatever the reason was, Bennett didn't question it. "Would you like to go?"

"Yes, I would." Hannah told herself it was because it would give her the opportunity to study him more closely, for professional reasons. She told herself it would give her the chance to see how well security worked away from the palace and the capital. But the truth was as simple as her answer. She wanted to go.

"Fine, then we'll fix it, and you can stand through the long and wordy welcoming ceremony with me."

"Hate to be bored alone, do you?"

Laughing, Bennett took her hand again. "Yes, I can see exactly why Eve brought you to us." Her hand was an inch from his lips when the murmur of voices came from below. Glancing down, more than a little annoyed, Bennett spotted Chantel.

"The anger has to show," she was insisting, walking so quickly the director had to lengthen his stride to keep up. "Julia is not a passive woman. She doesn't hide what she feels no matter what the consequences. Dammit, Maurice, I'll make it subtle. I know my job."

"Of course you do, *chérie*, that I don't question. It is simply that—"

"Mademoiselle." From the top of the stairs, Bennett looked

down. Hannah had a firsthand glimpse of how he smiled at a truly beautiful woman. Without thinking, she drew her hand from his and linked her fingers together.

Chantel, reaching one hand up to draw back her pale blond hair, tilted her head back. Even so dispassionate an observer such as Hannah had to concede that few women could claim such a combination of glamour, beauty and sexuality. Her lips curved. Her eyes, a deep, dreamy shade of blue, smiled with them.

"Your Highness," Chantel said in her rich, smoky voice as she dipped into a formal curtsy. She started up the stairs and Bennett started down. In the middle, they stopped, then Chantel reached up to touch his face before bringing him closer for a lengthy kiss. Above them, Hannah felt her teeth snap together. "It's been a long time."

"Too long." Bennett cupped her hand in both of his. "You're lovelier than ever. It's astonishing."

"It's genes," Chantel claimed, and grinned at him. "My God, Bennett, what a beautiful man you are. If I wasn't a cynic, I'd propose."

"If I wasn't terrified of you, I'd accept." They embraced again with the ease of old friends. "Chantel, it's good to see you again. Eve was turning handsprings when you agreed to take the part."

"It's a good play." Chantel gave a matter-of-fact shrug. "Even though I adore you, I wouldn't have come all this way to take a role in a bomb. Your sister-in-law's a talented woman." Chantel cast a look over her shoulder at the director waiting respectfully at the bottom of the stairs. "You might mention to her that I'm fighting to preserve the integrity of her Julia." As she turned back, she spotted Hannah standing on the landing. "Friend of yours?"

Glancing back, Bennett held out a hand. "Hannah, come meet the incomparable Chantel."

The stiffness in her movement only suited her character, Hannah told herself as she started down. All unremarkable women tensed up when slapped in the face with great beauty. She stopped on the step beside Bennett, but kept nearly a foot of space between them.

"Lady Hannah Rothchild, Chantel O'Hurley."

"How do you do?" Formal and proper, Hannah held out a hand. Chantel kept her face passive as she accepted it.

"I do fine, thank you." As a woman, as an actress who understood angles and role-playing, she wondered why someone with such good bone structure and a flawless complexion would deliberately make themselves appear plain.

"Lady Hannah is keeping Eve company for a few months."

"How nice. Cordina's a beautiful country. I'm sure you'll enjoy it."

"Yes, I already am. I also enjoyed watching you rehearse."

"Thanks, but we have a way to go." Chantel tapped a finger on the banister and wondered why she felt such instant distrust. Dismissing it as overwork, she turned back to Bennett. "I have to run. Try to make some time for me, darling."

"Of course. You're coming to dinner Saturday with the rest of the cast?"

"Wouldn't miss it. I'll see you there, Lady Hannah."

"Goodbye, Miss O'Hurley."

After giving Bennett a quick pat on the cheek, Chantel descended the stairs again and let the director trail behind her.

"She's quite a woman," Bennett murmured.

"Yes, she's very beautiful."

"There's that, too." Without looking at her, Bennett took Hannah's arm again. "I suppose I've always admired her willpower and ambition. She's determined to be the best and isn't afraid to work for it. Every time I see her on the screen, it's breathtaking."

Hannah dug her fingers into her purse and reminded herself

she was supposed to be unassuming. "You admire ambition, Your Highness?"

"Nothing's changed for better or worse without it."

"Some men still find ambition in a woman unflattering, or at least, uncomfortable."

"Some men are idiots."

"I couldn't agree more," Hannah said dryly, dryly enough that he lifted his brow as he gazed at her.

"Why am I never quite sure whether or not you're insulting me, Hannah?"

"I beg your pardon, sir, I was simply agreeing with you."

He stopped again. From the stage came the murmur of voices, but the hall was deserted. Bennett took her chin in his hand, ignoring her jolt of shock, and studied her face. "Hannah, why is it when I look at you I'm not convinced I'm seeing all there is?"

Alarm bells went off in her head. Her face paled a bit. She knew it, but thought, hoped, he would take that as natural. Not by another blink did she show concern. "I don't know what you mean."

"I wonder." He moved his thumb over her jawline, then just beneath where the skin was softer yet, and warm. "Yes, I wonder more than I should about you, Hannah. Do you have an answer for that?"

There were amber flecks in his eyes, turning what might have been plain brown into something tawny and compelling. He had the mouth of a poet and the hands of a farmer. Hannah wondered how it was possible to combine the two as her heart, always so steady, began to drum against her ribs.

"Your Highness—" It was both the lady without and the lady within who fumbled.

"Do you, Hannah?"

He saw her lips part. Strange, he hadn't noticed how attractive her mouth was before—soft, just a bit wide and beautifully shaped without cosmetics. He wondered if it would taste as cool as her voice or as rich as her eyes.

She had to stop this, here and now. The yearning building inside her could only be destructive. Even as she longed to reach out, she cast her eyes down. "No, sir, except that many times men are intrigued with a woman simply because she's not what they're accustomed to."

"We'll see." He backed off, though the effort it cost him was a surprise. "I'll take you back now, Hannah, and we'll both give it some thought."

CHAPTER 3

Hannah was given free run of the palace and the grounds. She had only to ask and her bath would be drawn or her bed turned down. If she developed a craving for hot chocolate at 3:00 a.m., she could pick up the phone beside her bed and request it. As a guest of the Royal Family, she was afforded every amenity the palace could offer.

And as a guest of the Royal Family, she was afforded her own guards.

Hannah considered them only a slight nuisance. It was a simple enough matter for someone of her talents to make them think she was tucked safely away in her rooms while she was somewhere else entirely. However, the fact that she was being watched made it difficult to set up a meeting with her contact on the outside.

Using the palace phones was out of the question. Too many extensions made it a risk that even a casual, coded conversation could be overheard. She'd briefly considered smuggling in a transmitter, then had rejected the notion. Transmissions could be traced. She hadn't spent two years of her life to get to this point to see it all wiped away because of some electronic foul-up. In any case, she preferred meetings of such importance to be face-to-face.

Two days after she arrived in Cordina, she mailed a letter. It was addressed to an old family friend in Sussex who didn't exist. Its destination was one of Deboque's many branches throughout Europe. If for any reason the letter was intercepted and opened, the reader would find nothing more interesting than a chatty note describing Cordina and the weather.

Once the letter reached its destination and was decoded, it would read differently. Hannah had given her name, her rank in the organization and had requested a meeting, detailing the time, date and place. The information would be fed back to the Cordina contact. All she had to do was get there, alone.

One week, Hannah thought once the letter was on its way. In one week she would well and truly begin what had been started so long ago. She had plenty to do to keep her busy in the meantime.

Princess Gabriella and her family were visiting the palace that evening. The staff had been in an uproar for the better part of the day, more, Hannah guessed, because the children were descending than for any other reason. Hannah had heard that the priceless collection of Fabergé eggs was to be put out of reach.

She spent the day quietly enough, visiting Eve and Marissa in the nursery, lunching with several members of the Historical Society, and in the lull of late afternoon, exploring the cellars for vulnerabilities.

Now, she clipped on her pearls and prepared to join the family in the main drawing room. It would be interesting to see them all together, she thought. In that way she could judge the interactions as well as the individuals. Before too much time had passed, she had to know them all as well as she knew herself. One mistake, one bad judgment call, and all could be lost.

"Come back here, you little demon!"

Hannah heard a loud laugh, a thud, then rushing feet. Before she had a chance to open the door to see for herself, it burst open. Barreling through it was a small boy with a thatch of dark hair that may or may not have been combed in the last week. He gave her an amazing grin, showing more than one gap before he scooted under her bed.

"Cachez-moi, s'il vous plaît!" His voice was muffled by the skirt of the spread before he disappeared.

Hannah opened her mouth again only to see Bennett filling the doorway.

"Did you see a small, miserably mannered boy?"

"I, ah—no," she decided on the spot and folded her hands. "I did think I heard someone go running past. What are you—"

"Thanks. If you see him, lock him in a closet or something." He started off down the hall. "Dorian, you nasty little thief, you can't hide forever."

Hannah walked to the door and looked out to see Bennett turning the corner before she closed it. Moving back to the bed, she crouched down and lifted the skirt. "I think it's safe now," Hannah told him in French.

The dark hair poked out first, then a sturdy little body dressed in short pants and a white linen shirt that were streaked with dirt. If Hannah hadn't already seen his picture, she would have taken him for one of the servants' offspring. But he was royal.

"You are English. I speak excellent English."

"So you do."

"Thank you for hiding me from my uncle." Young Prince Dorian bowed. Though he wasn't yet five, he executed it perfectly. "He was angry, but he doesn't stay that way long. I'm Prince Dorian."

"Your Highness." Hannah curtsied. "It's a pleasure to meet you. I'm Lady Hannah Rothchild." Then unable to resist, she bent down to his level. "What did you steal?"

Dorian glanced at the closed door, back at Hannah, then

grinned. Digging into his back pocket he pulled out a yo-yo. It might once have been blue, but now it was the gray of old wood with a few chips of brighter paint still holding. Hannah studied it with appropriate respect.

"This is Bennett's—His Highness's?" Hannah corrected.

"Merveilleux, n'est-ce pas? He's had it since he was five." Dorian turned the toy over in his hand, marveling that it had once been new and shiny when his uncle had been just the age he was now. "He gets angry when I go into his room and play with it, but how else am I going to be able to make it work?"

"Good point." Hannah barely resisted the urge to ruffle the royal head of hair. "And one would doubt he plays with it himself very often."

"He keeps it on a shelf. It isn't that he really minds me looking at it," Dorian explained, loyal to the core. "It's just that when I try to make it work, the string gets all tangled and knotted up."

"It takes a little practice."

"I know." He grinned again. "And I can only practice if I steal it."

"Your logic is flawless, Your Highness. May I see?"

Dorian hesitated only a moment, then graciously handed it over. "Girls usually aren't interested in such things." He made a grimace of masculine disgust. "My sisters play with dolls."

"Everyone has different tastes, I suppose." Hannah slid her finger into the loop, wondering how long it had been since Bennett's had fit there. The string wasn't as old as the toy itself. By her guess, it would have been replaced more than a dozen times over the years. On impulse, she let the yo-yo slide down, dangle, then brought it neatly up.

"Oh, nicely done." Charmed, Dorian watched her with wide eyes.

"Thank you, sir. I used to have one of my own. It was red,"

she remembered with a half smile. "Until my dog chewed it up."

"Can you do any tricks? I tried Round the World once and broke a lamp. Uncle Bennett scolded me, but then he tossed out the pieces himself so no one would know."

Because she could picture it so well, Hannah smiled. A loud roar, but little bite, she decided and wished she didn't like him the better for it. "A trick?" As she considered she took the yo-yo up and down. Then, with a quick flick of her wrist took it Round the World. When it snapped back in her palm, Dorian laughed and climbed on her bed.

"Do another, please."

Calling on memory, Hannah Walked the Dog and had the young prince bouncing on the bed and calling out for more.

"Well done, Lady Hannah," Bennett said from the doorway. "Obviously you have hidden talents."

Hannah had to bite off an oath as she brought the yo-yo back. "Your Highness." Toy in hand, she curtsied. "I didn't hear you knock."

"I didn't." Bennett pushed away from the doorjamb he was leaning on to walk to the bed. Unrepentant, his nephew grinned up at him.

"Isn't she wonderful, Uncle Bennett?"

"We'll discuss the Lady Hannah's attributes later." He gave Dorian's ear a twist before turning around. "My property, if you will."

Fighting to keep a straight face, Hannah handed it to him.

"This might seem to be nothing more than a simple child's toy," Bennett began as he slipped it into his pocket. "But in fact, it's an heirloom."

"I see." She cleared her throat on the laugh, but it escaped anyway. Hoping she looked contrite, she stared at the floor. "I beg your pardon, sir."

"The hell you do. And he was in here all along wasn't he?"

Bennett pushed his nephew flat on the bed and sent him into a fit of giggles. "You let me go running off all over the palace looking for this petty thief when all the time he was hiding behind your skirts."

"The bed skirts to be honest, sir." She had to clear her throat again, but managed to speak calmly. "When you rushed by with so vague a description, I had no idea you were looking for Prince Dorian."

"I admire a good liar," Bennett murmured as he moved closer. For the second time he caught her chin in his hand. But for the first time, she saw all of the arrogance he was capable of and felt all of its attraction. "And I grow only more intrigued."

"Lady Hannah can do a double Round the World."

"Fascinating." Bennett slid his hand away slowly as he turned back to his nephew. If he'd listened for it, he might have heard Hannah's slow sigh of relief. "I thought we had an agreement, Dorian."

Dorian's head drooped, but Hannah didn't notice that the light in his eyes dimmed in the least. "I only wanted to see it. I'm sorry, Uncle Bennett."

"Sure you are." Bennett hauled him up by the armpits, scowled, then kissed him soundly. "Your mother's downstairs. Don't slide in the halls on the way to the drawing room."

"All right." On his feet again, Dorian bowed to Hannah. "It was a pleasure meeting you, Lady Hannah."

"And you, sir."

He sent her a gap-toothed grin before he dashed off.

"Sweet talker," Bennett muttered. "Oh, you might think he's all charm, but he has a black heart."

"Strangely enough I was reminded of you."

With one brow lifted, Bennett rocked back on his heels. "Indeed, my lady, that is strange."

"He's a scoundrel, without question. And you love him."

"That's beside the point." Bennett stuck his hand in his pocket. "As to the matter of the yo-yo."

"Yes, sir?"

"Try to wait until I'm five feet away before you laugh in my face."

"As you wish, Your Highness."

"It was a gift from my mother when I was ill one summer. I've bought the little devil a dozen of them, but he keeps stealing mine. He knows if I don't get a son of my own by the time he's ten I'll make him a gift of it."

"I have a redheaded doll my mother gave me when I broke my wrist in a fall. I kept it when I outgrew all the others."

It wasn't until he'd taken her hand that she realized she'd told him something he didn't need to know, something she'd never told anyone else. Even as she warned herself such lapses were dangerous, his lips brushed her fingers.

"You, Lady Hannah, have a kind heart as well as a clever tongue. Come, walk downstairs with me and meet the rest of my family."

* * *

Reeve MacGee would be a formidable obstacle. Hannah had thought so before, but seeing him with his family, she was sure of it. She knew his background from the time he'd entered the police force as a rookie through his less publicized work for the United States government.

His involvement with Cordina and the Royal Family had the ring of romance, but Reeve was no poet. He'd come out of a self-imposed retirement at Prince Armand's request when Gabriella had been kidnapped. Though she'd escaped, her time in captivity had left its mark. Amnesia had plagued her and Reeve had been enlisted to protect her, and to investigate.

There had been no doubt that Deboque had been pushing

the buttons, but though his lover had been captured and imprisoned, she'd never implicated him. Like other powerful men, Deboque inspired loyalty. Or fear.

During the time that Gabriella was struggling to regain her memory, she and Reeve had fallen in love. Although Reeve had refused to accept a title when they married, he'd agreed to head security in Cordina. Even with Reeve's experience and skill, the palace had been infiltrated once again.

Two years ago, Alexander had nearly been assassinated. Since that time, Reeve had managed to block any and all attempts on members of the Royal Family. But Deboque was about to walk out of prison. With freedom would come more power.

Hannah watched Reeve now, seeing a quiet, introspective man who plainly adored his wife and children. He would use everything available to protect them from harm. So much the better.

With her hands folded and her skirts smoothed, Hannah sat and listened.

"We all know your play's going to be a wonderful success." Gabriella, with her hand caught loosely in Reeve's, smiled at Eve. Her rich red hair was styled with casual chic around a face that remained delicate and lovely. "That doesn't mean we don't understand you have to worry about it."

"I'm at the point now where I wish it was over." Eve drew Marissa into her lap.

"But you're feeling well?"

"I'm feeling fine." Eve let Marissa climb down again. "Between Alex's pampering and Hannah's eagle eye, I can hardly lift a finger without a doctor's certificate."

"It's so good of you to come." Gabriella smiled at Hannah before she sipped some sparkling water. "I know firsthand how comforting it is to have a friend nearby. Are we keeping you happy enough so that you're not homesick?"

"I'm very happy in Cordina." Hannah kept her back straight against the sofa.

"I hope you'll come out to the farm while you're here."

"I've heard a great deal about it." Gabriella had been kidnapped there while it had still been an overgrown plot of land. "I'd love to see it for myself."

"Then we'll arrange it." Reeve spoke quietly as he lit a cigarette. "You're enjoying your visit so far?"

"Yes, I am." Their eyes met and held. "Cordina is a fascinating country. It has a fairy-tale aura perhaps, but it's very real. I'm particularly interested in visiting the museum."

"I think you'll find we have some very unusual exhibits," Armand put in.

"Yes, sir. I did some research before leaving England. I have no doubt that my time in Cordina will be an education."

Marissa toddled over, still a bit unsteady on her year-old legs, and held her arms up. Hannah placed the child in her lap.

"Your father is well?" Reeve asked her through a haze of smoke.

Hannah jangled her pearls to entertain the baby. "Yes, thank you. It often seems that the older I get, the younger he gets."

"Families, no matter how large or how small, are often the focus of our lives," Reeve said quietly.

"Yes, that's true," Hannah murmured as she played with the baby. "It's a pity that families, and life, aren't as simple as they seem when we're children."

Bennett sat relaxed in his chair and wondered why he thought if he could read between the lines, he'd discover a great deal more than small talk.

"I wasn't aware you knew Hannah's father, Reeve."

"Only casually." When he leaned back, his smile was easy. "I heard that Dorian stole your yo-yo again."

"I should have locked it in the safe when I heard he was coming." Bennett patted the slight bulge in his pocket. "I'd have given the little devil a run for his money, but he had an accomplice." He turned his head to look at Hannah.

"I'll have to apologize for my son," Gabriella's lips curved as she lifted her glass again. "For drawing you into his crime, Lady Hannah."

"On the contrary. I enjoyed it. Prince Dorian is charming."

"We call him other things at home," Reeve murmured. The woman was a mystery, he thought. The harder he looked for chinks, the fewer flaws he saw. "With that in mind, I think I'll go out and look for the bunch of them. Adrienne's at the age where you can't be sure she'll mind them or urge them to wade in the fountain."

Bennett glanced toward the terrace doors. "God knows what havoc they might have wrought in the last twenty minutes."

"Wait until you have your own." Eve rose to take Marissa from Hannah. "You'll spoil them rotten. If you'll excuse me, I want to go up and feed Marissa."

"I'll go with you." Gabriella set her glass aside. "I thought we might talk over the plans for the Christmas Ball. You know I want to help as much as I can."

"Thank God I don't have to beg. No, Hannah, please, sit and relax," Eve continued as Hannah started to stand. "We won't be long."

"See that you're not." Bennett took out the yo-yo to pass it from hand to hand. "Dinner's in an hour."

"We all know your priorities, Ben." Eve bent to kiss his cheek before she left the room.

"I could use a walk myself." Rising, Alexander nodded to Reeve. "I'll help you round up the children." They were barely out the terrace doors when a servant appeared in the doorway.

"I beg your pardon, Your Highness. A call from Paris."

"Yes, I've been expecting it. I'll take it in my office, Louis. If you'll excuse me, Lady Hannah." Taking her hand, Armand bowed over it. "I'm sure Bennett can entertain you for a few moments. Bennett, perhaps Lady Hannah would enjoy seeing the library."

"If you like to look at walls of books," Bennett said when his father was gone, "you can't do much better."

"I'm very fond of books." Taking him at his word, Hannah rose.

"All right then." Though he could have thought of a dozen better ways to while away an hour, he took her arm and led her through the corridors.

"It's difficult to believe that the museum could have finer paintings than you have here in the palace, Prince Bennett."

"Le Musée d'Art has a hundred and fifty-two examples of Impressionist and Postimpressionist paintings, including two Corots, three Monets and a particularly fine Renoir. We've recently acquired a Childe Hassam from the United States. In return my family has donated six Georges Complainiers, a Cordinian artist who painted on the island in the nineteenth century."

"I see."

Noting her expression, Bennett laughed. "As it happens, I'm on the board of the museum. I may prefer horses, Hannah, but that doesn't preclude an affection for art. What do you think of this?"

He paused in front of a small watercolor. The Royal Palace was beautifully, almost mystically painted. Its white, white walls and turrets rose behind a pink mist that enchanted rather than concealed the building itself. It must have been dawn, she thought. The sky was such a delicate blue in contrast to the deeper sea. She could see the antiquity, the fantasy and the reality. In the foreground were the high iron gates and sturdy stone walls that protected the palace grounds.

"It's beautiful. It shows love as well as a touch of wonder. Who was the artist?"

"My great-great-grandmother." Pleased with her reaction,

Bennett drew her hand into the crook of his arm. "She'd done hundreds of watercolors and had tucked them away. In her day, women painted or drew as a hobby, not as a profession."

"Some things change," Hannah murmured, then looked back at the painting. "Some things don't."

"A few years ago I found her work in a trunk in one of the attics. So many of them had been damaged. It broke my heart. Then I found this." He touched the frame, reverently, Hannah thought. She looked from his hand to his face and found herself caught up in him. "It was like stepping back in time, generations, and discovering yourself. It could have been painted today, and it would look the same."

She could feel her heart moving toward him. What woman was immune to pride and sensitivity? In defense, she took a small step back. "In Europe, we understand that a few generations are only a blink in time. Our history stands before us, centuries of it. It becomes our responsibility to give that same gift to each new generation."

Bennett looked at her and found her eyes almost impossibly deep. "We do have that in common, don't we? In America, there's an urgency that can be exciting, even contagious, but here, we know how long it takes to build and secure. Politics change, governments shift, but history stands firm."

She had to turn away from him. It would only cloud the issue if she thought of him as a caring, sensitive man rather than an assignment. "Are there any others?" she said with a nod toward the painting.

"Only a handful, unfortunately. Most were beyond repair." For reasons he could only be half-sure of, he wanted to share with her things that mattered to him. "There's one in the music room. The rest are in the museum. Here, have a look." With his hand guiding her again, he took her down the hall into the next wing, their footsteps echoing off the mosaic tile.

Leading her through an open door, Bennett took her into a

room that seemed to have been fashioned to accent the white grand piano in its center.

There was a harp in the corner that might have been played a hundred years before, or last week. In a glass case were antique wind instruments and a fragile lyre. The flowers were fresh here, as they were in every room in the palace. Trailing blossoms of jasmine spilled out of glossy, Chinese red urns. A small marble fireplace was swept and scrubbed clean with a pile of fresh kindling stacked as though inviting the match.

With Bennett, she walked across an Aubusson carpet to look back in time. This painting was of a ball, festive in bright colors and bold strokes. Women, gloriously feminine in mid-nineteenth-century gowns, were whirled around a gleaming floor by dashing men. There were mirrors that reflected the dancers and doubled them while a trio of chandeliers glistened overhead. As Hannah studied it, she could almost hear the waltz.

"How lovely. Is this room here, in the palace?"

"Yes. It has hardly changed. We'll have the Christmas Ball there next month."

Only a month, she thought. There was so much to be done. In a matter of hours Deboque would be out of prison, and she would soon learn if her groundwork had been clever enough.

"This is a beautiful room." Hannah turned. Keep your conversation light, she warned herself. Keep your mind light, for now. "In our country house there's a small music room. Nothing like this, of course, but I've always found it so relaxing." She wandered to the piano, not so much to examine it as to give herself distance. "Do you play, Your Highness?"

"Hannah, we're alone. It isn't necessary to be so formal."

"I've always considered the use of titles as proper rather than formal." She didn't want this, she thought quickly. She didn't want him to close that gap of rank between them.

"I've always considered it annoying between friends." He walked behind her to touch her lightly on the shoulder. "I thought we were."

She could feel his hand right through the neat linen of her dress, through the skinny silk strap beneath and onto her flesh. Fighting her own private war, she kept her back to him. "Were what, sir?"

He laughed, then both hands were on her shoulders, turning her to face him. "Friends, Hannah. I find you good company. That's one of the first requirements of friendship, isn't it?"

She was looking up at him, solemn-eyed, with the faintest blush of color along her cheekbones. Her shoulders seemed so strong under his hands, yet he remembered how soft, how delicate the skin along her jawline had seemed.

Her dress was brown and dull, her face unpainted and unframed. Not a hair was out of place and yet he got a flash of her laughing, her hair unbound and her shoulders bare. And the laughter would be for only him.

"What the devil is it about you?" Bennett muttered.

"I beg your pardon—"

"Wait." Impatient, as annoyed with himself as he was with her, Bennett stepped closer. As she stiffened, he held his hands up, palms out as if to reassure her he meant her no harm. "Just be still a moment, would you?" he asked as he lowered his head and touched his mouth to hers.

No response, show no response. Hannah repeated it over and over in her head like a litany. He didn't press, he didn't coax or demand. He simply tasted, more gently than she'd known a man could be. And the flavor of him seeped into her until she was all but drunk with it.

His eyes remained open, watching hers. He was close, so close she could catch the scent of soap on his skin. Something that brought images of the sea. Hannah dug her fingers into her palms and fought to keep from showing him the turmoil within.

God, she wanted. How she wanted.

He didn't know what he'd expected. What he found was softness, comfort, sweetness without heat or passion. Yet he saw both in her eyes. He felt no driving need to touch her or to deepen the kiss. Not this first one. Perhaps he already knew there would be others. But this first one showed him an ease, a relaxation that he'd never looked for in a woman before.

He was man enough, experienced enough, to know there was a volcano inside of her. But strangely, he had no desire to push it to the eruption point, yet.

Bennett broke the kiss simply by stepping back. Hannah didn't move a muscle.

"I didn't do that to frighten you." He spoke quietly, for it was the truth. "It was just a test."

"You don't frighten me." He didn't frighten the woman he could see, but the one within was terrified.

It wasn't quite the answer he'd wanted. "Then what do I do to you?"

Slowly, carefully, she unballed her hands. "I'm afraid I don't understand what you mean, Your Highness."

He studied her another moment, then spun away. "Maybe not." He rubbed a hand along the back of his neck wondering why such an unassuming, placid woman should make him so tense. He understood desire. God knows he'd felt it before. But not like this. Never quite like this.

"Dammit, Hannah, isn't anything going on inside of you?"

"Of course, sir, a great number of things."

He had to laugh. He should have known she would put him in his place with logic. "Call me by my name, please."

"As you wish."

He turned back. She was standing in front of the glistening white piano, hands folded, eyes calm and quiet on his. He thought it the most ridiculous thing, but knew he was very close to falling in love. "Hannah—"

He'd taken no more than two steps toward her when Reeve walked into the room. "Bennett, excuse me, but your father would like to see you before dinner."

Duty and desire. Bennett wondered if he would ever find a full merging of the two. "Thank you, Reeve."

"I'll take Lady Hannah back in."

"All right." Still, he paused and looked at her again. "I'd like to talk with you later."

"Of course." She would move heaven and earth to avoid it.

She remained where she was when he left. Reeve glanced over his shoulder before he came closer. "Is there a problem, Lady Hannah?"

"No." She drew a deep breath, but didn't relax. "Why should there be?"

"Bennett can be . . . distracting."

This time when her eyes met his, she made certain they were slightly amused. A layer, the thinnest of the layers of her outer covering was dismissed. "I'm not easily distracted, particularly when I'm working."

"So I've been told," Reeve said easily enough. He was still looking for flaws and was afraid he might have found the first in the way she had looked at Bennett. "But you've never worked on an assignment quite like this one."

"As a senior agent for the ISS, I'm capable of handling any assignment." Her voice was brisk again, not the voice of a woman who'd been moved, almost unbearably, by a kiss. "You'll have my report by tomorrow. Now I think we'd better join the others."

She started by, but he took her arm and stopped her. "There's a great deal riding on this. On you."

Hannah only nodded. "I'm aware of that. You requested the best, and I am."

"Maybe." But the closer it came, the more he worried. "You've got a hell of a reputation, Hannah, but you've never come up against anyone like Deboque before."

"Nor he anyone like me." She glanced toward the hallway again, then lowered her voice. "I'm an established member of his organization now. It's taken me two years to get this close. I saved him two and a half million by seeing that that munitions deal wasn't botched six months ago. A man like Deboque appreciates initiative. In the last few months, I've been planting the seeds that will discredit his second in command."

"Or get your throat cut."

"That's for me to worry about. In a matter of weeks, I'll be his right hand. Then I'll serve him to you on a platter."

"Confidence is an excellent weapon, if it isn't overdone."

"I don't overdo." She thought of Bennett and strengthened her resolve. "I've never failed with an assignment, Reeve. I don't intend to begin with this one."

"Just make sure you keep in contact. I'm sure you'll understand when I say I don't trust anyone."

"I understand perfectly, because neither do I. Shall we go?"

CHAPTER 4

Hannah's plans to avoid driving with Bennett to Le Havre were neatly demolished. She'd justified her decision by convincing herself she could detail more useful information by concentrating on the palace. In order to remain behind, she'd come up with the credible, if unoriginal excuse of a headache.

Hannah had deliberately waited until Alexander had finished breakfasting with his family so that she could speak to Eve alone. It took Eve less than ten minutes to turn it on her.

"It's no wonder you're not feeling yourself." Eve sipped tea in the sunny nursery while she looked over her schedule. "I've kept you cooped up ever since you arrived."

"Don't be silly. The palace is the size of a small town. I've hardly been cooped up."

"However big it is, it still has walls. A nice drive along the coast is just what you need. Bernadette." She glanced up at the young nurse who was preparing to take Marissa for her morning walk. "Would you see that Princess Marissa has a hat? It's a bit breezy out."

"Yes, ma'am."

Eve held out her arms for her daughter. "Have a nice time, darling."

"Flowers," Marissa said, and laughed at her own voice.

"Yes, pick some flowers. We'll put them right here in your room." She kissed both of Marissa's cheeks then let her go. "I hate not being able to take her for a walk this morning, but I have a meeting at the Center in an hour."

"You're a wonderful mother, Eve," Hannah murmured when she saw the concern in Eve's eyes.

"I love her so much." With a long sigh, she picked up her tea again. "I know it's foolish, but when I'm not with her I think of dozens of things that might happen, that could happen."

"I'd say it was normal."

"Maybe. Being who we are, what we are, just magnifies everything." Unconsciously, she rested her hand where even now her second child slept. "I want so badly to give her a sense of normalcy, and yet . . ." Eve shook her head. "There's a price for everything."

Hannah remembered Alexander saying almost the same thing in referring to his wife.

"Eve, Marissa is a lovely, healthy and happy child. I'm not sure they get any more normal than that."

Eve stared at her a moment, then dropped her chin on her open palm. "Oh, Hannah, I'm not sure how I got through the last two years without you. Which brings me right back to where we were." Briskly, Eve refilled Hannah's cup. "You came here to visit and so far I haven't given you a moment's free time unless you were handcuffed to me. That makes me feel very selfish."

"The reason I'm here is to be with you," Hannah reminded Eve, as she felt herself rapidly losing ground.

"The reason you're here is because we're friends. As a favor, take the day, relax, enjoy the sea air. I promise you Ben can be wonderful company. I guarantee that five minutes after you're in the car, your headache will disappear."

"Someone have a headache?" Ben asked as he strode in. He

was wearing the white dress uniform with the red insignia that stated his rank as officer in the Cordinian Navy. On the left breast pocket was the royal seal that proclaimed him prince. Hannah had always considered the opinion that women fell for men in uniform nonsense. Until now.

He looked so . . . dashing, she admitted, though her practical side searched for a less dramatic word. The snowy white jacket accented his tan and the dark contrast of his hair. He grinned at her, making Hannah aware that he understood his effect. Automatically she rose to dip into a curtsy.

"Bennett, I'd forgotten what a heartbreaker you are in dress whites." Eve tipped her face up for a kiss. "Maybe I should tell Hannah to take an aspirin and stay behind after all."

"I think Lady Hannah can take care of herself. Can't you, *chérie*?"

Hannah decided then and there that if she had to fence with him, she would wield her foil well. "It's always been the case."

"You are a bit pale." He touched a finger to her cheek. "Are you really not well?"

"It's nothing." She wondered if he could feel her blood stir at the casual contact. "And Eve assures me that a drive along the sea is exactly the right prescription."

"Good. I'll bring her back with roses in her cheeks."

"If you'll give me a moment, I need to get my bag."

"Bennett." Eve stopped him before he could follow Hannah out. "Am I wrong, or did I see something just now?"

He didn't pretend to misunderstand her. "I'm not sure."

"Hannah's lived a very sheltered life. I suppose I don't have to tell you to be . . . well, careful?"

Though the sunlight streamed in behind him, his eyes cooled. "No, I don't have to be reminded who a man in my position can and can't have an affair with."

"I didn't say that to annoy you." Instantly Eve was on her feet, taking his hands. "We were friends long before we were family, Ben. I only ask because I'm fond of her and I know how irresistible you can be."

He softened, as he always did with Eve. "You always managed to resist."

"You always treated me like a sister." Eve hesitated again, torn between two loyalties. "Would I be pushing if I said she's not your usual type?"

"No, she's not. Perhaps that's what baffles me. Stop worrying." He bent to kiss her brow. "I won't damage your proper British friend."

"It could be I'm just as concerned about you."

"Then don't be." Giving her cheek a careless stroke, he walked to the door. "Tell Marissa I'll bring her some seashells."

Calm and resigned to her decision, Hannah met him at the top of the stairs. "I hope I didn't keep you waiting."

"We've plenty of time. I can promise the drive will be worth the pomp and speeches on the other end."

"I don't object to pomp and speeches."

"Then we're fortunate. Claude." Bennett nodded to the tall, sturdy man who waited beside the main doors.

"Good morning, Your Highness. Lady Hannah. Your car is ready, sir."

"Thank you, Claude." Bennett steered Hannah through the doors knowing the simple statement meant that the road between Cordina and Le Havre had been secured.

Hannah saw the car the moment they stepped outside. The zippy little French convertible sat at the foot of the steps flanked by two solid sedans.

"Do you drive that?"

"Looks like I should wind it up, doesn't it?" Bennett touched the shiny red hood with affection. "Handles like a dream. I've had her up to one-twenty on a straight."

She thought of how it would feel, speeding beside the sea with the wind on her face. Hannah pushed aside such wishes and tried for an uneasy look. "I hope you don't intend to try to break your record today."

With a laugh, he opened the door for her himself. "For you, I'll drive like a grandfather."

Hannah slipped into the seat and nearly sighed with pleasure. "It is rather small."

"Big enough for two." Bennett rounded the hood. Claude already had his door opened.

"But surely you don't travel without your security or an assistant."

"Whenever possible. My secretary will be in the car behind us. Let's give them a run, shall we?" He switched on the ignition. From the rich sound under the hood, Hannah decided it was filled with engine. Before she could draw a breath, Bennett sent the car speeding down the long, sedate drive. He drove the way he rode a stallion. Full speed.

"They're muttering already, I imagine." He gave the guards at the gates an easy salute. "If Claude had his way, I'd never go over thirty kilometers. I'd also be closed up in a bulletproof limo wearing a suit of armor."

"It's his job to protect you."

"A pity he has so little humor about it." Bennett downshifted, then sent the car squeaking around a curve.

"Did your grandfather live a long and fruitful life?"

"What?"

"Your grandfather," Hannah repeated as she folded her hands neatly in her lap. "I wondered if he lived a long life. It seems unlikely if he drove like this."

The wind was blowing his hair around his face as he turned his head to grin at her. "Trust me, *ma belle*, I know the roads."

She didn't want him to slow down. It was the first time she'd felt true freedom in months. She'd nearly forgotten how sweet it tasted. The sea shimmered blue and white beside the road as they traveled down from the heights of the capital. Palms twisted their way toward the sky, bending and swaying in the stiff breeze. Lush red flowers burst out of bushes that grew helter-skelter along the roadside. The air smelled of sea and perpetual spring.

"Do you ski?" Bennett asked her as he noticed her watching a man glide over the water behind a low-slung boat.

"I never have." It looked wonderful. "I'm sure you have to be fairly athletic. I'm more at home in libraries."

"One can't read all the time."

She watched the skier take a somersaulting tumble into the water. "I think perhaps I can."

Bennett grinned and roared though a lazy S-turn. "Life's hardly worth the trouble without a few spills. Don't you ever have the urge for adventure, Hannah?"

She thought of the last ten years of her life, of the assignments that had taken her from castles to ghettos and everywhere in between. French alleys. Italian waterfronts. She thought of the small-caliber pistol she carried in her bag and the pencil-slim stiletto tucked like a lover against her thigh.

"I suppose I've always preferred my adventures vicariously, through books."

"No secret dreams?"

"Some of us are exactly what we seem." Suddenly uncomfortable, she shifted away from the topic. "I didn't realize you were a naval officer." Another lie, she thought. But her profession was built on them.

"I served a couple of years. At this point, it's more of an honorary rank. Second sons are traditionally bound for the military."

"So you chose the navy."

"Cordina's surrounded by the sea. Our fleet is smaller than yours, certainly, but it's strong."

"And these are uneasy times."

Something came and went in his eyes. "In Cordina we've

learned that all times are uneasy times. We're a peaceful country, and because we want to remain so, we're prepared always for war."

She thought of the pretty white palace with its exotic gardens and fairy-tale turrets. Inaccessible by sea, with a cliff-top view that scanned miles with the naked eye. She sat back as the sea rolled by. Nothing ever was as simple as it seemed.

Le Havre was charming. Nestled at the base of a long hill, it clustered together with small white-washed buildings and clapboard cottages. Fishing and sail boats swayed quietly at neat docks at one curve of the harbor. Around the seawall of old stone, hardy blue flowers pushed their way through cracks. There were lobster traps and nets spread and drying in the sun. The scent of fish was heady and oddly pleasant in the early morning air.

At a glance, it could have been taken for any tidy fishing town that survived on and with the sea. But as they rounded the harbor the docks became more expansive, the buildings larger. Cargo ships with men hauling freight down gangplanks flanked an ocean liner. Like much of Cordina, Le Havre was more than it seemed. Through location and the skill of its people, it was one of the finest ports of call in the Mediterranean. It was also the center of Cordina's naval base.

Negotiating the narrow, winding streets, Bennett drove through a set of gates. He slowed only long enough to be acknowledged by the guards with snappy salutes. There were bungalows here painted a faded pink that reminded Hannah of the inside of a seashell. Palms and flowers grew in profusion, but she recognized the structure and order of a military facility. Moments later, Bennett drew up in front of a stucco building where seamen in whites stood at attention.

"For the next few hours," he murmured to Hannah, "we're official." Bennett reached in the back and picked up his hat. Even as he set it on his wind-ruffled hair, one of the seamen reached the door to open it for him. With the brim shading his eyes, Bennett returned the salutes. He knew the sedan had already pulled up behind him, but didn't look back as he guided Hannah into the building.

"First, we have a few formalities," he warned her, tucking his hat under his arm.

The formalities were a group of officers, from admiral down, and their wives and attachés who were waiting to greet and be greeted by His Royal Highness.

Hannah acknowledged the introductions and pretended not to see the looks of speculation. *Not the prince's type.* She could read it easily in every eye that met hers. She fully agreed.

They were given tea and a tour of the building—for her sake. Hannah feigned an ignorance of the equipment shown her, asking the proper questions and looking properly polite at the simplistic answers. She could hardly mention that the radar and communication systems were as familiar to her as they were to the trained operators. In a pinch, she could have rigged the equipment to contact the ISS base outside London or Deboque's headquarters in Athens.

She walked by display cases, listening with apparent fascination as an admiral explained to her the difference between a destroyer and an aircraft carrier.

The pomp and circumstance continued as they were escorted outside to await the docking of the *Indépendence*. The band, their white uniforms blinding in the sun, struck up a rousing march as Bennett stepped onto the dock. Crowds of people cheered from behind the military barricade. Babies and small children were held up so that they could catch a glimpse of the prince.

Hannah counted off a dozen security people mingled with the crowd in addition to the two men who were never more than an arm's span from Bennett's elbow.

Deboque is out, she thought. Everything is a risk.

The battle-gray destroyer maneuvered into position while the crowd applauded and the band continued to play. Seamen on the dock stood at attention as did seamen on deck. After six months at sea, the *Indépendance* was home.

The gangplank came ponderously down. The pipes were sounded. The captain strode down to salute the officers and bow to his prince.

"Welcome home, Captain." Bennett offered his hand, and the crowd cheered again.

There was, as there always was on such occasions, a speech to be made. Hannah kept her face attentive while she slowly scanned the crowd.

It was no surprise to find him there. The small, slightly stoop-shouldered man was on the edge of the crowd holding a small Cordinian flag. In his plain work clothes and quiet face, he would never be noticed or remembered. He was one of Deboque's best.

There would be no move on Prince Bennett today, she thought, though the back of her neck itched. Her successful planting at the palace had been one of her highest contributions to Deboque's organization. The working order now was for care and cleverness rather than a rash assassination attempt.

In any case, she knew Deboque wasn't as interested in Bennett as he was in Alexander, and in Alexander not so much as in Armand. He wouldn't settle for the second in line to the throne after so long a wait.

Still, she closed her hand over the handle of her bag. She shifted, only a matter of inches, but Bennett's body was now more than half shielded by hers.

Had the man been sent with a message for her? Hannah wondered. Or had he simply been ordered to stay close and watch? Instinct told her it was the second. Casually, she swept the crowd again. Her eyes met his and held for only a fraction of a second. There was an acknowledgment, but no signal.

Hannah let her gaze move on, knowing they'd meet within a few days at the museum.

The pretty ceremony with its brisk military music and banners continued with a tour of the ship and an inspection of the crew. Hannah walked with the admiral's wife as Bennett was led down the line of officers and seamen. Now and then he stopped to comment or ask a personal question of one of the men. More, she saw that he listened to the answers. Even a casual observer could have seen that he was given more than respect due his rank by the men he greeted. There was love, the kind Hannah was aware only men could give men.

Though she was certain Bennett had seen enough of ships to last a lifetime, he toured the bridge, the officers' quarters and the galleys with apparent fascination. The ship was as neat as a parlor, utilitarian certainly, but freshly scrubbed and without a sign of peeling paint or rust.

Bennett moved quickly through the ship, without seeming to hurry over the decks. There were questions that had to be asked, compliments that were deserved, but he knew duffel bags were packed and waiting. He clasped hands with the captain again, aware that the man had every right to be proud of his ship and his men. As he started down the gangplank, the cheers rose up again. Bennett had to wonder if they were for him or because the ceremonies were finally over and the men could go ashore.

Protocol demanded that he be escorted back through headquarters. It was here that Hannah began to sense his impatience to be off. Still, he was gracious, shaking hands, kissing hands, exchanging a last pleasantry. It wasn't until he was seated in his own car again that he let out a low oath.

"I beg your pardon, sir?"

Bennett merely patted Hannah's hand before he started the engine. "Four hours was a long time to keep you on your feet. Thank you for bearing with me."

"On the contrary, I found it fascinating." Nothing had ever seemed more wonderful than the wind blowing on her face again as the convertible picked up speed. "The tour of the ship was particularly educational. It was clever, wasn't it, for the ship's cook to frame a recipe for crepes where the flour was measured in pounds rather than cups?"

"Food becomes a priority after a few months at sea." He glanced over, surprised she'd been so well entertained by a ship and several pompous speeches. "If I'd known you were really interested I wouldn't have hurried things along quite so much."

"I suppose it becomes all routine and a bit boring for you after a while."

"I was thinking of the men. All they really wanted was to get ashore to their wives or lovers—or both." He was grinning when he turned his head toward her. "You can't imagine what four months at sea is like when the only woman you see is in a glossy photo with staple marks in the middle."

Her lips twitched, but she managed to hold the smile to a bare acknowledgment. "No, I'm sure I can't. But I think you enjoyed your time at sea, Bennett. It showed in the way you spoke with the men and looked at the ship."

He said nothing for a moment, surprised and not displeased that she had understood that so quickly. "I was more of an officer and less of a prince then. I can't say I have the sea in my blood the way Captain Dumont does, but it isn't something I'll forget."

"What is it you remember best?" she asked before she caught herself.

"Watching the sun rise at sea or better, riding out a storm. God, we went through one off Crete. The waves were a fifty-foot wall. The wind was like the wrath of God, so loud, so enormous that you could shout in someone's ear and not be heard. No sky, only water, wall after wall of it. An experience like that changes you."

"How?"

"It makes you realize that no matter who you are, what you are, there's something bigger, greater. Nature's a powerful equalizer, Hannah. Look at her now." With one hand he gestured toward the sea as he negotiated another curve. "Calm, almost impossibly beautiful. A hurricane doesn't make her less beautiful, only more dangerous."

"It sounds as though you prefer the danger." She understood that, perhaps too well.

"At times. Danger's its own seduction."

She could say nothing to that. It was something she had learned herself years before.

With the briefest of signals to the car behind him, Bennett pulled over. "At the moment I prefer the calm." He got out of the convertible, ignoring the guard who stood anxiously by the hood of the trailing car. "Walk with me on the beach, Hannah." He opened her door and held out a hand. "I promised Marissa some shells."

"Your security doesn't look pleased." Nor was she when she noticed how open they were.

"They'd only be pleased if I were sitting in a bulletproof globe. Come now, Hannah, didn't you tell me sea air was good for the constitution?"

"Yes." She laid her hand in his. He was safe, after all, as long as she played her part and played it well. "You'll have to find shells big enough that they can't be swallowed. At Marissa's age, children tend to eat the oddest things."

"Always practical." With an easy laugh, he lifted her by the waist over the low seawall. He saw her gaze focus over his shoulder and knew a guard would be following at a discreet distance. "You should take your shoes off, Hannah. You'll only get sand in them."

It was the practical thing to do, of course. The logical thing.

Hannah tried to tell herself she wasn't shedding part of her cover along with the pumps. "You must have some fascinating coral formations in these waters."

"Do you scuba?"

"No," she lied. "I'm not a very strong swimmer. I went to a marine exhibit in London a few years ago. Until then, I had no idea what an incredible variety of shells there were, or how valuable they can be."

"Lucky for me Marissa has simple tastes." With his hand on hers, he walked to the sea edge. "A couple of clam shells, and she'll be delighted."

"It's kind of you to think of her." He *was* kind, she thought. That itself was one of the most difficult things to overlook. "You seem to be a great favorite among your nieces and nephews."

"Oh, I suppose that's because I don't mind making a fool of myself now and then in a game. How about this one?" Bending, he picked up a long spiral that had broken off a larger shell and been worn smooth by the ebb and flow of the sea. At the top of the curve was a peaked cap that looked almost like a crown.

"Very suitable," Hannah commented when he handed it to her.

"Marissa doesn't care for suitable. She prefers pretty."

"It is pretty." With a smile, Hannah ran a finger along the curve that went from pale amber to polished pink. "She should have it in her windowsill where the sun would hit it. Oh look." Forgetting herself, she stepped into the surf and pried out an unbroken scallop shell. It was shaped like a fan, bone-white on one side, opalescent pink inside its shallow bowl. "You could tell her that fairies take their biscuits in it when they have tea."

"So Hannah believes in fairies," he murmured.

Caught up short, she handed him the shell. "No, but I think Marissa might."

Bennett slipped the shell into his pocket. "Your feet are wet."

"They'll dry quickly enough." She started to step back. He took her hand again, holding her in the shallow, foaming surf. "Since we're here, we ought to try for a couple more." Without waiting for a response he began to walk along the shoreline.

The water was warm and soft on her feet and ankles, but no warmer, no softer, than the air that blew in over it. Through the crystal water she could see the bed of white sand and the glittering sparkles of shells that had been crushed by waves. The surf was quiet here, all sighs and whispers.

There was nothing romantic in it, Hannah warned herself. She couldn't allow there to be. The line she walked was thinner and sharper than any she'd walked before. One misstep could mean tragedy at least, war at the worst. Determined to keep her place, she concentrated on the guards a few yards at their back.

"The ceremony today was lovely. I'm grateful you asked me to come."

"My reasons were purely selfish. I wanted your company."

Struggling not to be touched, she tried again. "In England there's often satire and criticism of the Royal Family, but beneath it all is a very real affection. I see that same kind of love and respect for your family here."

"My father would tell you that we serve as well as govern. He gives them solidity and confidence. Alex gives them the hope for the future. A continuation of tradition. In Brie they have glamour and intelligence as well as humanity."

"And in you?"

"Entertainment."

It annoyed her. She couldn't say why but his careless dismissal of himself made her stop and frown at him. "You underestimate yourself."

Surprised, Bennett cocked his head and studied her. It was there again, that something, that indefinable something in her eyes that had attracted him all along. "Not really. I'm well aware that I do my duty. My father raised all of us to understand that we didn't simply inherit a title or position. We had to earn it." He drew her back a bit so that the spray from the surf didn't dampen her skirt. "I won't rule. Thank God. That's for Alex and then for the son I continue to hope Eve gives us all this time around. Because I won't, I don't have to take myself as seriously as Alex, but that doesn't mean I take Cordina or my responsibilities to it lightly."

"I didn't mean to criticize."

"I didn't think you did. I only meant that above my official duties, my official position, I give the people something— someone to talk about over a glass of wine or an evening meal. I've been haunted by the title of Playboy Prince since I was in my teens." He grinned then and tucked a stray hair behind her ear. "I can't say I didn't do everything possible to earn it."

"I prefer literature to gossip," Hannah said primly as she started to walk on.

"Gossip has its place." Amused, Bennett stopped her.

"Apparently you enjoy it."

"No." His eyes darkened as he looked beyond her and out to sea. "I'm just accustomed to it. It's difficult, when you're twenty, to know that every time you look more than casually at a woman it's going to be splashed somewhere in bold print, pictures included. I like women." This time he smiled and looked back at her. "Since I didn't want to change that aspect of my personality, I decided to live with public speculation. If I've sinned, it was in lack of discretion."

"Some might say it was the quantity."

There was only the shortest of hesitations before he threw his head back and roared with laughter. "Oh, Hannah, what a gem you are. So you *have* whiled away some time with something besides Yeats."

"I may have skimmed a few headlines."

Laughing again, he swung her in a circle before she could prevent it. "Priceless. Absolutely priceless." His eyes were glowing as he set her back down. "I adore how you cut me down to size so skillfully."

Automatically, Hannah smoothed down her skirt. "I'm sure you've mistaken my intent."

"The devil I have. That's what delights me about you."

The frustrated look she gave him had nothing to do with the role she was playing. Delighting him had never been part of the plan. She was there to observe, to cement her position and to carry out a plan that was years in the making. Never before had the proper Lady Hannah had to worry about piquing a man's interest. Even as she calculated how to cancel it out again, he was reaching for her.

"Your hair's falling down." In a casual move he plucked a loose pin that was dangling near her shoulder. "My fault for not putting the top up."

"I must look as though I've been through a hurricane." She reached up to put the practical hairstyle back in place. Pins fell out in her hand, loosened by wind and weight. Even as she swore silently, her hair tumbled free, waterfalling past her shoulders to her waist.

"Mon Dieu." Before she could twist her hair back, Bennett had filled both hands with it. Twined around his fingers it was deep, honey blond and soft as silk. He stared, thunderstruck, by the transformation. It waved wild and free around her face, accenting the slash of cheekbones that only looked hard and angular without the framing. Her face no longer seemed thin and bony, but exotic. *"C'est magnifique. C'est la chevelure d'un ange."*

With her heart pounding, she tried to ignore what she saw in his eyes. It wasn't innocent delight or casual attraction now. Now there was desire, man for woman, basic, strong and as dangerous as the sea in a storm. She couldn't move back from him for his hands were buried in her hair. She couldn't deny the lunge of her own needs as he kept her close.

It wasn't supposed to happen. Even now she could tell herself it couldn't happen. Yet she wanted to be held by him, to be comforted, to be, though the words sounded foolish in her mind, cherished. Desired, needed, loved. All of those things were against the rules, but she found it hard to pull back.

"Angel hair," Bennett repeated in a whisper. "Why does a woman bind beauty up and hide it?"

No, she couldn't deny what was happening inside her, but she could, as she'd been trained, deny herself. "It's more practical worn up." She lifted her hands to scoop it from his and met resistance.

Yes, he'd been right all along. There was more, much more to her than she allowed to show on the surface. Perhaps it was that which continued to draw him in, make him want, make him need in a way he never had before. If it had been possible, he would have pulled her to him then. It wasn't the guards that stopped him, but the trace of anxiety he saw in her eyes.

"If that was true, my most practical Hannah, why haven't you simply cut it off?"

How many times had she nearly done so then pulled back at the last minute? Drawing a deep breath she offered the simple truth because truth was often the best cover of all. "Even I have some vanity."

"It makes you beautiful." He dragged his hands through her hair again, hardly able to believe it had been hidden by a handful of pins.

"Only different." Her smile hid the tension that was pulling her in two directions.

"Any man would approve of such a difference." She was stiff beneath his hands. With reluctance he acknowledged it and released her. "But then, you don't look for a man's approval, do you?"

"I've never found it necessary." With a few expert twists, she had her hair at the base of her neck again. The pins were pushed in until it was secure. She could almost, just almost feel secure herself. "We should be getting back. Eve may need me."

With a nod, Bennett began to walk back to the car with her. There would be another time and another place. He found in himself something he experienced rarely, particularly when it had to do with a woman. Patience.

"You can pin it up, Hannah. But now that I know what it looks like down, I'll see it that way whenever I look at you." When they reached the seawall, he again lifted her over, but this time stood, his hands around her waist and the wall between them. "Knowing this one secret makes me wonder how many others you have, and how soon I'll find them."

Anxiety and desire were a powerful combination. She felt her heart thud with both. "I'm afraid you'll be disappointed, Bennett. I have no interesting secrets."

"We'll see," he said, before he vaulted easily over the seawall.

CHAPTER 5

It wasn't often Hannah yearned to be beautiful. Her work had given her a fine appreciation for the beauty of being unremarkable, even forgettable. Over the years, she'd experienced a twinge now and then, but only a twinge when she thought of soft colors and filmy dresses. It had always been possible to release the urge when she was off duty and out of the country. Then her appearance could be changed with a more discerning choice of color and cut and a few clever strokes with a makeup brush.

There could be no release now, and no yearning.

Hannah knew everyone would look wonderful for Eve's dinner party. An affair at the palace was meant to be elegant, even extravagant. Hannah had no doubt every woman who attended would strive to live up to the occasion. Every woman, of course, except her.

She'd already seen Eve's glittery black dress with its swirls of material from waist to ankle and its daring draping back, Gabriella would no doubt wear something delicate that would accent her fragile, feminine looks.

Then there was Chantel O' Hurley. Hannah was certain the actress would be stunning whether she chose silk or sackcloth.

Remembering how Bennett had looked at her as he'd started down the stairs in the Center took no effort at all.

It shouldn't have mattered.

It mattered too much.

Lecturing herself, Hannah chose the best of the worst in a pale lavender gown with a fussy bodice that played down her curves. With her hair unpinned, it gave her the look of a wanton puritan. An image, she knew, that wouldn't go unnoticed. With only the smallest of sighs, she drew her hair back to begin the laborious job of braiding it into submission.

When it was neatly coiled at her neck, Hannah was satisfied that all traces of sexuality were tamed. She looked presentable, perfectly proper and sexless.

There could be no regrets, Hannah told herself as she slipped her pistol into her evening bag. Duty came above personal desire, and certainly far ahead of vanity.

* * *

He'd been waiting for her. The guests were being entertained in the Salle des Miroirs where they were served aperitifs by short-coated waiters. Both the cast and the crew of Eve's production had been invited so that conversation was a babble of noise underlaid with excitement.

Though impatient and distracted, Bennett performed his duty without a ripple. There were always polite questions to be asked, a hand to kiss and a joke to laugh at. Under usual circumstances, the party would have amused and entertained him, but . . .

Where was she? He found himself straining against the evening clothes he usually wore without a thought. All around him women glittered. Their scents mingled and mixed into one exotic fragrance that did nothing to tempt him. He wanted a moment alone with Hannah. He hadn't the least idea why it was so important, but he wanted it desperately.

He kept one eye on the doorway while he spoke with the wardrobe mistress. His gaze paused briefly on the ormolu clock while he listened to the director expound on the potential of Eve's play.

"Looking for me?" The sultry voice sounded in his ear just ahead of a cloud of scent.

"Chantel." Bennett kissed both her cheeks before drawing her back for a survey. "Stunning, as always."

"I do what I'm best at." Smiling, she accepted a glass from a passing waiter. Shimmering white left her shoulders bare, then dipped low enough to be tantalizing before it closely followed the subtle, feminine curves. "Your home is everything it's rumored to be." She lifted the wine to her lips as her gaze passed over the dozens of antique mirrors that graced the walls. "And how clever of you to choose such a room to entertain a group of narcissistic actors."

"We have our moments." He looked beyond her for a moment, but still saw no sign of Hannah. "I saw your last movie. You were extraordinary."

A woman who was accustomed to absorbing all of a man's attention knew instinctively when she had only a part of it. Still, Chantel only smiled and speculated. "I'm still waiting for you to come back to Hollywood."

"You seem to be keeping busy in the meantime." He reached in his pocket for a box of matches to light her cigarette. "How do you manage to divide your time among tennis stars, oilmen and producers?"

Chantel tilted her head as she blew out a thin stream of smoke. "Oh, much the same way I imagine you divide yours among countesses, marchesas and—was it a barmaid in Chelsea?"

Laughing, Bennett dropped the matches back in his pocket. "*Ma chère amie*, if either of us enjoyed all the incredible and innumerable affairs the press gifts us with, we'd be hospitalized."

With the true affection she felt for few men, Chantel touched a hand to his cheek. "To anyone else, I'd say speak for yourself. However, since we've never been lovers, regardless of the headlines to the contrary, I'll ask you how things are for you, romantically speaking."

"Confusing." At that moment, in the oval glass over Chantel's shoulder, he saw Hannah slip into the room. She looked like a dove lost in a group of peacocks. "Very confusing. Excuse me a moment, will you, love?"

"Of course." She'd seen which direction his attention had taken. "*Bonne chance*, Bennett."

A lifetime of experience allowed him to slip through the groups of people, exchanging a quick word, a smile or a murmured excuse without leaving any offense behind. Less than a minute after Hannah had settled into a corner, he was beside her.

"*Bonsoir*, Lady Hannah."

"Your Highness." She used his title and curtsied as protocol demanded. He caught her hands as she straightened, negating the formality.

"It's usual, when a woman is late, that she makes an entrance rather than slip into a corner."

Damn him for making her pulse skittish. Even as she tried to calm it again, she noted that more than one head was turned in their direction. So much for going unnoticed. "I prefer watching to being watched, sir."

"I prefer watching you." He signaled a waiter, then took a glass from the tray for her himself. "You move well, Hannah, as though you wouldn't make a sound in an empty room."

That had as much to do with her training in tae kwon do as her childhood lessons in ballet. "I was raised not to make disturbances." She accepted the glass because it freed one of her hands. "Thank you. This is a lovely room." She said it casually, as casual as the glance she sent sweeping over the guests. Her reflection was thrown back at her a dozen times. Hers, and Bennett's, close together.

"I've always been partial to it." Now that she was here, he was content. He'd almost heard the click of things falling into their proper place when he'd taken her hand in his. "As it happens it was another Bennett, some generations back, who started the collection. It seems he was miserably vain without much cause and continued to buy mirrors in hopes one would tell him a different story."

She had to laugh. For a moment she felt almost as though she belonged there with the gowns and the glass and the glamour. "I'd say you made that up, but it sounds foolish enough to be true."

"You have the most alluring laugh," he murmured. "It's a laugh that reminds me how you look with your hair down and your eyes dark."

She couldn't allow this. Hannah told herself she was foolish to be moved when she knew how clever he was with women. She was more foolish to be caught off guard when she knew what a dangerous game was being played. This time her voice was cool and formal.

"Shouldn't you see to your guests?"

"I have been." He passed his thumb gently over her knuckles. It was a small gesture and an intimate one that made her wish once again she could have been lovely for him. That she could, very simply, have been for him. "While I was waiting for you." He stepped closer. Because she was already wedged into a corner, there was no place to go. "You smell wonderful."

"Bennett, please." She almost lifted a hand to his chest before she remembered eyes were on them. In defense she lifted her glass instead.

"Hannah, I can't tell you how it pleases me to see you become unnerved. The only time you become at all unsure of yourself is when I'm just a bit too close."

It was true, and a bitter pill to swallow for a woman who survived by being sure of herself. "People are watching."

"Then walk in the gardens with me later, when we can be alone."

"I don't think that would be wise."

"Are you afraid I'd seduce you?"

There was both amusement and arrogance in his tone, but when Hannah looked back at him, she saw desire as well. She sipped again to moisten a throat that had gone bone-dry. "Not afraid. Uncomfortable seems a better word."

"It would give me great pleasure to make you uncomfortable, Hannah." His voice was low, a caress to accompany the brush of his lips over her knuckles. "I want to make love with you in some dark, quiet place. Very slowly and very gently."

The need sprinted inside of her until she had to fight off a shudder of anticipation. It could be like that, with him, it could be. If only . . .

There could be no "ifs" in her life. They meant uncertainty and uncertainty was lethal. Hannah, pulling herself steady by nerve ends, looked at him. He meant it. There was desire in his eyes—but more a kindness, a sweetness that was almost her undoing. She could marvel at the fact that he felt something real for her, that somehow, he'd looked beyond the surface and cared.

She could want it, but she couldn't accept it. There was only one way to stop what should never have started. She had to hurt him, and she had to do it now.

"I'm sure I should be flattered." Her voice was cool and calm again. "But if you'll forgive me, sir, I'm aware that your tastes are not very selective."

He stiffened his fingers on hers before he released her hand. She saw by his eyes that the arrow had hit its mark. "I'd appreciate an explanation for that, Hannah."

"The explanation seems obvious. Please let me pass, you'll cause a scene."

"I've caused one before." There was something new in his voice now. It was anger, certainly, but a reckless, heedless anger. Hannah knew that if she didn't play her game exactly right now, she'd find her name splashed in headlines for battling with Bennett in public.

"Very well." Setting her glass down on a nearby table, she folded her hands in her usual fashion. "I'm a woman, and therefore of some passing interest. To be blunt, the interest isn't returned."

"That's a lie."

"No." Firmer now, she cut him off. "Though it might be difficult for a man like you to understand, I'm a simple woman with simple values. As you told me yourself, your reputation precedes you." She paused just long enough to see him wince.

Oh, Bennett, I'm sorry. So sorry.

"I didn't come to Cordina to amuse you," she murmured as she took a step to the side.

He suddenly lifted his hand to stop her, and she waited. "You don't amuse me, Hannah."

"Then I must beg your pardon." Knowing it would be more insult than courtesy, she dipped into a curtsy. "If you'll excuse me now, sir, I'd like to speak with Eve."

He held her another moment. Hannah could feel his fury sear through his fingertips and burn her flesh. Then, in an instant, there was ice. "I won't keep you. Enjoy the evening."

"Thank you."

Despising herself, Hannah moved into the crowd. The lights were so brilliant, she told herself. That was why her eyes hurt.

"Lady Hannah, good evening." Reeve stepped beside her and took her arm. "Would you care for some wine?"

"Yes, thank you." Falling into step beside him, she accepted the glass he held out.

"Have you seen this collection of mirrors? I've always found these three particularly impressive. Are you all right?" he added in an undertone.

"Yes, they are lovely. I'm fine."

He cupped his hand around the end of a cigarette, glancing around casually to be certain no one was within earshot. "It looked as though you were having some trouble with Bennett."

"He's persistent." She sipped her wine, amazed that her nerves had yet to calm. "Surely this is eighteenth-century."

"Hannah." He pointed out another glass as they walked, but his voice softened. "I worked with your father when I first got my feet wet with the ISS. That makes me feel almost like family. Are you all right?"

"I will be." She drew a deep breath and smiled as if he'd said something amusing. "I caused him pain just now. I didn't enjoy it."

Reeve brushed a hand over hers in the most casual of gestures. The touch was as reassuring as a hug. "It's rare to get through an assignment without hurting someone."

"Yes, I know—the end justifies the means. Don't worry, I'll do my job."

"I wasn't worried."

"It would help a great deal if you'd see that Bennett was kept busy over the next week or so. Things should be coming to a head and I don't need him . . ."

"Distracting you?"

"Interfering," Hannah corrected. She glanced in one of the

mirrors and saw him across the room with Chantel. "Though I may very well have taken care of that myself. Excuse me."

* * *

He drove the horse hard, but still didn't find the level of release he'd been seeking. Swearing, Bennett plunged down the winding path, but neither joy nor excitement rode with him. Fury left little room.

He ached for her. He damned her to the devil and still ached for her. In the days that had passed since she'd turned him aside, the wanting hadn't eased. Now it was coated with self-derision and anger, but it hadn't eased.

He told himself she was a cold, insensitive prude with no generosity or heart. He saw her as she had been on the beach, with a shell in her hand, her eyes rich with laughter as the wind pulled pins from her hair.

He told himself she was hard as stone and just as unfeeling. Then he remembered how soft, how sweet her lips had been when his own had tasted them.

So he cursed her and rode harder.

The skies threatened rain, but he ignored them. It was the first time in days he'd been able to get away from obligations long enough to take Dracula out for more than cursory exercise. The wind whistled in off the sea and set waves dancing high.

He wanted the storm. By God, he wanted the wind and the rain and the thunder.

He wanted Hannah.

Imbécile! Only a fool wanted a woman when there was nothing returned. Only a madman thought of ways to have what had already been denied. He'd told himself all this before, but still he caught himself dreaming of ways he could gather her up and take her somewhere until he found the right way to show her. . . . Show her what? Bennett asked himself. Show her that it was different with her?

What woman would believe it?

Dozens, he thought, and his own laughter echoed bitterly behind him. He could certainly attest to that. But now when it was true, when it mattered the most, this woman wouldn't believe.

Because he'd acted like an idiot. Drawing the stallion to a halt, he stopped at a precipice over the sea and looked out. He'd pushed, too hard, too fast. It was humbling to admit he might have done so because he'd never met with a great deal of resistance before.

Women were drawn to him—because of the title and position. He wasn't so vain or so foolish not to know it. But they were also drawn to him because he enjoyed them. He liked their softness, their humor, their vulnerabilities. It was also true that he hadn't been intimate with as many as his reputation allowed, but there'd been enough women in his life for him to understand and appreciate that romance was a two-way street.

Hannah was young, inexperienced, sheltered. The term "Lady" wasn't merely a title, but a way of life. As far as men were concerned, it was doubtful she'd taken herself away from her books long enough to form any strong relationships.

With another oath, Bennett dragged a hand through his wind-tossed hair. And what had he done? He'd tried to seduce her at a dinner party. How could he have expected a woman of her breeding and sensitivity to be anything less than insulted? It had been the clumsiest, and perhaps the crudest of propositions.

Dracula danced impatiently, but Bennett held him steady another moment as he watched the storm roll slowly from the horizon toward the shore.

He hadn't told her, had never attempted to tell her what it

was she did to him inside, to his heart. Just talking with her, watching that solemn face and quiet manner excited him in a way the most exotic or flamboyant woman never had. It was something deeper, and so much richer. He'd never said that with her, he was on the edge of finding the love he hadn't been sure would ever be there for him.

He could hardly do all of that now that he'd alienated and insulted her. But he could do something else. His smile began as the first drops of water hit the sea. He could start at the beginning.

Bennett wheeled the horse around. As the first streak of lightning split the sky, they were racing for home.

Within an hour, in dry clothes and dripping hair, Bennett made his way up to the nursery. Bernadette barred him at the door.

"Your pardon, Your Highness, but it's Princess Marissa's nap time. Her Highness is resting with the baby."

"I'm looking for Lady Hannah." He leaned into the room, but Bernadette stood her ground.

"Lady Hannah isn't here, sir. I believe she went to the museum this afternoon."

"The museum." Bennett calculated a moment. "Thank you, Bernadette."

Before she could finish her curtsy, he was gone.

* * *

Le Musée d'Art was small and lovely as was the rest of Cordina. It was like a miniature palace itself with its marble floors and carved columns. In the main lobby was a high, domed ceiling of stained glass and a circling balcony that gave the illusion of space.

Rooms ran off this circular hub like spokes of a wheel. On the floor below was a moderately priced restaurant where diners could enjoy a view of the gardens through a wide glass wall.

Hannah had arrived early to take inventory of the entire building. Security was tight but people who rested on the benches near the exhibits were largely ignored. Groups of school children were led by, most of them more impressed with an afternoon away from classes than they were with the paintings and sculptures. Tourists, brochures in hands, muddled through with a weaving of French, Italian, British, and American accents.

On a rainy weekday afternoon, the museum was a pleasant pastime. A healthy number of people flowed in and out. Hannah decided she couldn't have planned it better.

At the time she'd requested in her message, she strolled toward a Monet seascape. She loitered there long enough to read the plaque and study the brushwork. Whoever she was going to meet was probably there, making his own study of the building, and of her. In a leisurely pattern, she moved from painting to painting.

Then she saw the watercolor and both heart and mind raced back to the music room, and Bennett.

The plaque read Her Serene Highness, Princess Louisa de Cordina, but in small letters in the corner of the painting was the signature. Louisa Bisset.

She'd titled it simply *La Mer*. It was indeed the sea, but from a view Hannah had yet to see in Cordina. There was a jagged fall of cliffs that gave way to a sheer incline and ended in a jumble of rocks. From there, the beach spread white to the blue verge of water. But it wasn't peaceful. In this painting, the artist had looked for and captured the power and the danger. The spray rose high, and on the horizon a storm was brewing.

He found this stored in a trunk, Hannah thought and had to resist the urge to touch the frame as he might have done.

He'd found it, she thought again, and perhaps had seen part of himself in it.

"An interesting subject."

The voice beside her was French, brusquely accented. Contact was made.

"Yes, the artist is very skillful." Hannah dropped her brochures. As she bent to pick them up she glanced around and was satisfied that no one was close enough to hear or even notice them. "I have information."

"You are to pass it through me."

She turned to smile at him as though they were exchanging a few pleasant remarks about the painting. He was of medium height, dark complexion with no scars. She gauged his age at fifty, though he might have been younger. Certain professions tend to age people quickly. He was not French by birth. The Germanic tone was faint, but she caught it and filed it away.

"There are certain aspects to some of my information that I feel must be given directly to the man who pays me."

"That is against the organization's policy."

"So I was told. However, I'm aware of what nearly happened six months ago because of policy. It wasn't looked on unfavorably when I used my own initiative and saved the organization, shall we say, certain embarrassments."

"*Mademoiselle*, I'm only here to receive your information."

"Then my information is this." Before speaking again, she moved toward another painting. Again, she took her time studying it. She lifted a hand as if to show her companion a certain combination of colors. "I have unlimited access to the palace. Neither my person nor my possessions are searched. I have already compiled the complete statistics on the security system both there, and at the Fine Arts Center."

"That will be most useful."

"And will be given to the man who pays me. That is *my* policy, *monsieur*."

"You are paid by the organization."

"And the organization is run by men. I know who I work for and why." She turned to him then, her smile very cool, very calm. They might have been discussing the weather. "I am not a fool. The . . . organization has certain goals. So do I. I am more than happy to have them merge to our mutual satisfaction. I will meet and speak with the highest authority. See that it's soon."

"Some people take a step and find themselves falling from a cliff."

"I'm surefooted. Pass this on, *s'il vous plaît*. What I know is worth a great deal. What I can find out is worth even more. You'll find enough to prove it in here." Hannah let her brochure fall to her feet, but this time she left it there. "*Bonjour, monsieur.*"

She turned, knowing that such demands would either take her to the next stage, or end in her being summarily disposed of. Nerves tingling, she began to wander toward the exit. Her heart stopped when Bennett walked in.

A dozen thoughts ran through her mind in a matter of seconds. Had she been set up? Had they used her to get him out in the open at a certain time and place? Had he come for her because Deboque had already struck somewhere else?

It took her only seconds more to dismiss them all as irrational. It was simply coincidence and bad luck that he should show up now on the tail of her meeting.

"I hope you don't mind company," Bennett said before she could think of a plausible opening.

"Of course not." She didn't dare look behind her yet to see if her contact was still there. She smiled, not quite sure how to behave since both she and Bennett had done an excellent job of avoiding each other for days. "The museum is even more beautiful than I'd been told."

"Have you seen everything? I'd be glad to show you around."

He took her hand in a casual, friendly way that she realized could only cement her position if Deboque's man was watching.

She let her fingers curl into his, hating herself for using Bennett's generosity against him. "I could spend days looking, but I'm a bit tired."

She saw him then. He'd moved into her peripheral vision. The brochure she'd passed him was in his hand, and though his back was to them, she knew he was listening.

Bennett didn't notice the man, but only her. "Let me give you coffee up in my office. I'd like to talk with you."

She felt the unexpected prick of tears. Everything he said, and the way he said it, only made her claims more plausible. "I'd love some coffee." Hannah let him take her arm and lead her out, knowing every detail would be reported back to Deboque.

With a silent and stone-faced bodyguard, they stepped into an elevator. Bennett used a key to send them up to the third floor.

They crossed pale gray carpet, past uniformed guards to a suite of rooms. Two secretaries, one manning a bank of phones, the other working on a state-of-the-art computer, rose as Bennett entered.

"Janine, could we have some coffee, please?"

"Yes, Your Highness. Right away."

With his hand still on Hannah's arm, Bennett opened a door. The moment it shut behind them, the whispers started. His Highness had never brought a woman to his office before.

It was a room that reflected a man who loved beautiful things. Grays and blues blended softly with ivory walls. Deep-cushioned chairs invited long stays and easy conversation while an ornamental lemon tree thrived in a corner. Glass shelves held small treasures, a china bowl, a T'ang horse, a handful of shells she imagined he'd gathered himself and a chipped demitasse cup that might have been picked up in a flea market.

Though there was a very businesslike antique desk and

chair, the essence of the room was relaxation. Hannah wondered if he came here when he needed to escape the palace and his title.

"Sit down, Hannah. If you've gone through the whole museum, you've been on your feet for hours."

"Yes, but I loved it." She chose a chair rather than the cozy lounge and folded her hands over each other on her lap. "I've always loved the Louvre, but this is so much more personal."

"The Board of Directors and the Chamber of Commerce will be delighted to hear it." He remained standing, his hands in his pockets, wondering just how to begin. "If you'd let me know you were coming today, I'd have enjoyed showing you through myself."

"I didn't want to disturb you. In any case, I rather liked just wandering."

Why, he's nervous, she realized. It might have pleased her in some secret place if she hadn't discovered she was nervous herself. It was the meeting, she told herself. No, it was Bennett. It was foolish to deny it.

"Do you work here often?"

"When necessary. It's often more convenient to work out of my office at home." He didn't want to talk about the museum. Bennett dug his hands deeper in his pockets. Since when had he had trouble talking to a woman? Since Hannah, he thought wryly, and tried again. "Hannah—"

The knock on the door had him biting off an oath. Bennett opened the door for Janine and the coffee tray. The pot was silver, Hannah noted, while the cups were violet bone china edged in gold.

"Yes, just set it down there, Janine. I'll see to it."

"Yes, sir." She set it down on the table in front of the lounge then curtsied.

Aware he'd been terse, Bennett smiled at her. "Thank you, Janine. It smells wonderful."

"You're welcome, sir." The door closed behind her with a discreet click.

"Looks like we're in luck." Bennett lifted the pot and poured. "These little pastries are from the restaurant downstairs. They're wonderful. Cream?"

"Yes, thank you. No sugar." How polite we are, she thought, as the tension began to spread from her neck to her shoulders. Like two strangers on a blind date.

"Will you come sit over here if I promise to behave?"

Though he said it lightly, Hannah heard the strain. She lowered her gaze to her hands. He couldn't know it was shame and not shyness. "Of course." Rising, she moved over and joined him on the lounge. She lifted her coffee while he left his alone.

"Hannah, I apologize for my behavior the other night. It's no wonder you were offended."

"Oh, please, don't." With a distress even her training couldn't smother, she set her cup down and started to rise. His hand reached for hers and held her still. "I don't want an apology." Fighting for control, she forced herself to look at him. "I wasn't offended, really. I was just—"

"Frightened then? That's just as inexcusable."

"No—yes." Which answer was the right one? In the end, she gave up. "Bennett, the truest thing I can say to you is that no one has ever confused me so well."

"Thank you."

"That wasn't a compliment, but a complaint."

"Hannah, thank God you're back." Laughing, he pulled both her hands to his lips. When she stiffened, he released them but continued to smile.

"Friends?"

Still wary, she nodded. "I'd like to be."

"Then friends it is." Satisfied the first hurdle was successfully negotiated, Bennett sat back. He would wait and be a great deal more cautious before attempting the second. "What did you like best about the museum?"

She didn't trust him. No, Hannah was far too good at game playing not to know when one was afoot. "The airy, unrestricted atmosphere, I think. Too often museums are solemn, serious places. Oh, I did see another of your ancestor's paintings. The one of the sea. It was stunning."

"One of my favorites." He was careful not to touch her again. "I was tempted to keep it locked in my room, all to myself, but . . ." With a shrug he picked up his cup. "It didn't seem fair."

"And you are fair," she murmured, knowing she'd used him.

"I try to be," he returned, knowing he would use fair means or foul to win her. "Hannah, you ride, don't you?"

"Yes."

"Ride with me tomorrow morning. It has to be early as the rest of my day is full, but it's been a long time since I had any company on a ride."

"I'm not sure I can. Eve—"

"Will be busy with Marissa until ten," Bennett finished.

How she would love a ride. An hour of freedom and movement. "Yes, but I've promised to go with her to the Center. She has appointments there at eleven."

"We'll be back by then if you're willing to start out early." He wasn't willing to lose the opportunity. In her eyes he saw hesitation and pressed his advantage. "Come, Cordina's at its best in the morning on horseback."

"All right then." It was impulse, she knew, but she could use an hour of relaxation.

In a matter of days, she would meet with Deboque. Hannah lifted her coffee again and sipped. Or she would be dead.

CHAPTER 6

He hadn't lied. Hannah had already thought Cordina beautiful, but in the early morning it was exquisite. With the dawn light, Cordina reminded Hannah of a young girl dressing for her first ball. The colors were soft, shimmering. Pinks and roses and misty blues still gathered to the east as they got mounted.

Settling into her own saddle, Hannah eyed Bennett's Dracula with a mixture of envy and anxiety. Her father's stables included some of the finest horseflesh in Britain, but he had nothing to compare with the black stallion. He looked fast and reckless and just a bit angry. Even as she imagined herself on his back, she could also picture Bennett being thrown.

"A mount like that would have a mind of his own," she commented when the old groom stepped back from the prince.

"Of course." Bennett steadied the stallion as he side-stepped. Then, misunderstanding her, he smiled in reassurance. "Your Quixote's strong, but quite the gentleman. Brie often rides him when she's here."

Hannah only lifted a brow, recognizing the soothing words for what they were. "Thank you, sir. It eases my mind to know you've given me a lady's mount."

He thought he caught a trace of sarcasm, but when he looked

at her he saw only calm eyes and a polite smile. "I thought we'd ride to the sea."

"I'd like that."

With a nod, Bennett turned his horse and started off at a gentle trot. "Are you comfortable?"

"Yes, thank you." As she settled into the easy rhythm, Hannah tried not to yearn for a wild gallop. "It was kind of you to invite me. I'm told your morning rides are sacred."

He grinned at her, pleased that she sat the horse well and confidently. "It's often true that I need an hour on horseback before I can be civil. Still, there are times I prefer company."

That hadn't been true lately. Since Deboque's release he felt he could never stretch his arms out without bumping a guard. And still nothing. His eyes clouded, as much with impatience as with anger. He wanted Deboque to move. He relished the thought of being able to deal with him personally, and finally. Instinctively he touched a hand to his shoulder where a bullet had entered. Yes, he would relish it.

The look in his eyes made her uneasy. There was something to watch for and defend against there. The man beside her was not the easygoing, easy loving prince she'd come to expect. Whatever, whoever he thought of seemed to communicate itself to his mount for Dracula shied nervously. She saw how easily he controlled the stallion, only a flexing of muscle. He could be kind or harsh, gentle or rough. Her own palm grew damp on the reins.

"Is something wrong?"

"What?" He glanced over. For an instant the look was still there, hard and dark enough to make her tense. Then it was gone and he was smiling again. There was no Deboque this morning, Bennett told himself. He was sick of having every aspect of his life and his family's lives clouded by one name. "No, nothing. Tell me what you do at home, Hannah. I can't picture you there."

"We live quietly in London." It was partially the truth. She wondered why she thought of it as partially a lie. "I do a great deal of my work at home, which makes it convenient for me to keep house for my father."

"Your work," he repeated. "Your essays?" He was leading her along the easiest route, where the incline was gentle.

"Yes." Again, there was a twinge of discomfort. "I hope to have them ready for publication in a year or two."

"I'd like to read them."

She shot him a look of surprise, then almost immediately felt her muscles tighten. It had nothing to do with fear. Even if he'd demanded to see her work, she had enough that would satisfy him. No, it wasn't fear but a certainty that if she had to continue to lie to him much longer, she would be physically ill.

"You're welcome to, of course, but I don't think my writing would be of great interest to you."

"You're wrong. You're of great interest to me."

She looked down, but not in the shyness he thought he saw. Once again it was shame. "It's lovely here," she managed after a moment. "Do you ride this way often?"

She wouldn't allow him to get too close. Bennett fought back frustration and reminded himself he was in for the long haul. "No, actually I haven't been this way in quite a while." When they reached the top of a rise, he stopped. Her gelding was content to busy himself with the grass alongside the path. Beside her, Dracula nearly shivered with energy. She thought she felt the same impatience from Bennett.

"A little distance changes things," he murmured.

Following his gaze, she looked back at the palace. From here it looked like an exquisite child's toy, a magnificent dollhouse a pampered child might find near the tree on Christmas morning. To the east was the sea, still hidden from view by the cliffs and trees and barely heard. Like the palace, it hardly seemed real.

"Do you need to get away from it so badly?" Hannah asked him quietly.

"Sometimes." It no longer surprised him that she read his moods. With a hand firm on the reins, he controlled the stallion and continued to look at his home. "I had my time at Oxford, and at sea. When I was away, I missed Cordina so badly it was like an ache. In the past six months, past year, I've felt a restlessness, a waiting for something to happen."

They both thought of Deboque.

"Often in England, especially at this time of year, I'll complain about the cold and the damp." She shifted in the saddle then smiled as she thought of her home. "I'll look out the window and think I'd almost sell my soul for a week of warm, sunny days. Then, when I'm away, I begin to miss the fog and the mists and the smells of London."

They began to walk the horses again while she cast her mind back to England. "There's a man who sells roasted chestnuts just around the corner from our house. You can buy a little bag and warm your hands on them and smell them, just smell them long before you ever eat them." Remembering made her smile again, but she had no idea how wistfully. "Sometimes I'd wonder how it could be Christmastime anywhere without roasted chestnuts."

"I didn't know you missed England so much."

Nor had she until that moment. "One always misses home. Our hearts are always there." And what she was, all that she had done, had always been for England first.

"I've often wondered how difficult it was for Reeve," Bennett said. The sounds of the sea became louder as they moved their way east. "Although he and Brie spend nearly six months every year at their farm in America. I know for Brie it's as much home as Cordina is."

"For many, real contentment comes with acclimation." Hadn't it been so for her, all of her adult life?

"It's a great deal harder for Eve. She has only a few weeks with her family in America."

"Some loves are greater than others. Some needs stronger." She was just beginning to truly understand it. "Eve would live anywhere as long as Alexander was with her. And I think the same is true for your brother-in-law."

Yes, it was true. Perhaps that was a part of the restlessness in him. Over the last few years he'd seen how beautiful, how strong, real commitment, real feelings could be. Somehow they always seemed so remote from him, so unattainable. Now there was Hannah.

"For love, could you turn your back on England?"

Hannah caught her first glimpse of the sea as they climbed higher. She concentrated on that, but saw, in her mind's eyes, the twisting charm of the Thames.

Could she? So much of her life, so much of her duty was bound with England. Even her current assignment had been as much to protect her country from Deboque as it had been to ensure the safety of the Royal Family of Cordina.

"I don't know. You especially would understand how strong some ties can be."

The trees thinned. Those that remained were bent and battered from the wind that swept in from the sea. The path grew rougher so that Bennett put himself between the edge and Hannah. Her mouth twitched at the move, but she said nothing. He could hardly know that she was capable of riding down the path pell-mell without saddle or reins. Besides, she found herself savoring the unaccustomed feeling of being protected.

Without the trees to break its power, the wind swirled from the sea to the top of the rise, carrying traces of salt. Even Hannah's tightly pinned hair couldn't resist it completely. Wispy tendrils escaped to dance around her cheeks. As she watched, a gull caught the current and glided peacefully up on a stream of air. Another, far below, skimmed the water looking for food.

"It's breathtaking." She relaxed enough to sigh.

He saw what was always in her heart, but which showed so rarely in her eyes. Her love of adventure, of power and of risk. It made her beautiful, arousing, mysterious. The need to reach out for her was so strong, he had to tighten his fingers on the reins to keep them still.

"I wanted to bring you here, but I worried that the height might bother you."

"No, I love it." Her horse shied a bit and she controlled him with the ease of long experience. "There are so many beautiful places in the world, but so few special ones. This is a special one. I think I could . . ." She trailed off as the full impact struck her. "This is the scene from the painting. There's no storm brewing, but this is it, isn't it?"

"Yes." He had no idea that her recognition of it would mean so much. Nor did he know what to do with the sudden, inescapable realization that he was in love with her. Completely. Unalterably.

He tossed his head back as the wind blew his hair into his eyes. He wanted a clear look at her, at this, perhaps the most important moment in his life.

She sat straight in the saddle, her eyes dark with appreciation of the scene spread out before and below them. Her profile was sharp, sculpted. The plain brown riding shirt and pants did nothing to enhance her pale skin. But when he looked at her, he saw the most beautiful, the most precious thing he'd ever found. And for the first time in his life, he had no words to tell her.

"Hannah." He reached out a hand and waited.

She turned. He was the most magnificent man she'd ever seen. More breathtaking than the view, more dangerous than a plunge to the rocks below. He sat on the huge stallion, straight as a soldier, as heartbreaking as a poet. In his eyes she saw both passion and compassion, both need and generosity.

Her heart betrayed her and was lost to him even before she could tell herself it couldn't be. As duty warred with emotion, she let her hand join with his.

"I know what you think I am."

"Bennett—"

"No." His fingers tightened on hers. "You're not far wrong. I could lie to you and promise to change, but I won't lie or promise."

Before she could stop herself, she softened. Only for this moment, she promised herself. There was magic, if only for the moment.

"Bennett, I don't want you to change."

"I meant what I said, though I said it badly the other night. I do want you, Hannah." Like her, he looked out to sea. "I also understand that it would be difficult for you to believe that I've never said that to another woman and meant it in the same way."

But she did believe him. It was thrilling, terrifying and forbidden, but she did. For one glorious moment, she let herself hope. Then she remembered who she was. Duty was first. Always.

"Please, believe me, if I could give you what you want, I would. It's just not possible." She drew her hand away because the contact was making her weak, making her dream.

"I've always believed anything is possible if you work hard enough for it."

"No, some things remain out of reach." She turned her horse away from the sea. "We should get back."

Before she could move, he'd backed up enough to cover the hands on her reins with his own. His arm brushed her arm, his leg, her leg. His face was close, too close, as their mounts stood in opposite directions.

"Tell me what you feel," he demanded. The patience was gone, dissolved in need and frustration. "Give me that much, dammit."

"Regret." As she spoke, the word shimmered with it.

He released her hands only to cup the back of her neck. "Tell me again how you feel," he murmured, then leaned toward her.

The kiss was like a whisper, soft, seductive, sultry. Hannah tightened her hands on the reins, then let them go limp as emotion swamped her. It wasn't supposed to be like this, so encompassing, so heady, so right. The wind ribboned around them. The sea crashed below. For a moment, just one moment, all rational thought fled, leaving only desires behind.

"Bennett." She only murmured his name as she started to draw away. He held her, firm, insistent.

"Another moment."

He needed it. He needed every scrap she would throw him. Never had he felt the desire to beg for what a woman could give or withhold. It wasn't just the passion he wanted; it was more than the physical. He wanted her heart with a desperation he'd never felt before.

It was that desperation that made him keep the kiss gentle, that made him draw back long before his craving for her was satisfied. If he wanted her heart, he would have to move slowly. His Hannah was delicate and shy.

"No regrets, Hannah," he said quietly, then smiled. "I won't hurt you, or push you further than you're ready for. Trust me. That's really all I want for now."

She wanted to weep. He was giving her a kindness, a sensitivity she didn't deserve. Lies were all she'd given him. Lies were all she would continue to give. To keep him alive, she reminded herself as the tears burned at the back of her eyes. To keep him and the people he loved safe and unharmed.

"No regrets," she told him, letting the words echo through her mind for herself. Tossing her head, she pressed her heels to the gelding's sides and took off in a gallop.

Bennett's first reaction was surprise. He hadn't expected her to ride so well or so forcefully. He took a moment to watch her race down the rise before he grinned and let Dracula have his head. Though she'd taken a good lead, Hannah heard them gaining ground behind her. Delighted, she bent lower over the gelding's neck as she urged him on.

"We can't beat them head-to-head," she called to her mount. "But we might outwit them."

The challenge was enough. Spurred by it, Hannah swung off the track and into the trees. The path here was narrow and rough, but what she sacrificed in speed, she gained in maneuverability. Bennett was hard on her heels, but she kept to the center giving him no room to pass. She burst through the trees and onto a field less than two lengths ahead. Instinct had her veering to the left and pounding up another rise so that Bennett had to check his momentum at the unexpected maneuver. Still, he continued to gain so that when the stables came into view they were nearly neck and neck. Laughing, she veered left again and headed for a hedge.

He felt an instant's panic as he imagined her flying off her mount onto the ground. Then they were sailing over, side by side. Heels down, knees snug, they thundered toward the stables.

Pipit stood with his hands on his hips. He'd watched them since they'd barreled over the rise with the gelding in the lead. Since they'd taken the jump, the stallion had pulled ahead with smooth, easy strides. To be expected, Pipit thought as he rubbed his hands on the thighs of his pants. There wasn't another horse in Cordina—or in Europe as far as he was concerned—that could match the stallion.

But he thought as he watched the woman keep the distance close that Prince Bennett had at last met his match.

Bennett reined in and slid from the horse's back with excitement still drumming in his head. She was only seconds behind him. Her laughter was low and a bit breathless as she started to swing down. Bennett was there to take her by the waist and turn her to him before her feet hit the ground.

"How did you learn to ride like that?"

She lifted her hands to his chest, as much to keep the distance as her balance. "It's the one thing I excel at other than literature. I'd forgotten how much I've missed it these last few months."

He couldn't take his eyes off her. It was pure desire now, basic, vital. The ride they could have together would be as wild, as reckless as the ride they'd just completed. Somehow he knew it, could almost taste it. For reasons he couldn't name, he felt that he was holding two women. One calm, one passionate. He wasn't sure which one drew him more.

"Ride with me tomorrow."

Once had been a risk and a delight. Twice, Hannah knew, would be a foolish mistake. "I don't think that's possible. With Eve's play about to open, there's so much to be done at the theater."

He wouldn't push. He'd promised himself that he would give her the time to become accustomed to having him with her. From the moment on the rise when he'd realized just what that meant to him, he'd been more determined than ever to court her properly.

A first for the Royal Rake, he thought as he stepped back to kiss her hand.

"The stables are at your disposal whenever you find the time to use them."

"I appreciate that." She reached up a hand to her hair to be certain her pins were in place. "I enjoyed this, Bennett, very much."

"So did I."

"Well, Eve will be waiting for me."

"Go ahead. Pipit and I will see to them."

"Thank you." She was stalling. The moment she realized it, Hannah drew herself in. "Goodbye, Bennett."

"Hannah." He nodded, then watched her walk back toward the palace. A smile tugged at his mouth as he patted his horse's neck. "I'm getting to her, *mon ami*," he murmured. "It's just going to take a bit of time."

* * *

Time moved so quickly. Locked in her room, Hannah held the letter from Sussex. Inside, she would find Deboque's answer to the demand she'd made only days before in the museum. Her hands were steady as she sat at her desk. With the ivory-handled letter opener provided her, she slit through the envelope. Inside was a casual, even uninspired letter from an acquaintance in England. It took Hannah less than fifteen minutes to decode it.

Request granted. December third, 23:30. Café du Dauphin. Alone. Contact will ask for the time, in English, then comment, in French, on the weather. Be certain your information warrants the exception to procedure.

Tonight. The next step would be taken tonight. Hannah folded the letter back into the envelope, but left it in plain view on her desk. Beside it was a single white rose Bennett had sent to her that morning. Hannah hesitated, then gave herself the pleasure of touching the petals.

If only life were as sweet and as simple.

Moments later, she was knocking on Prince Armand's office door.

It was opened by his secretary who bowed stiffly to her before announcing her to the prince. Armand stood behind his desk as he gave permission to admit her.

"Your Highness." Hannah made a deep curtsy. "I apologize for disturbing you."

"Not at all, Hannah."

"But you're busy." She stood just inside of the door, hands folded. "I only wished to ask your advice on something. If it's convenient, I'll come back later."

"It's convenient now. Please come in and sit. Michel, if you would see to those few matters now, I'll have a private word with Lady Hannah."

"Of course, Your Highness." Michel bowed his way out of the room. When the door was closed, Hannah dropped her hands to her sides. Her stride firm, she walked to the desk. "We've gotten a break. You'll have to call Reeve immediately."

* * *

I'm not easy about this," Armand said some time later when his son-in-law sat across from him. "How can we be sure Deboque will be fooled by the information Hannah will feed him?"

"Because it's so nearly the truth." Reeve downed his second cup of coffee. "Unless Hannah can give him something important, something he has no other way of getting, she'll never get close to him."

"But will he believe her?"

"It's my job to make sure he does," Hannah said quietly. "Your Highness, I know you've had objections to this operation all along, but up to this point it's worked exactly as we've wanted."

"To this point," Armand agreed, and rose. He gestured them both back into their seats so that he could pace in peace. "Now I'm in the position of asking a woman, a woman who both my family and myself have become very fond of, to go alone to meet a man who kills as much for pleasure as for profit."

"She won't be alone."

At Reeve's announcement, Hannah sat straight up. "I have to be. If Deboque or one of his men have the slightest clue that

I'm not, the whole operation goes up in smoke. I won't have it." Now, she rose as well. "I've given this two years of my life."

"And I intend to see that you live a bit longer," Reeve said mildly. "We suspect that Deboque has his headquarters in a small villa about five miles from here. We'll have men watching it."

"And they'll have Deboque's men watching them."

"Leave that part to me, Hannah, and do your job. You have the blueprints and the specs on the security systems?"

"Yes, of course." Annoyed, she sat again. "And I know I'm to give them to no one but Deboque."

"You also know that at the first sign that things are going wrong, you're to pull out."

She nodded, though she had no intention of doing so. "Yes."

"There'll be two men stationed at the café."

"Why don't you just send up a flare?" Hannah tossed back.

He understood her frustration, but merely poured a third cup of coffee. "It's a choice between that or wiring you."

"The last agent who attempted to get a wire into Deboque's organization was sent back to the ISS in three boxes."

Reeve moved his shoulders. "Your choice."

Again, Hannah rose. "I'm not used to being second-guessed, Reeve." When he said nothing, she set her teeth. "I realize that you're my superior on this assignment, so I don't believe I have much of a choice."

"As long as we understand each other." He rose then, and took her hand. "Hannah, I'm aware of your reputation. Why don't we just say I don't want to take any chances on losing one of the best?" Releasing her, he turned back to the prince. "I have a few things to put into motion. I'll keep in touch."

Armand waited until the door was closed again. "Another moment, please," he said to Hannah. "If you'd sit?"

She wanted to be alone, to plan each detail out carefully.

There was only a matter of hours left. Breeding was as strong as training, so she sat. "Would you like me to go over things with you again, sir?"

"No." His lips curved, just slightly. "I believe I grasp the situation well enough. I have a personal question, Hannah, and I ask you beforehand not to be offended." He sat across from her, militarily straight. "Am I mistaken, or has my son become fond of you?"

She linked her hands together immediately as her whole body went on alert. "If you mean Prince Bennett, sir, he's been very kind."

"Hannah, for my sake, please dispense with the evasions and the manners. Too often duty has interfered with the time I can spend with my family, but that doesn't mean I don't know my children and know them well. I believe Bennett is in love with you."

She went pale instantly. "No." She had to swallow, but the word came out a second time just as strongly. "No, he's not. Perhaps he's a bit intrigued, but only because I'm not the kind of woman he's used to spending time with."

"Hannah." Armand held up a hand before she could continue her rambling denial. "I don't ask in order to upset you. When I began to suspect this, it made me uncomfortable only because Bennett is unaware of your true purpose here."

"I understand."

"I'm not sure you do. Bennett is more like his mother than my other children. So . . . kindhearted. His temper has more of a lash, but his feelings are more easily reached. I only ask you this because if the answer to my next question is no, I must request that you tread softly. Do you love him, Hannah?"

Everything she felt was in her eyes. She knew it, and lowered her gaze quickly. "Whatever I feel for Bennett, for your family, won't interfere with my job."

"I know enough to recognize a person who will do what has

to be done." He felt a stirring for her, a grave kind of pity that twined with empathy. "But you didn't answer me. Do you love my son?"

"I can't." This time her voice wasn't strong and there were tears chasing behind it. "I've lied to him since the first, and I'll go on doing so. You can't love and lie. Please excuse me, Your Highness."

Armand let her go. For a moment, he sat back in the chair and closed his eyes. For the next few hours, he could do nothing more than pray for her.

*   *   *

The café wasn't one of the pretty little tourist spots in Cordina. It was a local waterfront bar that catered to the crews from the fishing and cargo boats. Inside it was cramped with tables, many empty, and smoke and the smell of liquor. Not as rough as they came, Hannah thought as she slipped inside, but neither was it a place where a woman alone would wander unless she was looking for trouble.

Still, she didn't cause much of a stir as she came in. In her plain gray sweater and slacks, she nearly blended into the walls. The handful of women who were already there were more interesting fare. If she could get this over with quickly, she might not have to discourage any of the locals.

Hannah chose a bar stool and ordered a bourbon, neat. By the time it was served, she had sized up the room. If Reeve had indeed planted two agents here, they were certainly good ones. It was a rare thing when Hannah couldn't spot one of her own.

She'd been drinking silently for ten minutes when one of the men stood from a table and wandered in her direction. Hannah continued to drink while every muscle tensed. When he spoke, it was in French and thickened by whiskey.

"It's a sad thing for a woman to drink alone."

Hannah relaxed only enough to be annoyed. She used her primmest British tones. "It's a sadder thing for a woman not to remain alone when she chooses to."

"When one is so plain, she shouldn't be so picky," he grumbled, but moved away again. Hannah nearly smiled, then another man came through the doors.

He was dressed in seaman's clothes, with his cap pulled low. Beneath it his face was deeply tanned and gaunt. This time she tensed because she was certain.

Still, she idly lifted her drink as he moved to sit beside her at the bar.

"You have the time, *mademoiselle*?"

"Yes, it's quarter to twelve."

"Thank you." He signaled for a drink. Another minute passed as he toyed with it. "*Il fait chaud ce soir.*"

"*Oui, un peu.*"

They didn't speak again. Behind them a group began to sing a song, in French and off-key. The wine was flowing freely and the night was still young. He finished his drink and left the bar. Hannah waited only a moment, then got up to follow.

He waited for her at the edge of the dock. There was little lighting here so that he was more shadow than man. Hannah moved toward him, knowing it could be the beginning or the end for her.

"You have the information." Again he spoke in English. It was bland and unaccented, just as his French had been. Deboque chose well, she thought and only nodded.

"We go by boat." He indicated the small open runabout.

Hannah knew she had no choice. She could refuse, or she could go on. Though she knew she would have no backup on the sea, she never even considered the first. Deboque was the destination. That was the bottom line.

Without hesitation, she lowered herself into the boat and took a seat at the stern. In silence, her contact got in beside her, cast off, and started the engine. It sounded like thunder on the open water.

Hannah took a deep breath. She was on her way.

CHAPTER 7

Reeve would be furious. Hannah rested a hand on the seat for balance as the boat picked up speed. He could afford to be, she thought, but she had to keep her head.

So Deboque wasn't on land in the villa as they'd expected. He was, unless the boat made a sudden and dramatic change in direction, at sea. No, there would be no backup now. Hannah drew another deep breath and watched the water wake behind them. She preferred working alone in any case.

Tonight, she would meet Deboque. She could feel it. Her pulse was slow and steady, her breathing even. The spray the boat kicked up teased her skin as she kept her expression placid. Nerves, what there were of them, couldn't be allowed to show. Her midnight cruise across the Mediterranean was bringing her closer to the goal she'd worked toward for just over twenty-four months.

Excitement, not fear, was building inside of her. Even that had to be controlled. Anything that made the pulse beat too fast or tempted the mind to swing too far ahead was dangerous. She couldn't make a mistake. Over the past two years she'd worked her way up in Deboque's organization, relying for the most part on her own skill. With the backing of the ISS she'd seen several jobs through to completion. Arms sold, diamonds liberated, drugs delivered.

The end justifies the means.

Rungs on the ladder, she thought. If she could continue to climb, it wouldn't be long before Deboque's kingdom of misery would come tumbling down on his own shoulders.

The trickiest rung had been making the well-placed Bouffe look incompetent. Deboque's senior lieutenant wasn't a fool and it'd taken a lot of guile and some risk to see that several of his assignments over the last few months had fallen through, without throwing suspicion back on herself. The biggest of these had been the arms deal with a terrorist group known for their lack of patience.

It had been sticky, but the timing had been perfect. Hannah had managed to make it seem as though Bouffe had nearly botched the deal before she had slipped in to make things right.

The terrorists had their arms—she had to leave the ISS to deal with that. And Deboque had his five million francs. It would be her pleasure to deal with that. And soon.

She saw the sleek white yacht anchored majestically in dark water. A thrill of anticipation moved through her. At the wheel, her contact signaled with an electric lantern. There was an answering flash from the ship. The engine was cut, throwing the night into silence as they drifted alongside the yacht.

Hannah reached out for the ladder and found the metal cool and hard. She knew she would be the same. Without a backward glance, she climbed up, and into the unknown.

"Lady Hannah."

There was a tall, dark-skinned man waiting for her. He took her hand and bowed over it. She recognized him from her last briefing, though she would have placed his accent as Jamaican in any case. He was Ricardo Batemen, a twenty-six-year-old islander, an ivy-league graduate with a degree in medicine. He still used a scalpel, but he preferred to wield it on the healthy and unanesthetized.

He had become a favorite of Deboque's.

"I'm Ricardo." His young, smooth face spread into a smile. "Welcome to the *Invincible*."

"Thank you, Ricardo." She gave a casual look around and counted five more men and one woman on deck. The men were dressed in dark suits and carried machine guns. The woman had a sarong draped over a bikini and looked bored. "Might I have a drink?"

"Of course." His eyes, she noted, were pale, an almost translucent green that never seemed to blink. His voice was like rich cream over hot coffee. "But first, you must excuse our precautions. Your bag, Lady Hannah."

She lifted a brow and met his eyes straight on. "I'll depend on you to see that everything in it is returned to me."

"You have my word." He bowed as she handed it to him. "Now, if you would go with Carmine. She will take you to your cabin. You may like to freshen up after she makes certain no one has planted any electronic devices on you."

A strip search, Hannah thought resignedly. "No one plants anything on me, Ricardo. But I admire a cautious man." Hannah crossed the deck to Carmine as though she was going to tea.

Moments later, Ricardo set Hannah's black alligator bag on a gleaming mahogany desk. "Carmine is seeing to her. She has a small-caliber pistol, her passport and identification and about three thousand francs along with a few cosmetics. There is an envelope, sealed."

"Thank you, Ricardo." The voice was deep and smoky with its traces of France. "You may bring her to me in ten minutes. Then we won't be disturbed."

"Oui, monsieur."

"Ricardo, your impressions?"

"Attractive enough, more so than her photograph. And cool, very cool. Her hand was dry and steady."

"Good." There was a trace of amusement in the voice now. "Ten minutes, Ricardo." He picked up the envelope and broke the seal.

A short time later, Hannah adjusted her sweater. She'd found the search more annoying than humiliating. Carmine had taken her stiletto, but she'd expected that. Ricardo had her pistol. For now, she was alone and unarmed in the middle of the sea. She still had her wits.

Hannah stood in the center of the cabin when Ricardo opened the door. "My apologies again for the inconvenience, Lady Hannah."

"A small annoyance, Ricardo." He hadn't brought back her bag, but she said nothing of it. "I hope there won't be too many more."

"None at all. If you'd just come with me."

Hannah followed him, walking easily as the boat swayed in the current. It was the size of a small hotel, she'd noted. And there were escape routes if it became necessary. The carpet they walked on was rich red. In the cabin where she'd been searched had been an antique mirror with beveled glass and a bedspread in velvet. There had also been a porthole big enough for a child, or a slender woman to work their way through.

Ricardo stopped by a glossy oak door and knocked twice. Without waiting for an answer, he turned the knob and gestured her inside. Hannah stepped through and heard the door click shut at her back.

It was opulent, elegant, even fanciful. Eighteenth-century France seemed to come alive. Now the carpet was the deep shimmering blue of kings and the paneled walls were polished to a mirrorlike gleam. Two delicate, glittering chandeliers sprinkled light over the antique wood and plush upholstery.

Brocade had been used lavishly to drape over and around a bed fit for a king. All the colors were vivid, almost shocking.

There was a scent of something floral and something old that merged together into one strangely compelling and oddly uneasy fragrance. With the gentle sway of the ship, a collection of crystal animals shuddered with life.

It only took Hannah seconds to absorb this. As grand and extravagant as the room was, the man who sat behind the Louis XVI desk dominated. She didn't feel the evil she'd expected to. With the truly wicked, Hannah knew you often experienced a chill or a dread. What she saw was a slender and attractive man in his fifties, with steel-gray hair flowing back in a mane from a chiseled, aristocratic face. He wore black. It seemed to accent his almost poetically-pale skin. His eyes were black, too, like a raven's. They studied her now as his full, rather beautiful mouth curved into a smile.

She'd seen pictures of him, of course. She'd studied every scrap of information that had been gathered on him in the last twenty years. And yet . . . And yet she hadn't been prepared for the shock of sensuality which seemed to emanate from him.

He was a man women had died for. And now she understood it. He was a man who other men had killed for without question. She understood that, too, as she stood ten feet away and felt the power.

"Lady Hannah." He rose, slowly, gracefully. His body was trim, almost delicate. His hand, as he offered it to her, was narrow and beautiful with a trio of diamonds on long fingers.

She couldn't hesitate, though she felt if her hand touched his she would be pulled out of what she knew into something foreign and frightening.

Hannah smiled and stepped forward. "Monsieur Deboque." She was glad to see his slight surprise at her use of his name. "It's a pleasure."

"Please sit. Will you have brandy?"

"Yes, thank you." She chose a soft high-backed chair that faced the desk. There was music playing through hidden speakers. Chopin. She listened to the notes as Deboque crossed to an enameled cabinet and withdrew a decanter. "Your ship is exquisite, *monsieur*." There was a painting behind his desk. One of six she knew had been stolen from a private collection only the year before. She herself had helped execute the theft.

"I appreciate beauty." He offered the brandy, then instead of going behind the desk again, sat beside her. "To your health, *mademoiselle*."

"And yours." She smiled at him again before she sipped.

"Perhaps you will tell me how you became aware of my name."

"I make it a habit of knowing who I work for, Monsieur Deboque." She shook her head as he drew out a cigarette case and offered her one. "I must congratulate you on your security and your staff. Discovering who, shall we say, reigned, was hardly an easy matter."

He drew in the smoke slowly, as a man who appreciated fine tastes. "Most have found it impossible."

Her eyes were cool and amused on his. "I find little impossible."

"Others have found it fatal." When she only smiled, he let it pass. She was, as Ricardo had said, very cool. "My reports on you are very flattering, Lady Hannah."

"Of course."

It was his turn to smile. "I admire confidence."

"And I."

"It appears I'm in your debt for smoothing over an exchange with our Mediterranean neighbors a few months ago. I would have been, to say the least, annoyed to have lost that contract."

"It was my pleasure. It would seem, *monsieur*, that you have a few weak links in the chain."

"It would seem," he murmured. He'd already debated hand-ing Bouffe over to Ricardo for disposal. A pity, Deboque thought. Bouffe had been a loyal and valued employee for over a decade. "You are enjoying your stay in Cordina?"

Her heart drummed lightly but she sipped again. "The pal-ace is quite lovely." She moved her shoulders as she let her gaze roam around the room. "I, too, appreciate beauty. It helps compensate for the fact that the Bissets are a bit boring."

"You're not impressed with the Royal Family, Lady Han-nah?"

"I'm not easily impressed. They are certainly very pretty people, but so . . . devoted." She tinted her voice with derision, lightly. "I prefer devoting myself to something more tangible than honor and duty."

"And loyalty, Lady Hannah?"

She turned to him again. He was looking deep, trying to see inside, trying to see beyond. "I can be loyal." She touched her tongue to the rim of her snifter. "As long as it's profitable."

It was a chance, she knew. Disloyalty in Deboque's organi-zation was punishable by death. She waited, outwardly cool while a single line of sweat beaded down her back. He studied her a moment, then threw his lion's head back and laughed. Hannah felt each individual muscle in her body sing with relief.

"An honest woman. I admire that. Yes, I admire that a great deal more than sworn oaths." He drew in the rich French smoke then exhaled again. "It would seem to my advantage to continue to make it profitable for someone of your skills and ambitions."

"I was hoping you'd see it that way. I prefer the executive branch, if you comprehend, Monsieur Deboque, but I'm will-ing to work my way to it. Delegation, organization, is so much more rewarding than execution, don't you think?"

"Indeed, yes." He studied her again, considering. She

appeared to be a mild, well-bred young woman of some means. He preferred a quiet, unassuming outer shell in a woman. He thought briefly of Janet Smithers who he'd used and discarded nearly a decade before. Lady Hannah, he thought, might prove to be a great deal more interesting, and more competent. "You've been with us two years now?"

"Yes."

"And in those two years, you've proven yourself to be very useful." He rose now and retrieved the envelope on his desk. "You brought this to me, I assume?"

"I did." She swirled her brandy. "Though I found the method with which it was delivered irksome."

"My apologies. This information is interesting, Lady Hannah, but I fear, incomplete."

She crossed her legs and relaxed back in the chair. "A woman who writes everything she knows on paper loses her value quickly. What isn't there, is in here." She laid a finger against her temple.

"I see." He admired an employee who knew her own worth, and guarded it. "If we say I'm interested in the security systems of the Royal Palace, the Fine Arts Center, the museum, for the purpose of emulating such systems for my own use, you would be able to fill in the blanks?"

"Of course."

"And if I asked how you came by such information?"

"This was the purpose of my visit to Cordina."

"One of them." Intrigued, he tapped the envelope on his palm. "It was fortunate that you were able to become close to Princess Eve."

"Fortunate, but not difficult. She was lonely for female companionship. I'm accommodating. I fuss over her daughter, listen to her fears and complaints. By easing some of her workload, I also earn the gratitude of Prince Alexander. He worries that his wife will tire herself while carrying his child."

"And you are trusted?"

"Implicitly. And why not?" she added. "My family is well respected, my breeding without mark. Prince Armand sees me as a young cousin of his dead wife. Your pardon, *monsieur*, but aren't these the reasons you enlisted me to find a place at the palace?"

"Yes, they are." He sat back. She pleased him, but he was a long way from giving her his full confidence. "I have word that the young prince is interested in you."

Something inside her froze at that. "Your network of information is admirable." Hannah glanced at her empty snifter, then tilted it in question. Deboque rose immediately to refill her glass. It was just enough time to regain her composure.

"Bennett is, as I'm sure you're aware, invariably interested in the female closest at hand." She gave a low laugh and tried not to hate herself. "He's really only a boy, and spoiled at that. I've found the simplest way to handle him is to act disinterested."

Deboque nodded slowly. "Then he pursues."

"Such men are always more—accommodating under those circumstances."

"I beg your pardon if I seem to be getting too personal, my dear, but how accommodating?"

"He's a bit bored, a bit reckless. His weakness for women should have its uses. I believe with a certain—flair—information can be drawn out of him. It was he, you see, who took me through the Center, and through the naval base at Le Havre." She sipped again, lingering over it. Deboque would already know about her tête-à-tête with Bennett at the museum. So, she would use his knowledge and twist the truth.

"It was a simple matter to ask questions and express interest in how the museum guards its treasures. With that, I was shown the setup, alarms, monitors, sensors." She paused again to let it sink in. "The more a woman pretends ignorance, the more she learns."

Deboque warmed the brandy in his hands. "Hypothetically, you understand, can the security at the palace be broken?"

At last, she thought, they were homing in. "Hypothetically, any security can be broken. I will say that Reeve MacGee has designed an admirable system, but not an invincible one."

"Interesting." He picked up a small china figure of a hawk and began to study it. The room fell into silence long enough for her to be sure he was trying to unnerve her. "And do you have a theory on how this system can be undermined?"

"From inside." She sipped her brandy again. "It's always cleaner from the inside."

"And the Center?"

"Much the same."

"This play the princess wrote, it opens in a few days. It would be amusing to cause a small disturbance."

"Of what nature?"

He only smiled. "Oh, I'm just speaking in theory, you understand. It seems to me that the Royal Family would be uncomfortable if something disrupted the evening. I should hate to miss it. You'll be there?"

"I'm expected." She needed to push him, push him into something definite. "I prefer knowing which door to walk into, *monsieur.*"

"Then you might be wise to remain in the audience. I wouldn't want to lose you now that we've become close."

She acknowledged this, but realizing he would demand the rest of the stats then dismiss her, Hannah changed gears. "As a matter of personal curiosity may I ask why you have such interest in the Royal Family? It intrigues me because I see you much as I see myself, as a person most interested in profit and personal gain."

"Profit is always desirable." He set the hawk down. He had hands that might have played a violin or written sonnets. They rarely killed, only gestured for others to do so. "Personal gain can have a multitude of variables, *n'est-ce pas*?"

"As long as it satisfies," she agreed. "Using the kidnapping of the Princess Gabriella or the threats on the Bissets as a lever to gain your release from prison was one thing. You're no longer in prison." Again she looked with admiration around the room. "I would think you would move on to more profitable waters."

"All business needs a completion." She saw emotion for the first time as his fingers tightened around his glass. "All debts require payment. The interest of ten years is dear, very dear. Do you agree?"

"Yes. Revenge, or retribution if you prefer. This I understand is as sweet as diamonds." And looking at him, she knew he would stop at nothing to collect. "*Monsieur*, you have arranged for me to be in the palace. I intend to continue to remain there until you alter the order, but I prefer to do so with some direction." She gestured casually, palm up. "The revenge, after all, is yours, not mine. I've never worked well blindfolded."

"A man who puts all of his cards on the table loses his edge."

"Agreed. So does a man who doesn't sharpen his tools and use them where they're best suited. I'm in, *monsieur*. Having a map of some sort would be useful."

He intended to use her, and well. Sitting back again, Deboque steepled his hands. His diamonds shot out violent light. He had failed, twice before he had failed to use the Bissets for his own purposes. He had failed to bring Armand to his knees. Whatever had to be done, whomever had to be used, he wouldn't fail this time. In Hannah, he thought he'd found the instrument.

"Let me ask you this. If one man wishes to destroy another, what does he do?"

"The simplest is to end his life."

Deboque smiled, and now Hannah saw the evil. It was coated with class, pampered with elegance, but very real. "I'm not a simple man. Death is so final, and even when it is slow, it's soon over. To destroy a man, the soul, the heart, requires more than a bullet in the brain."

He was speaking of Armand, she knew. It wasn't time to demand he name names and reveal his plan. He would tell her nothing and trust her less. Hannah set down her glass and tried to think as he did. "To truly destroy, you take away what is most valuable." Her heart began to beat in the back of her throat, clogging a wave of nausea. Still, when she spoke it was with cool admiration. "His children?"

"You are intelligent as well as lovely." Leaning over he placed his hand on hers. She felt it from him, the vile, dark movement of death. "To make a man suffer, to destroy his soul, you deprive him of what he loves best and leave him to live with it. His children and grandchildren dead, his country in chaos, a man would have nothing left but misery. And a country without an heir becomes unstable—and profitable—if one is shrewd."

"All of them," Hannah murmured. She thought of little Marissa, so pretty and soft, and Dorian with his smudged face and bright grin. Fear for them was suddenly so strong, so vital, she thought it had to show in her eyes. She kept them down, looking at his hand as it lay over hers and the cold, hard glint of the diamonds.

"All of them, *monsieur?*" When she thought she could trust herself again, she looked back at his face. He was smiling. In the fragile light of the chandeliers he looked wan as a ghost and infinitely more frightening. "Not an easy task, even for someone of your power."

"Nothing worthwhile is simple, my dear. But as you said, nothing is impossible—particularly when one is trusted and close."

Her brow lifted. She didn't shudder or draw away. Business, she told herself. Lady Hannah was all business. She was being offered a job, the most vital one Deboque had to offer.

"You were carefully chosen, Lady Hannah. For more than ten years, I've had one dream. I believe you are the instrument to see it to fruition."

She pursed her lips as if considering while her mind raced ahead. He was giving her a contract, a royal one. As she said nothing, his fingers played lightly over her knuckles. Like a spider, she thought, a handsome and very clever spider.

"Such a responsibility is weighty for someone in my position in your organization."

"That can be seen to. Bouffe is—retiring," he said softly. "I will be looking for a replacement."

She let her hand lie under his as she touched her tongue to her top lip. "A guarantee, *monsieur*."

"My word."

She smiled a little. "*Monsieur*."

With a nod of acknowledgment, he rose and pressed a button on his desk. Within seconds Ricardo appeared. "Lady Hannah will be replacing Bouffe. See to the arrangements, Ricardo. Discreetly."

"Of course." The pale green eyes half closed as if with pleasure.

Hannah waited for the door to shut again. A man's life was over. "The day may come when you decide to replace me as casually."

"Not if you continue to please me." He lifted her hand again and kissed it. "I have a feeling you will."

"I must tell you, *monsieur*, I have a distaste for killing children." His fingers tightened, very slightly on hers, but she didn't fidget. "I believe it will take five million American dollars to overcome this distaste."

She saw it in his eyes. He would break her fingers as easily as he would kiss them. Hannah kept her gaze steady on his and hoped she hadn't pushed her luck too far.

"Is it money that seduces you, *ma petite?*"

"Not seduces, pleases. I like to be pleased."

"You have two weeks to please me, Lady Hannah. Then I shall return the favor." He kept her hand in his as he drew her to her feet. "Now, as a show of faith, you will tell me what you failed to note down here."

Hannah walked over to the specs and prepared to lie to him.

* * *

She was exhausted. In a decade of assignments, nothing had left her feeling so empty and soiled. As she drove through the palace gates, she could only think about a long hot shower where she could scrub off whatever traces remained of Deboque's cologne. Reeve was standing a hundred feet beyond the gates. Hannah stopped the car and waited for him to slide in beside her.

"You were gone a long time." He gave her a long, thorough study. "It wasn't in the plans for you to be out of contact for over an hour."

"It was in the plans for me to get to Deboque."

"And you did?"

She rolled down her window a bit farther. "I met him on a yacht, the *Invincible*. It's anchored about five miles northwest. He has at least six armed guards, double that by a guess. He has the information we wanted him to have. I'm replacing Bouffe."

Reeve's brow lifted. "You must have impressed him."

"That was the idea." She wondered how soon she could wash the taste of his brandy from her mouth. "He's planning something for the opening of Eve's play." When Reeve stiffened beside her, she went on. "I don't believe it's going to be anything directly against the family. He seemed to think it would be entertaining to confuse matters. He's very careful how he phrases things. Nothing too direct. Even if I testified against him, it would be difficult to actually convict him of conspiracy. He hypothesizes, theorizes."

"Did he give you an idea where he intends to make his move?"

She listened for a moment to a bird that was singing its heart out. "He seemed most interested in the palace. It's the biggest challenge. We have two weeks."

"He moves in two weeks?"

"That's how long he gave me to murder your family." She turned to him then and saw his face was pale and set. "All of you but Armand, Reeve. The children, everyone. He wants to destroy Armand's soul and leave Cordina without an heir. If you trust my judgment, he wants this done as much for personal satisfaction as for the profit he might make when Cordina is thrown into chaos."

Reeve drew out a cigarette but didn't light it. "I trust your judgment."

"We have two weeks to stop him, or to convince him that I've done what he wants."

It was his family, his heart, yet he knew he had to think as coolly as she did. "Is he setting you up?"

She thought for a moment, then shook her head. "I don't think so. It's certainly possible that he'd dispose of me after I've finished the job, but I think it's more likely he'd continue to use me. We did a good job of planting information about me, and over the past two years I've saved him a bit of trouble and money. If he believes I can give him this, he'll sit back and wait."

"Armand will have to be told."

"I know." But not Bennett. Armand and only Armand.

"For now, just go on as usual." He indicated that she should drive ahead. "We'll need some time."

"Eve's opening is in a few days."

"We'll handle it. You get some sleep. As soon as we have a direction, I'll let you know."

Hannah got out of the car, then as Reeve stood on the other side she stopped. "I want him. I want him for myself. I know it's unprofessional and stupid. But if I have the chance, if I find the way, I'm going to take him out myself."

Reeve said nothing as she walked up the steps. He'd already vowed the same thing.

CHAPTER 8

I don't want you to go tonight."

"You know I have to." Eve stood, grim and stubborn, facing her husband. "It's my play, my troupe, my production. I don't have a choice, Alex."

"Excuses can be made." He looked at her, dressed in midnight blue that skimmed her shoulders and swirled to her ankles. Her hair was caught up in the back so that it fell over one shoulder like ebony. Even after all the years he'd known her, just looking at her made his pulse race. "You know how dangerous it could be. With the information we have now, we can be sure there'll be an incident tonight. I don't want you involved."

"I am involved." She was frightened. Ever since Reeve told them that he'd received a tip that there would be trouble at the theater on opening night, her nerves had been stretched tight. Yes, she was frightened, but she was no less determined. She crossed to the beveled mirror above the bureau as if checking the arrangement of her hair was of some importance. "I wrote the play, I produced it, and more important than either of those," she continued before he could interrupt, "I belong at the theater tonight because I'm your wife."

The fact that her arguments were valid meant nothing. He

wanted her in the palace, safe, untouchable. His heart would rest easy if he knew she was here, in the suite of rooms she'd decorated, tucked high in the palace that had been his family home for generations. Nothing could happen to her here. Anything could happen outside.

"My love, Reeve is rarely wrong. If he says there'll be trouble tonight, I want you well away from it. The fact that you're carrying a child is a very simple reason for you to be excused. I know the play is important to you, but—"

"Yes, it is," she interrupted. "But you're more important."

"Then do this for me, and stay home tonight."

She tilted her head, holding on to both her nerves and her temper. "Alexander, would you stay behind with me?"

"If it was possible, of course." Impatience had him dragging a hand through his hair. It was a ploy she'd used before, and one there was little argument against. "I can't close myself up every time there's a rumble from Deboque."

"For Cordina," she said quietly. "And Cordina is now my country, too."

"Eve." He thought he loved her as much as it was possible to love. Every day he learned there could be more. "You are the most precious thing in the world to me. I almost lost you once."

She crossed to him then, knowing the first step, the first touch should be hers. When both of his hands were in hers, she looked up into his eyes. "And I you, Alex. I'm going to sit in the Royal Box beside you, where I belong."

From outside the door, Hannah heard the conversation clearly enough. It was moments like this that made it difficult to think of what she was doing, what she had yet to do, as merely another assignment. There were people beyond the door who she'd come to care about. The Bissets were no longer names or symbols, but friends. After ten years of playing dangerous games, she knew how risky it could be to make friends.

She closed her eyes and drew her breath deep before she knocked.

"*Entrez.*" It was Alexander who answered, the impatience in his voice ripe. Hannah opened the door but didn't cross the threshold.

"I'm sorry. I'm disturbing you."

"Of course not." With the warmth that was so much a part of her, Eve smiled and gestured her inside. "I see you're ready for the evening." She felt a little twinge of regret at Hannah's severe beige dress and hairstyle. She'd hoped with a little time she could urge Hannah to soften her image. Tonight, however, there were more immediate matters of concern. "We were just about to come down ourselves."

Hannah saw Eve take Alexander's hand again. "I thought you might need some help."

"No, there's nothing." But the cloud of concern didn't leave Eve's eyes. "Hannah, I don't want you to feel obligated to go with the family. Knowing there's a possibility of an—incident," she began. "Well, it might be more comfortable for you here at home."

"Of course I'm going." With the hated secret tucked inside of her, she shifted the wrap on her arms. "And I really believe everything's going to be fine. If you don't need me then, I'll just go down."

"Please, let's not talk about it anymore," Eve said when Hannah shut the door behind her. "Let's go say good night to Marissa before we leave."

"Eve." Alexander gathered her close. He could feel the slight swell where another child lay. "I love you."

"Talk's cheap," she murmured, and tried for a laugh. "Promise to show me later, after the play."

He let his cheek rest on her hair. "You have my word."

Bennett was already waiting in the main hall. Even with the distance separating them, Hannah could feel the impatience coming from him. Impatience, she thought, mixed with a recklessness that the elegant evening clothes couldn't disguise. He was looking for trouble, Hannah realized. More, he was hoping for it.

"There you are." Though he smiled up at her, his mind was already on the evening ahead. Instinctively he took her hand, holding it as she reached the bottom of the stairs. "You don't have to go tonight, Hannah. I'd be happier if you didn't."

Guilt came so quickly that she had squeezed his hand in reassurance before she could stop herself. "Now even you sound like Eve," she said lightly. "I want to be there. A vague tip from an anonymous source is a foolish reason to miss a night at the theater."

He touched the pearl cluster at her ear. "Is that what we call British pluck?"

"It's what we call common sense."

"Whatever it's called I want you to stay close. There'll be enough guards to smother us, but I prefer to keep an eye on you myself." Before she could stop him, he was leading her toward the doors.

"Eve and Alexander are nearly ready. I said I'd wait for them."

"Security feels better splitting us up." He acknowledged Claude with a brief nod. "You'll ride with me. Father will come along after Alexander and Eve."

"All right." She walked out into the star-studded night, calmly holding the .22 that lay within her beaded evening bag.

* * *

The theater was sold out. Long before the first curtain, the seats were filled so that the babble of conversation rose up to the Royal Box. There was thunderous applause when the

Bissets entered. From the background as bows were made, Hannah held her breath and studied the sea of faces.

If Deboque had been there, she knew she would have found him.

"The Center's been swept twice," Reeve murmured in her ear. "There's nothing here."

She nodded and took her seat as the curtain rose.

The play was everything Eve had hoped for, though Hannah doubted anyone in the box had their full attention on the drama and pathos onstage. More than once, she cast a sidelong look at Bennett to find him studying the audience.

Deboque wasn't there. Hannah hadn't expected him. Whatever happened, whenever it happened, he would be far away with an alibi as solid as Cordinian rock.

So they would wait. And watch.

When the lights came up for intermission, Hannah could almost feel Eve relax. A false alarm? No. Though she preferred Eve believing it was so, Hannah knew better. There was an itch between her shoulder blades, vague but persistent. Some called it a hunch. Others called it instinct. Hannah had been in the game long enough to know when to wait and when to go with it.

"Would you like something to drink?"

She turned to Bennett, set to refuse. For personal reasons, she wanted him close at hand. "Yes," she heard herself saying, knowing this would be just one more deception. "I'd love something cool."

The moment he was through the doors behind them, Hannah leaned toward Reeve. "I'm going to look around."

"I'd stay close—I have a feeling." With him it was in the gut. He'd yet to let Gabriella move more than an arm's span away.

"I do too. Deboque said something about me staying in the audience. I want to take a walk backstage."

He started to object, but Gabriella took his hand and gave

Hannah the few seconds she needed to slip out. She made her way toward the ladies' lounge until she was certain no one was watching. With the ease of long experience, she slipped into a stairway and began moving down. She had ten minutes, Hannah thought as she checked her watch, before anyone would miss her.

There were costume changes and stretched nerves backstage when Hannah crossed the corridor. Most of the actors were too wound up to spare her a glance. Nothing out of place. Nothing out of synch. And yet, the itch between her shoulder blades persisted.

Chantel's dressing room door was half-open. The actress caught a glimpse of Hannah, hesitated, then called out. "Lady Hannah."

Because she saw no choice, Hannah stopped at the doorway. "Miss O'Hurley. Her Highness wasn't able to come down, but you should know she's delighted with your performance."

"Thank you." Chantel set down the grease pencil she'd been using to touch up her eyes. "And what do you think of the play?"

"It's gripping. Your interpretation of Julia is breathtaking."

With a nod, Chantel moved toward her. The exaggerated stage makeup only made her look more exotic. "You know, I was born into show business. It's in the blood, if you get my drift. And I've always thought one inveterate actor easily recognizes another."

Very cool, almost smiling, Hannah met her eyes. "I suppose that's true."

"Perhaps that's why while I'm still not sure if I like you, I know I don't trust you." Chantel adjusted the cuff of the dress she'd wear in the next scene. "I've always been very fond of Bennett. A woman like myself has few men she can call real friends."

There was something strong, something honest in the

woman who faced her. Hannah gave as much as she could. "I can tell you that Bennett is a special man, and one I care for very much."

Chantel was silent a moment, weighing, considering. "I'm not sure why, but I believe you." She shook her head. "I can't figure out why you're playing Jane Eyre, but I imagine you have your reasons."

"Places, Miss O'Hurley."

Chantel turned to give herself one last check in a full-length mirror. She lifted her chin to a different angle and became Julia. Her voice took on the slightest of drawls, an echo of the American South, as she turned back to walk past Hannah. "Darling," she said in character. "You must know beige is the worst possible color for you." Then she winked and walked to the wings.

Hannah let out a long breath. She'd seen nothing out of place, seen no one who didn't belong and had learned a lesson. Her cover wasn't as foolproof as she'd always thought.

She walked back down the corridor, turned into the stairway and started up. She heard the applause as the curtain came up. Then came the distant sound, the rumble and boom, of an explosion. The lights went out.

There were scattered screams as the theater plunged into darkness. From here, the warning rumble couldn't be heard. In the Royal Box, guards closed in like a wedge. Guns were drawn, and held ready.

"Stay where you are," Reeve ordered. He gave Gabriella's hand a quick, reassuring squeeze. "Two of you come with me." He moved into the hallway with two guards. "We'll need a light." Swearing, he dug in his pocket for a lighter. "We'll need someone to go over the PA and keep the audience from panicking." Even as he flicked the lighter on, throwing dull and shadowy light off his face, Chantel's voice came cool and clear through the speakers.

"*Mesdames and messieurs*, if you would stay seated for a moment or two. We seem to be having some difficulties with the lights. If you'd like to take advantage of the opportunity by getting to know your neighbor better . . ."

"Good girl," Reeve murmured as he heard the nervous laughter. "Let's get down to the main breakers."

Hannah hadn't come back. The words kept echoing over in Bennett's mind as he heard Alexander murmuring reassurances to Eve. She was out there somewhere, alone in the dark. Without hesitation, he was moving toward the door.

"Your Highness." The looming figure of a guard inched toward him. "If you would please remain seated."

"Let me pass."

"Bennett." His father's voice cut through the dark. "Please sit. This should be over in moments."

"Hannah's not here."

There was the briefest of silences. "Reeve will handle things."

There was duty, and the honor he'd never questioned. Now there was love. Bennett shoved his way through the door and went to find her.

* * *

Hannah had the gun in her hand as she stood in the stairwell. She didn't move, barely breathed, as she debated whether to go up and check on the Bissets, or whether to go down and check the power. If there had been one bomb, there could all too easily be another.

Her head told her that the Bissets were well guarded and her job was to find the source of the trouble. Her heart wanted only to see if Bennett was well and safe. Following it, Hannah started up the stairs. She'd climbed no more than three when she heard the sound of a door closing on the landing below.

With her finger wrapped around the trigger, she pointed the barrel of the gun up and started down again. She saw the beam of the flashlight before she heard the footsteps. Cautious ones. Quiet ones. Like a shadow, Hannah melted into a corner and waited.

She recognized him from the museum. He was dressed now in the dark blue uniform of the maintenance crew and carried a small toolbox. She almost nodded in approval. Anyone seeing him would simply assume he was assigned to fix whatever had gone wrong. The beam skimmed past the toes of her shoes before she stepped out and pressed the gun at his side.

"Be easy," she said in undertones. "I apologize for greeting you this way, but I didn't want a hole in my head before you recognized me."

"Mademoiselle." She heard the tightly controlled fury in his voice. No man liked to be caught unaware. "I was told you would remain out of the way this evening."

Hannah drew the gun back but kept it steady. "I prefer a firsthand look at what's going on. A dramatic distraction," she complimented him. "Are there other plans for tonight?" He was prepared to kill, she was certain. But was he armed? She knew if she detained him too long or pressed too hard, her cover would be in jeopardy.

"Only if the opportunity arises. You will excuse me?"

"Certainly." Her only thought now was to see him out of the theater and away before any opportunity arose. The theater was packed with people, the Royal Family was present. Now wasn't the time for a confrontation. "Can I assist you in making a discreet exit?"

"It's been seen to."

"Very well. Tell our employer that I won't be as dramatic, but I'll be effective." She turned toward the stairs when she heard the door above open.

"Hannah?"

At the sound of Bennett's voice her blood froze. Even as the man beside her made a move, she clamped a hand over his arm. She knew without seeing that he reached for a weapon.

"Don't be a fool," she hissed. "In this light you could too easily miss and ruin everything. Turn off that beam and let me handle it." She felt his resistance, but turned quickly and started up the stairs. "Bennett." She didn't have to fake the fear in her voice. He was hardly more than a shadow at the doorway but she put her arms around him and let her body block his.

"What are you doing down here?" he began.

"I lost my way when the lights went off."

"For God's sake, Hannah. How did you manage to get all the way down here?"

"I—I'm not sure. Please, let's go back."

"You could've broken your neck on these stairs." When he gave her a slight shake and started to draw her back she shifted to block him more thoroughly.

"Kiss me," she ordered in a whisper.

Almost amused now that he'd found her safe, Bennett tilted up her chin. In the dim light he could only make out the vague outline of her face and the glint of her eyes. "If you insist."

Even as he closed his mouth over hers, she gripped the door handle behind him, prepared to shove him through.

Then his fingers spread over her face, gently. His lips coaxed and comforted and asked so little in return. On the handle her fingers tightened as much in response to him as in fear for him. One hand settled at the small of her back, again to soothe. Hannah felt her heart tear. She loved him, yet knew she couldn't. She wanted the kiss to be no more than what it was, a merging of lips, a symbol of caring. But what it was, what it had to be was a tool to give the man below them the time to escape.

Then Bennett would be safe. For seconds only, she put her heart into the kiss. He would be safe, and she could breathe again.

He felt the change and his heart thudded with it. He had imagined her lost in the dark, alone and in need of comfort and physical contact. So thinking, he had buried his own needs and had kissed her as a friend might, with affection and understanding. Her response was thunder and lightning. His fingers tightened on her face as he murmured her name.

The lights came on in a flash.

It happened very quickly then, but Bennett would remember, for a lifetime, each movement, each sound. There was no time for fear, only for surprise, then disillusionment.

When the lights went on, he stiffened. She knew in that moment that Deboque's man had not made his escape as she had hoped, but was waiting to take advantage of the opportunity that had presented itself. Without hesitation she whirled out of Bennett's arms and half shoved him through the door. The man's gun was drawn, but so was hers. And she was very fast.

Bennett had seen the man, and his weapon. He had pushed himself off the door to shield her even as she'd fired. For a moment, he simply stared, stunned at seeing the man fall and lay still. Then he saw the pistol in Hannah's hand. Surprise came and went. His face became very impassive. When he spoke, his voice was neutral.

"What game are you playing, and for whom?"

She'd never killed before. She'd been trained to, of course, but had never actually ended a life by her own hand. As she stood looking down, the gun felt foreign and slimy in her hand. Her face was very pale, her eyes very dark when she turned to Bennett. "I'll have to explain, but there isn't time." She heard the sound of running feet and struggled to pull herself together. "Please trust me."

"That's an interesting request at this point." He started to brush by her to go to the man below.

"Bennett, please." Grabbing his arm, she drew up beside him. "I'll tell you whatever I can later. You can verify it all with Reeve or your father."

She felt his muscles tense. "My father?"

"Please, for his sake, the sake of your family, play this out with me." She pushed the gun into his hand just as Reeve arrived with five guards on his heels. Now she let reaction set it. Again, truth was often the best cover.

"He tried to shoot the prince." Hannah let her voice shake and leaned heavily against Bennett. "He was going to kill him. If Bennett hadn't . . ." Trailing off, she buried her face against Bennett's shoulder.

He didn't move, though he didn't contradict her, there was no comforting hand now, no murmured reassurances. Reeve bent over the body, then lifted his gaze and met Bennett's. "It's fortunate you were quick—and accurate." The .45 lying beside the body hadn't been fired. His eyes shifted over briefly to rest on Hannah. "We'll handle this quietly."

Bennett's lips curved, but it wasn't a smile. "Of course."

"If you'll go back to your box." Reeve signaled two of the guards to accompany him. "We'll say nothing of this to the family until we can be private." With a pencil, he lifted the .45 automatic by the trigger guard. "The police will come in the back way."

Bennett brushed the guards aside with a gesture. It was the first time Hannah had seen him use true royal arrogance. "I want to talk to you. Alone. Now."

"All right." He'd seen too much, Reeve knew. It had to be handled quickly. "Eve's office then. If you'd give me a few minutes to deal with this first."

"You have ten," Bennett said, and turned his back on all of them.

"I'd like to go back to the palace." Hannah stood on the steps, alone now. Her hands, white at the knuckles, clutched her bag. "I'm not feeling well."

"See to a car and driver," Reeve ordered one of the guards. To another he gave the dead man's weapon before he climbed the stairs to slip an arm around Hannah. "I'll walk you out." The moment they were out of earshot, his voice became curt and professional. "What happened?"

Her knees were shaking, but she schooled her voice to the same tone. Briefly, she gave him her report. "The entire thing couldn't have taken more than five minutes." It had seemed like hours.

"It was just bad luck all around that Bennett found you. Still, the story will hold. He has a reputation for being an excellent shot. All I have to do is calm him down." Reeve let out a long breath at that. He knew his brother-in-law well, just as he knew all the Bissets. Once their temper was lost, it wasn't easily regained. "We'll go over this in the morning so that the story you pass on to Deboque is the most advantageous one."

"He'll never forgive me."

Reeve was intuitive enough to know she wasn't speaking of Deboque now. "Bennett is neither unjust nor hardhearted. He'll be angry at being kept in the dark, but he won't blame you."

"Won't he?" Hannah walked through the doors and into the night air without looking back.

* * *

She sat by the window looking out at the garden. An hour had passed, then two while she watched the moonlight. The palace was quiet. Perhaps the others had come back, but she wouldn't have heard because her rooms faced the back. Guests were always given the loveliest views and the quietest spots.

She could imagine all too well how Bennett would have reacted to Reeve's explanations. But it wouldn't be Reeve he would blame. Hannah knew the blame would be hers and had accepted it. In the morning he would probably demand to speak with her privately.

She wouldn't apologize. Hannah lifted her chin a fraction higher. She would accept his anger and his coldness, but she wouldn't apologize for being who and what she was.

She loved him. He would hardly believe her now if she had the right to tell him. She would have died for him tonight, not only for duty, not only for honor, but so much more for love. He would never understand or believe that now. Perhaps it was best. If her feelings for him had gotten beyond her control, it was wiser, and safer, if his for her had deadened.

She still had an assignment to complete and two years of work to finish.

Hannah laid her head on the windowsill and wished she were in London where the night would be cold and damp and smell of the river.

He didn't knock. The time for manners, formalities and small kindnesses had passed. She was curled on the window seat with her arms folded on the sill and her head resting on them. She'd loosened her hair so that it fell over the shoulders and down the back of a plain white robe. A man could almost believe she was a woman lost in the night. Bennett no longer believed what he saw and little that he felt. When he shut the door behind him, she was up and standing quickly.

She hadn't expected him that night. Looking at his face, Hannah saw that she should have. Because she knew the worst when she faced it, she braced.

"You spoke with Reeve?"

"Yes."

"And your father?"

His brow lifted. Though he had discarded his formal jacket,

he could be very much the prince when he chose. "We talk to-morrow, though that doesn't concern you."

She acknowledged this with a slight nod. "Only inasmuch as it affects my position at the moment."

"Although you're obviously unaware of it, I'm not a fool. Your position remains." He took the small pistol from his pocket. After crossing to the stand beside her bed, he set it down. "Your property."

No, she would not be forgiven. She'd thought she'd been ready to accept it. She'd been wrong. "Thank you." As coolly as he, she walked to the stand, then placed the pistol in the drawer.

"You're an excellent shot, Lady Hannah."

The drawer shut again with the slightest of slams. "I've been well trained."

He caught her chin then, not gently. "Yes, by God, you have. What other talents do you have, I wonder? Deceit is certainly the sharpest. How many women can you be?"

"However many it takes to do my job. If you'd excuse me, I'm very tired."

"Oh, no." With his other hand, he gathered up her hair. He thought of what she'd put him through in one evening. Anxiety, outright terror and betrayal. "I'm afraid I won't fall for that again. With me, at any rate, the quiet, well-bred English lady is quite done. Cards on the table, Hannah."

It was fear, she realized, that had her stomach heaving. Not fear that he would hurt her physically, not fear that he would do something in temper that would jeopardize the operation, but fear, deadly and cold, that he would always look at her the way he was now.

"I doubt there's much I can tell you that Reeve hasn't. The operation was put in effect just over two years ago. The ISS needed an agent on the inside, so—"

"I've been apprised of the basic details." He let her go, dropping his hands to his sides. There, they balled into fists. "A bit late, but the information seems fairly complete. After establishing yourself with Deboque's organization, you pretended an affection for Eve so you could gain access to the palace." He saw the flicker of emotion cross her face at that but wasn't ready to interpret it. "In this way, Deboque would be deceived into believing he had one of his own on the inside. By playing both ends, you would be privy to his plans, and once he makes a move, the authorities would be able to close in and destroy his organization. I'm told I should be grateful you're so good at what you do."

"I don't need gratitude, just cooperation."

"Then perhaps you should have asked for it from the beginning."

She lifted her head. No, there would be no apologies. "I had orders, Bennett. You're no stranger to duty."

"No, but neither am I a stranger to honor. You played me." Anger broke through the ice so that he held both of her arms. "You used my feelings for you."

"You weren't supposed to have any," she snapped back.

"We can't always choose what we feel. But there are other choices. Did you need to use how I felt for you, Hannah?"

"I had a job to do." Her voice wasn't steady now because she couldn't be sure if she'd done what she'd done coolly or because of her own needs. "I tried to discourage you."

"You knew I cared, that I wanted you."

"I didn't want you to."

"You still lie."

"No." She yanked, but he held her firm. "I did nothing to attract you. Then again, perhaps a woman only has to exist for you to be attracted." She saw the fury bloom but ignored it. "Perhaps by refusing to sleep with you, I became more of a challenge. There are a lot of women who would gladly sleep with royalty."

"Do you believe if all I had wanted was you in bed that you wouldn't have been there a half-a-dozen times already?"

"I go nowhere I don't take myself." She tossed her head back. His voice had been too low, too precise, but she was past caring. "If you're angry because I'm not what you thought I was, it's because your ego's been bruised."

The rest of her words and her breath were knocked away as she fell under him on the bed. Before she could counter the move, her arms were pinned at her sides. She'd been warned about his temper. There had even been some documentation of it in his dossier. But none of that was nearly as awesome as seeing it firsthand.

"Ego?" He gritted out with his face only inches from hers. "So to you I'm still only what you've read, only what you've been told." It hurt, how it hurt. He could feel it shimmer inside of him until the only recourse was to turn it into anger. "I won't disappoint you then."

She scissored her legs and nearly succeeded in rocking him off. He shifted until her body was pressed flat against his. One hand rested dangerously on her throat. It gave him grim pleasure to feel her pulse flutter rapidly beneath his fingers.

"This won't prove anything." She managed to free one arm, but he caught it at the wrist. Her pulse beat there as well, fast, uneven. "You'll only demean both of us."

It didn't matter. He'd gone beyond right and wrong, truth and lies. "There was a time when I believed you to be shy and precious. That was a woman I only wanted to show tenderness to. For her I had such patience, such sweet feelings. But for you, we can dispense with such things, can't we?"

"Bennett, don't do this." She said it quietly, knowing it was already too late.

"Why not?" The recklessness was back, in full force, driven by betrayal. "It's a night for lies and passions."

She prepared to do battle, for herself and for him. "You won't rape me."

"No, I won't. But I will have you."

CHAPTER 9

It would be a battle of wits, a contest for control. Somehow it was easier for Hannah to think of that when Bennett's lips pressed down on hers. He didn't want to make love with her, but to punish, even to conquer. It was anger, not desire that had brought them here. She couldn't afford to forget it, not even for an instant.

Yet the kiss wasn't cruel. Hot and hard he moved his mouth over hers, more taunting than insistent. The hand on her throat didn't so much threaten as control. The callused fingers reminded her of the strength in his hands even as they stroked to arouse and seduce.

She made her body lie still and limp beneath his, waiting not just for a chance to fight back, but for a chance to fight and win.

But her blood was already beginning to stir.

He knew it. He was a man who understood passions, desires, vulnerabilities and how one would feed on the others. He'd used such things before, all in good humor, to give as much as to take. Now he would use them to wound as deeply as he had been wounded.

Women had frustrated him, amused him, baffled him and fascinated him. But no woman had ever hurt him before

Hannah. That she'd done so not inadvertently, not in a fit of temper, but coolly, passionlessly, made the sin unforgivable. For the first time in his life he held a woman in his arms with the sole intention of bringing her pain.

Or so he told himself.

There was only flesh beneath the robe. He knew it before he drew the material down her bare shoulder. There was strength there. He'd felt it once before. Now he felt the softness as well. Both moved him, just as, he discovered, his touch moved her. As she began her first struggles, he shifted so that her loosened robe parted for him.

She knew better than to panic, but her heart and her needs betrayed her. The moment he'd stroked his palm down her bare skin the flare of pleasure had opened the door to fear. To excitement. To passion. Her struggles took them rolling over the bed, locked in combat. His lean build and easygoing manner made the steely strength she discovered both a surprise and an arousal. Muscles bunched under his shirt as he countered her moves and took her where he wanted her to go. Hannah found herself trapped beneath him again with her arms pinned by the robe that had slipped down her back.

Breathless, she stared up at him. She was beaten, but far from ready to submit. Moonlight slanted in over her face so that her skin was milky pale, her eyes dark and glowing. The fear in them had turned to condemnation. In a mass of confusion, her hair spread over the bed, making him think of mermaids and witches.

"I'll despise you."

Something ripped quietly inside him. His heart or perhaps his soul. He ignored it and fixed on the need to punish her for making him love an illusion.

He lowered his mouth again, but she turned her head away. A small defense, and an unwise one as his lips found the soft, vulnerable curve of her throat. Her breath caught, then expelled again on a moan. The sound had his heart drumming as he found her taste as unique and as dangerous as his feelings for her.

He wanted to love her, and to hate her. He needed to comfort and to punish. He sought to hurt and to give pleasure. In the midst of his confusion, he forgot everything but Hannah.

Hardened from work, gentle by nature, his hands moved over her. With the tip of his tongue, he traced patterns, tormenting, tempting patterns over her skin. He could feel it heat beneath him so that the flavor and the softness seemed to intensify. She twisted one way under him, then the other so that her agitated movements only served to arouse them both.

All at once her body became very still, almost as if even breathing had stopped. Then the trembling began.

She'd never been more aware of herself, more distanced from rational thought. She wanted to remember why he was with her, why it was wrong for both of them, but could only feel. Reasons no longer mattered, consequences were forgotten. He wanted. She wanted. Right and wrong were for the sane.

When he brought his mouth back to hers again, she was waiting. He didn't find pliancy or panic, but the passion she had ruthlessly strapped down most of her life. For him it was free, and she had a fleeting moment to realize it would never fully be disguised again.

Impatience. Desperation. Together they rolled over the bed again but in a far different kind of combat. Her robe was lost so that her arms were free to capture him. In a move that might have told him everything, she locked him to her.

Stay with me. Love me. Understand me.

Then even that was lost in a torrent of heat that left them both gasping.

Once before he'd sensed a volcano inside of her. Now as it erupted around him, he was rocked by the power, the dark violence of it. The breeze that fluttered the curtains was cool and temperate. In the center of the bed was a furnace each of them stoked higher and higher.

Frantic for more of him, Hannah pulled his shirt open, scattering buttons over the mattress and floor. When her laugh came, it was low and sultry as he'd heard it before, but now it had an edge of something that might have been triumph. Then it was a sigh as she ran her hands up his chest. Her kiss was hot and hungry on his as naked flesh met naked flesh.

Something snapped inside him. As a lover he'd always been clever, considerate, caring. Love had never been a game to him, nor had it been a contest. Always, it had been a result of affection, a natural culmination of needs.

But he'd never needed like this.

Tenderness was forgotten as completely as revenge as he dove his hands into her hair and dragged her against him. His teeth nipped into her lower lip, sending dizzying sparks of pleasure through her. Then he began to move swiftly, leaving her lips unsatisfied while his kisses tortured and tamed wherever they reached.

There was panic again, but so twined with excitement she could recognize neither. Afraid, aroused, she tried to draw him back when with a suddenness that left her gasping, he drove her up and over. Her body contracted, almost in defense, then filled with a rash of heat that had her blood burning. Release came on a flood, on a cry of his name, and with the knowledge that no one would ever take her there but him.

She was weak and shuddering. The hands that had clutched the bed clothes went lax. For a moment, she began to float. Then he fanned the flames again.

This is what he'd wanted for her, from her. Her skin was damp and soft under his hands. Her muscles were limber as she began to move with him again. In the moonlight, he saw her face, dazed with passion, flushed with pleasure. Cupping her hips in his hands, he started a lingering line of kisses up her body. He could feel the moment the strength poured back into her.

Still shuddering, still breathless, she tugged at his slacks. She'd had a sample, a taste, and wanted more. She wanted all. As she pulled his clothes from him, he skimmed his fingertips over her inner thighs, hampering her progress, arousing her unbearably. He watched her eyes fly open with the shock of the fresh climax as her body arched up and strained toward the power. Then even as her muscles went lax, his mouth was on hers again and urging her along the next journey.

He was a drug. Her arms felt like lead as she tried to lift them for him. Her head was spinning from the flood of sensations. The ripe scent of passion covered both of them so that their skin was slick and hot. She could hear her own breath come in sighs and moans as she struggled to focus on his face.

His eyes were tawny, like a cat's before it springs. She remembered how he'd looked on the stallion, daring, dangerous. She shuddered once, then surrendered. With her eyes open and her heart willing, she gathered him close.

She opened. He filled.

The ride was fast and rough. Locked together, they raced. Without slackening pace, they plunged headlong over the cliff.

* * *

Silence seemed to last forever. Hannah curled herself into it and waited for him to leave her. Though her mind wasn't cool, some sanity had returned. Covered by the dark, she could admit to herself that she would never be the same. He'd broken through that carefully polished veneer and had conquered the inner woman, the woman he hated. She couldn't tell him that she loved, that she already mourned the loss of what she never really had and would spend the rest of her life wishing for it.

He wanted to reach out to her, to gather her close and stroke her hair in the moonlight. It wouldn't be possible to touch her again. He'd taken in anger what he'd once dreamed of taking in tenderness. The guilt was there, real and ripe even as the sense of betrayal crept back.

The woman he'd fallen in love with didn't exist. She'd been a lie even more than an illusion. Now he'd done what even in his wildest moments he'd avoided. He'd made love with a stranger. And God help him, he'd fallen just as deeply in love with her.

Had he hurt her? He wanted to ask, but held himself back. He couldn't afford to feel remorse or he would end up making a fool of himself over this new Hannah as well. Pride followed honor. Since he'd sacrificed one to temper and pain, he would hold firm to the other.

As he rose, he dragged a hand through his hair. How could he love her when he didn't even know her? How could he still love the woman he knew had never existed?

He dressed in silence while Hannah lay still as a stone on the bed.

"Now it seems we've used each other," he murmured.

She opened her eyes then. There were no tears in them. Thank God she still had the strength for that much. He was standing by the bed, naked from the waist up with the ruined shirt balled in his hand. "We can consider ourselves even."

"Can we?" His fingers went white on his shirt. He'd nearly taken a step toward her before he made himself turn and leave her alone.

Hannah lay and listened to the silence until dawn.

*　*　*

You have questions," Armand began as he faced his youngest son. The morning light was strong through the open windows and showed, all too clearly, the marks of a sleepless night on both faces. "I prefer it if you wait to ask them until after I've finished."

He'd been prepared to demand and to rage. The lines of strain and weariness made his father look suddenly old and much too vulnerable. Again, it was love rather than duty that guided him. "All right." Because he needed it, Bennett poured coffee and left it black.

"Will you sit?"

"No."

Armand's gaze sharpened at the tone. Then he, too, let love hold sway. "I shall." Once seated, he set his untouched coffee aside. "Two years ago, I sat in this office with Reeve and Malori. You and Alexander were also present. You remember?"

Bennett paced to the window and looked out. "Yes. We were speaking of Deboque and what could and should be done."

"Then you remember that Reeve, even then, had an operative in mind to infiltrate the organization."

"I remember, too, that it was decided that the name be kept from Alex and me." The trace of resentment he had felt then had grown to true bitterness in one night. "And that Malori was not completely satisfied with Reeve's choice."

"Malori has always been one of the most trusted members of the security staff in Cordina. But he's old-fashioned." Armand saw no need to add that he, too, had had his doubts. "He was concerned with using a woman."

Bennett downed half his coffee. "I felt then, as I feel now, that Alexander and I had a right to know what was being done. More, all of us had the right to know that the woman we accepted as friend was an ISS agent."

"I felt then as I feel now—" Armand's voice, though quiet, held the whip of authority "—that neither of you had a need to know. If I had become ill, Alex, of course, would have been apprised. However—"

"Do you think because I won't rule, Cordina is of less importance to me?" Bennett whirled on his father. The fury on his face was lethal. "All of my life I've been the younger brother. Alex was born to rule Cordina after you. He was molded for it, just as his son will be. Do you think because of that I cared less, loved less or would have offered less?"

Armand said nothing for a moment, knowing the words had to be chosen with care, even as they came from the heart. "Bennett, I've watched you grow from child to man and have waited for a sign, for a hint that you resented your position. You have been sometimes wild, always reckless and too often indiscreet, but never have I seen anything in you but love and devotion for your country and your family."

"Then why, when something threatens both, do you keep your plans from me?"

There was a headache drumming behind Armand's temple. He closed his eyes a moment, but didn't lift a hand to soothe it. "Two years ago, Lady Hannah Rothchild was chosen out of a half dozen highly qualified operatives to infiltrate and destroy Deboque's organization. We were aware, as she was, of the risks involved, and the time and skill it would take to succeed."

"Why her?" Bennett found he didn't want to think beyond that for a moment. It was an answer he had to have before he could deal with the others.

"Reeve felt Hannah's talents were uniquely suited to the operation. She's been with the ISS for ten years."

"Ten years?" Bennett roamed the room again as he tried to take it in. "How is that possible? She's so young."

"She's second generation," Armand said mildly. "Her father trained her himself while she was still in school. Lord Rothchild, though semiretired now, is one of the most valued agents in the ISS. He had some part in Reeve's early training, which was another reason Reeve leaned toward Hannah for this assignment."

"Ten years," Bennett repeated. How many women had she been? How many lies had she told?

"Apparently she had a natural aptitude for this kind of work." He saw his son's jaw set, but went on. "After reading Reeve's report on her, I had to agree that she was best suited for what we had in mind."

"Deboque often uses women," Bennett murmured.

"He feels they can be more cunning, even more cruel, than men." Armand remembered Janet Smithers and the bullet that had been dug out of his son's flesh. "His preference runs to a certain type, quiet, well-bred, spotless pedigrees."

"Hannah."

"Yes. It was those qualities in her which weighed the decision in her favor. With the cooperation of the ISS a deep background was created for her. The credentials she was given made it possible for her to slip into Deboque's company. In two years, she's moved from messenger to the top of the organization."

"The top?" The fear started then, like something foul in the back of his throat. "What do you mean?"

"She's met with Deboque himself, and by managing to discredit one of his top men, is now filling that position herself. Reeve explained to you that as far as Deboque knows, she's here at the palace as his instrument."

Bitterness was more palatable than fear. He concentrated on it. "She plays the game very well."

"An agent in her position plays the game well or loses her life. You know firsthand that Deboque doesn't hesitate to kill. Her name and the operation itself were kept in strictest confidence not to protect you or the rest of the family, Bennett, but to protect her."

Bennett set his cup down and stopped pacing. "In what way?"

"Three other agents have been killed trying to do what Hannah has nearly succeeded in doing. The last was butchered." He watched Bennett's face pale. He would have spared his son this, as a father. Now, as prince, he could spare him nothing. "By bringing her here in this way, letting you, all of you, believe what Deboque wanted you to believe, Hannah had the only protection we could offer. If she's discovered, even the ISS can't protect her. Now that you know all that you know, her risk is greater than ever."

In silence, Bennett crossed the room to sit across from his father. Though the turmoil was building all too quickly inside, his face was calm. "I'm in love with her."

"Yes." Armand sat back. "I was afraid you were."

"I will not stand still and watch Deboque hurt someone else I love."

"Bennett, there are times, too many times, when our personal feelings can't influence our actions."

"For you." Bennett's voice was still calm, but slightly colder. "Perhaps for Alex as well, but not for me. I prefer to kill him myself."

Armand felt a ripple of fear, a tingle of pride and controlled both. "If you do anything to interfere with the operation at this point, you could be responsible for Hannah's death, not Deboque's."

Pushed to his limit, Bennett leaned forward. "Do you understand, I'm in love with her? If you were in my position, could you do nothing?"

Armand studied his son's face and remembered the only woman he'd ever loved. "I can only say that I would do whatever was necessary to keep her safe. Even if that meant doing nothing." He rose and went to his desk. "Read these."

He lifted a small stack of files that carried the stamp of highest security. "These contain background information on Hannah, some of her own reports concerning certain assignments and most recently, her progress with Deboque. I'll leave you so that you can read them here. They mustn't leave this room."

Bennett rose to accept the files. "Where is she now?"

He had hoped the question wouldn't be asked. "She received a message early this morning. She's gone to Deboque."

* * *

She had to play this one very carefully. Hannah sat with her hands folded on her lap in the elegant salon of Deboque's rented villa. Though the meeting was on land this time, she knew if her cover hadn't held up, she was just as much alone as she had been on the yacht.

If he had a hint of the part she'd played in the events of the evening before, her throat would be slit before she could voice a denial. A risk every agent takes, she reminded herself. To test herself, she lifted the small china pot on the table in front of her and poured coffee. Her hand was steady.

It was imperative that her mind stay sharp and focused on the assignment.

Every other thought in her mind was of Bennett.

"Lady Hannah." Deboque walked into the salon then shut the double doors at his back. "How delightful to see you again."

She added a careful dollop of cream. "The message I received this morning left little option."

"Ah, I was brusque." He crossed to her, taking her hand and brushing his lips over it. "My apologies. The events of last night caused me some distress."

"And me." She drew her hand away. Instinct told her

annoyance was the wisest course. "I find myself wondering if I've chosen wisely."

Deboque chose the seat beside hers, then taking his time, chose a cigarette from a crystal holder. He wore emeralds today. "Meaning?"

"Only months ago, I found myself in the position of having to clean up for another of your employees." She sipped coffee. It was hot and Turkish. "Last night, another of them nearly ruined every carefully laid step I've taken toward the Bissets."

"May I remind you, *mademoiselle*, you were advised to stay out of the way?"

"I'll remind you, *monsieur*, that I haven't reached my current position by not looking toward my own interests. If I hadn't followed Bennett, you and I might even now be sitting in less agreeable quarters."

Deboque blew out smoke. "Explain."

"Bennett was a bit bored with the play and thought to wait in the American actress's dressing room until the curtain. Because I was aware that there were plans of some sort in the works, I decided it best to keep close. When the lights went out, I had to decide whether to go back or keep Bennett within reach. If I'd gone back, *monsieur*, the prince might indeed be dead."

"And for that you wish my gratitude?"

"He might be dead," Hannah repeated, "and a member of your organization would even now be in custody. Shall I pour you some coffee?"

"Merci." He waited patiently while she filled a second cup. At his nod, she added cream.

Hannah sat back again and folded her ringless hands. "Mac-Gee and the guards were already on their way. I spotted your man." She made a look of disgust. "He was bumbling his way around with a flashlight. I managed to distract Bennett by playing the hysterical female, but the idiot didn't take the opportunity to make good his escape. The lights came up again. Bennett saw him and his weapon. You should be flattered that since your release the prince has carried a small-caliber pistol with him. He used it, and for personal reasons, I'm grateful he used it well. Dead men can't name names." Playing up the role, she rose. "I ask you now, was the man under orders to kill one of the Bissets? Do you or do you not trust me to complete the contract?"

Say it! she ordered silently. Say it out loud, say it plainly so that this can be over.

Smoke curled up in a column toward the ceiling as he tapped the cigarette into an ashtray. "Please, my dear, be calm. The man you speak of may have been told to use initiative, but was never given a specific request. I have confidence in you, of course."

"We agreed. I would dispose of the Bissets in return for five million dollars."

He smiled, like a generous uncle. "We agreed that if such a thing were to happen, there would be some compensation."

"I'm tired of playing games." As if to prove it, Hannah picked up her bag. "If you won't speak frankly, if you won't honor our arrangement, there's no reason to go on with this."

"Sit." The order came sharp and clear as she walked to the door. Hannah stopped, turned, but didn't walk back. "You forget yourself. No one who works for me leaves until they are dismissed."

She knew there would be men outside the door, to detain or dispose of her at Deboque's whim. She gambled that he would respect audacity. "Perhaps it's best if I find other employment then. I'm not accustomed to being dealt only half the cards."

"Remember that I hold them. I ask you again, sit."

This time she obeyed. She let the impatience shimmer, but only enough to let him see her control. "Very well."

"Tell me how the Bissets cope this morning."

"With dignity, of course." She pretended to be amused. "Bennett's pleased with himself. Armand is worried. Eve is confined to bed for the day. Gabriella stays with her. MacGee is closeted with Malori—you know the name?"

"Yes."

"I would guess that they are trying to see what purpose the disturbance last night had. Your man did an excellent job on the main power, though I think the explosive was a bit over-stated." She shrugged as though it had been a hat with one too many feathers. "In any case, they ran on auxiliary for the rest of the evening and have a crew in the Center this morning for repairs. It's their belief that the power was blown so that the assassin could break his way into the Royal Box."

"A natural assumption," Deboque said as he went back to his coffee. And exactly the one he'd hoped for. "Though such a move would have been messy and unstylish. And you, my dear? How do you cope after witnessing a killing?"

"I've chosen to be shocked and weakened by the events. But brave, naturally. We British are, you know."

"I've always admired the quality." He smiled at her again. "I have to congratulate you on the depth of your skill. You look as though you didn't close your eyes all night."

It was a mistake to remember, to think even for an instant, of Bennett. "I drank enough coffee to keep me awake until dawn," she said easily as her stomach tied itself in knots. "At the moment I'm supposedly out for a walk to clear my head." To take his attention from that, she added the last of what she and Reeve had discussed. "Are you aware that the entire Royal Family will gather at the palace for the Christmas Ball?"

"So is tradition."

"With Eve being a bit delicate, the Princess Gabriella brings her family to stay for several days during the preparations. The MacGees share a wing with Alexander and Eve so that they can be close to the children."

"Interesting."

"And obliging. I'll require the makings for three plastic explosives."

Deboque only nodded. "The younger prince doesn't reside in the same wing."

"The younger prince will be fatally injured while trying to save the rest of his family. Leave it to me. Just make sure the five million is waiting." She rose again, then inclined her head as if waiting for his permission to leave. Deboque stood as well, then surprised her by taking both of her hands.

"I had thought that some time after the holiday I would take a long vacation. I have an urge to sail, to be in the sun. Vacations can be very dull without companionship."

Her stomach turned over. She prayed the revulsion wouldn't show, even for an instant. "I've always been fond of the sun." She didn't object when he stepped closer, but smiled. "You have a reputation for discarding women as easily as you collect them."

"When they bore me." He cupped a hand around her neck. His fingers were light, smooth, and still made her think of spiders. "I have a feeling you won't. I'm not attracted to looks, but brains and ambitions. Together, I believe we could be very comfortable."

If his lips touched hers, she would retch. Knowing it, Hannah tilted her head back just an inch. "Perhaps—after our business is completed."

The fingers on her neck tightened, then released. The marks they had left wouldn't fade for several minutes. "You're a cautious woman, Hannah."

"Cautious enough to want the five million before I sleep with you. Now if you'll excuse me, I should get back before I cause any concern."

"Of course."

She walked to the door. "I'll need those supplies by the end of the week."

"Expect a Christmas present from your aunt in Brighton."

With a nod, she swung easily through the door.

Deboque took his chair again and decided he'd become quite fond of her. It was a shame she'd have to die.

CHAPTER 10

It was midafternoon before Bennett went to find her. He'd read every word in the files Armand had given him. Though some had fascinated him, some had frightened him and some had angered him, he still wasn't sure he knew the woman.

Now he, too, was part of the deception, he thought as he made his way up to Eve's rooms. Nothing he'd read, nothing he'd been told could be confided to his brother. He couldn't comfort his sister or Eve with the fact that every move Deboque made was being monitored. He had, as he was coming to understand Hannah had, no choice but to play the game through. So he went to find her, knowing it was long past time they talked calmly.

He found Eve and Gabriella together at a table with piles of lists and a pot of tea.

"Bennett." Gabriella reached a hand out. "Just in time. We need a man's viewpoint on the Christmas Ball."

"Make sure there's plenty of wine." He bent to kiss both of her cheeks. Though she'd smiled at him, he'd recognized the signs of strain, just as he recognized them in Eve. "Hannah's not with you?"

"No." Eve set her pencil down as she lifted her face for Bennett's kiss. "I told her I wanted her to rest today. Last night . . ."

She tightened her fingers on his. "Last night must have been dreadful for her. And you."

He shrugged, remembering too clearly the way he'd left her—curled into a silent ball on the bed. "It wasn't a dull evening in any case."

"Don't joke, Ben. You could have been killed. All I can think is that it's the second time in the theater. The second time one of my plays—"

Keeping Eve's hand in his, he crouched down. "I wasn't hurt, and I don't want you letting that fertile imagination go. I'd be very annoyed if my nephew were born with worry lines. Where's Marissa?"

"Napping."

He rubbed a thumb under her eyes. "You should do the same."

Annoyance replaced the strain, as he'd hoped. "Now you sound like Alex."

"God forbid. Where is he, anyway?"

"Meetings." She nervously traced her fingers over the papers. "Most of the day. Everything's been switched to his offices here because of—because security prefers it."

"Then you should relax." He covered her hand with his. "You should know by now the Bissets are indestructible. At the least you should be grateful he's tied up for a while, otherwise he'd be in here hovering over you."

She managed to smile. "You do have a point."

Rising, he grinned down at Gabriella. "I suppose we can trust you to keep her in line—though you're not looking your best, either."

"Chivalry is never dead with you around."

"What are brothers for?" He wanted to gather them both close and tell them that nothing and no one would ever hurt them again. Instead, he gave his sister's hair a tug. "Now I'll let you two get back to what I'm sure is fascinating work." He'd gotten no farther than the head of the stairs when Gabriella caught up with him. "Ben."

He turned, and though he was ready with a smile, her expression stopped it.

Gabriella looked back over her shoulder to be certain they were far enough away from Eve's office, then laid a hand over his on the banister. "Reeve tells me little about certain matters." A trace of temper came into her eyes, then was dismissed. "That's something I have to live with. But particularly since I once lost everything, I have very good instincts when it comes to my family."

"I know you're worried," he began. "All of us are."

"It's more than that, though everything comes back to Deboque and his obsession with destroying us. I still have dreams, even after all these years." She could remember a cabin, and the dark, and the fear.

"Brie." He laid a hand on her cheek. "Nothing like that is ever going to happen again."

She closed her fingers lightly over his wrist. "And I remember seeing you shot and bleeding on the terrace floor. I remember sitting in the hospital while Eve hung between life and death. Deboque." Her face was very pale, but there was strength in it and in the hand that lay on his. "It's all been Deboque. And he isn't finished."

"He will be." Something dangerous came into his voice, into his eyes. "That I promise you."

"I want you to be careful, Bennett."

He smiled, so that the look vanished. "How can I be otherwise with a dozen guards smothering me?"

"Very careful," she repeated. "I've never known you to carry a pistol to the theater."

She knew it was a lie. He didn't have to hear her say it, only to look in her eyes. She knew, but didn't understand. And because she was Gabriella, she wouldn't stop until she did.

"Leave it for now."

"So Reeve told me," she said with an impatient gesture. "It's my family. How can I?"

"I only know it's going to be over soon. In the meantime we have to stand together. Something's being done, Brie. Hold on to that."

"I have been." She knew it was unfair to push, so released him. "I want you to promise you won't do anything rash."

"What is this reputation I carry with me?"

"Ben, please."

"All right, you have it." He kissed her again. "I adore you, even if you did bring Dorian into the world to pester me." He gave her hand a final pat before he started down the stairs. "*A bientôt.*"

She watched him go, but the worry stayed with her. "*A bientôt.*"

Hannah wasn't in her rooms. Bennett found himself frustrated yet again when he entered and found them empty. Had she gone out again? he wondered. Was she even now putting herself in danger to protect his family?

He hated it. The thought of her risking her life, of blocking his body with her own as she had done last night was impossible to accept. Whether it was family, friend or country, he protected. How could he do less for the woman he loved?

Wandering in her rooms, he moved to her dresser. There was a small enameled box with a peacock on the lid. He ran a finger over it, wondering where she had come by it. A gift? From whom? A purchase in some little shop in London? He needed to know even those inconsequential details about her. Couldn't she understand that in order to resolve his feelings he had to know the woman he'd given them to?

He looked up, and reflected in the mirror was the bed where they'd fought, and loved, the night before. If he stood very still, he could almost feel the echoes of passion and discovery in the air. Would she hate him for that? Even though the loving had been as intense and as stunning for her as for him, would she forgive him for forcing her to set the barriers aside?

He'd been rough. . . . Bennett looked down at his own hands, turning them over, spreading his fingers. And he hadn't cared. All of his life he'd taken such pains never to hurt a woman. Now, when he'd found the only woman, he'd set out to do just so.

Walking to the window he stared out and tried to sort out his feelings. He still resented her. No matter what his brain told him, his heart was still bruised by the deception. More, he couldn't shake off the feeling that he'd fallen in love with two women and could trust neither.

Then he saw her in the gardens below.

*　*　*

She needed some time, Hannah told herself. Just an hour alone to clear her mind and calm her nerves. She knew she'd handled Deboque as smoothly as possible that morning. If nothing went wrong, they would close the trap on him in a week. Then she would have succeeded. In her file would go another favorable report. A two-year assignment successfully tied up could very well mean a promotion. She was, she knew, only inches away from a captaincy. Why didn't it excite her as it once had?

Time, Hannah told herself again. She just needed some time.

She would take a much needed and well-earned vacation. Perhaps at last she would go to America—New York, San Francisco. Wouldn't it be possible to lose herself in such places for a while?

Or perhaps she would go back to England. She could spend time in Cornwall walking the moors or riding by the sea. In

England she couldn't lose herself, but perhaps she could find herself again.

Wherever she went, she would be leaving Cordina. And Bennett.

Wisteria rose up in an arch, sheltering a bench and inviting long, lazy contemplations. She sat, and closing her eyes, tried to bring her troubled mind to rest.

Who was she? For the first time in years she was forced to ask herself and admit she didn't know the answer. A part of her was the quiet woman who enjoyed a long afternoon with a book, who liked to talk of literature and art. A part of her was the woman who kept a weapon within reach and listened to footsteps behind her.

The fact that she could be both had always been a benefit before, never, as it was now, a painful puzzle to solve. She wished she could talk with her father, even for an hour. He understood what it was to live two lives and find contentment and challenge in each.

But she couldn't risk even that. In this, as in the assignment that had brought her here, she was alone.

He detested her. It was Bennett who had caused the ache and the doubts. It was Bennett who had forced her to question what she'd always taken for granted. Last night he'd taken her mind and heart and body, only because he'd wanted to humiliate her. And he had. No one, no one had ever shown her how much there could be, how much she could give. No one had ever left her so empty and alone.

He wouldn't know how much he'd hurt her. He couldn't know, she thought as the tears she'd held off throughout the night began to fall. Because he would never know how strong her feelings were for him, and how hopeless.

She had chosen her path, Hannah reminded herself, and she would live with it. In a matter of days it would no longer cross his.

He would be safe. His family would be safe. And she would be gone.

He found her sitting on the bench, her hands folded neatly in her lap, her eyes closed and her face wet with tears. So many feelings tumbled into him that he couldn't separate them. Regret, confusion, love, guilt.

She'd want to be left alone. He thought he understood her that well. There was still enough bitterness in him to want to leave her alone. He could no more have left her there than he could have left a wounded dog on the side of the road.

As he went closer, Hannah sprang up from the bench. He saw the shock and humiliation run across her face. For a moment, he thought she would turn and run. But she held her ground.

"I thought I was alone." Her voice was cold as she fought anger and embarrassment.

He took out a handkerchief and offered it. At the moment it was the only comfort he could give, or she accept. "I'm sorry I disturbed you." His voice was as stiff as hers. "I think we need to talk."

"Haven't we?" She dried her face then crumpled the linen in her hands.

"Would you like to sit?"

"No, thank you."

He slipped his hands into his pockets. She hadn't slept, he thought as he saw the shadows under her eyes. Neither had he. So perhaps there they were even. "I spoke with my father this morning. You've met with Deboque already today."

She started to cut him off, but relented. The garden was as secure as the palace—for the moment. "I don't report to you on those matters, Your Highness."

Temper narrowed his eyes and balled his hands into fists, but he spoke evenly. "No, but I'm now fully aware of the situation. I read your files."

Her breath came out on a huff of air. Was nothing she was

or had done hers alone any longer? "Very well then, your questions have been answered, your curiosity satisfied. You know everything there is to know about me—I hope you were entertained."

"I didn't read it to be entertained," he tossed back. "Dammit, Hannah, I have a right to know."

"You have no rights where I'm concerned. I'm neither servant or subject."

"You're the woman I took to bed last night."

"That's best forgotten. Don't." Her body went rigid as he started forward. "Don't you ever touch me again."

"Very well." He stiffened even as she did. "But we both know certain things can't be forgotten."

"Mistakes can," she countered. "I'm here as an agent of the ISS to protect you and your family, to stop Deboque's plans to ruin Cordina and avoid the repercussions in Europe. Whatever has to be done to assure that, I'll do, but I will *not* let you humiliate me again." The tears started again, blinding her. "Oh, damn you, can't you leave me alone? Wasn't last night enough retribution for you?"

That snapped the very tenuous control he had on his own temper. He grabbed her arm, closing his fingers over the firm muscle. "Is that all it meant to you? Retribution? Can you stand here now and tell me you felt nothing, feel nothing? How accomplished a liar are you?"

"It doesn't matter what I felt. You wanted to punish me, and you did."

"I wanted to love you, and I did."

"Stop." That hurt, more than she was able to stand. She pushed him away only to be caught closer. The movement sent wisteria blossoms raining. "Do you think I couldn't see how much you hated me? You looked at me and made me feel vile. For ten years I've been proud of what I do, and you took even that away from me."

"And what of you?" He kept his voice low, but the anger was just as potent. "Can you tell me you didn't know I was in love with you?" She started to shake her head in denial, but he tightened his fingers. "You knew I was in love with a woman who didn't even exist. A quiet, shy and honest woman to whom I only wanted to show tenderness and patience. For the first time in my life there was a woman I could give my heart and my trust to, and she was nothing but a mirage."

"I don't believe you." But she wanted to and her heart began to race. "You were restless, even bored. I entertained you."

"I loved you." He lifted his hand and held her face very still, very close. She saw his eyes as she had the night before, tawny with passion. "You'll have to live with that."

"Bennett—"

"And when I came to your room last night, I found another woman, one who had lied and used me." He dragged the hand up, raking through her hair so that pins scattered. "One who looked like a witch," he murmured as her hair fell heavily over his hands. "And I wanted her just as badly, but without those tender, those sweet feelings. God help me, I still want her."

When his mouth came down on hers, she didn't protest. She'd also seen the truth in his eyes. He had loved her. Or he had loved the pretense of her. If desire was all he could give her now, she would take it. For duty she had sacrificed love, but even for duty, she wouldn't sacrifice the crumbs she had left.

She wrapped her arms around him. Perhaps if she could give him the passion, someday he would forgive her the rest.

How easily he could lose himself in her. The passion was edgy and achy but it didn't seem to matter. Her mouth was warm, her body slender and straining. If it wasn't love she felt for him, at least there was need. He'd settled for no more than that before.

"Tell me you want me," he demanded as he moved his mouth desperately over her face.

"Yes, I want you." She hadn't known it possible to feel triumph and defeat at the same time.

"Come with me now."

"Bennett, I have no right to this." She turned her face into his throat, wanting to draw just a little more of him into her. "I'm here only because—"

With his hands on her shoulders he drew her away before she could finish the denial. "For today, for one day, we'll put your duty and mine aside."

"And tomorrow?"

"Tomorrow comes whether we want it to or not. Give me a few hours, Hannah."

She would have given him her life, and somehow knew that would be easier than what he was asking now. Still, she put her hand in his.

They went on horseback. As Hannah cantered beside him, she could see that Bennett knew the route to their destination well. They turned into the woods where they'd raced once before, and he took the lead. Each time doubts rose up to plague her, she beat them back. She would take the few hours she was being offered.

She heard the stream before she saw it. It was a simple, musical sound that suited the leafy shade and towering trees. When Bennett came to it, he turned his horse south. For a quarter of a mile they rode along the bank in silence.

The stream curved and twisted, then widened at a point where a trio of willows draped over it. Bennett stopped there and swung from the saddle.

"What a lovely spot." Hannah reined in, but found herself not quite courageous enough to dismount. "Every time I think I've seen the most beautiful place in Cordina, I find another. Do you often come here?"

"Not often enough." He'd secured his horse and now walked to her. Saying nothing, he held up a hand.

Here was the choice he'd refused to give her the night before. Perhaps he gave it to her now because he knew the decision had already been made. Hannah curled her fingers into his, held a moment, then dismounted. The silence continued while she tethered her horse beside his.

"I came here when my mother died." He didn't know why it seemed important that he tell her. "Not to grieve really, but because she always loved places like this. See the little white flowers along the bank?" His hand was on hers again as they moved closer to the stream. "She called them angel wings. They're sure to have a complicated Latin name, but angel wings seemed right."

Bending, he plucked one. It was no bigger than his thumb with thin petals cupped around a tiny blue center. "Every summer, before I'd have to go back to Oxford, I'd come here. For some reason it made leaving easier." He tucked the flower into her hair. "When I was a child, I thought the fairies lived here. I used to look for them in the clover and under toadstools."

She smiled and touched a hand to his cheek. "Did you ever find one?"

"No." With his hand on her wrist, he turned his head to press his lips to her palm. "But I think they're still here. That's why this place is magic. That's why I want to make love with you here."

Their lips were still an inch apart as they lowered to the grass. They remained a breath apart as they began to undress each other. Kneeling, gazes locked, they unfastened buttons. Sunlight dappled over skin as material was pushed aside. Their lips brushed, then clung.

He couldn't stop the rush of power, the flood of need. In seconds they were rolling over the grass. He caressed her everywhere, seeking, finding, exploiting until her moans shuddered into his mouth. The need to take her quickly, fiercely, couldn't be fought down, especially when her fingers were already tugging at the clasp of his jeans.

They waited only until all barriers were removed, then joined in a rocketing, furious journey that left them both sated.

Naked, with the grass tickling her back, Hannah looked up at the sunlight filtering through the leaves overhead. It had been moonlight before and she'd experienced a range of feelings from anger, shame, ecstasy and back to shame again. Today, in the sunlight, she no longer felt the shame.

What was between them could be, for this short time, between the man and the woman. Tomorrow they would be prince and agent again.

"What are you thinking?"

She was able to smile and turn her head toward him. "That this is a beautiful spot."

He'd wanted to bring her there before. He'd imagined it. How he would slowly, patiently, show her the pleasures of loving. Shaking off the mood, he drew her closer. This was a different day, and a different woman. "Are you warm enough?"

"Hmmm. But I . . ." she trailed off, knowing she'd sound foolish.

"But?"

"Well, I've never—" How to phrase it? "I've never lain naked in the grass under the sun before."

He laughed, not even realizing that the tone and the feeling behind it had come from the woman he'd first known. "Life should always include new experiences."

"I'm sure you've found yourself naked in all manner of unusual places."

The dry voice delighted him. Rolling over, he pressed a kiss to her mouth then drew back just to look at her. Her hair was fanned out over the dark grass. The tiny white flower was tangled in it as though it had grown there. Bruising shadows under her eyes made her look both wanton and delicate, as though she were a virgin who'd just spent a night being initiated into womanhood.

This was how he had once imagined her, how he had once wanted, how he had once loved.

"You're so beautiful."

She smiled, relaxed enough to be amused. "Now *that* I've never been."

He traced a fingertip along her cheekbone. "How unobservant of you, Hannah. Or how foolish. Making yourself look less attractive doesn't change the truth. Flawless skin." He traced his lips over it as if to taste. "These elegant bones that make a man wonder if you're made of flesh and bone or glass. Those calm, intelligent eyes that drove me mad wondering how they might darken and cloud if I could find the right way to touch you. And this." He rubbed a finger over her lips. "So soft, so generous." He lowered his head but only traced the shape with his tongue. "Do you remember the first time I kissed you?"

Her breath was already shaking, her eyes already closing. "Yes. I remember."

"I wondered how it was that such a quiet woman could make my knees weak with just a taste."

"Kiss me now," she demanded and drew him down to her.

It wasn't what she expected. There was tenderness instead of passion, patience rather than urgency. She murmured against his mouth in confusion. Bennett only stroked his fingers over her face and waited for her to relax. More, he waited for her to accept. Even when he deepened the kiss it remained gentle. The fire was there but smoldering rather than blazing.

He was making love to the Hannah he'd understood, she realized and wanted to weep. There was lust for one, affection for the other. How could she fight another woman when the woman was herself?

On a trembling sigh, she let her mind empty. She would give him whatever it was he needed today.

He felt the change—the slow, almost fluid surrender. With a murmured approval, he pressed his lips to her throat. He wanted to show her there could be more than flash and speed. If they only had a few hours, then he would use them to give her whatever sweetness she would accept from him.

Lightly he stroked the smoothness of her body. What he'd demanded from her the night before, he now requested, coaxed, offered. He took the time to watch her arousal grow as the sun filtered down on her face and the stream rushed by beside them. He murmured to her as he kissed her throat. There were promises, endearments, reassurances. She answered him in words so fragile they almost dissolved in the air.

She'd never been loved like this before—as though she was precious, as though she was special. Even with her mind fogging over she could hear the gentle hiss of water running over rock. She could smell the grass and the wild sweet flowers scattered through it. With her eyes half-opened, the sunlight seemed gold and bountiful over her lover's skin. She ran her hand over it, finding it smooth and taut and warm.

Her lover. Hannah brought his mouth back to hers and gave him everything that was in her heart. If the place was magic, then so was the moment. Dreams hadn't been a part of her life for too long to remember, but she opened herself to them now.

She was so giving, so pliant. He'd wanted too badly to feel this kind of emotion from her. It went far beyond heat, far above desire. She touched him as though she'd been waiting for him all of her life. She kissed him as though he were her first and only lover. The more she gave, the more he found in himself to give back. The shadows shifted and lengthened over them as they stroked and offered and discovered.

Even when he slipped into her, it was slow and easy. The

passion that had built was still harnessed by stronger emotions. They moved together in a harmony that seemed almost painful in its perfection while she framed his face with her hands and his lips met hers.

They glided over the top and settled softly.

* * *

You wanted to see me, Monsieur Deboque?"

"Yes, Ricardo." Deboque lifted his teapot and poured. He admired the British habit of tea in the late afternoon. It was so civilized. "I have a little shopping list for you." With one hand he gestured toward the desk by the window. "I'd like you to supervise it personally."

"Of course." Always pleased to be given trust, Ricardo picked up the list written on heavy cream-colored paper. His brow lifted only a fraction. "Shall I requisition this from within the company?"

"Please." Deboque added cream to his tea. "I prefer to keep this at home, so to speak. The delivery should be set up with Lady Hannah on . . . Thursday, I'd say. It's no use passing the merchandise along to her too soon."

"She risks much, smuggling such a—volatile package into the palace."

"I have implicit trust in our British friend, Ricardo." He remembered the way she'd sat across from him that morning. Trim, tidy and cultured. It gave his plans such a pleasant touch when they were carried out by delicate hands. "She has a certain style, wouldn't you say?"

"Class, even when so quietly cloaked, is still class, *monsieur.*"

"Precisely." Deboque smiled and sipped at his tea. "I have no doubt she will carry out her objective with class." He sipped his tea again and sighed. "I do admire the British, Ricardo. So traditional, so resilient. Not as passionate as the French, but so wonderfully pragmatic. In any case, see that the merchandise is shipped from the address on that list. I don't wish it to come through my hands."

"Of course."

"I'm preparing an itinerary, Ricardo. We'll be sailing the end of next week. I'll see Lady Hannah once more. You'll see to the details?"

"As you wish."

"Thank you, Ricardo. Oh, by the way, did you see that a wreath was sent to Bouffe's funeral?"

"Roses as you requested, *monsieur*."

"Excellent." Deboque chose one of the little sugared biscuits from the Wedgwood plate. "You're very dependable."

"I try, *monsieur*."

"Have a pleasant evening then, Ricardo. Do let me know if we get any further word on the accident at the theater. I'm very uncomfortable with the current report."

"I will. Good evening, *monsieur*."

Deboque sat back, nibbling on the cookie. Ricardo continued to please him a great deal. An intelligent man with sociopathic tendencies was an excellent addition to his staff. Deboque was certain Ricardo would be very grateful to have the assignment of dealing with Hannah when her job was completed. It was tempting, but Deboque discarded it.

He would deal with Hannah himself. After all, the least he could do after she'd given him his fondest wish was to see she died as painlessly as possible.

CHAPTER 11

Hannah appeared very calm as she sipped tea in the library. She listened to Reeve give an updated report to Malori, filling in occasionally when requested to, then lapsing back into silence.

Bennett had started to show her the library once. Then they'd detoured into the music room. And he'd kissed her. Was that when her life had really begun to change? she wondered. Had it been then, or the day on the beach when he'd given her a shell? Perhaps it had been that first night in the gardens.

"Do you agree, Hannah?"

She snapped back, cursing herself for letting her mind wander at such a crucial time. They had only thirty minutes for the briefing, half of which was already gone. Even within the walls of the palace it was dangerous for them to meet.

"I'm sorry. Could you repeat that?"

Armand had been watching her, wondering if her shoulders were strong enough to hold the fate of so much. "The last few days have been a strain." There wasn't criticism in his voice but concern. Hannah would have preferred the first.

"The last two years have been a strain, Your Highness." Then she lifted her shoulders in a gesture that was more acceptance than dismissal.

"If you're beginning to wear under it," Malori said in his clipped, no-nonsense voice, "it's best we know now."

"I don't wear." Her eyes met his without wavering. "I believe my record shows that."

Before Malori could speak again, Reeve cut in. She was wearing, he knew, but he had to gamble she'd hold out for a few more days. "If we could backtrack? We can assume that Deboque has already ordered the supplies you requested. An educated guess on where he'd procure them?"

"Athens," she said immediately. "I feel strongly that he'd draw from within his own organization. He feels totally secure, invulnerable if it comes to that. He wouldn't want to risk ordering from outside sources. From my other reports, we know that he keeps a warehouse in Athens. He has others, of course, but I think he'd go there because of its proximity to Cordina."

"We'll check our contact there and see if there's news of any explosives being moved." Malori noted it down. "With luck we'll close down his Athens branch once we have him here."

"The ISS won't move on Athens, Paris, London or Bonn until we have an airtight case on Deboque here." Hannah set down her tea. "That's a button I push, *monsieur.*"

"*Bien.*" Malori obviously didn't like it, but nodded.

"Will the case be strong enough when Hannah receives the explosives?" Armand glanced at Hannah, then at Reeve. "Hannah has taken the contract, requested the supplies. Once they are delivered, can that be the end of it?"

Hannah started to speak, then subsided. She would let Reeve explain. He was family. "We would have enough for an arrest, possibly for an arraignment. Even with the supplies being traced back to Athens or another of Deboque's companies, it wouldn't be enough for a conspiracy conviction. He's careful enough to divorce himself from business dealings of this kind."

Business dealings, Armand thought as he drummed his

fingers on the arm of the chair. "And his request that Hannah assassinate my family?"

"His hypothetical theory of what might happen if such a thing occurred," Reeve corrected. "Your Highness, I'm aware, very aware, of the frustration of not being able to close in on the evidence we have now. We had him once for over a decade, and it didn't stop him. If we want to crush Deboque once and for all, sever all these strings and hack away his control in Europe, we have to have solid and indisputable evidence of murder and conspiracy. Hannah will give us that in a matter of days."

Armand drew out a cigarette and shifted his gaze to Hannah. "How?"

"The payoff." She felt herself on solid ground again. It helped to have Malori there, sharp-eyed and just a bit disapproving. "When Deboque is convinced I've completed the job, he'll pay me off. As soon as money changes hands, we've got him."

"He's not a fool. You agree?"

"No, Your Highness, he's not a fool."

"But you will convince him you have murdered my family."

"Yes. If you would look at this diagram, sir?" She rose and waited for him to accompany her to a table. With Reeve's help, she stretched out a long roll of paper. "The blueprints I smuggled to Deboque show this wing as occupied by Prince Alexander and his family. I gave Deboque the information that Princess Gabriella and her family would also be staying here during the days before the Christmas Ball."

"I see. In truth, my son's family's wing is here." He skimmed his finger to the opposite side of the drawing.

"The night before the ball, I'll set some charges here, and here." She laid a fingertip on the areas. "They'll be much smaller than what Deboque assumes, but with Reeve's special effects added, it should be quite a show. There will be some damage, sir, but it will appear much worse, particularly from the outside, than it really is. You'll need to do some replastering and painting."

He lifted a brow, but she couldn't tell if he was amused. "There are areas of the palace that could do with some redecorating."

"It will be imperative, of course, to clear this wing. Discreetly."

"Of course."

"Ten minutes before the explosion, I will leave to meet with Deboque or his agent. The payment will be made after he considers the job done."

"Have you considered that he would want to have the deaths verified before he pays you?"

"Yes." Hannah straightened away from the diagram. "To some extent we'll use the press. In addition, I'm making it clear that payment must be made that night, as well as arrangements for my passage out of the country. Deboque has invited me to sail with him. I shall accept." She pressed her lips together as Malori grumbled. "The money will change hands because he'll believe I'll be easily accessible if anything has gone wrong."

"And will you be?"

"I'll be with him."

"The ISS will be covering both Deboque's villa and his yacht," Reeve cut In. "The moment we have Hannah's signal, we move."

"There is no other way?"

Again there was concern. This time Hannah found herself laying a hand on the prince's arm. On the arm of Bennett's father. "We could perhaps tie him to other crimes. With the information I've been able to dig up in the last two years, we would have something, but it would take months, even years and we would have no guarantee. This is the only way, Your Highness, to stop him once and for all."

With a nod, the prince looked over at Reeve. "You agree?"

"Yes."

"Malori?"

"It is more dramatic, and certainly more risky than one would like, but yes, Your Highness."

"Then I will presume that you two will see to whatever details have yet to be seen to. I will expect reports every four hours."

Recognizing dismissal Malori bowed. Even as Reeve rolled up the diagram again, Hannah was preparing to curtsy.

"Hannah, I'd like another moment, please."

"Yes, Your Highness." She stood by the table, stiff and tense as the two other men left them alone. He would know of her feelings for Bennett, Hannah thought. Even in the brief time she'd been in Cordina, she'd learned that Armand was both astute and observant. He didn't merely rule from a throne, but behind a desk and in boardrooms. If his country was at peace and prosperous, it was largely because he knew how to govern, how to make choices and how to remain objective.

Yes, he would know, she thought again. And he would not approve. She was European. She was an aristocrat. But she was by choice and by profession a spy.

"You're uncomfortable," Armand began. "Sit, please."

In silence she took a seat and waited.

She looked like a dove, he thought. A small gray dove who expected and accepted the fact that she was about to be mauled by a fox. Studying her, he had difficulty believing she would be the one to end the turmoil that had haunted his family for more than a decade.

"Reeve has confidence in you."

"I can promise it's not misplaced, Your Highness." She nearly relaxed. It wasn't about Bennett, but Deboque.

"Why did you agree to take this assignment?"

Her brow lifted because it seemed such a simple question with such a simple answer. "I was asked."

"And had the right to refuse?"

"Yes, sir. In such matters an agent always has a choice."

A prince didn't. He understood the difference, yet still didn't envy her. "You took the assignment because your superiors requested it."

"Yes, and because what Deboque does here has affected and could continue to affect my country and the rest of Europe. A terrorist, in whatever garb he chooses, remains a terrorist. England wants Deboque's hands tied, tightly."

"Your first consideration is country."

"It always has been."

He nodded again, knowing this could bring both joy and misery. "Did you choose your profession because you looked for adventure?"

Now she relaxed completely and laughed. The moment she did, Armand saw what had captivated his son. "Pardon, sir, I realize that the word 'spy' conjures up all sorts of glamorous images: foggy docks, Parisian alleyways, nickel-plated revolvers and fast cars. In truth, it's often tedious. In the past two years, I've done more work on telephones and computers than the average secretary."

"You wouldn't deny the danger involved."

"No." She sighed a little. "No. But for every hour of danger, there's a year of legwork and preparation. As for Deboque— Reeve, Malori, the ISS, have taken this plan step-by-step."

"Still, in the end, you'll be alone."

"That's my job. I'm good at it."

"Of that I have no doubt. Under normal circumstances, I would worry less."

"Your Highness, I assure you everything that can be done is being done."

He was aware of the truth of it and that, for the moment, his hands were tied. "And if a mistake is made, how will I comfort my son?"

She locked her fingers together. "I know, I promise you whatever happens, Deboque will be punished. If you—"

"I'm not speaking of Deboque now, but of you, and of Bennett." He held up a hand before she could speak again. "It is a rare thing for me to be able to speak as only a father. I ask you to allow me that luxury now, here in this room."

She drew in a breath and tried to be clear. "I realize Bennett is angry and upset because he wasn't told the reasons for my being here. I believe he feels a certain responsibility toward me because I'm here to protect his family."

"He's in love with you."

"No." The panic set in again, along with the shame and the desperate desire for it to be true. "That is, he thought, before when he believed me to be . . . At one time he began to feel a certain affection, but when he learned who—what I was, that changed."

Armand settled his hands on the arms of his chair. The ring of his office glinted in the lamplight. "My dear, are you any more clear on your feelings for him?"

She looked up. The dark eyes that watched her were kinder than they had been. Hard yes, he could be hard. But she could see now why his family and his country loved and trusted him. "Your confidence, sir?"

"You have it, of course."

"I love him more than I've ever loved anything or anyone. If I could change things, if I could go back and be what he thought I was, and only that, I swear to you I would." There were no tears. She had shed them once and had sworn not to do so again. Instead she looked down at her hands. "Of course, I can't."

"No, we can't change what we are. When we love, and love deeply, we can accept a great deal. Bennett's heart is very generous."

"I know. I promise you, I won't hurt him again."

His lips curved. She was so young, so valiant. "I have no fear of that. When this is done, I ask that you remain in Cordina for a few more days."

"Your Highness, I think it would be best if I returned to England immediately."

"We wish you to remain," he said again, and he no longer spoke as a father. He rose then, extending a hand. "You may want to rest before dinner."

Left without a choice, Hannah stood and curtsied. "Thank you, Your Highness."

* * *

Dinner was long and formal. Hannah was introduced to the Minister of State and his wife, as well as a German businessman who had interests in shipping and an ancient Frenchwoman who was some vague connection of the Bissets' and was visiting Cordina for the holidays. The Frenchwoman spoke in a husky grumble that kept Hannah straining to hear enough to make polite answers. The German spoke in short, loud blasts and was obviously delighted to have an invitation to the Royal Palace. Hannah was grateful that he was across the table so that she could avoid direct conversation with him.

Bennett wasn't there at all. A late board meeting at the museum had edged into a dinner for the Equestrian Society. Hannah tried to remember that Claude had been joined by two more guards who would keep Bennett annoyed and protected throughout the evening.

As the Frenchwoman hissed in her ear again, Hannah could only think Bennett the fortunate one.

Across the table, Eve sipped sparkling water and listened with apparent fascination as the German regaled her with stories of his business. Only when she turned to pick up her dessert spoon did her eyes meet Hannah's long enough for the humor to come through. Answering a question in low, polite tones, she rolled her eyes once, quickly, in a gesture that said everything. Then she was smiling at the German again and making him feel fascinating.

Hannah had to lift her glass to hide the grin. The royal were human after all. Not the same, not ordinary, but human. The child Eve carried might one day rule, but he would also laugh and cry and feel and dream.

She herself had loved a prince. Hannah picked up her spoon and began to toy with the elegant chocolate and cream concoction in front of her. She'd given her heart to a man who was second in line to one of the few remaining thrones in Europe. In a few days, she could very likely give her life for him.

For that was the truth of the matter, she thought as the woman beside her droned on. It might have started as duty, to her country and to the organization she had chosen, but when it ended, what she did would be for Bennett.

It would never be possible to tell him, just as it hadn't been possible to say as much to his father earlier that evening. If she admitted what she felt to a superior, even with all the planning, all the time lost, she could very well be pulled out.

So she would say nothing, but she would feel. And feeling as she did, she would see Deboque finished, if she lived. . . . And then, Hannah admitted, it would be a choice between her captaincy and retirement. Fieldwork would be all but out of the question now. She didn't believe that she could ever maintain the pose of quiet, unassuming Lady Hannah again. Not now that she had loved and been loved by a prince.

* * *

It was nearly midnight before escape could be politely made. Hannah deliberated over a hot bath or quick oblivion in bed as she stepped into her room. Eve was insistent about returning to the Center the next day, so she would have no choice but to go along. Would the message come the next day, or would Deboque take her right down to the wire?

She'd walked into the center of the bedroom when the warning signals began to throb at the base of her neck. There was no one in the room. A quick glance showed her nothing had been disturbed. But . . .

Hannah took a cautious step back and opened the drawer of the bedside table. She took out her weapon. The light was low and at her back as she began to move toward the adjoining room. The door was slightly ajar, but that could have been done by one of the maids. Her feet were silent on the carpet as she crossed to it. With one hand she pressed on the panel so that it opened slowly and without sound.

There was nothing in the room beyond—nothing except the neat sitting room that smelled of the gardenias that lay moist and lovely in a bowl.

So it had been a maid, she thought, relaxing gradually. One of them had set fresh flowers in the sitting room, and—

It was then she heard a sound, material against material, and tensed again. Keeping the gun secure in her hand, she slid against the wall and into the room.

The little settee faced away from the door so she didn't see him until she was fully inside. Bennett lay sprawled on it, his tie unknotted and hanging, his shoes off and his face buried in a blue velvet pillow.

Hannah swore, but softly, as she lowered the pistol. He looked exhausted, and very much at home, she thought as she lifted a brow. Her first instinct was to tuck a cover around him, but there was still enough of the proper Lady Hannah in her to know that it would never do for Bennett of Cordina to be found snoozing in her sitting room. She started to bend down to him, then remembered the gun in her hand.

Almost curiously, she turned it over in her hand. It looked

like a toy, but had already proven itself lethal. A part of her job, she thought. A part of her life. Yet she knew it was a part Bennett would find unpalatable. Moving back into her bedroom she secured it. She had to wake him and send him on his way, but she didn't have to keep a physical reminder of their differences close at hand.

She went back to him, and kneeling by the settee put a hand to his shoulder. "Bennett." She shook gently and received a mumbled response. Her lips curved. She had to resist the urge to brush at the hair tumbling over his forehead. In sleep, the energy, the amusement and the temper were put to rest. He looked as though he would be perfectly content to cuddle there, half on, half off the little sofa for days. Hannah bent closer and raising her voice gave him a quick, brisk shove. "Bennett, wake up."

He half opened his eyes, but Hannah noted that they focused quickly. Reaching up, he grabbed her earlobe. "Haven't you any respect for a dead man?"

"Ow!" She grabbed his wrist in defense, but she was already several inches closer. "If it's respect you want, I'll call a couple of the servants and have them carry you out, in state. Meanwhile, let go or I'll have to show you how easy it is to cause unconsciousness by applying pressure to certain nerves."

"Hannah, you've got to learn not to be so flighty and romantic."

"It's in the blood." She sat back on her heels to massage her ear. "Bennett, why are you sleeping on my settee instead of in your own bed?"

"I don't know who designed this thing. Another foot longer and a man could be comfortable." He dragged himself up a bit so that his feet dangled over the arm. "I wanted to talk to you." He rubbed both hands over his face. "When I got in, I saw that we still had guests. I took the coward's way and used the back stairs."

"I see. And Madame Beaulieu spoke so highly of you."

"Madame Beaulieu doesn't speak, she hisses."

"I know. I sat next to her at dinner."

"Better you than me."

"How gallant."

"You want gallant?" With one swing, he had her off the floor and stretched on top of him. He cupped the back of her neck with his hand, pressing as his mouth took hers quickly, completely.

"What does that have to do with gallantry?" she managed after a moment.

He smiled and ran a finger down her nose. "All the other women I've known have been impressed by it."

Hannah drew back another inch. Smiling, she ran a finger down his throat, then up again. "About those nerves I mentioned."

He caught one wrist, then the other. "All right then, tomorrow I'll look for a puddle to toss a cape over."

"A safe enough promise since it hasn't rained in days." She started to shift, but he brought her close again.

"Stay. I haven't seen you at all today." His lips were warm and coaxing against her cheek. "Do you know, Hannah, a man has to have you in his arms, has to have his lips against your skin before he catches your scent. Do you do that on purpose?"

She wore no perfume. It had to do with leaving no traces behind. "You said you . . ." He moved his lips to her ear. "You wanted to talk to me."

"I lied." His teeth closed gently over her earlobe. "I wanted to make love with you. In fact, I had a devil of a time keeping my mind off that thought throughout a long and frustrating board meeting and a noisy dinner." He drew down the zipper at the back of her dress. "I had to give a speech." He found silk, thin, fragile silk, beneath the linen. "It was difficult not to babble when I kept imagining myself here, with you."

"I don't want to interfere with your official duties." With her eyes closed, she pressed her lips to his neck and let herself enjoy the gentle stroking of his hands.

"But you do, *ma mie*. I sat listening to the huffing and puffing of ten stuffy men who are more interested in paintings than people, and I imagined you sitting there with your hands neatly folded and your eyes solemn. And you were wearing nothing but your hair."

She'd slipped off his tie, but paused now on the third button of his shirt. "In the boardroom?"

"In the boardroom." Would he ever stop being fascinated by that dry, serious tone and those dark eyes? "You can see why I had such a problem concentrating." He didn't tell her he'd also dealt with unexpected tingles of fear as he'd pictured her with Deboque, at his mercy, helpless, alone. It was an image he hadn't been able to drown out in innumerable cups of coffee or glasses of wine. "So I came in here to wait for you."

"And fell asleep."

"I'd hoped you'd see the irony and reverse the fairy tale. Wake the sleeping prince with a kiss. Instead I got a shove."

With her hands framing his face, she drew his head up. "Let me make up for it now then."

She touched her lips to his, brushed, retreated, teased then touched again. She felt him tense his fingers at her back as she toyed with his mouth. Her tongue traced, her teeth nipped as heat built to a flash point. She didn't object when he pressed her head closer, when his mouth closed hungrily over hers. If he had longed for her through the day, his need had been no sharper than her own. They would take the night hours together.

She had his shirt unbuttoned and open. Her dress had slipped down, revealing the shimmer of honey-colored lace beneath. Bennett let his fingertips play over it while he absorbed the contrasts and delights that were his Hannah. He drew the pins out of her hair so that it flowed over her shoulders and his. The scent of it was as light and elusive as the scent of her skin. What witchery she had was an innate part of her rather than something that came from bottles and pots.

Fresh, real, his. Delirious from her, he tugged the dress down her body and let it fall to the rug.

And his fingers slid over the stiletto strapped to her thigh.

She stiffened, remembering the weapon the instant he discovered it. Passion cooled so swiftly, she shivered. When she drew away he didn't stop her.

"Bennett, I'm sorry." She'd forgotten there could be no apologies, no regret. His eyes were on hers, blank and flat, as he sat up. Because there was nothing for her to say, no way for her to remove the barrier, she lapsed into silence.

Her hair was a riot of honey-toned waves that fell over her shoulders and the silk that echoed the color. Her eyes, darkly, richly green, were solemn now as she waited for him to speak. Or to leave.

Fighting the first stirrings of anger, he let his gaze pass over her, the milk-pale skin, the slender curves, the delicate silk. She was what she'd convinced herself she was not—beautiful, stunning, desirable. On one long slim thigh strapped by thin strong leather, was a knife associated with dark alleys and smoky bars. Saying nothing, Bennett reached for it. She automatically caught his wrist.

"Bennett—"

"Be quiet." His voice was as flat and cool as his eyes. Hannah let her fingers fall away. Slowly, he drew the weapon from its sheath. It was warmed from her skin, small enough to fit into the palm of his hand. Until he pushed the button and the thin blade slid silently, lethally out. It caught the lamplight and glistened silver.

She wore it intimately, he thought. He wanted to ask her if she'd used it, but a part of him knew it was best to keep the question to himself for now. It weighed nothing, but sat heavy as lead in his hand.

"Why do you need this in the palace?"

She pushed a strap back onto her shoulder, then rubbed the skin there that was growing colder and colder. "I'm expecting word from Deboque. I can't be sure when or where it will come from. Because I may have to respond to it immediately, it's best to be prepared."

"What kind of word?"

"I think you should ask—"

"I'm asking you." His voice carried a lash he used rarely, but effectively. "What kind of word, Hannah?"

Hannah drew her knees up to her chest, wrapped her arms around them and told him everything. There could be no objection now, she reminded herself. He already knew too much.

"So we sacrifice a part of the east wing. Camouflage." He twisted the blade under the light. He knew, without doubt, he could have plunged it into Deboque's heart.

"The more genuine things seem, the more easily Deboque will be convinced. He won't part with five million dollars until he's sure Cordina is left without an heir."

"He would kill the children," Bennett murmured. "Even Alexander's unborn child. All for what? Revenge, power, money?"

"For all three. He would have his revenge on your father, his own power would grow from the chaos, and money would follow. It's his greed that will topple him this time, Bennett. I promise you."

It was the passion in her voice that had him looking at her again. Her eyes were wide and dry, but the emotion almost leapt from them. To protect his family, he thought as he tightened his hand on the handle of the stiletto. To protect herself. As suddenly as he'd fallen in love, he realized the full truth. Whatever she did, whatever she used didn't matter, as long as she kept herself safe.

He pressed the release and sent the blade back home. And he would see to that himself. After setting the knife aside, he reached over to unsnap the strap from her thigh. Her skin had gone cold, he discovered, though the room was warm. It stirred something in him that he recognized again as a need to protect. She didn't move, didn't speak and flinched only slightly when he rose. She was waiting for him to reject her, to dismiss her, to leave her.

He felt both her surprise and her doubt as he gathered her up into his arms. "You should trust me more, Hannah," he said quietly.

When she relaxed against him, when she let her head rest on his shoulder, he carried her to bed.

CHAPTER 12

The package was delivered in the most pedestrian of ways. It was carried by Dartmouth Shippers, one of Deboque's less profitable but most useful tentacles. It was marked with the return address of Hannah's aunt in England and stamped FRAGILE.

The only difficulty came from the fact that Eve was present when it was delivered.

"Oh, what fun!" Eve hovered around the package. "It's a Christmas present, isn't it? Why don't you open it?"

"It isn't Christmas," Hannah said mildly, and set the package on the shelf in her closet. She would turn it over to Reeve at the first opportunity.

"Hannah, how can you be so casual about it?" With nerves just below the surface, Eve poked around the room. "Didn't you ever search under beds and in closets for packages at this time of year?"

"No." Hannah smiled and went back to arranging the flowers Eve had brought her. "I never wanted to spoil Christmas morning."

"It doesn't spoil it, it only adds to the excitement." Eve glanced back at the closet. "Couldn't we just peek?"

"Absolutely not, though I can tell you the package probably contains five dozen homemade cookies—as hard as bricks. Aunt Honoria is nothing if not predictable."

"It doesn't feel like Christmas." Moody, Eve wandered to the window. She laid one hand protectively over the swell of her belly and fidgeted nervously at the curtain with the other. "The ballroom's being scrubbed and polished for the holiday, the tree's already trimmed. If I walk by the kitchens there are the most glorious scents, but it just doesn't feel like Christmas."

"Are you homesick, Eve?"

"Homesick?" Puzzled for a moment, she turned around, then smiled. "Oh, no. Alex and Marissa are here. I do hope my sister manages to get away from her art gallery for a week or two, but I don't miss the States really. It's just that everyone tries to pamper me, protect me by hiding things." Sighing, she moved to Hannah's dresser to toy with the little enameled box Bennett had admired. "I know how tense and worried Alex is, no matter how hard he tries to pretend everything's fine. Even when I talk to Bennett, his mind only seems to be half with me. It has to stop, Hannah. I can't bear to see the people I love torn apart this way."

She too would pamper, and protect by hiding things, but it was the only comfort Hannah could allow herself to give. "It's this Deboque, isn't it?"

Eve set the box down again. "How can one man bear so much hate? How can one man cause so much pain? I know, though after years I still can't really understand, I know that he won't be satisfied until he's destroyed us."

"It isn't possible for most of us to understand real evil," Hannah began, though she could and did understand it. "But I think we only add to it when we let our lives be affected so strongly."

"You're right, of course." Eve held out both hands. "Do

you know how grateful I am that you're here? Without you I'm afraid I'd be moody and brooding all of the time. Brie's coming later today with all the children. We still have florists and musicians to deal with." She squeezed Hannah's hands as she drew a deep breath. "I hate being helpless. What I'd like to do is to go up and spit in Deboque's eye, but if all I can do is make things easier here, then I'll have to be content with that."

Hannah vowed, at the first opportunity, to spit in Deboque's eye for her. "Why don't you take me up to the ballroom and show me what's been done? I'd like to help." She wanted to help—and she wanted Eve away from the package that sat on the shelf in the closet.

"All right, but I want you to come to my room first. I have a present for you."

"Presents are for Christmas," Hannah reminded her as they walked to the door.

"This one can't wait." She had to get her mind off the undercurrents that were pressing on them all. Dr. Franco had already warned her that her tension could affect the child. "Pregnant princesses must be indulged."

"How clever of you to use that to your advantage when it suits you." They climbed a short flight of stairs and crossed to the next wing. "You said Gabriella would be here soon. Is the whole family coming today?"

"In force, this afternoon."

Hannah relaxed a little. It would be easy to transfer the package to Reeve and continue on with the plan. "Has Bennett put his treasure in the vault?"

"Treasure? Oh, his yo-yo." With her first easy laugh of the day, Eve entered her bedroom. "He adores that child, you know. I've never known anyone quite as good with children as Bennett. He puts an enormous amount of time into the Aid for Handicapped Children even though it takes away from his free days with his horses." She walked into the adjoining dressing room as she spoke. "Another reason I suppose I've been moody is that I know Bennett should be on top of the world right now, and he looks as though he rarely closes his eyes."

"On top of the world?"

"It's taken him six months and a lot of frustration to get approval for the children's wing in the museum. He finally pushed it over the top at the board meeting the other night, but not without a lot of work and fast talking. He didn't mention it to you?"

"No," she said slowly. "No, he didn't mention it."

"It's been his pet project for a couple of years. It took him months to find the right architect, one who'd mesh practicality with the essence of what Bennett wanted to do. Then, because the board wouldn't give an inch, he had the plans drawn up at his own expense. They're wonderful." Eve came back into the room carrying a long box. "You should ask him to see them sometime. He wanted it open, lots of windows so that the kids wouldn't feel closed in. The board mumbled and grumbled when he talked of sculptures the children could make contact with and illustrations from storybooks instead of Rubenses and Renoirs and Rodins under glass."

"I didn't realize he was so . . . involved."

"Whatever Bennett does he does with total involvement. His idea was to introduce children to art through media they could understand and enjoy. Then there's a section that's reserved for paintings and models the children make themselves."

Eve set the box on the bed and smiled. "I'm surprised he didn't tell you about it. Usually no one's safe. It's taken him two years of planning and six months of fighting to get this project off the ground."

"It sounds lovely." She felt her heart twist and expand and

fill with more love. "One often thinks of him as a man only interested in horses and the next party."

"He enjoys the image, but there's more to Bennett than that. I thought that the two of you had gotten quite close."

"Bennett's very kind."

"Hannah, don't disappoint me." A little tired, Eve sat on the edge of the bed. "He watches you walk out of a room and waits for you to come into one."

"He does?"

"Yes." Now she grinned. "He does. With all the anxiety and all the tension of the last weeks, at least I've had the pleasure of seeing Bennett fall in love. You do care, don't you?"

"Yes." It was almost over. Some deceptions were no longer necessary. "I've never known anyone like him."

"There isn't anyone like him."

"Eve, I don't want you to think, or to hope, for something that isn't going to happen."

"I'm entitled to think and hope as I choose." She lay a hand on the box beside her and patted the lid. "But for now, open your present."

"Is this a royal command or a request?"

"Whatever it takes to get you to open it. Please, I'm dying to see if you like it."

"Well, it's against my principles to open a present before Christmas, but . . ." Giving in, Hannah lifted the lid. She pushed aside the layers of tissue paper, then stood staring.

It glittered like a jewel and shimmered like fire. The dress was the rich, luscious green of emeralds with thousands and thousands of tiny beads that caught the afternoon light.

"Take it out," Eve insisted, then too impatient for Hannah, drew it out of the box herself.

The silk swayed, whispered and settled. It was cut straight, with a high neck that glistened with its beaded band at the throat. The arms would be bare well onto the shoulders as would the back before the material draped again and followed a long line to the floor. It was a dress made to glitter under chandeliers and shimmer under moonlight.

"Tell me you like it. I've driven the dressmaker crazy for a month."

"It's beautiful." Tentatively Hannah reached out. The dress shivered with life at the barest touch. "Eve, it's the most beautiful thing I've ever seen. I don't know what to say."

"Say you'll wear it to the Christmas Ball." Delighted with herself Eve turned Hannah toward the mirror and held the dress in front of her. "Look what it does to your eyes! I knew it." Laughing, she pushed the dress into Hannah's hands so she could step back and take it in. "Yes, I was sure of it. With that skin of yours . . . Oh yes," she said as she tapped a finger to her lips. "Bennett's going to take one look and babble like an idiot. I can't wait to see it."

"I don't think I should—"

"Of course you should, and you will because I refuse to take no for an answer." She stepped forward, eyes narrowed to pull free a lock of Hannah's hair. "My hairdresser's going to have a whack at you, too."

"That sounds a little ominous." As much as she longed to, she couldn't let herself go. The plain and proper Lady Hannah Rothchild wouldn't have had the nerve to wear such a dress. "Eve, it's lovely, you're lovely, but I don't think I'm made for a dress like this."

"I'm never wrong." Eve brushed off denials with a careless flick of her wrist. She may have been a princess for only two years, but she'd always been determined. "I've spent too long in the theater not to know what suits and what doesn't. Trust me, and if that's too much, do me a favor as a friend."

They *had* become friends, no matter what the initial reasons were or the ultimate goal. What harm would it do to accept? It was very possible that she wouldn't even be in Cordina for the ball. "I'll feel like Cinderella," she murmured, and wished it could be so.

"Good. And you should remember the clock doesn't always strike twelve."

*　*　*

B ut it did. Hannah remembered Eve's words as she and Reeve moved silently through the palace. The game was almost up, and so was her time.

The package had contained the explosives she'd requested and a coded message. She was to make her move that night and meet Deboque's agent at the docks at 1:00 a.m. The payoff would come then.

"This has to work," Hannah muttered as she carefully set the first charge. The equipment she used now was ISS-approved. The package she'd received was already being traced. Deboque would soon lose Athens and very much more.

"From outside the walls, it'll look as though the fire's burning out of control," Reeve said, working as quickly and competently as she. "The blasts are rigged for more noise than power. We'll blow out a few windows and put on a hell of a show while Malori and his men will remain here to bank it if necessary."

"Is the prince with them now?"

"Yes, Armand is filling the rest of the family in. Malori objects, but I think you're right. No harm can come from them knowing what's under way at this point, and a lot of anxiety can be relieved." He thought of Gabriella. After tonight, perhaps even the nightmares would fade.

"I couldn't bear to think of Eve waking up to the explosion and thinking it Deboque's doing. And Bennett? He's safe in the family wing?"

"Bennett's safe," he said, and left it at that. "I'm giving you ten minutes. That's enough time for you to get off the grounds. The dock's secure, so that if anything goes down there, we'll be on top of you. I'll be on the boat that has Deboque's yacht under surveillance. We'll move in the moment we have your signal. Hannah, I know the wire's risky. If you're searched—"

"If I'm searched, I'll deal with it." The mike was an ISS masterpiece that resembled an intricately worked locket that rested inches below the pulse in Hannah's throat.

"If he sees through this, he'll move fast."

"I'll move faster." She laid a hand on his when he started to speak again. "Reeve, I have a stake in this too. I don't want to die."

He looked at her for a moment as a woman. "I have a reputation for keeping my partners alive."

She was grateful he could make her smile. "I'm counting on it. But if something goes wrong, would you give Bennett a message for me?"

"Of course."

"Tell him . . ." She hesitated, unused to trusting her feelings to anyone. The clock struck the hour, midnight, and she prayed the magic would hold. "Tell him I loved him, both parts of me loved him. And there are no regrets."

She left through the main door and drove slowly toward the gates. In minutes, the guards who'd not been informed of the camouflage would react in precisely the way it was expected. Anyone watching the palace would see the shock and the action. For now, she passed through the gates with only the briefest of checks.

She kept an eye on her watch as she drove, hearing the minutes tick off and thinking of Bennett. He would be safe now. Whatever happened that night, he and his family would be safe. If Deboque paid her, he would be arrested for conspiracy. If he killed her, he would be arrested for the murder of an ISS agent. The end justified the means.

Hannah stopped the car, waited and heard the explosion. Mallori had promised loud, and had delivered. She opened the door and stood beside the car a moment. The palace was a dim white blur against the night sky, but the east wing was lit like day. The fire was impressive from here, and knowing that none of Deboque's men could get much closer, she was satisfied. Within twenty minutes one of Malori's men would leak word that the Royal Family, save Armand, had perished in the explosion.

By the time she arrived, the docks were deserted. Word of trouble had already spread this far. Hannah parked her car in the shadows, then left it behind to wait in the light. She made an excellent target.

*　*　*

The boat anchored off the coast appeared to be a small, expensive pleasure yacht. Several times during the day, a dark-haired woman had appeared on deck, to sun, to read. From time to time, she'd been joined by a man, bare chested, young, bronzed. They'd sipped wine, cuddled, slept. The watch on the *Invincible* had kept it under surveillance, and had taken bets as to whether the two lovers would have sex under the sun. They'd been disappointed.

Below deck, the ISS had everything from television monitors to grenade launchers. Eight men and three women crowded into the hulled-out cabin and waited.

Bennett had been confined to the cabin since an hour after dawn. For the past three hours, he'd swallowed nothing but coffee and impatience. He'd watched the monitor until his eyes had blurred. Not once had Deboque appeared in the focus of the long-range camera. He wanted to see him. By God, he wanted to look into his eyes as the trap snapped shut. But more, so much more, he wanted to hear over the transmitter that it was done, and Hannah was safe.

"MacGee's boarding." The man with the headphones spoke, and continued to smoke. Seconds later, Reeve slipped into the already crowded cabin. He was dressed in black from head to foot. Even his face and hands were smeared with it. He took off his sailor's cap and tossed it aside.

"First stage is finished." He nodded toward Bennett. "From beyond the gates, it looks as though the east wing is devastated. The ISS is theatrical."

"The family?" Bennett asked as he looked back to the monitor.

"Safe."

He reached for the bitter, cooling coffee beside him. "Hannah?"

"Word should be coming in within minutes. Some of our best men are on the docks as backup."

Bennett shot him a look that held for a long moment. He'd wanted to be at the docks, as close by as possible. He'd run into the stone wall of his father, Reeve and Malori on that, and eventually had had to concede. If he'd been spotted, the entire operation would have been put in jeopardy.

Now it was only Hannah, he thought, only Hannah who risked it all.

"Deboque hasn't been seen all day."

"He's there." Reeve lit a cigarette and prepared to wait. "He wouldn't want to be too far away tonight."

"Contact." An agent on the port side of the cabin lifted a hand to his headphones. "She's made contact."

* * *

The breeze off the water was cool and the night was clear. Hannah recognized the man who approached her as the one who had come into the smoky little bar. He came alone and empty-handed.

"Mademoiselle."

"My part of the bargain is met, *monsieur*. You have the compensation?"

"It's a nice night for a ride on the water."

The yacht. She felt a ripple that was both unease and excitement. "You understand I'm no longer in a position to return to Cordina?"

"This is understood." He gestured toward a small motorboat. "Your needs will be seen to."

As before, she had a choice. She could draw her weapon now and take him in. If luck was with them, he would trade his own freedom for Deboque's. She couldn't risk Bennett's safety to luck. Without a word, she stepped into the boat and sat.

Her life was in her own hands now, Hannah thought, and folded them. However the night turned out, Deboque would be ruined.

Her contact didn't speak again, but his gaze shifted back and forth over the dark water. They were all waiting and watching now. Because the night was clear, Deboque's yacht stood out white and stark on the sea. She could see three men on deck, Ricardo and two others. It was Ricardo who assisted her onto the yacht.

"Lady Hannah, it's a pleasure to see you again."

There was something in his eyes, something smirking and self-satisfied. She knew then, as surely as if he'd held a knife to her throat, that she wasn't meant to leave the *Invincible*. Her voice was cool and calm when she spoke, and she hoped, clearly received across the span of water.

"Thank you, Ricardo. I hope this won't take long. I'm forced to admit I'm uneasy in Cordinian waters."

"We sail in an hour."

"For?"

"A more comfortable climate. The radio has announced the tragic deaths of several members of the Royal Family. Prince Armand is grieving in seclusion."

"Of course. Cordina is left without its heart, and without its heir. Monsieur Deboque has been informed?"

"He waits for you in his cabin." Ricardo reached out a hand for Hannah's bag.

"Are employees always searched, Ricardo?"

"We can dispense with that, Lady Hannah, if you will allow me to hold your weapons." He drew out her pistol and pocketed it. "And your knife?"

With a shrug, Hannah lifted her skirt to her thigh. She watched Ricardo's gaze dip and hold there as she drew out the knife. She pushed the release. On either side of her guns clicked.

"An admirable weapon," she said mildly as she held the blade up to the light. "Quiet, stylish, utilitarian." She smiled and sent the blade sliding back into place. "And one I would hardly use on the man who is about to give me five million American dollars." She dropped the knife into Ricardo's palm, knowing she had only her wits as defense now. "Shall we go? I enjoy the smell of money when it's still warm."

He took her arm in his surgeon's hand and with considerable panache, led her belowdeck to Deboque's cabin.

"Lady Hannah." The cabin was lit with a dozen candles. It was a Beethoven sonata this time that poured gently through the speakers. He wore a burgundy jacket and rubies. Blood colors. A magnum of champagne sat nestled in a silver bucket. "How prompt you are. You may leave us, Ricardo."

Hannah heard the door shut behind her. She didn't have to be told Ricardo would be stationed outside it.

"A pleasant ambience," she stated. "Most business isn't transacted in candlelight."

"There's no need for formalities between us now, Hannah." He was smiling as he moved to the champagne. "The announcements from Cordina are a bit hysterical and tragic." The cork rushed out. Wine bubbled to the lip. "I felt a small, tasteful celebration was in order."

"I rarely refuse champagne, *monsieur*, but its taste goes down so much more smoothly when I have money in my hand."

"Patience, my dear." He filled two tulip glasses and offered one. His face was marble pale in the dim light, his eyes almost black and full of pleasure. "To a job well done and a rich, rich future."

She touched her glass to his then sipped. "An excellent vintage."

"I've come to understand you prefer the excellent, and the expensive."

"Precisely. *Monsieur*, I hope you won't be offended if I say while I appreciate the wine and soft light, I would appreciate them more after our business is completed."

"So mercenary." He ran his fingers down her cheek. The candlelight flattered her, he thought. In time she would bloom under his hands. A pity he couldn't take the risk and keep her with him for a few months. He had only an hour for her. But much could be accomplished in an hour. "You'll forgive me, but my mood is very light. I find myself wanting to celebrate your success, our success."

His hand roamed down her throat, within inches of the microphone. She caught it at the wrist and smiled. "You set the mood, *monsieur*, first by taking my weapons. Do you prefer defenseless women?"

"I prefer amenable women." He lifted his hand to her hair, digging his fingers into its richness. Hannah steeled herself for the kiss. She could show resistance, but not revulsion. "You're strong," he murmured and brought his mouth to hers again. "I prefer that as well. When I take you to bed, you'll give me a fight."

"I'll give you more than that. After I've seen the money."

He tightened his fingers, bringing pain quickly enough so that she gasped. Then they relaxed with his laugh. "Very well, *mon amie cupide*. You will see your money, and then you'll give me something in return."

When he turned his back to reveal a hidden safe, Hannah scrubbed her lips with the back of her hand. "I've already given payment for payment."

"The lives of the Royal Family." He spun the dial as Hannah's heart began to drum. "Five million dollars to assassinate the Bissets. Five million dollars to give me a full plate of revenge and the sweet dessert of power. Do you think it so much?" His eyes glittered as he turned back to her with a large case. "My dear child, you could have asked ten times as much. For over ten years I've plotted, and twice very nearly succeeded in killing a member of the Royal Family. Now, for the paltry sum of five million dollars, you have disposed of them all for me."

* * *

That's it," Reeve announced as Deboque's voice came over the receiver. "Move in. Slowly."

Bennett's hand closed over his brother-in-law's. "I board with you."

"It's out of the question."

"I board with you," Bennett repeated in a hard, icy voice. Moment by moment, he had listened and sweated as Hannah stood alone with Deboque. As Deboque put his hands on her. As Deboque prepared to pay her for the murder of everything and everyone he loved. "Give me a weapon, Reeve, or I go unarmed."

"My orders are to keep you here."

"If it were Brie?" Bennett's eyes were hot and reckless. "If it were Brie, would you stay behind and let others protect her?"

Reeve looked down at the hand closed over his. It was strong and capable. And young. Then he looked into the eyes that were darker than his wife's but that held the same passions. Rising, he took a. 45 automatic from the arsenal.

* * *

They would move now, Hannah thought and struggled to keep her voice impassive. "Do you tell me this now so I can regret?" She laughed and walked to the desk. "Five million will do me nicely. I plan to invest and to live quietly in Rio for the next few years."

He kept his eyes on hers as he unlocked the case. The money was there, but would be for his own uses. "You have no desire to continue in my employment?"

"Unfortunately, that would be risky for both of us after the events of tonight."

"Yes." His thoughts exactly. But he opened the lid so that she would at least have the pleasure of seeing the money before he killed her.

"Lovely." Clinging to the role, Hannah stepped forward and lifted a thick stack of crisp hundreds. "Do you know how sensual new money smells?" She fanned the stack.

"Indeed." He slid the top drawer of his desk open. Inside was an elegant pearl-handled revolver. He thought it just to kill her with style. He closed his fingers over it when the first shots were heard from above.

Hannah swung toward the door, hoping he would take excitement for alarm. "What game is this?" she demanded. She slammed the lid on the case, and taking the money headed for the door. Her hand closed over the knob.

"Remain still." Deboque warned. The gun was in his hand now and pointed at her heart. A fine film of sweat pearled over his brow as the sound of running feet pounded over their heads. He held the trigger lightly, but didn't press home. Whatever trouble was on deck, he didn't want to draw it down to him. "The case, Hannah."

"A double cross?" Her eyes narrowed as she calculated how much time she dared stall him. "Yes, you would easily have paid me ten times this if you never intended to pay me at all."

"The case." He started toward her, slowly. Fear was blossoming inside him, not of death, not of defeat, but of prison. He would never survive behind bars again.

Hannah waited until he was two feet away, then with both hands on the handle, swung the heavy case at his gun arm.

* * *

Deboque's men, whether in loyalty or fear, fought madly. Gunfire exploded back and forth from the two boats. A spray of bullets from a machine gun smashed in the wood above Bennett's head and sent splinters raining down his back. He watched a man fall over the rail of the yacht and into the water below.

Already the firing from Deboque's side was coming more sporadically, but time was speeding by. And Hannah was still with Deboque. Alive, Bennett told himself as he aimed and fired. She was alive. He'd know if it was otherwise because his heart would have stopped. But there was an urgency churning in him, more than the wild night and the scent of blood. Moving with it, he worked his way to stern and slipped into the water.

The night was rent with shooting and the shouts of men. He saw a man dive from Deboque's yacht and swim frantically toward a shore that was ten miles off. His hand brushed a body that floated facedown. ISS or the enemy, he didn't know. While the fighting raged, he swam silently around the yacht.

Because it was nearly over, Reeve signaled for his men to close in. It was then he noticed that Bennett was no longer beside him.

"The prince." His throat went dry with panic. "Where is Prince Bennett?"

"There." One of the men spotted Bennett just before he disappeared around the stern of Deboque's yacht.

"In the name of God," Reeve breathed. "Move in fast. Prepare to board."

There was no one on the starboard side as Bennett dragged himself on deck. There was the occasional blast and rip of bullets, but the shouting had died. He'd spent an hour during that long, endless day below deck studying Hannah's diagram of Deboque's yacht. He went to find her.

* * *

She'd managed to knock the gun across the room, but he was faster and stronger than he appeared. Even as she dove after it, Deboque was on top of her. One hand closed over her throat, shutting off her air. Hannah freed one arm and brought her fist into his windpipe. Then both of them were gasping. She reached forward and her fingers scrabbled over the handle of the gun. She swore in both pain and fury as he dragged her back by the hair. For thirty grim and exhausting seconds, they struggled on the cabin floor. Her blouse tore at the seam. Beneath, bruises were already forming. She bloodied his mouth but was frustrated, unable to land a disabling injury.

Wrapped like lovers they rolled toward the gun again. She reached again, nearly grasping it. Out of the corner of her eye, she saw the fist coming and dodged. The blow was glancing, but strong enough to send her reeling. Then she was looking into the barrel of his gun.

She'd prepared herself to die. Struggling for breath, she braced. If she could do nothing else, she could fulfill her vow to spit in his eyes. "I'm an ISS agent. The Bissets are safe, and you've nowhere to run."

She saw the fury come into his eyes. She smiled at him and waited for the bullet.

When Bennett broke into the room, he saw Deboque crouched over Hannah, pointing a gun at her head. It happened in flashes, so quick that immediately afterward he couldn't be sure who had fired first.

Deboque's head swung around. Their eyes met. As the gun swiveled from Hannah's head toward Bennett's, she screamed and swung out. Two triggers were pressed. Two bullets exploded.

Bennett felt one whiz by him, so close that his skin shuddered and heated from it. He saw the blood bloom on Deboque's chest an instant before he crumpled onto Hannah.

She started shaking then. All the years of training dissolved as she lay trembling under the dead man. She'd prepared for her own death. That was duty. But she'd seen the bullet smash into the wood less than an inch from Bennett's face.

Even when he came to her, pushing what had been Deboque aside and gathering her close, the trembling didn't pass. "It's over, Hannah." He cradled her, rocked her, pressed kisses to her hair. "It's over now." Instead of the satisfaction, even the glory he'd expected to feel there was only relief. She was safe. And he was going to see that she stayed that way.

"You might have been killed. Damn you, Bennett, you were supposed to be home."

"Yes." He glanced up as Reeve rushed into the room. "We'll both go there soon."

There were tears on her cheeks. Brushing them aside, Hannah struggled to stand. She faced Reeve, but had to draw several breaths. "I'm ready to make my report."

"The hell with that." Bennett swept her into his arms. "I'm taking her home."

EPILOGUE

She'd slept around the clock. It wasn't until over twenty-four hours had passed that Hannah realized that Dr. Franco, the Bissets' personal physician, had given her a sedative.

She'd woken rested and resentful. And though she'd hated to admit it, aching.

The doctor had fussed for another full day, murmuring over her bumps and bruises in his kind but implacable tones. Because his orders to keep her in bed had come from His Royal Highness, neither doctor nor patient had a choice but to obey.

She complained. Even though visitors came often, she fidgeted at the inactivity. Word was delivered through Reeve from ISS headquarters, word that should have delighted her. Deboque's operation had crumbled. She'd been given her promotion. Hannah sulked in bed and wished for escape.

It was Eve who ultimately provided it on the night of the Christmas Ball.

"You're awake. Wonderful."

"Of course I'm awake." Cranky from two days in bed, Hannah shifted. The fact that her ribs were still sore to the touch only made it worse. "I'm going crazy."

"I'm sure you are." Smiling, Eve sat on the edge of the bed. "And I'm not going to embarrass you by going on again about how grateful we all are for everything you did. What I'm going to do is give you Dr. Franco's latest orders."

"Oh, spare me."

"Which are, to get up, get dressed and dance until dawn."

"What?" Hannah pushed herself up, wincing only a little. "I can get up? Do you mean it?"

"Absolutely. Now here." Rising, she lifted Hannah's robe. "Put this on. My hairdresser's expected any minute and she's going to do her magic on you first."

"Magic." With a sigh, Hannah lifted a hand to her hair. "More like a miracle at this point. Eve, as much as I want to get up and be doing, I don't think the ball is the best idea."

"It's the perfect idea." After helping Hannah into her robe, she leaned over to smell the clutch of gardenias by the bedside. "From Bennett?"

"Yes." Hannah gave in enough to touch the waxy leaves with her fingertips. "He brought them this morning. I haven't seen a great deal of him." Shaking off the mood, she tied the belt of the robe. "I know how busy you've all been, with the press conferences and public statements to clear up the entire mess."

Eve lifted a brow. She decided against telling Hannah that Bennett hadn't moved from her bedside throughout the first night. There was enough romance in her for her to want them to discover each other for themselves.

"Speaking of messes, you should see the east wing. Mostly glass. It'll take the maids weeks to get it all. Hannah." On a long breath, Eve took both her shoulders. "I'm going to embarrass you. I know it was an assignment, but whatever reasons brought you to us, you've given us peace. There's nothing I can say or do that can repay that. My child . . ." She smiled a little. "Marissa and this one are safe. I know what Deboque had planned to do."

"It's over now, Eve."

"Yes." Solemn, Eve kissed both of Hannah's cheeks. "I owe

you my life, and the lives of all of my loved ones. If there's anything I can ever do, and I speak as your friend and as the wife of the heir of Cordina, you have only to ask."

"Put it behind you, and me. Eve, I've never been able to make and keep friends. I'd like to feel that's changed."

Eve studied the woman she was just beginning to know. "I have two sisters, the one I was born with and the one I was given by Alexander." She held out a hand. "I'd like to have three."

"Your Highness." One of the young maids hovered at the doorway. "I beg your pardon, but Madame Frissoutte is here."

"Wonderful." Eve hooked her arm through Hannah's. "Prepare to be transformed."

*   *   *

It was a transformation, Hannah thought as she studied herself in the glass. Her hair, curled wildly down her back, was caught away from her face with two glittering combs. The dress sparkled and shimmered as it draped from her throat to her ankles. She was clever enough with makeup to have covered the bruises on her arms and face.

All she needed were glass slippers, she thought with a half laugh. More illusion. But if this was to be her last night with Bennett, she would take it. There would be no regret when the clock struck twelve.

There was already music in the ballroom. Hannah slipped in, as was her habit, and absorbed the brilliance. Mirrors were polished to reflect the glitter and glamour of gowns and jewels. Chandeliers shone like stars. It was all shimmering silver and icy blue with draping garlands and shiny balls. On a tree that towered to twenty feet were a thousand crystal angels that caught the light.

He'd been watching for her. Waiting. When he saw her the

breath simply left his body. The couple he'd been chatting with fell silent, brows lifting as he walked away without a word.

He caught both her hands even as she dipped into a curtsy. "My God, Hannah." For the first time in his life his tongue tied itself into knots. "You're exquisite."

"It's Eve's doing." He wore dress whites, with the insignia of his rank and a sword at his side. However many ways she remembered him, and she knew there would be many, she would never forget how he looked just now. "Everything is so beautiful."

"It is now." His hand slipped around her waist as he swirled her into the waltz.

* * *

It was magic, she thought. The music, the lights, the mirrors. For hours they danced together, spinning around and around the room, leaving the food and the wine for others. When he circled her out to the terrace, she didn't object. There were still a few minutes until midnight.

Drawing away, she went to the rail to look out at Cordina. Lights glowed in festive colors for the holiday. The breeze held a springtime warmth and scent.

"Do you ever tire of looking at it?"

"No." He stood beside her. "I think it means even more now."

She understood, but wanted to keep even Deboque's ghost at bay. "In England, it would be cold, sleeting. There might be snow by morning, or we'd have gray, heavy skies. All the fires would be lit and the rum warmed. The cooks would have all the puddings and turkeys cooking so that you'd smell Christmas everywhere."

"We can't give you snow." He lifted her hand and kissed it. "But we could offer the fire and warm rum."

"It doesn't matter." She drew a deep breath. "When I'm

home, I'll remember standing here with Christmas almost upon us. I'll remember it smelled like roses and jasmine."

"Would you wait here a moment?"

"All right."

"Just here," he said, and kissed her hand again. "I'll only be a minute."

When he was gone, she turned back to look out again at the lights and the sea. She would be home in a few days, and in time, perhaps Cordina would seem like a dream. Cordina, she thought, but never Bennett. She lifted her face to a star but didn't dare wish.

"I have something for you."

With a half smile, she turned, then caught the scent. "Oh, chestnuts!" With a laugh, she took the bag he offered. "And they're warm."

"I wanted to give you something from home."

She looked up. There was so much to say, and nothing that could be said. Instead, she rose on her toes to kiss him. "Thank you."

He brushed his fingers over her cheek. "I'd thought you'd share."

Hannah opened the bag and with her eyes closed, drew in the scent. "Isn't it wonderful? Now it feels like Christmas."

"If Cordina can be enough like home, perhaps you'll stay."

She opened her eyes, then lowered them quickly to the bag. "I have orders to return at the end of the week."

"Orders." He started to reach for her, but held himself back. "Your position in the ISS is important to you." He couldn't prevent the trace of resentment. "I'm told you received a promotion."

"A captaincy." She bit her bottom lip. "I'll be working behind a desk for a good while. Giving orders." She managed to smile.

"Have you ever considered giving it up?"

"Giving it up?"

It was the blank, puzzled look that worried him. Was it possible she could think of nothing else but her duty to her organization? "If you had something to replace it. Is it the excitement that pulls you?" He cupped her face in his hand, turning it toward the light so that the bruise Deboque had put there showed in a shadow.

"It's simply what I do." She drew a breath. "Bennett, we never talked about what happened on the yacht. I never thanked you for saving my life. I suppose it's because I've been used to taking care of myself."

"I would have killed him for this alone," he murmured as he traced the bruise on her cheek. She started to step back, but a look from him stopped her. "Don't back away from me. I haven't spoken before this because Franco was concerned with keeping you quiet and undisturbed. But dammit, I'll speak of it now."

He stepped closer so she could feel it, the recklessness, the barely controlled fury. "I had to sit and wait and listen to you deal with that man. I had to stay where I was, helpless while you were alone with him. And when I broke into that cabin and saw him holding a gun at your head, I had one hideous flash of what life would be like if you weren't in it. So don't back away from me now, Hannah."

"I won't." She steadied her breathing then lay a calming hand on his. "It's over, Bennett. The best thing for everyone is to put it aside. Cordina is safe. Your family is safe. And so am I."

"I won't accept your risking your life again for anyone."

"Bennett—"

"I won't." He caught her hair in his hands and kissed her, but this time with a force and power that left her breathless. He dragged himself away, reminding himself he had a plan and meant to see it through. "Are you going to try those chestnuts or just stand there smelling them?"

"What?" She had the bag locked in a viselike grip. She swallowed and opened it again. "I'm sure they're wonderful," she began, knowing she was going to babble. "It was so thoughtful of you to . . ." She broke off when she reached in and touched a small box. Puzzled, she drew it out.

"There's an American tradition. A box of candied popcorn with a prize in it. I had an urge to give you your Christmas present early."

"I've always been very strict about waiting until Christmas morning."

"I could make it a command, Hannah." He touched her cheek again. "I'd rather not."

"Well, since it *is* the Christmas Ball." She opened the lid and for the first time in her life felt faint.

"It was my grandmother's. I had it reset but it meant more to me to give you this than to choose another from a jeweler." He touched her hair, just the ends of it with his fingertips. "She was British, like you."

It was an emerald, fiery, stunning, made only more brilliant by the symphony of diamonds that circled it. Just looking at it made her light-headed. "Bennett, I couldn't take something like this. It belongs in your family."

"Don't be thick-headed." He took the bag from her to set it on the wall. The scent of chestnuts mixed with the summer fragrance of roses. "You know very well I'm asking you to marry me."

"You—you're carried away," she began, and this time did step back from him. "It's everything that's happened. You're not thinking clearly."

"My mind's never been more clear." He took the box from her, slipped the ring out and tossed the container aside. "We'll do it my way then." Taking her hand, he pushed the ring on. "Now, I can drag you back inside and announce our engagement—or we can talk about it reasonably first."

"Reasonably." How was it she needed to laugh and cry at the same time? "Bennett, you're being anything but reasonable."

"I love you—unreasonably then." He pulled her into his arms and covered her mouth with his. He could feel her heart thud, hear her breath shudder, taste both need and fear. "I'm not letting you go, Hannah, not now, not tomorrow, not ever. You'll have to exchange captain for princess. Believe me, it can be every bit as wearing."

Was it magic, or was it a dream come true? Her head was still spinning as she tried to get a grip on common sense. "You know I'm not the woman you cared for. Please, Bennett, listen to me."

"Do you think I'm a fool?" He spoke so mildly she was deceived into thinking him calm.

"Of course I don't. I only mean that—"

"Shut up." He caught her face in his hands, and she saw by his eyes he was anything but calm. "I thought the woman I first fell in love with was an illusion." He gentled as he brushed his lips over her cheeks. "I was wrong, because she's right here. There was another woman who made my mouth dry every time I looked." His kisses were more urgent now, more possessive. "She's here as well. It's not every man who can love two women and have them both. And I will have you, Hannah."

"You already have me." She was almost ready to believe it could be real, and true and lasting. "But even you can't command a marriage."

He lifted his brow, arrogant, confident. "Don't be too sure. You told me once you wanted me. Was it a lie?"

"No." She steadied herself with two hands on his chest.

She was crossing a line in her life, one that allowed for no deceptions. He was offering her a chance to be herself, to love openly and honestly. "No, it wasn't a lie."

"I ask you now if you love me."

She couldn't speak. From deep within the palace the clock began to strike. Midnight. She counted off the gongs and waited for the illusion to fade. Then there was silence and she was still in his arms. Looking down, she saw the ring glow against her finger. A promise. A lifetime.

"I love you, and nothing's ever been more true."

"Share my home." He caught her ring hand in his and pressed his lips to the palm.

"Yes."

"And my family."

She twined her fingers with his. "Yes."

"And my duty."

"From this moment."

She wrapped her arms around him. She lifted her face for his kiss. Below and as far as eyes could see, Cordina spread out before them and prepared to sleep.

The Name of the Game

To Faye Ashley.
Now you'll have to leave me the bracelet.

CHAPTER 1

"Marge Whittier, this is your chance to win *ten thousand dollars*. Are you ready?"

Marge Whittier, a forty-eight-year-old schoolteacher and grandmother of two from Kansas City, squirmed in her chair. The lights were on, the drum was rolling and the possibility of her being sick was building. "Yes, I'm ready."

"Good luck, Marge. The clock will start with your first pick. Begin."

Marge swallowed a lump of panic, shuddered with excitement and chose number six. Her sixty seconds began to dwindle, and the tension grew as she and her celebrity partner picked their brains for the right answers. They leaped over such questions as who founded psychoanalysis and how many yards in a mile, then came to a screeching halt. What element do all organic compounds contain?

Marge went pale, and her lips quivered. She was an English teacher and a bit of a history and movie buff, but science wasn't her strong suit. She looked pleadingly at her partner, who was better known for her wit than for her wisdom. Precious seconds ticked away. As they fumbled, the buzzer sounded. Ten thousand dollars flowed through Marge's sweaty fingers.

The studio audience groaned their disappointment.

"Too bad, Marge." John Jay Johnson, the tall, sleekly polished host, laid a sympathetic hand on her shoulder. His rich, rolling voice expressed just the right combination of disappointment and hope. "You were so close. But with eight correct answers you add another eight hundred dollars to your total. An impressive one." He smiled at the camera. "We'll be back after this break to total up Marge's winnings and to give you the correct answer to the stumper. Stay with us."

The music was cued. John Jay kept his avuncular smile handy. He used the timed ninety-second break to come on to the pretty celebrity panelist.

"Pompous jerk," Johanna muttered. The pity was that she was too aware his smooth looks and slick manner were keeping *Trivia Alert* up in the ratings. As producer, she'd learned to accept John Jay as part of the set. She checked the second hand of her watch before walking over to the losers. Putting on a smile of her own, she commiserated and congratulated as she eased them along. She needed them in camera range for the finish.

"Coming up on five," she announced, and signaled for applause and music. "And cue."

John Jay, his arm around Marge and his three-thousand-dollar caps gleaming, closed the show.

They were one big happy family as the assistant director shut off his stopwatch. "That's a wrap."

Kiki Wilson, Marge's partner and the current star of a popular situation comedy, chatted a few moments longer with Marge in a way that would have the schoolteacher remembering her warmly for years to come. When Kiki rose, her smile was still firmly in place as she walked the few steps to John Jay.

"If you ever pull something like that again," she said quietly, "you'll need a paramedic."

Knowing she was referring to his quick—and, if he did say

so, clever—hand maneuver just before the end of the break, John Jay smiled. "Just part of the service. About that drink, sweetheart . . ."

"Kiki." In a smooth move that didn't appear nearly as rushed and harassed as it was, Johanna swung over and scooted the actress away. "I want to thank you again for agreeing to do the show. I know how hectic your schedule must be."

Johanna's warm voice and soothing manner brought Kiki's blood pressure down slightly. "I enjoyed it." Kiki pulled out a cigarette and tapped it absently against an enameled case. "It's a cute show, moves fast. And God knows the exposure never hurts."

Though Johanna didn't smoke, she carried a small gold lighter. Pulling it out, she lit Kiki's cigarette. "You were wonderful. I hope you'll consider coming back."

Kiki blew out smoke and regarded Johanna. The lady knew her job, Kiki admitted. Even though she looked like some cuddly little model for shampoo or yogurt. It had been a long day, but the catered dinner break had been first-class, the studio audience generous with their applause. In any case, her agent had told her that *Trivia Alert* was *the* up-and-coming game show of the year. Considering that, and the fact that Kiki had a good sense of humor, she smiled.

"I just might. You've got a good crew, with one notable exception."

Johanna didn't have to turn to know where Kiki's narrowed gaze had landed. With John Jay it was either love or disgust, with little middle ground. "I have to apologize for any annoyance."

"Don't bother. There are plenty of jerks in the business." Kiki studied Johanna again. Quite a face, she decided, even with the minimal makeup. "I'm surprised you don't have a few fang marks."

Johanna smiled. "I have very thick skin."

Anyone who knew her would have attested to that. Johanna Patterson might have looked soft and creamy, but she had the energy of an Amazon. For eighteen months she had slaved, hustled and bargained to get and keep *Trivia Alert* on the air. She wasn't a novice in the entertainment business, and that made her all the more aware that behind the scenes and in the boardrooms it was still a man's world.

That would change eventually, but eventually was too long a wait. Johanna wasn't patient enough to wait for doors to open. When she wanted something badly enough, she gave them a push. For that she was willing to make certain adjustments herself. The business of entertainment was no mystery to her; nor were the deals, the concessions or the compromises. As long as the end product was quality, it didn't matter.

She'd had to swallow pride and sacrifice a principle or two to get her baby off and running. For example, it wasn't her name, but her father's logo that flashed importantly at the end of the show: Carl W. Patterson Productions.

His was the name the network brass related to, and his was the one they trusted. So she used it—grudgingly—then ran things her way.

Thus far, the uneasy marriage was into its second year and holding its own. Johanna knew the business—and her father—too well to take for granted that it would continue.

So she worked hard, tying up loose ends, hammering out solutions to problems and delegating carefully what couldn't be handled personally. The success or failure of the show wouldn't make or break her, financially or professionally, but she had more than money and reputation tied up with it. She had her hopes and her self-esteem.

The studio audience had been cleared. A few technicians remained on the set, either gossiping or tidying up last-minute business. It was just past eight o'clock, and moving into hour fourteen for Johanna.

"Bill, do you have the dupes?" She accepted the copies of the day's tape from her editor. Five shows were produced and recorded in one full-day session. Five costume changes for the celebrity panelists—Johanna had a policy against referring to them as guest stars. Five wardrobe trips for John Jay, who insisted on a change from underwear out for each show. His natty suits and coordinated ties would be sent back to the Beverly Hills tailor who provided them free in exchange for the plug at the end of each show.

His job was over, but Johanna's was just beginning. The tapes would be reviewed, edited and carefully timed. Johanna would oversee each step. There would be mail to go through, letters from home viewers who hoped to be chosen as contestants, more letters from people who disagreed with certain answers. She'd go head-to-head with her research coordinator to check facts and select new questions for upcoming shows. Though she couldn't personally interview and screen each potential contestant, she would go over her contestant coordinator's selections.

The game-show scandals of the fifties were long over, but no one wanted a repeat of them. Standards and Practices was very strict, their rules and regulations very clear. Johanna made it a habit never to relax her own, and to check each detail herself.

When screened contestants arrived at the studio for a day's taping, they were turned over to staff members who sequestered them from the crew, the audience and their prospective partners. They were entertained and soothed, literally cut off from the show until their turn came to participate.

Questions were locked in a safe. Only Johanna and her personal assistant had the combination.

Then, of course, there were the celebrities to deal with. They would want their favorite flowers and choice of beverage in their dressing rooms. Some would go with the flow and make her life easier, and others would be difficult just to show they were important. She knew—and they knew she knew—that most of them appeared on morning game shows not for the money or the fun but for the exposure. They were plugging series and specials, placating their networks or scrambling to keep their face familiar to the public.

Fortunately, a good percentage of them had fun once the ball was rolling. There were still more, however, who required pampering, cajoling and flattery. She was willing, as long as they helped her keep her show on the air. When a woman had grown up with artistic temperaments and the wheeling and dealing of the entertainment business, very little surprised her.

"Johanna."

Regretfully Johanna put her fantasy of a hot bath and a foot massage on hold. "Yes, Beth?" She slipped the tapes into her oversize tote and waited for her assistant. Bethany Landman was young, sharp and energetic. Just now she seemed to be bubbling over. "Make it good. My feet are killing me."

"It's good." A bouncy dark contrast to Johanna's cool blond looks, Bethany gripped her clipboard and all but danced. "We've got him."

Johanna secured the tote on the shoulder of her slim violet-blue jacket. "Who have we got and what are we going to do with him?"

"Sam Weaver." Beth caught her lower lip between her teeth as she grinned. "And I can think of a lot of things we could do with him."

The fact that Bethany was still innocent enough to be impressed by a hard body and tough good looks made Johanna feel old and cynical. More, it made her feel as though she'd been born that way. Sam Weaver was every woman's dream. Johanna wouldn't have denied him his talent, but she was long past the point where sexy eyes and a cocky grin made her pulse flutter. "Why don't you give me the most plausible?"

"Johanna, you have no romance in your soul."

"No, I don't. Can we do this walking, Beth? I want to see if the sky's still there."

"You read that Sam Weaver's done his first TV spot?"

"A miniseries," Johanna added as they wound down the studio corridor.

"They aren't calling it a miniseries. Promotion calls it a four-hour movie event."

"I love Hollywood."

With a chuckle, Bethany shifted her clipboard. "Anyway, I took a chance and contacted his agent. The movie's on our network."

Johanna pushed open the studio door and breathed in the air. Though it was Burbank air and therefore far from fresh, it was welcome. "I'm beginning to see the master plan."

"The agent was very noncommittal, but . . ."

Johanna stretched her shoulders, then searched for her keys. "I think I'm going to like this *but*."

"I just got a call from upstairs. They want him to do it. We'll have to run the shows the week before the movie and give him time to plug it every day." She paused just long enough to give Johanna a chance to nod. "With that guarantee they'll put on the pressure and we've got him."

"Sam Weaver," Johanna murmured. There was no denying his drawing power. Being tall, lanky and handsome in a rough sort of way didn't hurt, but he had more than that. A bit part in a feature film five, maybe six years before had been a springboard. He'd been top-billed and hot box office ever since. It was more than likely he'd be a pain in the neck to work with, but it might be worth it. She thought of the millions of televisions across the country, and the ratings. It would definitely be worth it.

"Good work, Beth. Let's get it firmed up."

"As good as done." Bethany stood by the spiffy little Mercedes as Johanna climbed in. "Will you fire me if I drool?"

"Absolutely." Johanna flashed a grin as she turned the key. "See you in the morning." She drove the car out of the lot like a bullet. Sam Weaver, she thought as she turned the radio up and let the wind whip her hair. Not a bad catch, she decided. Not bad at all.

*   *   *

Sam felt like a fish with a hook through his mouth, and he didn't enjoy the sensation. He slumped in his agent's overstuffed chair, his long, booted legs stretched out and a pained scowl on the face women loved to love.

"Good Lord, Marv. A game show? Why don't you tell me to dress like a banana and do a commercial?"

Marvin Jablonski chomped a candied almond, his current substitute for cigarettes. He admitted to being forty-three, which made him a decade older than his client. He was trim and dressed with a subtle flair that spoke of wealth and confidence. When his office had consisted of a phone booth and a briefcase, he'd dressed the same. He knew how vital illusions were in this town. Just as he knew it was vital to keep a client happy while you were manipulating him.

"I thought it was too much to expect that you'd be open-minded."

Sam recognized the touch of hurt in Marv's tone—the poor, self-sacrificing agent, just trying to do his job. Marv was far from poor and he'd never been into personal sacrifice. But it worked. With something like a sigh, Sam rose and paced the length of Marv's glitzy Century City office. "I was open-minded when I agreed to do the talk-show circuit."

Sam's easy baritone carried a hint of his native rural Virginia, but his reputation in Los Angeles wasn't that of a country gentleman. As he paced, his long-legged stride made the observer think of a man who knew exactly where he was going.

And so he did, Marv thought. Otherwise, as a selective and very successful theatrical agent he would never have taken the struggling young actor on six years before. Instinct, Marv was wont to say, was every bit as important as the power breakfast. "Promotion's part of the business, Sam."

"Yeah, and I'll do my bit. But a game show? How is guessing what's behind door number three going to boost the ratings for *Roses*?"

"There aren't any doors on *Trivia*."

"Thank God."

Marv let the sarcasm pass. He was one of the few in the business who knew that Sam Weaver could be maneuvered with words like *responsibility* and *obligation*. "And it'll boost the ratings because millions of sets are tuned in to that half-hour spot five days a week. People love games, Sam. They like to play, they like to watch and they like to see other people walk out with a free lunch. I've got miles of facts and figures, but let's just say that most of those sets are controlled by women." His smile spread easily, shifting his trim, gray-flecked mustache. "Women, Sam, the ones who buy the bulk of the products the sponsors are hyping. And that fizzy little soft drink that's the major sponsor for *Roses* also buys time on *Trivia*. The network likes that, Sam. Keeps things in the family."

"That's fine." Sam hooked his thumbs in the pockets of his jeans. "But we both know I didn't take the TV deal to sell soda pop."

Marv smiled and ran a hand over his hair. His new toupee was a work of art. "Why did you take the deal?"

"You know why. The script was gold. We needed the four hours to do it right. A two-hour feature would have meant hacking it to bits."

"So you used TV." Marv closed his fingers together lightly, as if he were shutting a trap. "Now TV wants to use you. It's only fair, Sam."

Fair was another word Sam had a weakness for.

A short four-letter epithet was Sam's opinion. Then he said nothing as he stared out at his agent's lofty view of the city. He wasn't so many years off the pavement that he'd forgotten what it felt like to have the heat bake through his sneakers and frustration run through his blood. Marv had taken a chance on him. A calculated risk, but a risk nonetheless. Sam believed in paying his dues. But he hated making a fool of himself.

"I don't like to play games," he muttered, "unless I set the rules."

Marv ignored the buzzer on his desk; it was the prerogative of a man in demand. "You talking politics or the show?"

"Sounds to me like they've been lumped together."

Marv only smiled again. "You're a sharp boy, Sam."

Sam turned his head just a fraction. Marv had been hit by the power of those eyes before. They were one of the reasons he'd signed an unknown when he'd been in a position to refuse the business of well-established luminaries. The eyes were big, heavy lidded and blue. Electric blue, with the power of a lightning bolt. Intense, like his long-boned, narrow face and firm mouth. The chin wasn't so much cleft as sculpted. The kind of chin that looked as though it could take a punch. The nose was a bit crooked, because it had.

California sun had tanned the skin a deep brown and added the interest of faint lines. The kind that made a woman shiver, imagining the experiences that had etched them there. There was a mystery about his face that appealed to females, and a toughness that drew approval from other men. His hair was dark and left long enough to go its own way.

It wasn't a face for a poster in a teenager's room, but it was the kind that haunted a woman's secret dreams.

"How much choice do I have on this?" Sam asked.

"Next to none." Because he knew his client, Marv decided it was time to bare the truth. "Your contract with the network ties you to promotion work. We could get around it, but it wouldn't be good for you, this project or any future ones."

Sam didn't give a damn if it was good for him. He rarely did. But the project was important. "When?"

"Two weeks from today, I'll move the paperwork through. Keep it in perspective, Sam. It's one day out of your life."

"Yeah." One day, he thought, could hardly make much difference. And it wasn't easy to forget that a decade before he'd have considered an offer to do a game show as much of a miracle as manna from heaven. "Marv . . ." He paused at the door. "If I make an ass out of myself, I'm going to dump Krazy Glue on your hairpiece."

* * *

It was strange that two people could have business in the same building, often ride the same elevator, but never cross paths. Sam didn't make the trip from Malibu to his agent's office often. Now that his career was on the rise he was usually tied up in rehearsals, script meetings or location shoots. When he had a few weeks, as he did now, he didn't waste it battling L.A.'s traffic or closing himself up inside Century City's impressive walls. He preferred the seclusion of his ranch.

Johanna, on the other hand, made the trip to her Century City office daily. She hadn't taken a personal vacation in two years, and she put in an average of sixty hours a week on her show. If anyone had tagged her as a workaholic she would have shrugged off the label. Work wasn't an illness, as far as Johanna was concerned; it was a means to an end. The long hours and dedication justified her success. She was determined that no one accuse her of riding on Carl Patterson's coattails.

The offices maintained by *Trivia*'s staff were comfortable but understated. Her own was large enough to prevent her from feeling claustrophobic and practical enough to make the statement that this was a place of business. She arrived like clock-work at eight-thirty, broke for lunch only if it included a meeting, then worked straight through until she was finished. Besides her almost maternal devotion to *Trivia*, she had another concept on the back burner. A word game this time, an idea that was nearly refined enough to take to the network brass.

Now she had her jacket slung over her chair and her nose buried in a week's worth of potential questions passed on to her by Research. She had to get close to the words because she refused to wear the reading glasses she needed.

"Johanna?"

With little more than a grunt, Johanna continued to read. "Did you know Howdy Doody had a twin brother?"

"We were never close," Bethany said apologetically.

"Double Doody," Johanna informed her with a nod. "I think it's a great one for the speed round. Did you catch today's show?"

"Most of it."

"I really think we should try to lure Hank Loman back. Soap stars are a big draw."

"Speaking of big draws . . ." Bethany set a stack of papers on Johanna's desk. "Here's the contract for Sam Weaver. I thought you'd like to look it over before I run it up to his agent."

"Fine." She shuffled papers before drawing the contract close enough to focus on it. "Let's send him a tape of the show."

"The usual fruit and cheese for the dressing room?"

"Mmm-hmm. Is the coffee machine fixed?"

"Just."

"Good." She took a casual glance at her watch. It was a simple affair with a black leather band. The diamond-encrusted one her father's secretary had picked out for her last birthday was still in its box. "Listen, you go on to lunch. I'll run these up."

"Johanna, you're forgetting how to delegate again."

"No, I'm just delegating me." Rising, she shook the creases out of her pale rose jacket. After picking up the remote channel changer from her desk, she aimed it at the television across the room. Both picture and sound winked off. "Are you still seeing that struggling screenwriter?"

"Every chance I get."

Johanna grinned as she shrugged into her jacket. "Then you'd better hurry. This afternoon we need to brainstorm over the home viewer's contest. I want that rolling by next month." She picked up the contracts and slipped them and a cassette into a leather portfolio. "Oh, and make a note for me to slap John Jay's wrist, will you? He charged a case of champagne to the show again."

Bethany wrote that down enthusiastically and in capital letters. "Glad to do it."

Johanna chuckled as she swung out the door. "Results of the contestant screening by three," she continued. "That tech's wife—Randy's wife—she's in Cedars of Lebanon for minor surgery. Send flowers." Johanna grinned over her shoulder. "Who says I can't delegate?"

On the ride up in the elevator, Johanna smiled to herself. She was lucky to have Beth, she thought, though she could already foresee the time when her assistant would be moving up and out. Brains and talent rarely settled for someone else's dream. She liked to think she'd proved that theory for herself. In any case, Johanna had Beth now, and with the rest of her bright young staff, Johanna was on her way to establishing her own niche in the competitive world of daytime television.

If she could get her new concept as far as a pilot, she had no doubt she could sell it. Then maybe a daytime drama, something with as much action as heartache. That story was already in its beginning stages. In addition to that, she was determined to have a nighttime version of *Trivia* syndicated to the independents. She was already on the way to achieving her five-year goal of forming her own production company.

As the elevator rose, Johanna automatically smoothed down her hair and straightened the hem of her jacket. Appearances, she knew, were as important as talent.

When the doors opened, she was satisfied that she looked brisk and professional. She passed through the wide glass doors into Jablonski's offices. He didn't believe in understatement. There were huge Chinese-red urns filled with feathers and fans. A sculpture of what might have been a human torso gleamed in brushed brass. The carpet was an unrelieved white and, Johanna's practical mind thought, must be the devil to keep clean.

Wide chairs in black and red leather were arranged beside glass tables. Trade magazines and the day's papers were set in neat piles. The setup told her Jablonski didn't mind keeping clients waiting.

The desks in the reception area followed the theme in glossy red and black. Johanna saw an attractive brunette seated at one. Perched on the corner of the desk and leaning close to the brunette was Sam Weaver. Johanna's brow lifted only slightly.

She wasn't surprised to see him flirting with one of the staff. Indeed, she expected that kind of thing from him and others like him. After all, her father had had an affair with every secretary, receptionist and assistant who had ever worked for him.

He'd been the tall, dark and handsome type, too, she thought.

Still was. Her only real surprise at running into Sam Weaver was that he was one of that rare breed of actor who actually looked better in the flesh than on the screen.

He packed a punch, an immediate one.

Snug jeans suited him, she acknowledged, as did the plain cotton shirt of a working man. No gold flashed, no diamonds winked. He didn't need them, Johanna decided. A man who could look at the receptionist the way Sam was looking at that brunette didn't need artifice to draw attention to him.

"She's beautiful, Gloria." Sam bent closer to the snapshots the receptionist was showing off. From Johanna's angle it looked as though he were whispering endearments. "You're lucky."

"She's six months old today." Gloria smiled down at the photograph of her daughter, then up at Sam. "I was lucky Mr. Jablonski gave me such a liberal maternity leave, and it's nice to be back at work, but boy, I miss her already."

"She looks like you."

The brunette's cheeks flushed with pride and pleasure. "You think so?"

"Sure. Look at that chin." Sam tapped a finger on Gloria's chin. He wasn't just being kind. The truth was, he'd always gotten a kick out of kids. "I bet she keeps you busy."

"You wouldn't believe—" The still-new mother might have been off and running if she hadn't glanced up and seen Johanna. Embarrassed, she slid the pictures into her drawer. Mr. Jablonski had been generous and understanding, but she didn't think he'd care to have her spending her first day back on the job showing off her daughter. "Good afternoon. May I help you?"

With a slight inclination of her head, Johanna crossed the room. As she did, Sam swiveled on the desk and watched her. He didn't quite do a double take, but damn near.

She was beautiful. He wasn't immune to beauty, though

he was often surrounded by it. At first glance she might have been taken for one of the hordes of slim and leggy California blondes who haunted the beaches and adorned glossy posters. Her skin was gold—not bronzed, but a very pale and lovely gold. It set off the smoky blond hair that fluffed out to tease the shoulders of her jacket. Her face was oval, the classic shape given drama by prominent cheekbones and a full mouth. Her eyes, delicately shaded with rose and violet, were the clear blue of a mountain lake.

She was sexy. Subtly sexy. He was used to that in women as well. Maybe it was the way she moved, the way she carried herself inside the long loose jacket and straight skirt, that made her seem so special. Her shoes were ivory and low-heeled. He found himself noticing even them and the small, narrow feet they covered.

She didn't even glance at him, and he was glad. It gave him the chance to stare at her, to absorb the sight of her, before she recognized him and spoiled the moment.

"I have a delivery for Mr. Jablonski."

Even her voice was perfect, Sam decided. Soft, smooth, just edging toward cool.

"I'll be happy to take it." Gloria gave her most cooperative smile.

Johanna unzipped her portfolio and took out the contracts and tape. She still didn't look at Sam, though she was very aware he was staring. "These are the Weaver contracts and a tape of *Trivia Alert*."

"Oh, well—"

Sam cut her off neatly. "Why don't you take them in to him, Gloria? I'll wait."

Gloria opened her mouth, then shut it again to clear her throat as she rose. "All right. If you'd just give me a moment," she said to Johanna, then headed down the corridor.

"Do you work for the show?" Sam asked her.

"Yes." Johanna gave him a small and purposefully disinterested smile. "Are you a fan, Mr.—?"

She didn't recognize him. Sam had a moment to be both surprised and disconcerted before he saw the humor of it and grinned. "It's Sam." He held out a hand, trapping her into an introduction.

"Johanna," she told him, and accepted the handshake. His easy reaction made her feel petty. She was on the verge of explaining when she realized he hadn't released her hand. His was hard and strong. Like his face, like his voice. It was her reaction to them, her quick and intensely personal reaction to them, that drove her to continue the pretense and blame it on him.

"Do you work for Mr. Jablonski?"

Sam grinned again. It was a fast, crooked grin that warned a woman not to trust him. "In a manner of speaking. What do you do on the show?"

"A little of this, a little of that," she said, truthfully enough. "Don't let me keep you."

"I'd rather you did." But he released her hand because she was tugging at it. "Would you like to have lunch?"

Her brow lifted. Five minutes ago he'd been cuddling up to the brunette; now he was inviting the first woman who came along to lunch. Typical. "Sorry. I'm booked."

"For how long?"

"Long enough." Johanna glanced past him to the receptionist.

"Mr. Jablonski will have the contracts signed and returned to Ms. Patterson by tomorrow afternoon."

"Thank you." Johanna shifted her portfolio and turned. Sam laid a hand on her arm and waited until she looked back at him.

"See you."

She smiled at him, again disinterestedly, before she walked

away. She was chuckling when she reached the elevators, unaware that she'd tucked the hand he'd held into her pocket.

Sam watched her until she'd turned the corner. "You know,
Gloria," he said, half to himself, "I think I'm going to enjoy
playing this game after all."

CHAPTER 2

On the day of a taping, Johanna was always on the set by nine. It wasn't that she didn't trust her staff. She did. She simply trusted herself more. Besides, last week they'd had a few mechanical glitches with the moving set that swung the contestants and their counters stage center for play, then off again for the championship round. Small problems like that could delay taping anywhere from five minutes to two hours. By checking everything through personally beforehand, she sweetened the odds.

All the lights on the display board had to be tested, and the dressing rooms had to be primped and fresh coffee and cookies arranged for the prospective contestants.

They weren't due until one, but experience told Johanna that most would arrive early so they could chew their nails in the studio. Soothing them was one job she gladly delegated. The celebrities were also due at one so they could do a run-through and still have plenty of time for hair, makeup and wardrobe.

John Jay would arrive at two to complain about the suits that had been selected for him. Then he would close himself in his dressing room to sulk before his makeup call. When he was suited up, powdered and sprayed he would emerge, ready to shine for the cameras. Johanna had learned to ignore his artistic temperament—for the most part—and to tolerate the rest. There was no arguing with his popularity quotient. It was largely due to him that the line would form outside the studio for tickets for the day's taping.

Johanna checked off her duties one by one, then double-checked everyone else's. Over the years, efficiency had grown from a habit to an obsession. At noon she downed something that resembled a shrimp salad. The taping should start at three and, if God was in his heaven, be over by eight.

Fortunately, the female celebrity was a repeater who had done *Trivia* at least a dozen times, along with numerous other game shows. That gave Johanna one less headache. She hadn't given Sam Weaver a thought.

So she told herself.

When he arrived, she would turn him and his entourage over to Bethany. It would give her assistant a thrill and keep God's gift to women out of her hair.

She only hoped he could handle the game. The questions were fun, for the most part, but they weren't always easy. More than once she'd had a celebrity grumble and complain because an inability to answer had made him or her look stupid. Johanna made it a policy to see that each show's batch of questions contained the obvious and amusing, as well as the challenging.

It wouldn't be her fault if Sam Weaver turned out to have an empty head. He would only have to smile to gain the audience's forgiveness.

She remembered the way he'd smiled at her when she'd asked if he worked for Jablonski. Yes, that was all it would take to make every woman at home and in the studio turn to putty—except her, of course.

"Check the bell." Johanna stood in the middle of the set and directed her sound technician. At her signal the bright, cheery beep of the winning bell rang. "And the buzzer." The flat drone of the loser sounded. "Bring up the lights in the winner's circle." She nodded in satisfaction as the bulbs flashed.

"The contestants?"

"Sequestered." Bethany checked her clipboard. "We have the accountant from Venice returning from last week. He's a three-game winner. First challenger's a housewife from Ohio in town visiting her sister. Nervous as hell."

"Okay, see if you can help Dottie keep them calm. I'll give the dressing rooms a last check."

Mentally calculating her time as she went, Johanna scooted down the corridor. Her female celebrity was Marsha Tuckett, a comfortable, motherly type who was part of the ensemble of a family series in its third year. A nice contrast for Sam Weaver, she thought. Johanna made sure there were fresh pink roses on the dressing table and plenty of club soda on ice. Satisfied the room was in order, she walked across the narrow hall to the next room.

Because she hadn't thought roses appropriate for Sam Weaver, she'd settled on a nice leafy fern for the corner. As a matter of course she checked the lights, plumped the pillows on the narrow daybed and made certain the towels were fresh and plentiful. A last look showed her nothing he could find fault with. Carelessly she stole a mint from the bowl on the table and popped it into her mouth, then turned.

He was in the doorway.

"Hello again." He'd already decided to make it his business to find her, but he hadn't expected to be quite so lucky. He stepped into the room and dropped a garment bag negligently over a chair.

Johanna pushed the candy into the corner of her mouth. The dressing room was small, but she couldn't recall feeling trapped in it before. "Mr. Weaver." She put on her best at-your-service smile as she offered a hand.

"It's Sam. Remember?" He took her hand and stepped just

close enough to make her uncomfortable. They both knew it wasn't an accident.

"Of course. Sam. We're all delighted you could join us. We'll have our run-through shortly. In the meantime, you can let me or one of the staff know if you need anything." She looked past him, puzzled. "Are you alone?"

"Was I supposed to bring someone?"

"No." Where was his secretary, his assistant, his gofer? His current lover?

"According to my instructions, all I needed was five changes. Casual. Will this do to start?"

She studied the navy crewneck and the buff-colored slacks as though it mattered. "You look fine."

She'd known who he was all along, Sam thought. He wasn't so much annoyed as curious. And she wasn't comfortable with him now. That was something else to think about. Making a woman comfortable wasn't always a goal. After reaching for a mint himself, he rested a hip against the dressing table. It was a move that brought him just a little closer. Her lipstick had worn off, he noticed. He found the generous and unpainted shape of her mouth appealing.

"I watched the tape you sent."

"Good. You'll have more fun if you're familiar with the format. Make yourself comfortable." She spoke quickly but not hurriedly. That was training. But she wanted out, and she wanted out now. That was instinct. "One of the staff will be along to take you to Makeup."

"I also read credits." He blocked the door in an offhand way. "I noticed that a Johanna Patterson is executive producer. You?"

"Yes." Damn it, he was making her jittery. She couldn't remember the last time anyone had been able to make her nervous. Cool, controlled and capable. Anyone who knew her would have given that description. She glanced deliberately at her watch. "I'm sorry I can't stay and chat, but we're on a schedule."

He didn't budge. "Most producers don't hand-deliver contracts."

She smiled. Though on the surface it was sweet, he saw the ice underneath and wondered at it. "I'm not most producers."

"I won't argue with that." It was more than attraction now, it was a puzzle that had to be solved. He'd managed to resist any number of women, but he'd never been able to resist a puzzle. "Since we missed lunch before, how about dinner?"

"I'm sorry. I'm—"

"Booked. Yeah, so you said." He tilted his head just a bit, as if to study her from a new angle. It was more than the fact that he was used to women being available. It was the fact that she seemed bound and determined to brush him off, and not very tactfully. "You're not wearing any rings."

"You're observant."

"Involved?"

"With what?"

He had to laugh. His ego wasn't so inflated that he couldn't take no for an answer. He simply preferred a reason for it. "What's the problem, Johanna? Didn't you like my last movie?"

"Sorry. I missed it," she lied, smiling. "Now if you'll excuse me, I've got a show to see to."

He was still standing at the door, but this time she brushed past him. And against him. Both felt a jolt, unexpected and tingling.

Annoyed, Johanna kept walking.

Intrigued, Sam kept watching.

She had to admit, he was a pro. By the middle of the taping of the first show, Sam had gotten in a casual and very competent plug for his new miniseries *No Roses for Sarah*. So effective, that Johanna knew she'd tune in herself. The sponsors and the network brass would be delighted. He'd charmed his partner, the mother of two from Columbus, who had walked onto the set so tense that her voice had come out in squeaks. He'd even managed to answer a few questions correctly.

It was hard not to be impressed, though she worked at it. When the lights were on and the tape was rolling he was the embodiment of that elusive and too often casually used word: *star.* John Jay's posturing and flashing incisors shifted to the background.

Not all entertainers were at ease in front of a live audience. He was. Johanna noted that he was able to turn on just the right amount of enthusiasm and enjoyment when the cameras were rolling, but also that he played to the studio audience during breaks by joking with his competitor and occasionally answering a question someone shouted out at him.

He even seemed to be genuinely pleased when his partner won five hundred in cash in the bonus speed round.

Even if he was just putting on a good face, Johanna couldn't fault him for it. Five hundred dollars meant a great deal to the mother of two from Columbus. Just as much as her moment in the sun with a celebrated heartthrob.

"We've got a very tight game going here, folks." John Jay smiled importantly at the camera. "This final question will determine today's champion, who will then go to the winner's circle and try for ten thousand dollars. Hands on your buzzers." He drew the card from the slot on his dais. "And the final question, for the championship, is . . . who created Winnie the Pooh?"

Sam's finger was quick on the trigger. The woman from Columbus looked at him pleadingly. John Jay called for a dramatic silence.

"A. A. Milne."

"Ladies and gentlemen, we have a new champion!"

As the cheers got louder and his partner threw her arms

around his neck, Sam caught Johanna's look of surprise. It was easy to read her mind and come up with the fact that she didn't see him as a man who could read and remember storybooks—especially not classic children's books.

John Jay said the official goodbyes to the accountant from Venice and broke for a commercial. Sam had to all but carry his partner to the winner's circle. As he settled back in his chair, he glanced at Johanna.

"How'm I doing?"

"Sixty seconds," she said, but her voice was friendlier because she saw he was holding his partner's hand to calm her.

When the minute was up, John Jay managed to make the woman twice as nervous as he ran down the rules and the possibilities. The clock started on the first question. They weren't so difficult, Sam realized. It was the pressure that made them hard. He wasn't immune to it himself. He really wanted her to win. When he saw she was beginning to fumble, he blanked out the lights and the camera the way he did during any important scene. The rules said he could answer only two questions for her. Once he did, letting her keep her viselike grip on his hand, she was over the hump.

There were ten seconds left when John Jay, his voice pitched to the correct level of excitement, posed the last question. "Where was Napoleon's final defeat?"

She knew it. Of course she knew it. The problem was to get the word out. Sam inched forward in the impossibly uncomfortable swivel chair and all but willed her to spit out the word.

"Waterloo!" she shouted, beating the buzzer by a heartbeat. Above their heads, *10,000* began to flash in bold red lights. His partner screamed, kissed him full on the mouth, then screamed again. While they were breaking for a commercial, Sam was holding her head between her knees and telling her to take deep breaths.

"Mrs. Cook?" Johanna knelt down beside them and monitored the woman's pulse. This wasn't the first time a contestant had reacted so radically. "Are you going to be all right?"

"I won. I won ten thousand dollars."

"Congratulations." Johanna lifted the woman's head far enough to be certain it was merely a case of hyperventilation. "We're going to take a fifteen-minute break. Would you like to lie down?"

"No. I'm sorry." Mrs. Cook's color was coming back. "I'm all right."

"Why don't you go with Beth? She'll get you some water."

"Okay. I'm fine, really." Too excited to be embarrassed, Mrs. Cook managed to stand, with Johanna taking one arm and Sam the other. "It's just that I've never won anything before. My husband didn't even come. He took the kids to the beach."

"You'll have a wonderful surprise for him," Johanna said soothingly, and kept walking. "Take a little breather, then you can start thinking about how you're going to spend that money."

"Ten thousand dollars," Mrs. Cook said faintly as she was passed over to Beth.

"Do you get a lot of fainters?" Sam asked.

"Our share. Once we had to stop taping because a construction worker slid right out of his seat during the speed round." She watched a moment longer until she was satisfied Bethany had Mrs. Cook under control. "Thanks. You acted quickly."

"No problem. I've had some practice."

She thought of women fainting at his feet. "I'll bet. There'll be cold drinks and fresh fruit in your dressing room. As long as Mrs. Cook's recovered, we'll start the tape in ten minutes."

He took her arm before she could move away. "If it wasn't my last movie, what is it?"

"What is what?"

"All these little barbs I feel sticking into my heart. You have a problem with me being here?"

"Of course not. We're thrilled to have you."

"Not we. You."

"I'm thrilled to have you here," she corrected, wishing he didn't make it a habit to stand almost on top of her. Her low heels brought her eyes level with his mouth. She discovered it wasn't the most comfortable view. "This series of contests, like your movie, will be shown during the May sweeps. What could be better?"

"A friendly conversation, over dinner."

"You're persistent, Mr. Weaver."

"I'm puzzled, Ms. Patterson."

Her lips very nearly twitched. There was something cute about the way he drawled her last name. "A simple no shouldn't puzzle a man who obviously thinks so well on his feet." Deliberately she looked at her watch. "Half your break's up. You'd better change."

* * *

Because things ran smoothly, they were able to tape three shows before the dinner break. Johanna began to have fantasies about finishing on time. She kept them to herself, knowing how easy it was to jinx success. The dinner spread wasn't elaborate, but it was plentiful. Johanna didn't believe in pinching pennies over such minor matters as food. She wanted to keep her celebrities happy and her contestants at ease.

During the break she didn't sit, but grabbed a plate and a few essentials and kept herself available. The audience had been cleared, and new ticketholders would be allowed in for the two final tapings. All she had to do was avoid any crises, keep the energy level up and make certain John Jay didn't proposition any of the females on set.

With the first in mind, Johanna kept her eyes on the new challenger, a young woman from Orange County who appeared to be about six months pregnant.

"Problem?"

She'd forgotten that her other prerequisite had been to avoid Sam Weaver. Reminding herself to keep the celebrities happy, she turned to him as she plucked a small chilled shrimp from her plate. "No, why?"

"You don't relax, do you?" Without expecting an answer, he chose a slim carrot stick from her plate. "I've noticed you're watching Audrey like a hawk."

She wasn't surprised that he already knew the expectant mother by her first name. "Just being cautious." She bit into the shrimp and unbent enough to smile at him. After all, the day was nearly over. "During one of my early shows we had an expectant mother go into labor in the winner's circle. It's not an experience you forget."

"What did she have?" he asked, testing.

"A boy." Her smile became more generous as her eyes met his. It was one of her best memories. "By the time she was half-way to the hospital the staff had a pool going." She swallowed the last of the shrimp. "I won."

So she liked to bet. He'd keep that in mind. "I don't think you have to worry about Audrey. She's not due until the first part of August." He caught Johanna's curious look. "I asked," he explained. "Now, can I ask you a question? Professional," he added when he sensed her withdrawal.

"Of course."

"How often do you have to wind John Jay up?"

She had to laugh, and she didn't bother to object when he snitched a cube of cheddar from her plate. "Wind down's more like it. He's harmless, really. Only he thinks he's irresistible."

"He told me the two of you were . . . cozy."

"Really?" She glanced briefly over in the show's host's

direction. The haughty look was so casual and innate that Sam grinned. "He's also an optimist."

He was glad to hear it. Very glad. "Well, he does his job. Somehow he manages to hit the note between cheerleader and father confessor."

Covering her personal opinion with her professional one was an old habit. To her, entertainment was first and last a business. "Actually, we're lucky to have him. He hosted another show about five years back, so he's not only familiar but also has a strong appeal to the home viewer."

"Are you going to eat that sandwich?"

Without answering, Johanna took half of the roast-beef-and-Swiss and handed it to him. "Are you enjoying yourself so far?"

"More than I'd expected." He took a bite. So she had a taste for hot mustard. He was fond of spice himself, and in more than food. "Will you be offended if I tell you I kicked a bit about doing it?"

"No. I'm the first to admit that the show isn't Shakespeare, but it serves its purpose." Leaning against a wall, she watched one of the crew heap on a second helping. "What have you found appealing about it?"

He avoided the obvious answer. Her. The one he gave was equally true. "I got a kick out of seeing those people win. Of course, I developed a soft spot for Mrs. Cook. Why do you do it?"

She avoided several possible answers. The one she settled on was true enough. "I enjoy it." When he offered her his glass of sparkling water and lime, she accepted without thinking. She was relaxed, optimistic about the rest of the day and, though she didn't realize it, comfortable in his company.

"I hesitate to point this out, but it looks like we're having dinner after all."

She looked at him again, slowly, gauging him and her

reaction to him. If she'd had a different background, different memories, fewer disillusionments, she would have been flattered. More, she would have been tempted. He had a way of looking at her as though they were alone; as though, if they'd been in a room with hundreds of other people, he would have picked her, and only her, out.

Trick of the trade, she told herself, disliking her own cynicism.

"Isn't it handy we got that out of the way?" She handed him back his glass.

"Yeah. It should make it easier for us to do it again."

Casually she signaled to the crew to begin clearing up. "I don't want to rush you, but we'll start taping again in fifteen minutes."

"I never miss my cue." He shifted his body just enough to prevent her from walking by him. He had the moves, Johanna thought. Very smooth. Very slick. "I get the impression you like to play games, Johanna."

There was a dare in his voice. She caught it, and was trapped. Though her voice was cool again, she stood her ground and met his gaze. "Depends on the stakes."

"Okay, how's this? If I win the next two games you'll have dinner with me. I set the time and the place."

"I don't like those stakes."

"I haven't finished. If I lose I come back on the show within six months. No fee." That had her attention, he noted, pleased with himself. He hadn't misjudged her dedication to her show or her weakness for a dare.

"Within six months," she repeated, studying him to assess whether he could be trusted. Not an inch, she decided, on many matters. But she didn't see him as a man to welsh on a bet.

"Deal?" He made his voice deliberately challenging as he held out a hand.

It was too good a bet to turn down. His eyes were too mocking to ignore. "Deal." She set her palm against his, then removed it and stepped away. "Ten minutes, Mr. Weaver."

Johanna had a very bad feeling when Sam and his teammate took the first game. Since the conception of the show, she'd had a strict personal policy against rooting for either side. It didn't matter that no one could read her thoughts. She knew them, and prejudice of any kind was unprofessional. She certainly would never have imagined herself actually rooting against a certain team. She did now.

It was because she wanted him back on the show, she told herself when the last taping of the day began. The producer, not the woman, had made the bet. It was ridiculous to think that she was afraid, even uneasy, about having a meal with him. That would only be a small annoyance—like a spoonful of bad-tasting medicine.

But she stood behind camera two and cheered inwardly when the opposing team took the lead.

He didn't show nerves. Sam was much too skilled an actor to show nerves in front of a camera. But they dogged him. It was the principle, he told himself. That was the only reason he was so determined to win and make Johanna pay the price. He certainly wasn't infatuated. He'd been around too long to be infatuated just because a woman was beautiful. And aloof, his mind added. And contrary and stubborn. And damn sexy.

He wasn't infatuated. He just hated to lose.

By the beginning of the final round, the two teams were neck and neck. The studio audience was loud and raucous, the contestants wired. Johanna's stomach was in knots. When Sam turned and winked at her during the commercial break she nearly bared her teeth.

Positions jockeyed back and forth. Professionally Johanna knew that when the show aired it would pull the television audience in. That was, after all, the name of the game. Personally, she'd hoped for a landslide, however boring.

When the final question came up, she held her breath. Sam was quick to push the button, but his partner was quicker. He nearly swore. The expectant mother from Orange County had more than her own fate in her hands.

"Surrender, Dorothy!" she shouted. When the lights went on, Sam took her face in his hands and kissed her. Hard. Audrey would be able to dine out on the moment for months. Sam kept his arm around her as they walked toward the winner's circle. Once she was settled, he strolled casually over to Johanna and bent closer to her ear.

"Saturday night, seven. I'll pick you up."

She only nodded. It was hard to speak when your teeth were clenched.

*   *   *

Johanna found several vital tasks to perform after the taping was completed. She did not, as was her habit, say a personal thank-you to both guest stars. That job was handed over to Bethany. She made herself scarce for thirty minutes so that she could be sure Sam Weaver was off and out of her hair. Until Saturday.

She couldn't quite drum up the job-well-done mood the end of the day usually brought her. Instead she made a list of details to see to the following day that would keep her occupied from the time she got up until she crawled back home again. Business as usual, she told herself, and broke the tip off her pencil.

"Everybody's happy," Beth told her. "The questions we didn't use in the speed round are locked back in the safe. The contestants we didn't get to are ready and willing to come back next week. Your dupes." She handed Johanna the tapes. "We've got some great shows. Especially the last one. Even the techs were getting into it. They loved Sam." Bethany pushed back a lock of hair. "And you know how jaded techs can be. Anyway, it's nice to know that besides being gorgeous and sexy he's got some smarts."

Johanna grunted and dropped the tapes in her carryall.

Bethany tilted her head. "I was going to ask you if you wanted to take some of the leftover fruit home, but it looks more like you'd prefer raw meat."

"It's been a long day."

"Uh-huh." Beth knew her boss better. Johanna had pulled a roll of antacids out of her bag and had popped two of them. A sure sign of trouble. "Want to have a drink and talk about it?"

Johanna had never made it a habit to confide in anyone. There simply hadn't been enough people in her life she could trust. Johanna knew Beth. Her assistant was young and energetic, but she was also trustworthy. She was also the closest thing Johanna had ever had to a foul-weather friend.

"I'll pass on the drink, but how about walking me out to my car?"

"Sure."

The sun hadn't set. Johanna found something reassuring about that after having been inside all day. She'd put the top down, she thought, and take the drive home through the Hills fast. Maybe a bit recklessly. She had a taste for the reckless, a taste she usually controlled. It came from her father. But tonight it might do her good to give in to it for a little while.

"What did you think of Sam Weaver?"

Bethany cocked a brow. "Before or after I stopped drooling?"

"After."

"I liked him," she said simply. "He didn't expect the red carpet, he wasn't condescending and he wasn't snickering behind his hand at the contestants."

"Those are all negative virtues," Johanna pointed out.

"Okay, I liked the way he joked around with the crew. And the way he signed autographs as though he wanted to instead of acting as though he were granting a favor." She didn't add that she'd asked for one herself. "He acted like somebody without making sure everybody remembered that *somebody* was in all capital letters."

"Interestingly said," Johanna murmured. "Are you still keeping that little book with the list of celebrity panelists?"

Beth colored a bit. She was in the business, but that didn't stop her from being a fan. "Yeah. Sam gets five stars."

Johanna's lips twitched a bit at her assistant's top rating. "I guess I should be relieved to hear it. I'm having dinner with him on Saturday."

Bethany's mouth went into the O position. There were stars in her eyes. She simply couldn't help it. "Wow."

"It's confidential."

"Okay," Bethany said, and Johanna knew she was as good as her word. "Johanna, I know you were raised in the business and Cary Grant probably bounced you on his knee, but doesn't it give you a tingle?"

"It gives me a pain," Johanna stated bluntly as she pulled open her car door. "Actors aren't my type."

"Too general."

"Okay, blue-eyed lanky actors with a drawl aren't my type."

"You're sick, Johanna. Very, very sick. You want me to go as proxy?"

She chuckled as she lowered herself into the car. "No. I can handle Sam Weaver."

"Lucky you. Listen, not to pry or anything . . ."

"But?"

"You will remember the details? I might want to write a book or something."

"Go home, Beth." The engine sprang to life as she twisted the key. Yes, she definitely wanted power and speed tonight.

"Okay, just let me know if he always smells so good. I can live on that."

Shaking her head, Johanna roared out of the lot. She hadn't been interested enough to notice what Sam Weaver had smelled like.

Like a man, her memory informed her. He'd smelled very much like a man.

CHAPTER 3

It was only dinner. Nothing to worry about. Certainly nothing, after several days to put it in perspective, to be annoyed about. They would no doubt go to one of L.A.'s flashier restaurants, where Sam could see and be seen. Between the pâté and the double chocolate mousse he would greet and chat with the other glamorous types who patronized that kind of eatery.

Meat houses, her second stepmother had called such places. Not because of the menu but because of the flesh exposed. Darlene had been one of the most honest and least affected of her father's attachments.

If she wanted to stretch a point, Johanna could consider it a business dinner. She found she wanted to stretch a point. She could tolerate this, as she had tolerated many other meals, as a part of the game everyone who wanted to remain part of the business learned to play. Since it was business, she would be charming and chatty, even gracious, until it was over and she could close the door on the entire episode.

She didn't like persistent men.

She didn't like men with reputations.

She didn't like Sam Weaver.

That was before the flowers arrived.

Johanna had spent Saturday morning gardening and half-hoping Sam Weaver wouldn't find her address. He hadn't called to ask her for it or to confirm plans. Waiting for him to do just that had left her jumpy and out of sorts all week. That was just one more sin to lay at his door.

It was her habit whenever she worked outside to take her cordless phone with her. Business could crop up even on weekends. Today, however, she pretended to have forgotten it and spent a warm and pleasant morning tending a plot of columbine.

This was her respite, even her vice, in a way. The flowers she planted were nurtured and cared for. They rewarded her by renewing themselves year after year. Their continuity soothed her. This, as was the case in other areas of her life, was something she'd done with her own hands. Whatever rewards she reaped, whatever failures she suffered, were her own.

The flowers lasted. The people in her life rarely did.

Her jeans were scruffy at the knees and her hands stained with mulch when the delivery man pulled up. Johanna shaded her eyes as she rose.

"Miz Patterson?"

"Yes."

"Sign here, please." The deliveryman met her halfway across her lawn, handing her first his clipboard and then a long white box embossed with a florist's name and tied with a red satin ribbon. "Nice garden you got there," he said with a tip of his hat as he climbed back into the truck.

She was a sucker for flowers. Without waiting to go in and wash up, Johanna opened the box. They were roses. Not a dozen red or two dozen pink, but one long-stemmed sample of every color she'd ever seen, from the purest white to the deepest red, and all the pinks and golds between. Charmed, she lowered her face to the box to draw in their scent.

Heady. Roses were always heady, lush and unashamedly sensual.

It wasn't her birthday. In any case, her father—or rather her father's secretary—wasn't imaginative enough to have thought of such a sweet and charming gift. Though her fingertips were soiled, she pulled open the card that had come with the box.

I don't know your favorite color. Yet. Sam.

She wanted to shrug it off. Pretty gestures came so easily to some. It would have taken only a casual order to an assistant to have them delivered. How well she knew it. So he'd found her, she thought with a shrug as she started back across the lawn. The deal was still on, and she'd live up to her end of it.

She tried, really tried, to set them aside and go back to work on the buds she'd planted herself. But she couldn't dismiss the roses, didn't have the heart to dampen her own pleasure. She was smiling when she sniffed the flowers again. Smiling still when she went into the house to arrange them.

*   *   *

He hadn't looked forward to an evening quite so much in a long time. It was easy to compare it to a winning poker hand or a successful day at the track. He'd never cared half as much for the purse as for the winning. He'd have preferred to think of it in those terms, but the truth was that he was looking forward to spending a few hours in Johanna Patterson's company.

Maybe he was intrigued because she was so disinterested. Sam took a turn sharp and fast while the radio blared through the open windows. What man didn't appreciate a challenge? If she'd taken him at his word on their first meeting, they might have enjoyed a pleasant lunch and an easy hour. He'd never know if that would have been the end of it. The fact that she'd refused, and had continued to refuse, only made him more determined to wear her down.

Women came easily to him. Too easily. Sam wouldn't deny he'd gone through a stage when he'd taken advantage of that. But his background, and what many might have considered the rather quaint and traditional values that had gone into it, had surfaced again.

The press could beat the drum of his romantic adventures all they liked. The truth was, he *was* a romantic. Rolling from one bed to the next had never been his style.

There were two Sam Weavers. One was intensely private, guarded about matters like family and relationships, the things that really mattered. The other was an actor, a realist who accepted that the price of fame was public consumption. He gave interviews, didn't bother to dodge the paparazzi and was always willing to sign an autograph. He'd learned to shrug off whatever reports were exaggerations or outright lies. They were the public Sam's problem. The private one couldn't have cared less.

He wondered, given what he now knew about Johanna Patterson's background, which Sam Weaver she would understand.

She was the only child of the respected producer Carl Patterson, the product of his first, and reportedly most tempestuous marriage. Her mother had disappeared or, as some reports put it, "gone into seclusion," after the marriage had failed. Johanna had grown up in the luxury of Beverly Hills, had attended the best schools. Some rumors stated that she adored her father, others that there was no love lost between them. In either case, she was the only offspring Patterson had after four marriages and numerous affairs.

He was surprised that she lived back in the Hills. He'd

expected some slick condo in the city or a wing in her father's Beverly Hills estate. The sharp professional woman he'd met seemed out of place so far from the action. He was more surprised when he found the house.

It was tiny. Like a dollhouse, but without the gingerbread. Hardly more than a cabin, it was rustic and sturdy, with the wood unpainted and the panes of glass sparkling in the evening sun. There wasn't much land before the trees and the hills took it over. What was there was uneven and rocky. To compensate—more, to enhance it—flowers and budding vines were everywhere. The dashing little Mercedes parked in the driveway looked as though it had been left there by mistake.

Hands in pockets, he stood beside his own car and looked again. She didn't have any close neighbors, and the view was nothing to write home about, but it seemed as though she'd carved out her own corner of the mountainside. He knew about that. Appreciated it.

When he reached the door, he caught the scent of sweet peas. His mother planted them each spring, outside the kitchen windows. Johanna opened the door and found him smiling.

"Brigadoon," he said, and watched her polite smile turn to an expression of puzzlement. "I was trying to think what your place reminded me of. Brigadoon. Like it's only here once every hundred years."

Damn him, she thought, feeling almost resigned. She'd barely managed to put the roses in perspective and here he was, charming her again. "I wasn't sure you'd find it."

"I have a good sense of direction. Most of the time." He glanced toward the flowers that flanked both sides of her house. "From the looks of things, the roses were overkill."

"No." It would have been petty not to let him know they'd pleased her. "It was sweet of you to send them." He wasn't wearing a dinner suit, but a breezy linen shirt and pleated slacks. Johanna was glad she'd guessed right when she'd bypassed glitz for the subtler lines of a slim-skirted white dress. "If you'd like to come in a minute, I'll get my jacket."

He did, though he thought it would be a shame to cover up her arms and shoulders. The living room was small enough to be cozy. She'd arranged deep chairs by a white bricked fireplace and had added dozens of pillows. It made Sam think that when Johanna was finished with work she liked to take off her shoes and snuggle in.

"This isn't what I expected."

"No?" She pulled on a sizzling tomato-red jacket. "I like it."

"I didn't say I didn't like it, I said it wasn't what I expected." He noted his roses had been given a place of honor on the mantel, tucked prettily in a clear, widemouthed vase that glinted at the bottom with colored pebbles. "Do you have a favorite?"

She glanced at the roses. "No. I just like flowers." The clusters of rubies at her ears glinted as she adjusted them. "Shall we go?"

"In a minute." He crossed to her, noticing with some interest the way she stiffened up. Despite it, he took her hand. "Are you going to be a good sport about this?"

She let out a little sigh. "I've thought about it."

"And?" It was the easy curving of his lips that made her relax. "I decided I might as well."

"Are you hungry?"

"Some."

"Mind a bit of a ride?"

Curious, she tilted her head. "No, I suppose not."

"Good." He kept her hand in his as they walked outside.

* * *

She should have known he was up to something. They didn't drive into the city as she'd expected. Rather than comment, Johanna let the conversation flow as she wondered how to handle him. Actors were a tricky bunch. They knew how to set the stage, how to read their lines, how to put on whatever face was most appropriate to the situation. At the moment, it seemed Sam had chosen to be the casually friendly companion a woman could relax with. Johanna wasn't ready to give him an inch.

He drove fast, just faster than the law allowed and just under the edge of safety. Even when they left the freeway for a road that was rough and sparsely populated, he continued at the same steady clip.

"Mind if I ask where we're going?"

Sam negotiated a lazy turn. He'd wondered how long it would take before she asked. "To dinner."

Johanna turned to study the landscape. The land rolled by, wide and dusty. "Something over an open fire?"

He smiled. She'd used her haughty tone again, and damned if he didn't enjoy hearing it. "No, I thought we'd eat at my place."

His place. The thought of dining privately with him didn't alarm her. She was too confident of her ability to handle whatever situation cropped up. She was more curious about the fact that he would have a *place* this far from the glitz. "You have a cave?"

Because there was amusement in her voice now, his smile widened. "I can do a little better than that. I only eat in restaurants when it's necessary."

"Why?"

"Because you end up doing business, or being stared at. I wasn't in the mood for either tonight." Pebbles spit from under the tires as he turned to drive through a plain wooden gate.

"That's part of the game, isn't it?"

"Sure, but there has to be a reason to play it." He whizzed by a pretty white house with blue shutters, giving two blasts of his horn. "My foreman and his family live there. If he knows it's me he won't come looking for trespassers."

They passed barns and sheds, and she was surprised that they looked as though they had a purpose other than a decorative one. She spotted paddocks with split-rail fencing and dark, rich dirt. A dog—or what sounded like a pair of them—began to bark.

The road forked, and then she saw the ranch house. It, too, was white, but the shutters were gray and the three chimneys it boasted were brick weathered to a dusky rose. It was low and spreading, shaped like an H turned on its side. For all its size, it didn't overpower. There were rockers on the porch, sturdy wooden ones that gave the impression that someone sat in them often. Window boxes had been freshly painted a bright, sassy red. Tumbling out of them were pansies and bushy impatiens. Though the air here was hot and dry, they were thriving and well tended.

Johanna stepped out of the car to turn a slow circle. It certainly looked like a working ranch. "Quite a place."

"I like it," he said, mimicking her earlier remark.

She acknowledged that with a quick, though cautious, smile. "It must be inconvenient to commute."

"I keep a place in L.A." He shrugged it off as though it were no more than a storage closet. "The best thing about finishing a film is being able to come back here and dig in for a while. Before I got hooked on acting, I'd wanted to come west and work on a ranch." He took her arm as they walked up the two wooden steps to the porch. They creaked. For some reason, Johanna found that endearing. "I was lucky enough to do both."

She glanced at the pansies, with their arrogant Alice-in-Wonderland faces. "Do you raise cattle?"

"Horses." He'd left the door unlocked. It was a habit he'd

grown up with. "I bought the place about three years ago. Convinced my accountant that it'd be a great tax shelter. It made him feel better."

The hardwood floors were polished to a high gloss, scattered with hand-hooked rugs in muted pastels. In the entrance a collection of pewter—bowls, spoons, mugs, even a dented candlestick—was arranged on a waist-high table. The early twilight crept through the windows.

It had a good feel, a solid feel. Though she would never had admitted it out loud, Johanna had always felt strongly that houses had their own personalities. She'd selected her own house because it had made her feel warm and comfortable. She'd left her father's because it had been possessive and dishonest.

"Do you get to stay here often?" she asked him.

"Not often enough." He glanced around at the walls, which he'd painted himself. The house, like his career, was something he never took for granted. Though he'd never known poverty, he'd been taught to appreciate security, and that nothing replaced sweat for earning it. "Would you like a drink, or would you rather go for dinner?"

"Dinner," she said firmly. She knew better than to drink, socially or otherwise, on an empty stomach.

"I was hoping you'd say that." In the casual way he had, he took her hand and led her down the hall. The wing of the house ran straight. At the end it opened up into a large country kitchen. Copper pots hung from hooks over a center island. The room was flanked by counters and cabinets on one side and a small stone hearth on the other. A ribbon of windows gave an open view of dusk settling over a brick terrace and a mosaic pool. She'd thought to find a servant or two busily preparing the evening meal. Instead, all she found was the scent of cooking.

"It smells wonderful."

"Good." Scooping up two hot pads, Sam bent down to the oven. "I left it on warm." He drew out a casserole of bubbly lasagna.

Food wasn't something that usually excited her, but now the scent alone drew her over to his side. How long had it been since she'd seen someone take a homemade meal out of an oven? "It looks wonderful, too."

"My mother always told me food tastes better if it looks good." He picked up a long loaf of Italian bread and began slicing.

"You didn't cook this."

"Why not?" He glanced over his shoulder, amused that she was frowning again. She looked so thoughtful that he was tempted to run a fingertip down the faint line that formed between her brows. "Cooking's a very manageable skill if you approach it properly and have the right incentive."

Johanna stuck with carryout or prepackaged microwave meals. "And you have both?"

"I wanted to be an actor, but I didn't have any desire to be a starving actor." He poured garlic butter over the bread, set the oven, then slid it in. "After I came to California, I kicked around from audition to audition and from greasy spoon to greasy spoon. A couple of months of that and I called home and asked my mother for some recipes. She's a great cook." Sam drew the cork from a bottle of wine, then set it aside to breathe. "Anyway, it took me a lot less time to figure out how to sauté trout than it did for me to get a memorable part."

"Now that you've had a number of memorable parts, what's your incentive?"

"To cook?" He shrugged and took a leafy spinach salad from the refrigerator. "I like it. We're about ready here. You want to grab the wine? I thought we'd eat outside."

The trouble with Hollywood, Johanna thought as she

followed him out, was that things were never what they seemed. She'd been sure she had Sam Weaver pegged. But the man she'd assessed and dismissed wouldn't have copied recipes from his mother.

Nor was he the type, she thought as she set the wine down, who would have prepared a charming dinner for two, alfresco, with pretty blue stoneware plates and thick yellow candles. It was every bit as friendly as it was romantic. The romance she'd expected, and she knew just how to discourage it. The offer of friendship was another matter.

"Light those candles, will you?" He glanced around briefly, checking the way a man did when he was already certain things were just as he wanted them to be. "I'll get the rest."

Johanna watched him go back inside. Did someone who walked like that, she wondered—as though he were heading toward a shoot-out—really prepare spinach salad? She struck a match and held it to the wick of the first candle. Apparently so. There were more important things to lie about than cooking. She held the match to the second candle, then deliberately blew it out. She wouldn't have called avoiding three on a match superstitious. Just practical.

She heard the music he put on, something low and bluesy, with a lot of sax. While he brought out the rest of the meal, she poured the wine.

His instincts had been right, Sam thought as they settled at the wicker table. He'd been on the verge of making dinner reservations at some tony restaurant when he'd pulled back. He'd cooked for women before, but never here. He never brought anyone to the ranch, because the ranch was home. Private. Off limits to the press and the public, it was both refuge and sanctuary from a world he was a voluntary member of—when he chose to be. At the time, he hadn't been sure why he'd wanted to break his own rule with Johanna. Now he began to understand.

At the ranch he could be himself—no pretenses, no roles. Here he was Sam Weaver from Virginia, and here he was most comfortable. He didn't have to be *on* here. And he wanted to be himself with Johanna.

She wasn't without pretenses, he mused as he watched her. Not entirely. Unless he missed his guess, most of her resentment had faded, but not her distrust. He'd already decided to ease his curiosity and find the reason for it.

Maybe she'd been stung in an affair that had gone sour. Broken hearts often mended jaggedly. If she had been betrayed by a man she'd cared for and trusted, it would be logical that she would put up some defenses. It might take some time before he could wear them down, but he had a feeling it would be worth it. He'd start with what he believed was the focus of her life: her work.

"Were you happy with the taping the other day?"

"More than." She was too fair-minded not to give him his due. "You were really good, not just as far as the answers went, but overall. A lot of times you can have people zip right through the questions and be a dead bore." She broke off a piece of bread, then nibbled at the crust. He'd hit the right tone. It was always easy for her to relax when the subject was business. "And, of course, it was a coup to have you."

"I'm flattered."

She studied him again with those cool blue eyes. "I doubt it would be that easy to flatter you."

"An actor always wants to be wanted. Well, to a point, anyway," he added with another quick grin. "Do you know how many game shows I've turned down in the last couple of days?"

She smiled and sipped her wine. "Oh, I could hazard a guess."

"How'd you get into it? Producing?"

"Heredity." Her lips tightened only briefly. After taking a

second sip, she set her glass down. "I guess you could say I like pulling the strings."

"You'd have learned young with Carl Patterson as your father." He saw it, very briefly but very clearly. More than resentment, less than pain. "He's produced some of the best, and most successful television shows, as well as an impressive number of features. Being second-generation can be a strain, I imagine."

"You get past it." The lasagna was cheesy and rich with spices. Johanna concentrated on it. "This really is terrific. Your mother's recipe?"

"With some variations." So her father was off limits. He could respect that—for now. "How about the show itself? How did that get started?"

"With the flu." At ease again, she smiled and took another bite.

"Care to elaborate?"

"I had the flu, a nasty bout of it, a couple of years ago. I had to stay in bed for a week, and since it hurt my eyes to read, I lay there hour after hour and watched television. The game shows hooked me." She didn't object when he topped off her glass. The wine was very mellow and dry, and she knew her limit right down to the swallow. "You get involved, you know, in the games, and the people playing them. After a while you start rooting for them, tensing up in an effort to help them. When someone wins, the vicarious thrill is automatic. And then you have the advantage of almost always being smarter at home, because there's no pressure. That's a nice smug feeling."

He watched her as she spoke. She was animated now, the way she'd been while she'd rushed around the set making sure things fell into place. "So after your bout with the flu you decided to produce one."

"More or less." She could remember running into the brick wall of the network brass and ultimately having to appeal to her father. "In any case, I had the concept, and the experience in producing. I'd done a couple of documentaries for public television and had worked on a prime-time special. With a little string-pulling, we got a pilot done. Now we're only a couple of ratings points from being on top. I'm waiting for the go-ahead to start evening syndication."

"What happens then?"

"The demographics open. You get the kids who've finished their homework, the business crowd who want to put their feet up for a half hour. You up the ante. Give away some cars, bigger bucks."

She was surprised to discover she'd cleared her plate. Usually she ate a few bites, then ended up picking at the rest, impatient for the meal—and the time sitting down—to be over.

"Want some more?"

"No. Thanks." She picked up her wine as she studied him. "I know I lost the bet, but it looks as though I got the best part of the deal."

"Not from where I'm sitting."

The shades came down. Just like that. One compliment, however offhand, and she pulled back. Seeing it, Sam rose and offered a hand. "Want to walk? There's enough moonlight."

There was no point in being ungracious, Johanna told herself. She hated it when she became prickly over something unimportant. "All right. The only ranches I've ever seen have been on the back lot."

He bundled up the last of the bread, then handed it to her. "We'll go by the pond. You can feed the ducks."

"You have ducks?"

"Several overfed ducks." He slipped an arm around her shoulders to steer her. She smelled like the evening they walked through, quiet and promising. "I like looking at them in the morning."

"Your Jake in your last movie would have eaten them for breakfast."

"So you did see my last movie."

She took a quick nip at the tip of her tongue. "Oh, was that your last one?"

"Too late. You've already boosted my ego."

When she looked at him, his smile was appealing and too easy to respond to. *He* was too easy to respond to. In self-defense she looked back at the house.

"It's lovely from out here, too. You live all alone?"

"I like a little solitude now and then. Of course, I've got a few hands who look after things while I'm working, and Mae comes in a couple times a week to scoop at the dust." His hand slipped down to take hers. "My family comes out a few times a year and shakes everything up."

"Your parents visit you here?"

"Them, my brother, my two sisters, their families. Assorted cousins. The Weavers are a large and loud bunch."

"I see." But she didn't. She could only imagine. And envy. "They must be proud of you."

"They were always supportive, even when they thought I was crazy."

The pond was almost a quarter mile from the house, but the going was easy. It was obvious he walked the path often. She caught the scent of citrus, then the stronger scent of water. The moonlight struck it, highlighting the grass which had been left to grow ankle-high. Sensing an audience, several brown and speckled ducks paddled over to the water's edge.

"I've never had the nerve to come out here empty-handed," he told her. "I think they'd follow me home."

Johanna opened the linen cloth and broke off a crust of bread. It didn't even hit the water before it was gobbled up. She laughed; it was a low, delighted sound deep in her throat. Immediately she tore off another piece and, tossing this one farther out, watched a drake zoom in on it.

"I've always wanted to watch them from underneath so I could see their feet scramble." She continued to break off and toss. Ducks pursued the bread in groups and squabbled over it with bad-tempered quacks and competitive pecks. "My mother and I used to go out and feed the ducks. We'd give them silly names, then see if we could tell them apart the next time."

She caught herself, amazed that the memory had surfaced, stunned that she'd shared it. Her hand closed into a fist over the bread.

"There was a pond about five miles away when I was a kid," Sam said, as if he hadn't noticed her change in mood. "We used to ride our bikes to it during the summer, after we'd stolen a pack of crackers or whatever from the kitchen. We'd toss it out for the ducks—and a couple of pushy swans—and accidentally fall in as often as possible." He glanced out over the water. "Looks like someone's had a family."

She followed his gaze and saw a brown duck gliding along, trailed by a long shadow. As it came closer, Johanna saw that the shadow wasn't a shadow, it was fluffy ducklings. "Oh, aren't they sweet?" She crouched down for a closer look, forgetting about the hem of her skirt. The babies followed Mama on their evening swim, straight as an arrow. "I wish there was more light," she murmured.

"Come back when there is."

Johanna tilted her head up. In the moonlight his face was stronger, more attractive, than it had a right to be. The eyes, eyes that invariably drew women in, were as dark as the water.

And, as with the water, Johanna didn't know what lay beneath the surface. Turning away again, she continued shredding the bread and tossing it.

He liked the way her hair haloed around her face, stopping just inches from her shoulders. A man could fill his hands with it. It would be soft, like the hand she rarely offered but he continued to take. It would carry that same subtle scent.

Her skin would be like that, on the back of her neck beneath all that heavy blond hair. He had an urge to touch it now, to skim his fingers over it and see if she trembled.

The ducks stopped their chatter when the last of the bread was consumed. A few hopefuls hung around the edge of the pond for a minute longer, then, satisfied the treat was done, glided away. Into the sudden silence came a night bird's song, and the rustle of a rabbit running into the brush.

"It's a lovely spot," she said, rising and brushing the crumbs from her fingers. "I can see why you like it so much."

"I want you to come back."

It was said very simply, so it shouldn't have meant so much. Johanna didn't back away, because that would have been admitting it did. If her heart was beating a little faster, she could pretend otherwise. She reminded herself that things often seemed more important in the moonlight than they did in the day.

"We had a bet. I lost." She said it lightly, already aware that the tone wouldn't matter. "But that's been paid up tonight."

"This has nothing to do with bets or games." He touched her hair as he'd wanted to. "I want you to come back."

She should have been able to shrug it off, to nip it before whatever was beginning to grow would blossom. It wasn't as easy as it should have been to dredge up the cool smile and the careless refusal. She looked at him, really looked at him, and could think of only one thing to say.

"Why?"

His lips curved. She watched the smile move slowly over his face, the angles shifting, the shadows playing. "Damned if I know. But when you do come back, maybe we'll both have an answer. Meanwhile, why don't we get this one question out of the way?"

He leaned toward her. She'd told herself she didn't want to be kissed. She wouldn't like it. She wasn't a demonstrative person, and for her a kiss wasn't merely a touching of lips. Even though she'd grown up in a world where a kiss was nothing more than a handshake—and often less binding—to her it was a personal thing that meant affection, trust, warmth.

She'd told herself she wouldn't be kissed. But that had been before the moonlight and the bird's song. That had been before he'd touched her.

Her eyes were wary. He saw that even as he brushed his lips lightly over hers. He'd meant it to be light, casual, hardly more than a peace offering. She was so cool and lovely, and so firmly on guard, that he'd been unable to resist.

An easy kiss. A friendly kiss. That was where he'd meant to begin and end it. That was before he'd tasted her.

He drew back, not quite sure of his footing. He hadn't been prepared for whatever had rushed into him, not for the punch of it. With the water lapping beside them, he stared down at her. Moonlight was on her face, and he touched her cheek where the light played. She didn't move. He couldn't know that her own stunned reaction had left her rooted to the spot.

He touched her again, drawing his fingers back through her hair until they gripped it. Still she didn't move. But when his lips came to hers again, hard, hungry, she met passion with passion.

She'd never wanted it to be like this. Desire raced through her, pushing her to keep pace with it. His mouth ran along her jaw, across her face, making her shiver with pleasure, but she twisted until their lips joined again.

A craving she'd never known she had . . . a dream she'd never allowed into her waking hours . . . that was what he was. Wherever his hands touched, they lingered, as if he couldn't get enough. Lost in the first wave of pleasure, she pressed against him.

No, he couldn't get enough. He pulled her head back and deepened the kiss. She tasted like the night, dark, haunted. The thin silk under her jacket teased and shifted until he had to force back the urge to tear it away. He wanted her, all of her. There, in the tall, damp grass, he wanted to discover all her secrets and make them his own.

She was breathless when they drew apart. That frightened her. Caution and control had been hard-learned lessons, and she always, without exception, applied them to all the areas of her life. She'd lost them both in the flash of an instant, in the brush of his lips.

She had to remember what he was: an artist, both in his craft and with his women. More, she had to remember what *she* was. There was no room in her life for reckless passion in the moonlight.

He reached for her again, just to trace his knuckles along her cheek. Because even that affected her, she moved aside.

"This isn't the answer for either of us." She didn't like hearing the strain in her own voice, or the lingering huskiness he'd caused.

"It was a lot more than I bargained for," he admitted. The defenses were going up again. He took her hand before she could withdraw behind them completely. "I felt something the first time I saw you. Now I begin to see why."

"Lust at first sight?"

"Damn it, Johanna."

She'd hated herself the moment she'd said it, but she couldn't back down. If she backed down, she'd give in. "Let's let it go,

Sam. I'll be honest and say that was more than nice, but I'm just not interested in the sequel."

Anger stirred. He knew his own temper well enough to take things slow. He'd never decked a woman. Yet. "What are you interested in?"

She recognized barely restrained fury when she heard it. It was almost a relief. If he'd been kind, if he'd been the least bit persuasive, she would have crumbled. "My job." She tried for a smile and almost managed it. "That's really enough complications for me."

"Lady, anybody who can kiss like that is just asking for complications."

She hadn't known she could kiss like that. She certainly hadn't known she'd wanted to. And what was even more unnerving was that she wanted to kiss him again. "I suppose that's a compliment. Shall we just say it was an interesting evening and leave it at that?"

"No."

"That's the best I can do."

He touched her hair again. It wasn't a testing gesture this time, it was a possessive one. "Okay. You'll learn as you go along."

She couldn't pretend to be amused, because he was frightening her. It wasn't a fear that he would drag her to the ground and finish what they'd both started, but it was a fear that he would prove to be stronger-willed and much more determined than she.

Stay out of his way, her mind warned her. And get started on it now.

"It was much too nice an evening to end it with an argument. I appreciate the meal and the walk. Now it's getting late, and since it's a long drive, we should be going."

"All right." He was much too annoyed to fight with her.

Better, he thought, that he do exactly as she asked, then re-evaluate the situation. Turning homeward, he reached out to guide her so that she wouldn't stumble. When she jerked at his touch, he smiled again, and most of his annoyance left him.

"The longest trips are often the most eventful, don't you think?"

She thought it best to leave that question unanswered.

CHAPTER 4

"Just how many cases of Diet Zing do we have?" Johanna waited for Bethany to run down her list.

"Considering what the crew pinched, about a hundred and fifty cases. We're square on the porto-vacs and the gift certificates and, of course, the encyclopedias." Bethany turned over the list of parting gifts. Though she thought it odd that Johanna was staring out the window rather than checking off her own list, she didn't comment. "About the home viewers' contest," Bethany began.

"Hmmm?"

"The home viewers' contest?"

"Oh." Johanna swore at herself, then pulled her gaze away from the window and her mind away from Sam Weaver. Daydreaming was always a waste of time, but it was a sin during office hours. "I want to get that nailed down this morning." She unlocked the top drawer of her desk and pulled out a file. "I have several potential questions. Research put in a lot of extra time on it last week. The idea is to have John Jay announce a different one every day, somewhere during the program." She glanced down the list again to satisfy herself. "I don't want him to do it at the same time every day, particularly not at the beginning. If we're going to draw people in, I want them to watch all day, all week. Is the deal on the car set?"

"Almost. We're going with the American product and tying it in with the drawing the week of the Fourth of July."

"Fine, but I want two."

"Two what?"

"Two cars, Beth. Watch *Trivia Alert* and win." She smiled a bit and tapped the end of her pencil on the desk. "Two luxury cars. One should be a convertible. People in Omaha with two kids don't usually buy convertibles. Let's make it a red one, at least for the ads. We'll have the full-sized car in white and John Jay in a blue suit."

"Hit them over the head with patriotism?"

"Something like that. See if we can bring the total value up to fifty thousand."

"Sure." Bethany blew her bangs away from her eyes. "I'll use charm. And if that doesn't work I'll use Mongo the enforcer."

"Use the ratings," Johanna suggested. "I want a big ad in the *TV Guide* and the Sunday supplements. Black and white for the guide, color for the supplements." She waited while Bethany made her notes. "The ten-second spot at ten is already set. We'll tape it as soon as the cars are delivered. We have to pick five questions from the list." She handed Bethany a copy. "And the list doesn't go out of this office."

Bethany skimmed down. "Where did Betty meet the leader of the pack?" Lips pursed, she glanced up. "Betty who?"

"Brush up on your girl groups. Early-sixties rock and roll."

Bethany merely made a face. "These are pretty tough."

That was exactly what she'd wanted to hear. "They're worth fifty thousand."

Giving a quiet murmur of agreement, she checked another question. "Johanna, how could anyone know how many witches were burned at the stake in Salem?"

"None." Sitting back, Johanna ran the pencil through her fingers. "They were hanged."

"Oh. Well, so far I'm batting a thousand." When Johanna's phone rang, Bethany took another hard look at the questions.

"Mr. Weaver's on the line, Ms. Patterson."

Johanna opened her mouth and was surprised when nothing came out.

"Ms. Patterson?"

"What? Oh, tell Mr. Weaver I'm in a meeting."

When she hung up, Beth glanced over. "I wouldn't have minded waiting."

"I doubt he's calling to discuss the show." Telling herself to dismiss it, Johanna picked up her list and made her eyes focus. "What do you think about number six?"

"I don't know that answer, either. Johanna . . ." Outgoing and candid herself, Bethany nonetheless understood and respected her boss's restraint. "Did everything go okay the other night?"

It would have been foolish to pretend to misunderstand. "It went fine. Very pleasant." Johanna dug into her pocket for a roll of antacids. "I'm leaning toward numbers one, four, six, nine and thirteen."

Beth looked at each one, decided she might have an inkling about question thirteen, then nodded. "Let's go for them." She handed the list back so that Johanna could lock them up. "Could we pretend we're out of the office, maybe at home with our feet up and a nice bottle of wine already half-gone?"

Johanna turned the key and pocketed it. "Do you have a problem, Beth?"

"No, but I'd swear you did."

"I'm fine." Johanna began to stack and straighten papers on her desk. "We had a friendly dinner, some pleasant conversation, and that was that. I have no idea why Sam's calling me at the office, but I don't have time to chat with him."

"I didn't mention Sam," Bethany pointed out. "You did. I

only mentioned a problem." She smiled sympathetically. "I get the feeling they're the same thing."

Johanna rose and, with her hands in the deep pockets of her skirt, walked to the window. "He just can't get it through his head that I'm not interested."

"Are you? Not interested, I mean," Bethany supplied when Johanna turned her head.

"I don't want to be interested. It's the same thing."

"No. If you weren't interested you'd be able to smile, maybe pat him on the head and say thanks but no thanks. Not wanting to be interested means you are and you get around it by avoiding phone calls and making excuses."

Johanna pushed a thumb into the ivy geranium hanging in a basket at her window. The soil was moist. She'd watered it herself that morning. "How did you get to be an expert?"

"Unfortunately, most of it comes from observation rather than execution. He seems like a nice guy, Johanna."

"Maybe, but I don't have room for men right now, and less than none for actors."

"That's a hard line."

"It's a hard town."

Bethany wasn't willing to buy that. True, she'd only lived in L.A. for three years, but it still fascinated her. To her it remained the town where dreams could be chased and caught. "I hope you're not going to break my heart and tell me he's a jerk."

"No." With a reluctant smile, Johanna turned again. "No, he's not a jerk. Actually, you're right, he's a very nice guy, charming, easy to talk to—" She caught herself. "For an actor."

"He makes my insides tingle," Bethany confessed, unashamed and artless.

Mine, too, Johanna thought. Which was precisely why she wasn't going to see him again. "You're supposed to be concentrating on your screenwriter," she said briskly, then stopped when she saw Beth's expression. "Trouble?"

"He dumped me." She shrugged her shoulders in an uncon- cerned gesture. Johanna only had to look at Beth's eyes to see how much she was hurting. "It's no big deal, really. We weren't serious."

Maybe he wasn't, Johanna thought with a mixture of sym- pathy and resignation. "I'm sorry. Everyone has spats, Beth."

Bethany understood that, had even expected it. She hadn't expected deceit. "We went a little beyond that. It's better this way, really it is. I thought he was interested in me, you know, but when I found out he was more interested in my position—" She caught herself, swore silently, then smiled. "Doesn't mat- ter. He was just one of the many toads you have to go through to find the prince."

"What about your position?" It never took Johanna long to put two and two together. Screenwriter, assistant producer. Toss in ambition and it added up perfectly. "Did he want you to hawk a script?"

Uncomfortable, Bethany shifted. "Not exactly."

"Spit it out, Beth."

"All right. He had the idea that I could influence you to in- fluence your father to produce his screenplay. When I told him it wouldn't work, he got mad, then I got mad, and one thing led to another." She didn't add that it had been ugly. She didn't have to.

"I see." Why were there so many creeps in this world? Johanna wondered. So many users. "I am sorry, Beth."

"Bruises fade," Beth said easily, though she was aware hers would last a long time. "Besides, I've got the satisfaction of hoping he sells nothing but commercial jingles for the next ten or twenty years."

"Do yourself a favor," Johanna advised her. "Fall in love

with an insurance salesman." She glanced toward the door as her secretary popped a head in.

"Telegram, Ms. Patterson."

With a murmured thank-you, Johanna took it. Stupid, she told herself as her fingers tensed on the paper. It had been almost twenty-five years since she'd gotten that brief and heartbreaking telegram from her mother. She hadn't even been old enough to read it herself. Shoving back the memory, she tore the envelope open.

I can be as stubborn as you. Sam.

Johanna scowled at the single line, read it twice, then crumpled it into a ball. But instead of tossing it in the waste-basket, she shoved it into her pocket.

"Bad news?" Bethany asked.

"A weak threat," Johanna said, picking up her remote. "The show's starting."

* * *

The damn woman was making him crazy. Sam groomed the mare, who'd been bred only hours before to his prize stud. She was still skittish and prone to nip. High-strung, pedigreed and temperamental, she reminded Sam of Johanna. That made him smile, if a bit grimly. He didn't think Johanna would appreciate being compared to a horse, not even a purebred.

She hadn't returned one of his calls. *Miss Patterson is unavailable. Miss Patterson is in a meeting.*

Miss Patterson is avoiding you like the plague.

He was beginning to feel like a gawky teenager with a crush on the class princess. More than once he'd told himself to write her off, to find some less complicated woman to spend an evening with.

The mare turned her head and took aim at his shoulder.

Sam merely shifted out of range and continued to stroke and soothe. He didn't want to spend the evening with a less complicated woman. He wanted to spend it with Johanna. Just a test, he told himself, to see if whatever had happened by the pond would happen again. And if it did, what the hell was he going to do about it?

He was better off not seeing her again. A man had a lot more freedom when he cluttered up his life with many women than when he found himself concentrating on only one. He wasn't trying to concentrate on her, he reminded himself. He just couldn't get her out of his head.

What secrets did she have tucked away inside her? He had to find out.

When she'd kissed him . . . there had been no secrets there. She'd been open, passionate and as honest as a man could hope for. It hadn't been ordinary. He knew what it was to kiss a woman for pleasure, for obligation or because the script called for it. That moment with Johanna had been nothing so simple as pleasure, and it had been nothing so casual as obligation. The reaction—his *and* hers—hadn't been in any script.

She'd been as stunned as he was, and as unnerved. Didn't she want to know why?

The hell with what she wanted, Sam decided as he shut the stall door. *He* had to know why. Whether she wanted to or not, Johanna was going along for the ride.

* * *

She was beat. Johanna downed two aspirin and a carton of yogurt at her kitchen sink. Her afternoon had been taken up by back-to-back meetings, and though she should have been celebrating the nighttime syndication of *Trivia*, she'd opted for a quiet evening at home. She'd have to set up a party for the crew next week. They deserved it. And she'd see that Beth got a raise. For tonight, she didn't want to think about production meetings or sponsors. Her flowers needed tending.

The sun was warm on her face and arms as she walked outside to her garden. The roses that climbed the trellis along the side of the house needed pinching off. Snapdragons and hollyhocks needed weeding. Some of the taller and heavier-bloomed plants would require staking. Pleased with the scents and colors, she dug in.

She'd spent many quiet afternoons with the gardener on her father's estate, learning the names of the plants and the care they required. He'd let her have a plot of her own and had shown her how to turn soil and plant seeds, how to separate at the roots and prune. She'd learned how to blend plants for color, texture, height and flowering periods from him. On rainy days, or during cold snaps, he'd let her explore the greenhouse, where fragile seedlings had been nursed or exotic bulbs forced for early blooming.

The scents there had never been forgotten, the sultriness, the heat, even the damp smell of watered soil. He'd been a kind man, a little stoop-shouldered and thick through the middle. During one brief fantasy she'd imagined he was her father and they'd gone into business together.

She hadn't known until she'd heard him talking with another servant that he'd felt sorry for her.

All the servants had felt sorry for her—the little girl who was only brought out and paraded at her father's whim. She'd had a three-story dollhouse, a tea set of English china and a white fur coat. There had been ballet lessons and piano lessons and French taught by a private tutor. Other little girls would have dreamed of having what Johanna had only had to lift a hand for.

At six, her picture had been splashed across the press. She'd worn a red velvet dress that had skimmed her ankles and a tiny diamond tiara as flower girl at her father's second wedding. A Hollywood princess.

The bride had been an Italian actress who enjoyed having tantrums. Her father had spent a good deal of that two-year union on the Italian Riviera. Johanna had spent most of it in the gardens of his Beverly Hills estate.

There had been a scandal and a mudslinging divorce. The actress had kept the Italian villa, and her father had had a blistering affair with the lead in his next production. Johanna, at age eight, had already developed a cool and all-too-adult view of relationships.

She preferred her flowers. She didn't like wearing gloves. She felt that she got a better sense of the soil and the fragile roots with her hands uncovered. When she managed to squeeze in time for a manicure, she was usually met with shock and dismay. As a matter of routine, Johanna kept her nails clipped short and didn't bother with enamel.

Unfeminine. That was what Lydia had called her. Lydia had been one of her father's more vocal and longer-lasting distractions. Lydia had been palely beautiful and unceasingly selfish. Fortunately, she hadn't wanted to marry Carl Patterson any more than he had wanted to marry her.

Send the girl to the nuns in Switzerland, darling. Nothing like nuns for teaching a girl a little femininity and grace.

Johanna, at twelve, had lived in terror that she would be sent away, but Lydia had been replaced before she'd managed to pressure Carl into paying the tuition.

Unfeminine. The word still cropped up in Johanna's head from time to time. She usually ignored it; she'd found her own style of womanhood. But now and again, like an old scar, the word caused an itch.

On her hands and knees, she brushed through her patio dahlias, back to the freesia that would bloom in another few weeks. With care and precision, she pulled out any weeds that had had the audacity to sprout. It had been a dry spring, and after testing the soil she decided she'd give everything a good soak before calling it a day.

She heard the car but didn't bother to glance up, because she expected it to drive by. When it didn't, Johanna had just enough time to look around before Sam swung out of the driver's side.

She said nothing and remained kneeling, speechless.

He was furious. The long drive from his ranch had given him plenty of time to work on his temper. Here he was chasing after some cool-eyed go-to-hell blonde and all he could think of when he saw her was how she'd looked in the moonlight.

It was dusk now, the light soft and tenuous. She was kneeling in front of a bank of flowers like some pagan virgin sacrifice. She didn't rise, and her hands were stained with soil and grass. The air smelled like sin, dark and rich.

"Why the hell do you have a secretary and an answering machine if you don't intend to answer messages?"

"I've been busy."

"What you are is rude."

She hated that. Hated knowing it was true. "I'm sorry." She put on her coolest and most professional smile. "The show's going into syndication and I've been tied up with meetings and paperwork. Was there something important?"

"You know damn well it's important."

She spent the next ten seconds carefully wiping the worst of the dirt from her hands onto her jeans and staring at his boots. "If there's a problem with your contract—"

"Cut it, Johanna. We've done our business. That's over."

She looked at him then. "Yes, that's right."

He stuck his hands in his pockets. If he'd had them free much longer he might have throttled her. "I don't like feeling like a fool."

"I'm sure you don't." She rose, careful to keep an arm's

length of distance between them. "I'm losing the light, Sam. If there's nothing else . . ." The rest of the words slid down her throat when he grabbed her by her shirtfront.

"You're going to turn away from me once too often," he said quietly. Much too quietly. "I've always considered myself fairly even-tempered. Seems I was wrong."

"Your temperament's not my problem."

"The hell it isn't." To prove his point, he yanked her against him. Her hands came up automatically for balance and defense. But his mouth was already on hers.

There was no testing kiss this time, no friendly overture. There was only the outpouring of urgency and demand that had clawed inside him for days. She didn't struggle. He hated to think of what he might have done if she had. Instead, she went very still, and for a moment nearly fooled them both into thinking she was unaffected.

Then she moaned. The sound went from her mouth into his, filled with surrender and despair. Before the sound had died her arms were around him, her fingers digging into his shoulders.

Twilight deepened, cooling the air, but she felt only the heat from his body as she pressed against him. He smelled of horses and leather. Dazed, she thought that the scent must be part of some deeply buried fantasy. Knight on white charger. But she didn't want to be rescued. Like a fool, she'd thought she could escape, from him, from herself. It only took a moment to show her how firmly she was already bound.

He brushed his mouth across her face, drawing in the taste, the softness. Her lips skimmed his jaw as she, too, searched for more. He tightened his arms around her. He'd thought he'd understood what it was to ache for a woman. Nothing had ever come close to this. He hurt everywhere, with a pain more erotic than anything he'd ever imagined. The more he touched, the more he hurt. The more he hurt, the more he was driven to touch.

"I want you, Johanna." His hands were in her hair now, as if he couldn't trust them to wander over her again. "I haven't been able to stop thinking about you for days. For nights. I want to be with you. Now."

She wanted it, too. A shudder ran through her as she clung to him. She wanted him. She wanted to let go of her control, of her caution, and just feel—the way he could make her feel. Somehow she already knew that he could bring her things she'd never believed in. Once he did, she'd never be the same.

For a moment longer, she held on. Regret, more than she'd ever known, replaced desire as she drew away. With an effort she managed a smile as she glanced at the smudges on his shoulders. "My hands were dirty."

He took them both. "Let's go inside."

"No." Gently she drew her hands from his. "It wouldn't work, Sam. *We* wouldn't work."

"Why?"

"Because I wouldn't want it to. I wouldn't let it work."

He took her chin in his hand. "Bull."

"I wouldn't." She wrapped her fingers around his wrist. The pulse was fast there, as fast as her own. "I'm attracted to you, I won't deny that. But it can't lead anywhere."

"It already has."

"Then it can't lead any farther. Believe me when I say I'm sorry, but we're both better off facing up to it now."

"I'm sorry, too, but I can't accept it." He moved his hand to her cheek in a gesture that pierced her with its tenderness. "If you're expecting me to walk away and leave you alone, you're going to be disappointed."

She took a deep breath and met his eyes squarely. "I'm not going to sleep with you."

His brow lifted. "Now, or ever?"

The last thing she'd expected to do was laugh, but the chuckle bubbled out. "Good night, Sam."

"Hold on. We're not finished." There was amusement in his voice as he gestured toward her front steps. "Why don't we sit down? It's a nice night." When she hesitated, he lifted his hands, palms out. "No contact."

"All right." She wasn't completely at ease with it but felt perhaps she owed them both that much. "Would you like a drink?"

"What have you got?"

"This morning's coffee."

"I'll skip it, thanks." He settled comfortably next to her, hip to hip. "I do like your place, Johanna," he began, wondering if he would be able to understand her better through it. "It's quiet, private, well looked-after. How long have you had it?"

"About five years."

"Did you plant all this?"

"Yes."

"What are those?"

She looked over to the edge of one of her borders. "Soapwort."

"Ugly name for such a pretty thing." The little pink flowers looked delicate, but he could see that they spread exactly as they chose. "You know, it occurs to me that we don't know each other very well." He leaned back against the next step, stretching his legs out. Johanna thought he looked very much at home.

"No," she said cautiously. "I suppose we don't."

"You believe in dating?"

She hooked her hands around her knees and smiled. "It's a nice occupation for teenagers."

"You don't figure adults can pull it off?"

On guard again, she moved her shoulders. "Most people I know have lovers, not boyfriends."

"And you don't have either."

"I like it that way."

The way she said it made him glance back at the little pink flowers again. "Why don't we shoot for another term, like companion?" He turned to study her profile. "We could try being companions for a while. That's an easy, uncomplicated term. No strings."

It sounded that way, but she knew better. "I meant what I said before."

"I'm sure you did." He crossed his feet at the ankles. "That's why I figured you wouldn't be afraid to get to know me better."

"I'm not afraid," she said immediately, showing him that he'd hit the right button.

"Good. There's a benefit Friday night at the Beverly Wilshire. I'll pick you up at seven."

"I don't—"

"You support raising funds for the homeless, don't you?"

"Of course I do, but—"

"And since you're not afraid, it wouldn't bother you to be my companion. It's formal," he continued smoothly. "I don't care much for that kind of evening myself, but it's for a good cause."

"I appreciate the offer, but I simply couldn't manage to get home from work and change in time for a formal function at the Wilshire by seven." And that, she thought, should be the end of that.

"All right, I'll pick you up at your office. That way we can make it seven-thirty."

She let out a huge breath, then shifted so that she could look at him directly. "Sam, why are you trying to maneuver me this way?"

"Johanna . . ." He took her hand and kissed her fingers, too quickly for her to object. "I can maneuver much better than this."

"I'll just bet."

Delighted, he grinned. "I love it when you use that tone. It's so proper. Makes me want to muss you up."

"You didn't answer my question."

"Which question? Oh, that one," he finished when she narrowed her eyes. "I'm not trying to maneuver you, I'm trying to make a date with you. No, not a date," he corrected. "No dates for adults. We can't call it a meeting, that's too businesslike. How about encounter? You like encounter?"

"I don't think so."

"One thing I've found out about you already, Johanna, is that you're a hard woman to please." He stretched out again with a sigh. "But that's all right. I can sit right here until you come up with the right choice of words. Stars are coming out."

Involuntarily she glanced up. She often sat out by herself in the evening. She'd been content to look at the stars alone. Somehow the night seemed more appealing with him there, and that worried her. Depending on someone else for your contentment was a big mistake.

"It's getting chilly," she murmured.

"Are you asking me in?"

She smiled, then rested her elbow on her knee. "It's not that chilly." They were silent for a moment. Then the silence was broken by a nighthawk. "Why aren't you down in the city at some club being seen with some up-and-coming actress with lots of teeth?"

As if he were thinking it through, Sam rested his elbows on the back of the step. "I don't know. Why aren't you down in the city at some club being seen with some hotshot director with a perfect tan?"

Still pouting a bit, she kept her head still but shifted her gaze over to him. "I asked you first."

"I love acting," he said after a moment. His voice was so calm and serious that she turned her head again. "I really love it when it all comes together—the script, the moves, the crew. And I don't mind being paid well for it, either. I've got a couple of weeks before we start shooting. Once we do, there are going to be a lot of very long and very demanding days. I don't want to waste the little time I have in a club." He touched her hair. They both remembered he'd promised there would be no contact, but she didn't object. "Are you going to come back and feed my ducks, Johanna?"

It was a mistake, she told herself as she smiled at him. A stupid one. At least she was making it with her eyes open. "I think I can make it Friday night, if you don't mind leaving the benefit a bit early. I'll have put in a full day at the office."

"Seven-thirty, at your office?"

"Fine. No strings?"

"Deal."

The minute he leaned toward her, she held up a hand. "Don't kiss me, Sam."

He backed off, not without effort. "Now, or ever?"

She rose and brushed off the seat of her jeans. "Now, anyway. I'll see you tomorrow."

"Johanna." She paused at the top of the steps and looked back. "Nothing," he told her. "I just wanted to look at you again. Night."

"Drive carefully. It's a long trip."

He threw her a grin over his shoulder. "It's getting shorter all the time."

CHAPTER 5

By five-thirty the offices were like a tomb. Johanna was happy enough to have an extra hour to herself. Paperwork that never seemed to diminish during the normal working day could be gotten through in an uninterrupted hour. Questions for Monday's taping had been chosen and checked, but Johanna took the time to go over them herself to be certain they were as entertaining as they were educational.

She answered a pile of memos, read and signed letters and approved a stack of bills. The beauty of game shows, she thought as she worked, was that they were cheap to produce. In a big week they could give away over fifty thousand dollars and still come in at a fraction of the cost of a thirty-minute situation comedy.

She was still determined to get her other concept on the air, and was ready to make her pitch for the pilot so that when things clicked the show could debut in the fall. And they would click, Johanna promised herself. One more success, one more solid success, and her own production company could begin its struggle for survival.

Garden Variety Productions. She could already see the logo. Within two years others would see it, as well. And remember it.

She'd continue to do the games, of course, but she'd begin to expand her own horizons, as well. A daytime drama, a couple of prime-time movies, a weekly series. She could already see it building, step by step. But for now she had to concentrate on getting through the rest of the day. And the evening.

After her desk was cleared, Johanna brought out her secret. She'd hidden the bag in her bottom drawer, behind the office stationery. There'd been enough commotion over her bringing an evening dress to the office. Now Johanna pulled the box from the bag, opened it, then read the instructions through twice. It didn't seem that complicated. She'd make it an adventure, she told herself, even if it was silly. She'd told herself it was silly even as she'd let the clerk talk her into buying them.

Johanna set her equipment in orderly lines, with the instructions handy, then examined her hands, back, then palms. The clerk hadn't been wrong about her nails being a mess. And what was wrong with trying something new? Johanna picked up the first fake fingernail and began to file it. She tested it often, placing it on her short, unpainted thumbnail until she was satisfied that the length wasn't extravagant. Only nine more to go, she thought, and began to attack the rest.

As she worked, she slipped out of her shoes and curled her legs under her. It was a position she never would have permitted herself to take if anyone had been in the office. Alone, she switched to it without thinking. Once she had ten uniformly filed nails on her blotter, she went on to the next stage.

The instructions told her it was easy, quick and neat. Johanna peeled off the adhesive and pressed it against her nail. Easy. With the tweezers she carefully caught the tip of the backing and began to peel it off. The adhesive rolled into a ball. Patiently Johanna removed it and tried again. The third time she managed to make it stick. Pleased, she picked up the first nail and aligned it carefully over her own. After pressing down, she examined the result.

It didn't look like her thumb, but it was rather elegant. After she painted it with the Shell-Pink Fizz enamel the clerk had sold her, no one would know the difference.

It took her twenty minutes to complete one hand, and she had to resort to digging out her reading glasses—something else she never would have done unless completely alone. She was swearing at the clerk, at herself and at the manufacturer when the phone rang. Johanna hit line one and popped the nail off her index finger.

"Johanna Patterson," she said between her teeth.

"It's John Jay, honey. I'm so glad you're a workaholic."

Johanna glared at her naked index finger. "What is it?"

"I've got a teeny little problem, sweetheart, and need you to come to my rescue." When she said nothing, he cleared his throat. "Listen, it seems my credit card's at the limit and I'm in a bit of an embarrassment. Would you mind talking to the manager here at Chasen's? He says he knows you."

"Put him on." Disgusted, she ran her hand through her hair and popped off another nail. It took less than two minutes to squeeze John Jay out of his embarrassment. After she hung up the phone, Johanna looked at her hand. Two of the nails she'd meticulously placed were gone, and her fingers were smeared with adhesive. Letting out a long breath, she began to remove the rest.

She was an intelligent, capable woman, she reminded herself. She was a hop and a skip away from being thirty and she held down a complex and demanding job. She was also probably the only woman in the country who couldn't attach fake nails.

The hell with it. She dumped everything, including the bottle of enamel, into the trash.

She did what she could with her hair in the women's lounge. Then, because she was feeling unfeminine and klutzy, she went dramatic with her makeup. Dressed only in thigh-high stockings and tap pants, she unzipped the garment bag. She'd only worn the gown once before, a year ago. It was strapless and clingy, a far cry from her usual style. With a shrug, Johanna stepped into it, and shimmied it up, then fought to reach the zipper. She swore again and wondered why she'd allowed herself to be talked into going out at all. Once the dress was secured, she tried to see as much of herself as possible in the waist-high mirrors.

It was a good fit, she decided as she turned to the side. And the color—which, she remembered grimly, would have matched the enamel now in the trash—was flattering. Though she couldn't see it, the hem skimmed her knees in the front, then graduated down to full-length in the back. Johanna changed her everyday earrings for pearl-and-diamond circles, then clasped on a matching choker.

As good as it gets, she thought, and zipped her office clothes in the bag. She'd have her secretary send them to the cleaners on Monday. With the bag slung over her arm, she started back to her office. She'd been wise to have Sam meet her here, Johanna decided. Not only did it make it less like a date, there was the added security that she'd have to be dropped off back in the parking garage so that she could drive herself home.

The coward's way. She shrugged her shoulders with a touch of annoyance as she walked. The safe way, she corrected. Whatever she was feeling for Sam was a little too fast and a little too intense. Having an affair wasn't in her plans, professionally or personally. She'd simply lived through too many of her father's.

Her life would never be like his.

As far as Sam Weaver was concerned, she would be sensible, cautious and, above all, in complete control of the situation.

Oh, God, he looked wonderful.

He was standing in her office by the window, his hands in the pockets of his tux and his thoughts on something she couldn't see. Pleasure, hardly comfortable, slammed into her. If she'd believed in happily-ever-afters, she would have believed in him.

He hadn't heard her, but he'd been thinking about her hard enough, deeply enough, that he'd known the moment she'd stepped into the doorway. He turned, and his image of her dissolved and reassembled.

She looked so fragile with her hair swept up off her neck and her shoulders bare. The business-first office had suited the woman he'd first met. The pretty garden and isolated house had suited the woman who'd laughed with him beside the pond. But this was a new Johanna, one who seemed too delicate to touch.

As ridiculous as it made him feel, he had to catch his breath. "I thought you'd skipped out."

"No." When she realized her knuckles were turning white clutching her summer bag, she relaxed them. "I was changing." Because she wanted badly to act natural, she made herself move to the closet. "I'm sorry if I'm a bit behind. I got caught up. Work," she said, and with a quick glance made certain the fiasco of plastic nails and polish was out of sight.

"You look wonderful, Johanna."

"Thanks." She shut the closet door, trying to take the compliment with the same ease with which it was given. "So do you. I'm ready whenever you are."

"I need another minute." He crossed to her, catching the quick surprise in her eyes just before he covered her bare shoulders with his hands and kissed her. He lingered over the kiss, struggling to keep the pressure light, the demand minimal. "Just wanted to see if you were real," he murmured.

She was real, all right, so real that she could feel her own blood pumping hot and, quick. "We should go."

"I'd rather stay here and neck. Well, maybe some other time," he added when he saw her brow lift. With her hand in his, he started out of the office toward the elevators. "Listen, if this is really boring we could leave early. Take a drive."

"Hollywood galas are never boring." She said it so dryly that he laughed.

"You don't like them."

"I don't often find it necessary to attend them." She stepped into the elevator as the door opened.

"It's hard to be a part of a world and ignore it at the same time."

"No, it's not." She'd been doing it for years. "Some of us do better behind the scenes. I saw one of the early ads for your miniseries," she continued, changing the subject before he had a chance to probe. "It looked good, very classy, very sexy."

"That's marketing," he said dismissively as the elevator reached the underground parking garage. "It's not really sexy. It's romantic. There's a difference."

There was indeed, but it surprised her that he knew it. "When you've got your shirt off and your chest is gleaming, people think sex."

"Is that all it takes?" He opened the passenger door of his car. "I can be out of this cummerbund in under five seconds."

She swung her legs into the car. "Thanks, but I've already seen your chest. Why television?" she asked when he'd joined her. "At this point in your career, I mean."

"Because the majority of people won't sit still in a theater for four hours, and I wanted to do this movie. The small screen's more personal, more intimate, and so was this script." The car's engine echoed in the nearly empty garage as he backed up and began to drive out. "The character of Sarah is so fragile, so tragic. She's so absolutely trusting and naive. It knocked me out the way Lauren pulled it off," he added, referring to his co-star. "She really found the essence of that innocence."

And, according to the press, he and Lauren had had as many

love scenes away from the cameras as they had in front of them. It would be wise, Johanna reminded herself, to remember that. "It's not usual to hear an actor talk about a character other than his own."

"Luke's a bastard," Sam said simply as he stopped at a light. "An opportunist, a womanizer and a heel. A very charming, glib-tongued one."

"Did you capture his essence?"

He studied Johanna before the light changed. "You'll have to watch and tell me."

Deliberately she turned away. "What's your next project?"

"It's a comedy."

"I didn't know you did comedy."

"Obviously you missed my tour de force as the Raisin Crunch man a few years ago."

The chuckle welled up. "I'm embarrassed to say I did."

"That's all right. I'm embarrassed to say I didn't. That was right before I did the Mano cologne commercials. 'What woman can resist a man who smells like a man?'"

She would have laughed again if she hadn't remembered her own reaction to everything about him, including his scent. "Well, no one can say you haven't paid your dues."

"I like to think I have, and I'm also aware that the Mano campaign got me a reading for *Undercover*."

She was sure it had. Johanna hadn't missed those particular ads. In them, Sam had been blood-pumpingly sexy, intensely male and cocky enough to make a woman's mouth water. His character in *Undercover* had been precisely the same, but with an underlying depth that had surprised both the audience and the critics.

"Those kind of breaks don't happen very often," she said aloud. "When they do, they're usually deserved."

"Well . . ." He drew the word out. "I think that was a compliment."

She shrugged. "I've never said you weren't good at what you do."

"Maybe we could turn that around and say the problem from the outset has been that I am." She said nothing, but he thought that was answer enough.

Her brow creased a bit as they drove up to the well-lit limousine-adorned Beverly Wilshire. "Looks like quite a crowd."

"We can still go back to your office and neck."

She gave him a brief, very bland look as one of the uniformed staff opened her door. The moment she was on the curb, strobe lights and cameras flashed.

She hated that. She didn't have the words to explain even to herself how much she hated it. With a gesture that could be taken for one of aloofness rather than panic, she turned away. Sam slipped an arm around her and by doing so caused a dozen more flashes.

"They hound you less if you smile and cooperate," he murmured in her ear.

"Mr. Weaver! Mr. Weaver! What can you tell us about your upcoming television miniseries?"

Sam aimed his answer at the crowd of reporters and personalized it with a smile even as he started to walk. "With a quality script and a cast that includes Lauren Spencer, I think it speaks for itself."

"Is your engagement to Miss Spencer off?"

"It was never on."

One of the reporters got close enough to grab Johanna's arm. "Could we have your name, Miss?"

"Patterson," she said, and shook him off.

"Carl Patterson's girl," she heard someone in the crowd say. "That's the old man's daughter. Ms. Patterson, is it true your father's marriage is on the rocks? How do you feel about him being linked with a woman half his age?"

Saying nothing, Johanna swept through the front doors into the lobby.

"Sorry." Sam kept his arm around her. She was trembling a bit with what he took for anger.

"You had nothing to do with it." She only needed a moment, she thought, to calm down. Yes, there was anger, but there was also that stomach-churning distress that swooped down on her whenever she was confronted with cameras and demanding questions about her father. It had happened before and would happen again, as long as she was the daughter of Carl W. Patterson.

"You want to slip into the bar and get a drink? Sit in a dark corner for a minute?"

"No. No, really, I'm fine." As the tension eased, she smiled up at him. "I'd hate to go through that as often as you must."

"It's part of the job." But he lifted her chin with a finger. "Are you sure you're okay?"

"Of course. I think I'll just—"

But her plans for a brief escape were scotched when several people walked over to greet Sam.

She knew them, some by sight, others by reputation. Sam's co-star in his last feature was with her husband and happily pregnant with her first child. The elite of the press who had been permitted inside took the photo opportunity.

As they inched their way to the ballroom, others came by to renew an acquaintance or be introduced. Through her father she knew a great many of them herself. There were cheeks to be kissed, hugs to be given, hands to be shaken. A veteran actor with a silver mane of hair and a face that still graced billboards squeezed her. With an affection she felt for few, Johanna hugged him back. She'd never forgotten how he had come up to her room and entertained her with stories long ago, during one of her father's parties.

"Uncle Max, you're even more handsome than ever."

His laugh was low and gravelly as he kept his arm around her. "Jo-Jo. Looking at you makes me feel old."

"You'll never be old."

"Mary will want to see you," he said, speaking of his long-time and only wife. "She's run off with a safari to the ladies' room." He kissed her cheek again, then turned to size up Sam. "So you've finally broken down and taken on an actor. At least you've chosen a good one. I've admired your work."

"Thank you." After six years in the business, Sam had thought he was immune to being starstruck. "It's an honor to meet you, Mr. Heddison," he said, and he meant it. "I've seen everything you've ever done."

"Little Jo-Jo always had taste. I'd like to work with you sometime. Not many of this generation I'd say that to."

"Tell me when and where."

With his eyes narrowed, Max gave a slow nod. "I've a script I've been considering. Maybe I'll send it along and let you have a look. Jo-Jo, I'd like to see your pretty face more often." He kissed her again, then strode off to find his wife.

"I believe you're speechless," Johanna commented when Sam only continued to watch Max's back.

"There's not another actor alive I admire more than Max Heddison. He doesn't socialize much, and the couple of times I've seen him I didn't have the nerve to wangle an introduction."

"You, shy?"

"Intimidated is a mild way to put it."

Johanna took his hand again, touched that he could be. "He's the kindest man I know. Once for my birthday he gave me a puppy. My father was furious—he hates dogs—but he couldn't say anything because it was from Uncle Max."

"Jo-Jo?"

She shot him a look. "Uncle Max is the only one who has ever, or who will ever, call me that."

"I like it." He ran a finger down her nose. "It makes me wonder how you'd look in pigtails and a straw hat. Oh, God." She saw his expression change from one of amusement to resignation just before he was enveloped by slim white arms.

"Oh, Sam, I just can't believe how long it's been." The woman with the mane of red curls turned her face just enough to let the camera get her best side. "Darling, where *have* you been hiding?"

"Here and there." He managed, with considerable skill, to untangle himself. "How are you, Toni?"

"Well, how do I look?" She threw back her magnificent head and laughed. Johanna noted that her dress was cut to the lowest degree that the law would allow. "I've been so terribly busy I've lost touch. I've just started filming and could barely fit this little event into my schedule. It's so boring not being able to see friends."

"Johanna Patterson, Toni DuMonde."

"It's nice to meet you." Johanna knew DuMonde's reputation as a mediocre actress who traded more on sex appeal than talent. She'd married well twice, and both husbands had boosted her career.

"Any friend of Sam's—" she began, then stopped. "You aren't Carl's daughter, are you?" Before Johanna could answer, she threw her head back again, making sure her hair cascaded as she laughed. "What a riot! Darling, I've just been dying to meet you!" Placing a hand on Johanna's shoulder, she scanned the room. Her eyes, sharp and tawny, skimmed over minor celebrities, smiled at those worth noticing and narrowed when focused on a rival. When she found her objective, her smile turned up several hundred kilowatts. Johanna noticed the flashy diamond on her left hand as she signaled.

"This is such a happy coincidence," Toni continued. "I'm sure you'll understand how very delighted I am. Sweetheart, look who I found."

Johanna looked at her father as Toni snuggled against him. The move was calculated so that the diamond on her finger winked hard and cold and in plain sight.

"Johanna, I didn't realize you were attending." Carl brushed his cheek against hers, as he would have with any of his hundreds of acquaintances.

He was a tall man, with broad shoulders and a flat stomach. He'd allowed his face to line because he had a fear of going under the knife, even cosmetically. But he'd never permitted his body to sag. At fifty-five, Carl W. Patterson was in his prime. Women were as drawn to him now as they had been thirty years before. Perhaps more, as power added to his sex appeal.

"You're looking well," Johanna told him. Sam noted that there was none of the warmth here that there had been when she'd greeted Max Heddison. "Carl Patterson, Sam Weaver."

"A pleasure." Carl took Sam's hand in his hefty, well-manicured one. "I've kept my eye on your career. Word is you're starting a film with Berlitz soon. We go back a ways."

"I'm looking forward to it."

"Isn't this cozy?" Toni put in, clipping her free hand through Sam's arm. "The four of us running into each other this way. We'll have to get a table together, won't we, Carl? After all, I'll want to get to know your daughter, now that we're going to be family."

Johanna didn't freeze. She didn't even react. By this time she was past being surprised by her father. "Congratulations." She winced only slightly when a camera flashed, catching the four of them together.

"We haven't set the date yet." Toni beamed up at Carl. "But we plan to make it soon—well, as soon as a few minor matters are taken care of."

Which would be the legal disposal of his fourth wife, Johanna surmised. Fortunately, she was no longer affected by the whims or variable presence of stepmothers. "I'm sure you'll be very happy."

"We intend to be." Carl patted Toni's hand, looking at her rather than at his daughter.

"Do let's get a table, Carl, and have a drink to celebrate." Toni kept a casual grip on both men. So casual that it was barely noticeable when Sam removed her hand and took Johanna's. Hers was ice-cold and rigid.

"I'm sorry, we can't stay long." Sam's smile was charming and faintly apologetic.

"Oh, pooh, you've time for one quick drink before this place turns into a zoo." Toni trailed her fingertips up Carl's arm. "Darling, you'll have to insist."

"No need to insist." She wouldn't be ill, Johanna told herself. She wouldn't even be upset. Neither did she smile as she looked up at her father. "The least I can do is drink to your happiness."

"Wonderful." Toni thought it more than wonderful to be seen with a man as important as Carl and a man as attractive as Sam at the same time. "Now, Johanna darling, you mustn't believe all those naughty things you must have read about Sam and me. You know how people in this town love to talk." She turned to be escorted inside and shot a smile over her shoulder, daring Johanna not to believe every word.

"Why in the hell are you doing this?" Sam demanded.

"Because it's part of the game." Chin up, Johanna stepped into the ballroom.

* * *

The room was full of babble. It glittered as such events are meant to, and it would make excellent copy in *People*. It would raise a great deal of money—a hundred, perhaps a hundred and fifty thousand dollars—while making the evening worth the price of the meal. And the food was lavish.

She didn't eat. Johanna barely noticed what was placed in front of her, though Toni cooed over each course and made noises about calories. The ring on her hand flashed triumphantly every time she moved her fingers. She made coy little remarks about Sam behaving like a gentleman with her almost-step-daughter, giggled delightedly about having a daughter the same age as herself and snuggled kisses on Carl's cheek when she wasn't flirting elsewhere.

He was dazzled by her. Johanna sipped champagne and watched her father preen whenever the redhead stroked his ego. She'd never known him to be dazzled by a woman before. Desirous, covetous, infuriated, but never dazzled.

"Just a teeny bit more," Toni said when Carl poured more wine. "You know how silly I get when I drink too much." She shot him an intimate look that promised she could get a great deal more than silly. "Isn't this a wild crowd?" She waved cheerily to someone at another table. "God, what a hideous dress. All those diamonds don't make up for plain bad taste, do they? Sam, darling, I heard Lauren's seeing some French race-car driver. Did she break your heart?"

"No," he said flatly, and shifted away when she patted his knee.

"That's because you always do the heartbreaking. Be very careful with this man, Johanna dear, better women than I have shed a tear over him."

"I'm certain," Johanna said sweetly, and sipped more champagne.

"Tell me, why haven't you had your daddy put you in the movies?" Toni gave her a cool woman-to-woman look over her glass.

"I don't act."

"What do you do?"

"Johanna produces daytime television," Carl put in. "The latest reports that crossed my desk were excellent, by the way."

"Thank you."

"Evening syndication is moving forward?"

"Yes, we just finalized it. I would have sent you a memo, but I thought you were out of town."

"We just spent two weeks on the most dismal location shoot in Arizona." Toni patted Carl's hand. "Thank God Carl was there to be sure I wasn't worn to a frazzle. Sam, I've heard the most marvelous things about your television thing. That'll be aired in a couple of weeks, won't it?"

He smiled at her again and nodded. He knew she'd tested for the part of Sarah and had yet to forgive him for not pulling strings to get it for her.

"We really should do a movie together, with Carl producing."

When hell freezes over, Sam thought. "I really hate to cut this short, but Johanna and I are already late." He rose before anyone could protest and offered a hand. "A pleasure meeting you, Mr. Patterson, and my compliments on your finest production." Taking Johanna by the hand, he grinned at Toni. "Don't ever change, darling."

"Good night," Johanna said to her father. "Best wishes." She didn't object to Sam's supporting arm as he guided her out of the ballroom. "You didn't have to cut your evening short on my account," she began.

"I didn't cut it short, and I'm not leaving only on your account. I don't like socializing with piranhas like Toni." He drew out the claim check for his car and handed it to the boy on the curb. "Besides, you look like you could use some fresh air."

"I'm not drunk."

"No, but you were heading there."

"I never get drunk, because I don't like to be out of control." Truer words had never been spoken, he was certain. "Fine, but I'm going to get you something to eat anyway." He handed the boy who brought his car a twenty and ushered Johanna in himself. "Could you handle a burger?"

"I'm not hungry."

Stubborn, he thought, and just this side of sulking. "Okay, I want a burger."

She started to snap and realized just in time that she was being nasty. "Sam, I appreciate it, but I really don't want anything. Why don't you just drop me off so I can get my car?"

"You had five glasses of wine. I counted." He'd nursed one the moment he'd seen what kind of mood she was in. "I'm driving you home—after we eat."

"I can't leave my car in town."

"I'll have someone drop it off to you tomorrow."

"That's too much trouble. I can—"

"Johanna . . ." He pulled over to the curb and waited until she looked at him. "Let me be a friend, okay?"

She shut her eyes, wanting badly to do something else she never allowed herself. To cry, hard and long and for no reason at all. "Thanks. I guess I could use some food and some air."

In his tux, Sam ran into a bright fast-food restaurant, ordered burgers, fries and coffee, signed half a dozen autographs and ran out again. "Life's rarely simple anymore," he told Johanna as he tucked the bag between her feet. "The little girl behind the counter wanted to pay for them, and I know damn well she stuck her phone number in the bag. She must have been all of nineteen."

"You should have let me go in."

"We all have our crosses to bear." He headed out. "Johanna, I don't make it a habit to pay attention to what's said about me in print—unless it's a review—but I'd like to make an exception and tell you that Toni and I were never together."

"Sam, it's none of my business."

"Whether you think it's your business or not, I'd like you to believe me. If you've already got a picture of her and me, it's bad enough. When you add that to the fact that she's apparently going to marry your father, it's ludicrous."

Johanna opened her eyes and studied him as he drove. It hadn't occurred to her before. She'd been too wrapped up in her own thoughts and feelings to notice. But she saw it now. "She embarrassed you. I'm sorry."

"I just didn't like her implying—" Implying, hell, he thought. She'd practically taken out an ad. "I'd feel better if you understood there'd never been anything between us." He wanted to say more but found it difficult to say what he thought about the woman who was going to become a part of Johanna's family. "Anyway, it wasn't quite the evening I had in mind."

In a little while he pulled up at the crest of a hill. Below, spread out like a game of lights, was the Los Angeles Basin. He put the top down. Far off in the distance she heard the call of a coyote.

"We're not dressed for burgers, but I got plenty of napkins." He reached down for the bag and the back of his hand brushed her calf. "Johanna, I have to tell you something."

"What?"

"You have incredible legs."

"Give me a hamburger, Sam," she said, and took off her shoes.

"Smells better than the veal medallions."

"Is that what we had?"

"No, that's what you didn't have. Here's the ketchup." He passed her a handful of little plastic bags, then waited until he was satisfied she was eating. If he'd ever seen anyone more miserable than Johanna had been at that pretty, flower-bedecked table with stars glittering in every corner, he couldn't remember. The worst of it was that she'd been struggling to be valiant about it.

"Want to talk about it?" When she only shrugged, he pressed

a little harder. "I take it you didn't know your father was planning to get married again."

"I didn't know he was planning to get divorced again. He
doesn't check these things through with me."

"Are you fond of your current stepmother?"

"My father's current wife," she corrected automatically,
which told him a great deal. "I don't know, I've only met her
a couple of times. I think she moved back to New York a few
weeks ago. I was just surprised because he doesn't usually stack
one marriage on top of the other. Generally there's a space of
a year or two between legal contracts."

"He'll have a few months to get to know Toni better. He
could change his mind."

"I'm sure he knows exactly what she is. One thing Carl isn't
is stupid."

"Sometimes if you tell someone when you're angry with
them it loosens things up."

"I'm not angry with him, not really."

He brushed his knuckles along her cheek. "Hurt?"

She shook her head, unable to trust herself to speak for a moment. "He lives his own life. He always has. And that makes it
easier for me to live mine."

"You know, I had some real matches with my father." He
shook the bag of fries, urging them on her.

"Did you?"

"God, did we fight." With a laugh, Sam opened his coffee
and began to sip. "The Weavers have tempers. We like to yell.
I think I spent most of the years between fifteen and twenty
going head-to-head with my old man. I mean, just because I
plowed the car through Greenley's fence was no reason to con-
fiscate my license for six weeks, was it?"

"I imagine Greenley thought it was. Did you ever get your
own way?"

"I figure that was about seventy-five, twenty-five, with him holding the lion's share. I probably got as much as I did because he was busy yelling at my brother or one of my sisters."

"It must be different, having a big family. I always imagined . . ."

"What?"

The wine cushioned embarrassment. Without it, she might never have said it out loud. "I sometimes thought it would be nice when I was little to have brothers and sisters . . . I don't know, grandparents to visit, family squabbles. Of course, I had stepsiblings from time to time. Things were usually finished before we'd gotten used to each other."

"Come here." He shifted over so he could put an arm around her. "Feel any better?"

"A lot." She sighed and rested her head. "I appreciate it."

Her hair smelled like the air outside the windows. Clean, quiet. The urge to turn his face into it was natural, and he did it without thinking. "I wish you hadn't had so much wine."

"Why?"

"Then it wouldn't be against the rules for me to seduce you."

She surprised herself by turning her face to his. She didn't like the word "seduce." It implied a lack of will. But just now it sounded liberating, and more than tempting. "You live by the rules?"

"Not many of them." He brought his hand to her hair. "I want to make love with you, Johanna, but when I do I want you to have your wits about you. So for now I'll settle for a little less."

He nipped at her lower lip, testing its softness, experimenting with tastes. Here was warmth, just edging toward heat, and acceptance, only a step away from surrender.

Of all the visions and fantasies he'd already had of being with her, the one that was the strongest was of him just holding her like this, with the stars overhead and the night breezes blowing cool and clean.

She could have pulled away. His touch was so gentle she knew he would never have pushed. Not this time. There would be others. She already accepted that. On another night when the breeze was just ruffling the leaves he'd hold her like this, and his mood wouldn't be as patient. Nor, she was afraid, would hers. Something had taken root, no matter how hard she'd tried to pull it free. With a little sigh, she brought a hand to his face.

It was torture, but he ran his hand along her bare shoulders. He wanted to take the feel of her with him when he drew away. Just as he would take the taste of her, the scent of her skin, with him on the long, lonely trip home.

"I wish I knew what I was feeling," she murmured when she could speak again. It wasn't the wine. It would have been a lie to blame it on anything so ordinary. Her eyes were heavy, a bit dazed. Her mouth was soft. Just by looking at her Sam knew he could have her. One more easy nudge and they would be lovers.

He reminded himself about rules and fragile women.

"We're going to have to talk about it." He kissed her again, briefly. "Then we're going to have to do something about it. But right now I'm going to take you home."

CHAPTER 6

Johanna considered Saturdays the day the work force had been given to catch up on everything their jobs had forced them to ignore during the week. Rather than a day off, she thought of it as an alternate. Saturdays weren't for sleeping late—even if you were slightly hung over and punchy. They were for weeding the garden, marketing, dealing with personal correspondence and bookkeeping. Her Saturdays, like the rest of her days, had a routine she rarely varied. Johanna depended on organization because a well-ordered life was a safe one.

She dealt with the cleaning first. Though she'd never thought of herself as particularly domestic, Johanna had never considered hiring someone to do the housekeeping. The house was her personal life, and as in all areas of that life, she preferred to handle it herself.

The vacuuming and dusting, the scrubbing down and polishing up, were never mundane chores. There was a certain basic pleasure in them, but more compelling was the feeling that her house, her things, deserved her attention. It was as simple as that. She could haul a bucket and dust rags from room to room with the same dedication and enjoyment she put into reading contracts or balancing budgets.

She preferred the radio loud so that she could hear it in

whatever corner of the house she decided to tackle first. This was a day for both production and solitude. Over the years, Johanna had developed a dependency on both.

She did think about the car, and thinking of that naturally turned her thoughts to Sam. She hoped he didn't forget his promise to have someone drop it off, but if he did she'd simply forgo her Saturday marketing and have Bethany pick her up on Monday morning.

Johanna never depended on promises or other people's memories.

But she did think of him, and if her thoughts weren't completely comfortable she couldn't forget that he'd been kind, and gentler than she'd expected. She remembered, a little too well, how she'd felt when she'd kissed him. Full, edgy, tempted. Just a little more tempted each time she was with him to throw away the pact she'd made with herself so many years ago. The pact said no relationships that couldn't be controlled, by her, from the outset—no dependencies, no promises, long- or short-term.

It was a sensible pact, unwritten but binding. The fact that Sam had nearly lured her into forgetting it worried her. But it made her wonder more.

Just what was it about him that made her lose a bit of ground every time they were together? She could discount his looks, however delightful they were. She might appreciate a great physique, but she wouldn't swoon over one.

Not that she was swooning over Sam Weaver, Johanna reminded herself as she poured hot water into her bucket. She thought very little of women who built fantasies or relationships around cleft chins and bulging biceps.

Nor was it his reputation. That, in fact, worked against him. Johanna dunked her mop in hot, soapy water, then began to wash her kitchen floor. The fact that he was an actor was a strike against him. The fact that he was an actor with a reputation with women was a bigger one.

Of course, she knew that such reports were usually exaggerated and often outright lies. But there were times . . . There were times, Johanna thought as she swiped the mop back and forth, that the press didn't even come close to making rumor as outrageous as the truth.

The press had never known her truth. Her mother's truth. With the care and firmness of experience, she locked that thought away.

So it wasn't his looks or his reputed way with women. It certainly wasn't his fame. Growing up as she had, Johanna had had to tolerate vicarious fame all her life. It wasn't his talent, either, though she certainly respected that. She knew people were often drawn to talent and power. Her father, and the stream of women in his life, were proof of that. They were also drawn to wealth and position. Johanna was too ambitious and had spent too much time trying to perfect her own skills to be swayed by anyone else's.

So if it wasn't one of the attributes he was so obviously endowed with, just what was it that was making her think about him when she shouldn't?

It hadn't started with that first kiss. It would have been easy to blame it on basic sexual attraction, but Johanna preferred honest self-analysis. The seed of something had been there from that first meeting. If not, she wouldn't have gone out of her way to give him a hard time.

Defense mechanism, Johanna thought, recognizing and acknowledging it.

There was his charm, of course. She wrung out the mop and began to rinse. It wasn't stylized or deliberate. That she would have been immune to. It was natural, easy, even friendly. The roses had managed to turn the key in an old, well-guarded lock.

The kiss had managed to blow it open briefly, just long enough to give her cause for alarm.

Alarm. Yes, that was what she'd felt overlaying every other emotion he'd drawn out of her. Now that she'd admitted it, she had to decide what to do about it.

She could ignore him. But she didn't believe that would do much good. She could—cautiously—go along with his suggestion that they get to know each other better. Slowly. And she could stick to her guns and not get involved beyond a wary friendship.

The solution had to be in there somewhere, she thought. She'd come up with it, and the next time she had to deal with him she'd be prepared.

She was incredible. Sam stood in the kitchen doorway and watched her mop the kitchen floor. He'd knocked, but the music she had blaring in the other room had drowned out the sound. Since the door hadn't been locked, he'd simply walked in and wandered through until he'd found her.

Johanna Patterson. She was just a bit different every time he saw her. Sophisticated one minute, wonderfully simple the next. Alluring, then cool. Nervous, then tough. A man could take years getting to know all of her. Sam figured he had time.

Right now she was dressed in faded cotton pants rolled up at the ankles and a big man-styled shirt pushed to her elbows. Her feet were bare, and her hair was pinned up untidily. She handled the mop with smooth, easy strokes, not skimming over the job and not swearing over it. He imagined she took to such things as housekeeping with the same steady drive she took to everything else. He liked that, and he liked her for it.

He knew exactly why he was attracted to Johanna. She was beautiful, but that wouldn't have been enough. She was smart, but though he respected a sharp mind that wouldn't have kept him coming back. She was vulnerable. Normally that would have made him take a cautious step back instead of these continued steps forward. She had an edge to her that in another few years might become hard. But now, just now, Johanna was a cautious woman with a few bruises who wasn't easily impressed by status. The combination was more than enough to keep pulling him toward her.

And she'd rather he didn't, Sam thought. On the surface, at least, she'd have preferred that he step out of her life and stay out. But deep down, he believed, she was looking for someone, for something, just as he was.

He wasn't naive enough to believe it was so just because that was what he wanted, but he was determined to find out.

He stood where he was as the strokes of the mop brought her closer. When she rammed into him, he took her arm to keep her from overbalancing.

Johanna whirled around, automatically gripping the mop like a weapon. The relief when she saw him turned quickly to anger.

"How the hell did you get in here?"

"The door," he told her easily. "It wasn't locked. I did knock. I guess you didn't hear me."

"No, I didn't." She was shouting to be heard over the music. "Apparently you took that as an invitation."

"I took it to mean you didn't hear me." He held up the keys she'd given him the night before. "I thought you'd want your car back."

"Thanks." She stuffed them in her pocket. It wasn't anger nearly as much as it was embarrassment. She didn't care to be sneaked up on unaware.

"You're welcome." He handed her a bouquet of painted daisies and snapdragons. As he'd suspected they would, her eyes softened. "I stole them from Mae's garden. I figured she wouldn't notice."

"They're pretty." With a sigh that was only partially one of resignation, she took them. "I do appreciate you bringing my car back." She knew she was weakening, and she struggled not to. "You've caught me at a bad time. I can't even offer you a drink because the floor's wet, and I'm really busy."

"I'll take you out for one. Better, let's go have some lunch."

"I can't. I've only half finished here, and I'm not dressed to go out. Besides, I—"

"Look fine," he finished for her. "You'd better put those in water. They're starting to droop."

She could have been rude. Johanna knew she was capable of it, but she found she hadn't the heart. Instead, she said nothing. She plucked an old square bottle from a shelf and went into the bathroom to fill it. As she did, she heard the volume of the music go down several notches. He was in the living room studying her collection of antique glass when she came back.

"My mother used to have some plates like this green stuff here. Depression glass, right?"

"Yes."

"I thought that meant it made her sad. I could never figure out why she kept it."

She wouldn't be amused, Johanna told herself. At least not very. "Sam, you really shouldn't keep whoever followed you up waiting outside."

"No one followed me up." He hooked his thumbs in his pockets and smiled. Some might have thought the look sheepish, but Johanna wasn't fooled.

"Now I suppose you want me to drive you back."

"Sooner or later."

"I'll call you a cab," she said, turning to the phone. "I'll even pay for it."

He put his hand over hers on the receiver. "Johanna, you're being unfriendly again."

"You're being pushy."

"Yeah, but subtleties don't work with you." He reached over to stick a loose pin back in her hair. He'd have preferred to have pulled it out, and the rest of them besides, but bided his time. "So how about lunch?"

"I'm not hungry."

"So, we'll take a drive first." He skimmed his hand from her hair to her cheek. "I really think we should, because if we stay in here too much longer I'm going to want to make love with you, and since I figure you're not ready, a drive's a better idea."

Johanna cleared her throat and took another stab at persuasion. "I appreciate your logic, but I don't have time for a drive, either."

"You've got an appointment?"

"No," she said, then wished she could bite off her tongue. "That is, I—"

"You already said no." He watched her eyes narrow and thought she was almost as pretty annoyed as she was amused. You're already sunk waist-deep, Sam, he told himself. Another few steps and you're over your head. But what the hell. "It's too nice a day to stay indoors cleaning a house that's already clean enough."

"That's my business."

"Okay, then I'll wait for you to finish before we go out."

"Sam—"

"I'm persistent, Johanna. You told me so yourself."

"I'll drive you home," she said, giving up.

"Not good enough." He caught her again, this time by the shoulders. There was something about the way he spread his fingers over her, about the way his palm fit so truly over her. His expression had changed just enough to make her uneasy. The amusement was gone, but it hadn't been replaced by anger. She wouldn't have been uneasy about anger. This was determination, solid and unshakable. "I want to spend the day with you. You know damn well I want to spend the night with you, as well, but I'll settle for the day. Give me five reasons why not and I'll walk down to the freeway and hitch a ride."

"Because I don't want to."

"That's a statement, not a reason. And I don't buy it, anyway."

"Your ego won't buy it."

"Suit yourself." Refusing to be annoyed, he sat on the arm of her couch, absently picked up one of her pillows and began to toss it. "Look, I've got all day. I don't mind sitting around until you've stopped fussing with your imaginary dust. Hell, I'll even give you a hand, but then we're going to have to get out of here, because being alone with you for long periods of time isn't easy." She opened her mouth, but he continued before she could make a suggestion. "I keep wanting to touch you, Johanna, in all kinds of interesting places."

"We'll go out," she said quickly, before she could admit she wanted it, too.

"Good idea. Listen, why don't I drive?"

She started to protest even that—on principle—then decided he'd be less likely to give her trouble if he had his eyes on the road. "Fine." After switching off the radio, she dumped the keys back in his hands. "It'll take me a few minutes to change."

"You look fine," he said again, and took her hand. "I happen to like this Johanna every bit as much as the others I've met over the last couple of weeks."

She decided not to ask him what he was talking about. "We'll have to make it a very informal lunch, then."

"It will be." He opened the door of the car for her. "I promise."

He was as good as his word.

The hot dog dripped mustard, and the noise level was intense. Johanna sat almost in the shade and watched pink elephants circle overhead. It wasn't a dream, or the last remnants of a hangover. It was Disneyland.

"I don't believe this." She took another bite of the hot dog as a boy in mouse ears dashed by, yelling for his parents to hurry up.

"Pretty great, isn't it?" Sam wore sunglasses and a low-brimmed cowboy hat that Johanna was forced to admit suited him. So did the chinos and the simple T-shirt. The disguise wasn't very imaginative, and it would have been transparent as glass if anyone had looked closely enough. Sam had told her that the best place to be anonymous was a crowd. They certainly had one.

"You come here for lunch often?"

"Great hot dogs in Fantasyland." He took an enormous bite to prove his point. "Besides, I'm hooked on the Haunted Mansion. It's terrific, don't you think?"

"I don't know. I've never been in it."

"Never?" His tone of quick astonishment wasn't feigned. Wanting a better look, he tipped down his tinted glasses and studied her. "You grew up here, didn't you?"

She only shrugged. Yes, she'd grown up a short drive from Anaheim, but neither her father nor her succession of stepmothers or "aunts," as she'd been taught to call the other women in her father's life, had been inclined to take a day trip to an amusement park.

"You're not telling me you've never been to Disneyland at all?"

"It's not a requirement."

He pushed his glasses back on his nose as she wiped her hands on a napkin. He remembered the impersonal non-kiss her father had given her the night before. His family was always, had always been, demonstrative, both physically and vocally. No, Disneyland, like other small pleasures, wasn't a requirement. But it should be.

"Come on, your education's lacking."

"Where are we going?"

"To take Mr. Toad's Wild Ride. You're going to love it."

Oddly enough, she did.

It was fast and foolish and certainly designed for the younger set, but Johanna found herself gasping and giggling as the car swerved and twisted through the tunnels. She'd barely put her foot on the ground again before Sam was dragging her off to the next line.

They rode down a mountain in a raft, and the final waterfall drop surprised a scream out of her. Wet and breathless, she didn't even protest when he pulled her along again. By the time they'd done Fantasyland to his satisfaction, she'd been spun, twirled, flown and floated. The Mad Hatter's Tea Party had left her giddy and weak-kneed and without the least notion that she was being educated.

He bought her mouse ears with her name stitched across the front, using her own hairpins to secure it even when she grumbled.

"Looks cute," he decided, then kissed her. She might not have known it, Sam thought, but she was more relaxed than he'd ever seen her. "I think you're ready for the Haunted Mansion."

"Does it spin?"

"No, it strikes terror into your heart. That's why you're going to hang on to me and make me feel brave." He swung an arm around her shoulders and began to walk. Johanna had already discovered he knew the park very well.

"You really do come here a lot, don't you?"

"When I first came to California I had two priorities. Get a job—an acting job—and go to Disneyland. Whenever my family comes out we always spend at least one day here."

Johanna looked around as they walked. There were families, so many families. Infants and toddlers pushed in strollers, children with sticky faces riding piggyback and pointing toward the next adventure.

"I guess it is an amazing place. Everything seems real while it's going on."

"It is real when it's going on." He stepped to the back of the line, undaunted by its length. After a moment's hesitation, he took a chance. "I was Pluto for six weeks."

"Pluto?"

"The dog, not the planet."

"I know who Pluto is," she murmured. Absently adjusting her hat, she frowned at him. "You actually worked here?"

"In a dog suit. A very hot dog suit—no pun intended. It paid my first month's rent."

"What exactly did you do?" The line shifted up.

"Marched in the parade, posed for pictures, waved and sweated a lot. I really wanted to be Captain Hook, because he gets to have sword fights and look evil, but Pluto was all that was open."

Johanna tried to imagine it, and nearly could. "I always thought he was cute."

"I was a terrific Pluto. Very lovable and loyal. I did cut it from my résumé after a while, but that was on Marv's suggestion."

"Marv? Oh, your agent?"

"He thought playing a six-foot dog was the wrong image to project."

While Johanna thought that one through, they were ushered inside. The spiel was camp and full of bad puns, but she couldn't help being pulled in. The pictures on the walls changed, the room shrank, the lights went out. There was no turning back.

By the time they were in their tram and starting on the tour she was, so to speak, entering into the spirit of things.

The producer in her couldn't fail to be impressed by the show. Holograms, music and elaborate props were blended to entertain, to raise goose pimples and nervous chuckles. Not so scary that the toddlers in the group would go home with nightmares, but not so tame that the adults felt cheated out of the price of a ticket, Johanna decided as she watched ghosts and spirits whirl around in a dilapidated, cobweb-draped dining room.

Sam had been right about one thing. It was real while it was going on. Not everything in life could be trusted to be the same.

She didn't have to be prodded any further, not to visit a pirate's den and dodge cannon fire, nor to take a cruise up the Amazon or a train ride through Indian territory. She watched mechanical bears perform, ate dripping ice cream and forgot she was a grown woman who had been to Paris and dined in an English manor but had never been to Disneyland.

By the time they started back to the car she was exhausted, but in the most pleasant way she could remember.

"I did not scream," she insisted, holding the small stuffed Pluto he'd bought her in a headlock.

"You never stopped screaming," Sam corrected. "From the minute that car started moving through Space Mountain until it stopped again. You've got excellent lungs."

"Everyone else was screaming." In truth, she hadn't a clue whether she'd screamed or not. The car had taken its first dive, and planets had raced toward her. Johanna had simply squeezed her eyes shut and held on.

"Want to go back and do it again?"

"No," she said definitely. "Once was quite enough."

Sam opened the car door but turned before she could climb in. "Don't you like thrills, Johanna?"

"Now and again."

"How about now?" He cupped her face in his hands. "And again later."

He kissed her as he'd wanted to do since he'd seen her

studiously mopping her floor that morning. Her lips were warm, as he'd known they would be, but softer, incredibly softer, than he'd remembered. They hesitated. There was a sweetness in that, a sweetness that was its own allure.

So he lingered, longer than he'd intended. He wanted, more than was wise. When she started to back away, he gathered her closer and took, more than either of them had expected.

It wasn't supposed to be like this, Johanna told herself even as she stopped resisting both of them. She was supposed to be strong, in charge, reachable only when and if she chose to be. With him, he only had to touch . . . No, he only had to look and she began losing ground.

All her careful analysis that morning was blown to dust the minute his mouth was on hers.

I don't want this. Her mind tried to cling to that thought while her heart beat out steadily: But you do, yes, you do. She could almost feel herself separating into two parts, one aloof, one almost pitifully vulnerable. The most frightening thing was that this time she was more than afraid that vulnerability would be the stronger.

"I want to be alone with you, Johanna." He said it against her lips, then again against her cheek as he trailed kisses there. "Anywhere, anywhere at all as long as it's only you and me. I haven't been able to get you out of my system."

"I don't think you've been trying."

"You're wrong." He kissed her again, feeling her renewed resistance swerve toward passion. That was the most exciting, the most irresistible thing about her, the way she wanted, held back and wanted again. "I've actually given it a hell of a shot. I kept telling myself you're too complicated, too uptight, too driven." He felt her lips move into a frown and was seduced into nibbling on them. "Then I find ways to see you again."

"I'm not uptight."

He sensed her change of mood but could only be amused

by it. Johanna, outraged, was fascinating. "Lady, half the time you're like a spring that's wound to the limit and just waiting to bust out. And I damn well intend to be there when you do."

"That's ridiculous. And don't call me lady." She snatched the keys from him, decided she'd do the driving this time.

"We'll see about that." He climbed into the car and nearly managed to stretch out his legs and get comfortable. "Going to give me a lift home?"

She was tempted, more than tempted, to order him out and strand him in the parking lot, right under Donald Duck's cheerful beak. Instead, she decided to give him the ride of his life. "Sure." Johanna put the car in gear.

She drove cautiously enough through the lot. It was, after all, full of pedestrians, many of them children. Things changed when she hit the freeway. She whipped around three cars, settled in the fast lane and rammed down on the gas pedal.

Drives like she's ready to bust, too, Sam thought, but said nothing. Her speedometer might have been hovering around ninety, but her hands were competent on the wheel. And she might, he thought, burn off that temper that had fired up when he'd called her uptight.

She hated it that he was right. That was the worst of it. She knew very well that she was full of nerves and hang-ups and insecurities. Didn't she spend most of her time fighting them off or blanketing them over? It didn't do her any good to hear Sam pinpoint it so casually.

When she'd made the conscious and very calculated decision to make love with a fellow college student, he, too, had called her uptight. Sexually. "Loosen up" had been his sage advice. She hadn't been able to, not with him, who she'd been fond of, nor with any of the men she'd developed careful relationships with. So she'd stopped trying.

She wasn't a man-hater. That would be absurd. She simply didn't want to be tied to one, emotionally or sexually. Her eyes had been opened young, and she'd never forgotten how those two tools could be used. So perhaps she was uptight, though she detested the word. Better that than loose enough to tumble for a pair of wonderful blue eyes or a lazy drawl.

Mad as hell, Sam thought. That was fine. He preferred strong emotion. As a matter of fact, he preferred any emotion at all when it came from Johanna. He didn't mind her being angry with him, because if she was angry she was thinking. About him. He wanted her to do a lot of that.

God knew he'd been thinking about her. Constantly. He'd been telling her no less than the truth when he'd said he'd tried to get her out of his system. When it hadn't worked, he'd decided to stop beating his head against the wall and see where the road would lead.

It was a bumpy ride, but he was enjoying every minute of it.

He was going to have her, sooner or later. Sooner, he hoped for the sake of his sanity. But for now he'd let her drive awhile.

When he saw she was going to miss the exit, he gestured. "You want to get off here."

Johanna switched lanes, aggressively challenging traffic, and breezed onto the ramp.

"How about dinner next week?" He said it casually, as though the interlude in the parking lot had been as make-believe as the rest of the day. When she said nothing, he fought back a grin and tossed his arm over the seat. "Wednesday's good for me. I can pick you up at your office."

"I'm busy next week."

"You've got to eat. Let's make it six."

She downshifted for a turn. "You're going to have to learn to take no for an answer."

"I don't think so. Take the left fork."

"I remember," she said between her teeth, though she didn't.

She drove in silence, slowing down only slightly when she passed through the gate of his ranch. Sam leaned over casually and tooted her horn. When she stopped in front of his house he sat there a moment, as though gathering his thoughts.

"Want to come in?"

"No."

"Want to fight?"

She would not be amused or charmed or soothed. "No."

"All right, we can fight some other time. Want to hear a theory of mine? Never mind," he said before she could answer. "Listen anyway. The way I figure it, there are three stages to a relationship. First you like somebody. Then, if things work out, you start to care for them. When the big guns hit, you fall in love with them."

She kept her hands on the wheel because they'd gone damp all at once. "That's very interesting. If only life worked that neatly."

"I've always thought it does—if you let it. Anyway, Johanna, I went past liking you last night and went straight into the second stage. A woman like you wants reasons for that kind of thing, but I haven't got a handle on them yet."

Her hands had stopped sweating and were now as cold as ice, though the heat was baking right through the windshield. "Sam, I said before I don't think this is a good idea. I still believe that."

"No, you still want to believe that." He waited patiently until she looked at him. "There's a difference, Johanna. A big one. I care for you, and I figured we'd do better if I let you know." He leaned over to kiss her. A very gentle threat. "You've got until Wednesday to think about it."

He got out of the car, then leaned in through the window. "Drive carefully, will you? You can always kick something when you get home if you're still mad."

CHAPTER 7

I t had been a long day. In fact, it had been several long days.
Johanna didn't mind. The pressure to solve problems and
work through a few minor crises had kept her mind off her personal life.

Her lighting director had chosen Monday, taping day, to
have an appendectomy. She sent flowers and wished him—not
for totally altruistic reasons—a speedy recovery. John Jay, in
the middle of contract negotiations, had decided to have lar-
yngitis. Johanna had been forced to pamper and cajole—and
make a few veiled threats—to work an instant and miraculous
cure. Her assistant lighting man had proven to be competent
and unruffled, even after three technical hitches. Still, the day
had been lengthened by two hours.

Tuesday had stretched even further with meetings to discuss
the photo sessions for the ads and the final preparations for the
following week's contest. Security had been strengthened to
guard that set of questions. A special safe had been purchased,
and only she had the combination. Only she and Bethany knew
which five questions had been sealed inside. Johanna began to
feel like the head of the CIA.

A meeting with her father had been draining and difficult.
They'd both been professional, executive producer to producer,

as they'd discussed the show's status and plans for expansion. He'd absently mentioned an engagement party and told her his secretary would be in touch.

And, of course, because she considered it part of her job, Johanna watched *Trivia* every morning. It was just a nasty trick of fate that Sam's appearance ran this week. It was difficult enough not to think of him, and impossible when she was forced to watch him every day—long shots, close-ups. By Wednesday they had already received a stack of mail from delighted viewers.

Wednesday.

He'd given her until Wednesday to think about it. To think about him. Them. She just hadn't had the time, Johanna told herself as she turned up the volume and prepared to watch the day's segment. If she'd allowed herself to think about it she would have come up with a way, a polite and reasonable way, to get out of a dinner she hadn't even accepted.

The bright, bouncy opening theme came on, the lights flashed. The two celebrity panelists walked through the arch, then paused for applause before they took their seats. Johanna struggled to look at the big picture, but she kept focusing on him.

Relaxed. He always looked so relaxed, so confident about who he was. That was something she couldn't help but admire about him. He was at ease and put his partner at ease while still maintaining that larger-than-life quality people expected from stars.

So he was good at his job, Johanna told herself as she paced back and forth during the commercial break. That didn't mean she was infatuated with him.

When the show came back on, she took her chair again, wishing she didn't need to have that very small and indirect contact with him.

It's my job, Johanna reminded herself. But she lost track of the game as she watched him. And she remembered, a bit too clearly, that after this segment had been taped she had had her first real conversation with him. She'd taken a dare, and had lost. Since that one miscalculation, nothing had been the same.

She wanted it to be the same. The quick panic surprised her, but she fought it back and tried to think logically. She did want it to be the same as it had been before, when her life had been focused on career and nudged by ambition, both heated and cooled by pride. There hadn't been any sleepless nights then. Tension and self-doubt, perhaps, but no sleepless nights.

And there hadn't been any rides down a mountain on a raft, either, her mind echoed.

She didn't need them. Sam could keep his thrills. All she required was peace of mind.

He was in the winner's circle, surrounded by lights and the audience's total support. Johanna remembered that the quick, cocky grin had been for her benefit. The minute the congratulatory applause began, she snapped off the set.

On impulse, she went to the phone. Rather than going through her secretary, Johanna dialed direct. Such minor precautions were a bit late, since her picture—with Sam—had already been in the paper, and the speculation about them as a couple had already begun. Johanna had decided there was no use adding to the gossip that was already buzzing around the office.

She was calm, she told herself even as she wound the phone cord around her fingers. She wasn't being stubborn or spiteful, but sensible.

A woman's voice answered. Hearing it gave Johanna all the justification she needed. A man like Sam would always have women around. And a man like that was precisely what she wanted to avoid.

"I'd like to speak with Mr. Weaver. This is Johanna Patterson calling."

"Sam's not in. I'd be happy to take a message." On the other end of the line, Mae was digging for the notepad she always carried in her apron pocket. "Patterson?" she repeated, then shifted the phone and grinned. "Sam's spoken about you. You're the one who does *Trivia Alert*."

Johanna frowned for a moment at the idea of Sam talking about her to one of his women. "Yes, I am. Would you mind—"

"I never miss it," Mae continued conversationally. "I always keep it on when I'm cleaning. Then I see if Joe can answer any of the questions that night at dinner. Joe's my husband. I'm Mae Block."

So this was Mae, the one who shoveled out the dust and grew the snapdragons. Johanna's vision of a pretty morning visitor faded and left her more than a little ashamed. "I'm glad you like the show."

"Crazy about it," Mae assured her. "As a matter of fact, I just had it on. Got a real kick out of seeing our Sam on it. Thought he did real good, too. I even put it on the VCR so Joe could see it later. We're all just crazy about Sam. He speaks real kindly of you, too. Did you like your flowers?"

Having at last found a space in Mae's rapid-fire conversation for a word, Johanna managed to insert one. "Flowers?"

"Sam doesn't think I saw him snitch them."

"They were lovely." Despite all her resolutions, Johanna felt herself soften. "I hope you didn't mind."

"Plenty more where they came from. I figure flowers should be enjoyed, don't you?"

"Yes. Yes, I do. Mrs. Block—"

"Mae. Just Mae, honey."

"Mae, if you could tell Sam I called." Coward, her mind said all too clearly. Johanna closed herself off from it and continued. "And that—"

"Well, you can tell him yourself, honey, 'cause he just this minute walked in. Hold on now."

Before Johanna could babble an excuse, she heard Mae yelling. "Sam, that lady you've been mooning about's on the phone. And I'd like to know what you're thinking of wearing a white shirt when you're wrestling with horses. How you expect me to get out those stains is more than I can understand. Did you wipe your feet? I just washed that kitchen floor."

"Yes, ma'am. It's an old shirt," he added in a half apology Johanna recognized even over the wire.

"Old or not, it's a dust rag now. A boy your age oughta know better. Don't keep your lady waiting all day. I'll make you a sandwich."

"Thanks. Hello, Johanna."

Mae hadn't mentioned her name. *The lady you've been mooning about.* That was something Johanna would have to think about later. "I'm sorry to bother you in the middle of the day. You must be busy."

"Having my wrist slapped." He pulled out a bandanna and wiped the line of sweat from his temple. "I'm glad you called. I've been thinking about you."

"Yes, well . . ." Where were all the neat excuses she'd thought up? "About tonight."

"Yes?"

Very carefully she unwrapped the cord from around her fingers. "We'd left things a bit unstructured, and as it turns out, I have a late meeting. I can't be sure what time I'll wrap things up, so—"

"So why don't you drive out here when you're finished?" He recognized a lie when he heard one. "You should know the way by now."

"Yes, but it might run late. I don't want to mess up your evening."

"The only way you'd mess it up is not to come."

She hadn't a clue as to how to respond to that. "I never actually agreed to come." Her conscience insisted on reminding her she hadn't stuck by a refusal, either. "Why don't we make it some other time?"

"Johanna," he said, very patiently, "you don't want me to camp on your doorstep, do you?"

"I just think it would be better—"

"Safer."

Yes. "Better," she insisted.

"Whatever. If you don't show up by eight I'm coming after you. Take your choice."

Bristling wasn't nearly as effective over the phone. "I don't like ultimatums."

"That's a pity. I'll see you when you get here. Don't work too hard."

Johanna scowled at the dial tone, then dropped the phone on the hook. She wouldn't go. She would be damned if she did.

Of course, she went.

Only to prove that she wasn't a coward, Johanna assured herself. In any case, avoiding a situation didn't solve anything, it only postponed things. Loose ends were something she invariably tied up.

It was true that she enjoyed his company, so there was no reason to be out of sorts. Except for the fact that she'd been maneuvered again. No, he hadn't done the maneuvering, she corrected. She'd done that all by herself, thank you very much. If she hadn't wanted to go, she would never have called him to say she wasn't going to. Deep down she'd wanted to keep the engagement because she'd always had a need to face up to whatever could be faced.

She could certainly face Sam Weaver.

A simple dinner, she decided. Between friends. They could, cautiously, be called friends by this time. A little conversation never hurt, particularly between two people who were in the same business. Game shows or movies, it all came down to entertainment. She picked up speed a bit, and the plastic bags over this week's dry cleaning snapped and rustled on their hangers behind her.

At least this time she had her own transportation. She would leave when she was ready to leave. There was some security in that.

When she passed through the gates leading to the ranch, she promised herself that she would enjoy the evening for what it was. A simple dinner with a friend. She stopped her car in front of his house and stepped out, refusing to glance in the visor mirror. She wouldn't fuss with or freshen her makeup any more than she had fussed with her outfit. Her gray suit was stylish but certainly businesslike, as were the three hanging in the car. Her low-heeled pumps were comfortable, purchased as much for that as for fashion.

She glanced at her watch and was pleased with the time. Seven-thirty. Not so early that it would appear that she'd been cowed, nor so late that it made her look spiteful.

She looked as she had on that first day, Sam thought. Composed, coolheaded, subtly sexy. His reaction to her now was exactly the same as it had been then. Instant fascination. Stepping out on the porch, he smiled at her.

"Hi."

"Hello." She didn't want to be unnerved, not again, not the way she seemed to be every time she saw him. She answered his smile, though cautiously, and started up the steps. His next move was so unexpected that she had no chance to block it.

He cupped a hand around the base of her neck and kissed her, not passionately, not urgently, but with a casual intimacy that shot straight through her. Welcome home, it seemed to say, and left her speechless.

"I love the way you wear a suit, Johanna."

"I didn't have time to change."

"I'm glad." He glanced beyond her at the sound of a truck. With a half smile, he shaded his eyes. "You forgot to blow your horn," he told her.

"Everything all right here, Sam?" In the cab of a pickup was a man of about fifty with shoulders like cinder blocks.

"Everything's fine." Sam slipped an arm around Johanna's waist.

The man in the truck chuckled, then spun the wheel and made a U-turn. "I can see that. Night."

"That was Joe," Sam explained as they watched the truck cruise down the hard-packed road. "He and Mae keep an eye on the place. And me."

"So I see." It was entirely too easy, standing on the porch, his arm around her, as the sun lowered. Johanna didn't deliberately step away. The move was automatic. "Your housekeeper told me she watches *Trivia*."

She also said you were mooning over me. Johanna kept the fact that she'd overheard that little piece of information to herself. It was ridiculous, of course. Men like Sam Weaver didn't moon over anyone.

"Religiously," he murmured, studying her. She was nervous. He'd thought they'd passed that point, and he wasn't sure whether to be pleased or frustrated to discover otherwise. "In fact, Mae considers my, ah . . . performance so far this week the height of my career."

The smile came quickly. Her fingers relaxed their grip on the railing. "Emmy material, I'm sure."

"Is that a smirk?"

"I never smirk, and especially not about my show. I suppose I'll have to risk inflating your ego, but we've already gotten a tremendous amount of mail. 'Sam Weaver is the cutest thing on two legs,'" Johanna quoted, and was amused when he grimaced. "That was from a seventy-five-year-old woman in Tucson."

"Yeah." He took her hand and drew her inside. "When you've finished smirking—"

"I told you, I never smirk."

"Right, and when you're finished we'll see about dinner. I figured we'd barbecue, since I wasn't sure when you'd wind up that meeting."

"Meeting?" The lie had slipped away from her. Remembering, Johanna did something else she couldn't remember having done before. She blushed. Just a little, but enough. "Oh, well, it moved along faster than I'd expected."

"Lucky for both of us." He could have pinned her on it, Sam mused, but decided to let her escape. If he understood Johanna as well as he believed he was coming to understand her, she was already berating herself for the excuse, and for botching it. "I've got some swordfish. Why don't you pour yourself some wine and I'll heat up the grill?"

"All right." The bottle was already open. Johanna filled the two glasses he'd set on the kitchen counter as he breezed through the back door.

He'd known the meeting was nothing more than a weak excuse. She couldn't remember ever having been quite so transparent. Johanna sighed, sipped, then sighed again. He was letting it go so that she wouldn't be embarrassed. That only made it worse. The least she could do, she thought as she picked up his glass, was to be pleasant company for the rest of the evening.

The pool looked cool and delightfully inviting. Swimming had been a daily habit when she'd lived in her father's house. Now she couldn't seem to find time for the health club she'd conscientiously joined. She skirted around the pool to where Sam stood by the stone barbecue pit with two fish steaks on a platter, but she did glance at the water rather wistfully.

"You want to take a quick swim before dinner?" he asked.

It was tempting. Johanna found herself tempted too often when around him. "No, thanks."

"There's always after." He set the steaks on the grill, where they sizzled. Taking his glass from her, he clinked it lightly against hers, then drank. "Go ahead and sit down. These won't take long."

Instead, she wandered a short distance away, looking at his land, the tidy outbuildings, the isolation. He seemed so comfortable here, she thought, so much at home. He could be anybody, an ordinary person. But she remembered that she'd read about him just that morning.

"There's a very hot write-up in this week's *TV Guide* about *No Roses for Sarah*."

"I saw it." He saw, too, how the sun bounced off the water of the pool and onto her skin, making her seem like an illusion. The trim gray suit didn't make him think of offices or board meetings, but of quiet evenings after the day was over.

"*Variety* was equally enthusiastic. 'Gripping, not to be missed,' and so on." She smiled a little as she turned to him again. "What was the adjective used to describe you . . ." She trailed off as if she couldn't quite remember, though the exact quote had engraved itself on her brain. "'Weaver executes a'— Was it 'sterling performance'?"

Sam flipped the steaks, and they hissed. Smoke rose up, hot and sultry. "'Sizzling,'" he corrected, knowing when he was being strung along.

"Yes, sizzling." She paused to touch her tongue to her upper lip. "'A sizzling performance as a down-on-his-luck drifter who seduces Sarah and the audience with equal panache.' Panache," she repeated. "That one rolls around on the tongue, doesn't it?"

"I didn't realize you were such a smart aleck, Johanna."

She laughed and crossed over to him. "I'm also human. Nothing could drag me away from my set on Sunday night when the first part's aired."

"And Monday?"

"That'll depend, won't it?" She sipped her drink and sniffed appreciatively at the mesquite smoke. "On how *sizzling* you were on Sunday."

The grin was fast and crooked, as if he had no doubt where she would be at nine o'clock Monday night. "Keep an eye on these, will you? I'll be right back."

She'd keep an eye on them, but she hoped the steaks didn't do anything they weren't supposed to do until he got back. Alone, she stretched her arms and worked the muscles in her back. The late meeting had been a lie, but the long day hadn't. Wistfully she glanced at the pool again. It really was tempting.

If she were just anyone—if he were just anyone—she could share this meal with him, laugh a little over something that had happened during the day. Afterward, while the wine was still cool and the air still hot, they could slide into the water and relax together. Just two people who enjoyed each other and a quiet evening.

Later, when the moon came out, they might stay in the water, talking quietly, touching, easing gently into a more intimate form of relaxation. He would have music on again, and the candles on the table would burn down and drown in their own melted wax.

When something brushed against her legs, she jolted, sloshing wine over her hand. The fantasy had come through a bit too clearly, too compellingly, and that wasn't like her. Johanna turned away from the pool and the ideas it had had stirring inside her. With a hand to her heart, she looked down at a fat gray cat. He rubbed up against her calf again, sent her a long, shrewd look, then settled down to wash.

"Where did you come from?" Johanna wondered as she bent to scratch his ears.

"The barn," Sam told her, coming up from behind her. "Silas is one of the barn cats, and I'd guess he got a whiff of the fish and came down to see if he could charm any out of us."

She didn't look at Sam right away, concentrating on the cat instead. The daydream was still a bit too real. "I thought barn cats were fast and skinny."

Not when someone was always taking them down scraps, Sam thought ruefully as he set the bowl of pasta salad on the table and flipped the fish onto a platter. "Silas can be pretty charming," he said, and pulled out a chair for Johanna.

"Silas is pretty huge."

"You don't like cats?"

"No, actually, I do. I've even thought of getting one myself. Why Silas?"

"Marner," Sam explained easily as he served her. "You know how he hoarded gold. Well, this Silas hoards mice."

"Oh."

He laughed at her expression and topped off her wine. "You wanted to know. I've been meaning to ask you," he said, thinking she deserved a change of subject, "when you go on nighttime."

"Two weeks." Johanna told herself she wasn't nervous, not nervous at all. "We tape in two weeks, actually, and go on in four."

"Adding more crew?"

"Some. For the most part it just means that we'll be taping two days a week instead of one. Interested in making another appearance?"

"I'm going to be a bit tied up for a while."

"The new movie." She relaxed a few more degrees. This was how her practical mind had imagined the evening. Shoptalk, nothing more. "When do you start?"

"Any day, theoretically. Realistically, in a week or two. After some preproduction and studio work here, we'll head east. They figure about three weeks on location in Maryland, in and around Baltimore."

"You must be anxious to begin."

"I always get lazy between pictures. Nothing like a few 6:00 a.m. calls to get you back in gear. How's your fish?"

"It's wonderful." And once again, she'd all but cleared her plate without realizing it. "I bought a grill a few months ago, but I burned everything I put on it."

"A low flame," he said, and something in his voice made her skin tingle. "A careful eye." He took her hand, linking their fingers. "And patience."

"I—" He brought her hand to his lips, watching her over it as he kissed her fingers. "I'll have to give it another try."

"Your skin always smells as though you've walked through the rain. Even when you're not here I can't help thinking about that."

"We should—" Stop pretending, she thought. Acquiesce. Take what we want. "Go for a walk," she managed. "I'd like to see your pond again."

"All right." Patience, Sam reminded himself. But the flame wasn't as low as it had been. "Hold on a minute." He tossed a few scraps onto the grass before gathering up the dishes. She knew she should have offered her help, but she wanted, needed—badly needed—a moment alone.

She watched the cat saunter over to the fish with an arrogance that told her he'd been certain all along he'd get what he'd come for. Sam walked like that, Johanna thought, and suddenly cold, she rubbed her hands over her arms.

She wasn't afraid of him. She reminded herself of that to boost her confidence. But it was no less than the truth. She wasn't afraid of Sam: fear of herself, however, was another matter.

She was here because she wanted to be here. Wasn't it time to face that one fact? She'd already admitted that she hadn't come because he'd maneuvered her. She'd maneuvered herself, or that part of herself that was still determined to stand apart.

There was another part of herself, a part that was slowly

taking charge, that knew exactly what she wanted. Who she wanted. That was a part that had already made an enormous mistake by falling in love with Sam.

Before she had a chance to deal with the enormity of that realization, he was back, carrying a plastic bag filled with crackers.

"They'll expect to be— Are you all right?"

She was pale, and her eyes were huge. If Sam hadn't known better he would have sworn someone had come along and given her a fast, unexpected backhand.

"I'm fine." Thank God her voice was steady. She still had that much under control. "Your pets keep you under their thumb, don't they?"

Her smile didn't quite reach her eyes, but he nodded. "It looks that way." He touched her face. She didn't flinch, but he felt the muscles of her jaw tense. "You look a little dazed, Johanna."

Terrified was the word. In love with him, her mind repeated. Good Lord, when, how and, most of all, *why?* "It's probably the wine. I'll walk it off."

It had nothing to do with the wine, but he let it go. Taking her hand firmly in his, he started toward the path. "Next time you come, you're going to have to dress for this. As sensible as those shoes are, boots or sneakers are better for the hike."

Sensible. Frowning, Johanna looked down at her trim, low-heeled Italian pumps. Damn it, they were sensible. She managed to bite off the sigh. Sensible. Like her. "I told you I didn't have time to change."

"That's okay, I can always carry you."

"That won't be necessary."

There it was again, that low, cool tone. He didn't bother to fight back the smile as he steered her along.

The sun was nearly down, so the light was soft and pearly. There were wildflowers along the path that hadn't yet bloomed the last time they'd taken this walk. He imagined Johanna could name them for him if he asked, but he preferred to let them pop out of the ground anonymously.

He could smell the water now, and could just hear its faint lap against the high grass. Every time he'd walked there in the last few weeks he'd thought of her. The birds were quiet now, settling down for the night. Those that called the night their own had yet to stir. He liked the quiet of dusk, the aloneness of it, and wondered if she felt the same. He remembered how she'd knelt in front of a bank of flowers at sundown and figured that she did.

The water of the pond was darkening, like the sky. The shadows of the trees were long and dim across it. It still made her smile to see the ducks gliding over it, preening a bit in anticipation of an audience.

"I take it Silas and his companions don't bother them."

"Too much effort to come all the way out here and get wet when they've got the barn. Here." He handed her the bag. As she had before, Johanna laughed at the ducks' antics as she tossed the crackers to them.

"I guess no one spoils them like this when you're away."

"Mae does. She wouldn't admit it, though."

"Oh, I didn't see the drake close up before." She skimmed a cracker to him. "He's beautiful. And look how the babies have grown." She scattered crumbs on the water until the bag was empty. Without thinking, she tucked it into her pocket. "It's so nice here," she murmured. "Just the water, and the grass." And you, she thought. But she didn't look at him, not until his hand was on her cheek, gently urging her to.

It was just as it had been the first time. And yet it was nothing like it. This time she knew exactly how she would feel, how she would want, when he kissed her. She knew he would touch her hair before he drew her close. She knew her mind would cloud and her pulse would quicken.

She knew, but it still stunned her.

He felt as though he'd waited forever. It hadn't been merely weeks since he'd first seen her. She'd been under his skin, inside his heart, for as long as he could remember. A dream, a half-formed wish that had only taken one look at her to click solidly into place. It was so right. Somehow it was exactly right when his mouth found hers.

She still wasn't sure. He could feel the hesitation even as he felt the passion that drummed beneath it. But he was sure enough for both of them.

It was meant to be here, here where those first shock waves had passed through both of them. It was meant to be now, before night fell.

She tightened her grip on his shirt, holding on, holding back. In a moment, she knew, she wouldn't be able to think clearly. It would be wise to withdraw now, to leave things as they had been. But his lips coaxed her to stay. To trust.

She murmured, tensing up when she felt him slip the jacket from her shoulders. A step was being taken. Then he was soothing her, giving her time, plenty of time, but no choice at all. The buttons that ran down her back were loosened one by one in an agony of sweetness and promise. When she felt his fingers brush her skin, she shuddered at the contact and searched for the will to end it.

But his lips skimmed her throat as he peeled the blouse from her. She was helpless, but the sensation was no longer frightening.

Is this what it felt like to give in, at last, fully, completely give in to something not quite known but only sensed? Hadn't she waited for it, anticipated it, even while she'd struggled against it? Now the struggle was almost over.

He had to use every ounce of self-control not to rush her. He knew she needed time and care, even as his own needs balled like fists inside him. He'd already imagined what it would be like to touch her like this, to feel her tremble when he did. Her skirt slid down her hips. His hands followed it.

The sun had dropped away, but he could see her, her hair haloed around her face, her eyes wide and uncertain. He kissed her again, slowly, trailing his lips over her jaw as he shrugged out of his shirt. He saw her start to reach for him, then hesitate just short of contact. Taking her hand, he brought it, palm up, to his lips and felt her go limp.

He lowered her to the grass.

It was cool, soft and damp with early dew—a sensation Johanna knew she would remember always. He was over her, so she could only see his face, then only his eyes. She heard the first owl call before he bent to her. Then there was only him.

He touched. She shuddered, no longer from fear or from doubt, but from a pleasure so pure she could never have described it. He tasted. She floated, no longer helpless, but a willing partner. And when she reached for him, drew him closer, the world was shut off for both of them.

She was so soft, so generous. He wondered that he could still be surprised by how many facets there were to her. She'd opened to him now, as completely as he could have hoped.

If her touch was still shy, it was only more endearing. He wanted it to be sweet for her, memorable, and as special as he already knew it would be for him. Somewhere along the line she had stopped being a woman, however desirable, however fascinating, and had become his woman.

He took her, gently, higher.

When she moaned, desire thrummed in him, hard, demanding. He fought it back, wanting her to ride the wave as long as they could both stand it. Slowly, drawing out the process, he slipped her teddy down to her waist, then to her hips, letting the hunger build inside him.

Her fingers dug into the grass as he brushed his lips over her. She could feel her skin tremble wherever he chose to linger. Then, abruptly, the pleasure rocketed up, beyond anything she'd dreamed possible. She cried out his name, her body arching up. Pleasure doubled back, and he was with her again. Now her fingers dug into his shoulders desperately.

Stars began to wink to life above them.

The breath was dragging in and out of his lungs when he filled her. Now he was helpless, his face buried in her hair, his body more her prisoner than she had ever been his. Need expanded and became the focus of his world, and then even that shattered, leaving only her.

CHAPTER 8

He couldn't speak. At the moment Sam wasn't sure his mind would ever be able to direct that basic function again. He knew he should shift his weight from her but couldn't bear to break the bond.

Whatever else it had been—passion, desire, chemistry—it had forged a bond.

Overhead, the stars were still coming out. Johanna could see them now, but all she could think of was the way Sam's heart still raced against hers. She hadn't known she was capable of giving or receiving that kind of pleasure. Though the heat had eased, his body was still warm, a continuing contrast to the cool grass that waved around them. The water, pushed by the night breezes, lapped only a few feet away.

It had been a shock to realize she was capable of feeling anything this intensely, but more, she had seen his eyes, felt his body shudder, and had known for the first time in her life that she could give.

Hardly realizing she was doing so, she lifted a hand to stroke his hair. Sam was aware, even if she wasn't, that it was the first time she'd touched him without being backed into a corner. He closed his eyes and held on to that thought. What would once have been a small thing to him was now an enormous one. He'd slipped into the third phase, into love, almost painlessly.

"Johanna." When he could speak, her name was the first thing that formed. Because he wanted to see her, he found the strength to raise himself onto his elbows. Her hair was spread out on the grass that had bent under them. Her eyes were half-closed, but what he could see was still dazed with pleasure. "You're so lovely."

Her lips curved a bit, and she touched him again, her fingers on his face. "I didn't think this would happen. I didn't think it could."

"I imagined it, here, just like this." He lowered his head, just to brush his lips against hers. "But my fantasy didn't even come close to the real thing. Nothing ever has." He felt her withdraw at that, just a fraction, but enough that he felt compelled to take her face in his hand. "Nothing and no one, Johanna."

His eyes insisted that she believe him, and she wanted to, but there was still too much of a block within her to make that possible. "I've wanted you." At least she could be honest with both of them. "I can't think about what happens next."

"We're both going to have to. I've no intention of letting you go." She opened her mouth to protest, to make some excuse, and only managed to moan as she felt him harden inside her. "Not a chance," he murmured, before desire clouded his mind completely.

When she could think again, she tried to draw away. She was going to need time to put this in perspective, to work out the steps. The first was to be an adult, and not to expect.

They had shared something. Perhaps it hadn't been casual for her, but she'd always understood that every relationship had its limitations. Better to remember that now and face it from the outset. She cared, too much for her own good, but she still knew better than to cuddle up at his side and start thinking about tomorrows.

"It's late." She pulled her hands through her hair as she sat up. "I have to go."

He'd have been surprised if he could have moved again for eight hours. "Go where?"

"I have to go home." She reached for her teddy but missed by an inch when his hand braceleted her wrist.

"If you expect me to let you go anywhere tonight, you're crazy."

"I don't know what you're talking about." Her voice was amused as she tugged on her hand. "In the first place, it's not a matter of you *letting* me go anywhere." After picking up her teddy, she shook it out. "And I can hardly sleep in the grass all night."

"You're absolutely right." If she hadn't been so relaxed, she would have realized he'd given in too easily. "Here, put on my shirt. It'll be easier for you to dress inside."

Because it made sense, Johanna allowed him to bundle her into it. It carried his scent. Unconsciously she rubbed her cheek against the collar as Sam pulled on his jeans.

"Let me give you a hand with those." Sam took her now-folded clothes and draped them over his arm. "Better let me go first. There isn't much light tonight."

Johanna followed him down the path, hoping she seemed as casual and at ease as he. What had happened by the pond, weeks ago and now tonight, had been beautiful. She didn't want to lose the importance of it. But she didn't want to exaggerate its importance, either.

Nothing and no one else.

No, she'd be a fool to believe it—to hope for it. He might have meant it at the moment he'd said it. She could believe that because she'd come to understand that Sam wasn't a man for lies, even pretty ones. She could believe, too, that he cared for her—again, for the moment.

Intense feelings rarely lasted, and all the hopes and promises built on those feelings eventually crumbled. So she didn't allow herself to hope and refused to make promises.

They still had a long way to go, Sam mused. She wasn't ready to take what he'd discovered he was ready to give. The trouble was, now that he was in love with her he wouldn't be able to be so patient. Johanna was just going to have to keep pace.

As they stepped onto the terrace, he set her clothes neatly on the table. A frown formed between her brows as he casually stripped off his jeans.

"What are you doing?"

He stood before her, undeniably magnificent in the light of the moon. With a smile that warned her an instant too late, he hauled her into his arms.

"It's what *we're* doing," he said simply, and jumped into the pool.

The water was several degrees warmer than the night air, but it was still a shock. Before it closed over her head, she had time for one surprised shriek. Her legs tangled with his as the plunge separated them and the shirt billowed up around her head. Then her feet touched bottom, and instinctively she pushed upward. Gasping, she surfaced, blinking water from her eyes.

"Damn it!" She drew her arm through the water, hand fisted, and shot a spray into his grinning face.

"Nothing like a midnight swim, is there, Jo-Jo?"

"Don't call me that. You must be out of your mind."

"Only about you," he told her, then sent an unloverly splash in her direction.

Johanna dodged it, barely, telling herself she wasn't amused. "What the hell would you have done if I couldn't swim?"

"Saved you." He trod water with little effort. "I was born to be a hero."

"Jerk," she corrected. She turned, and in two strokes had reached the side. Before she could haul herself out, Sam caught her by the waist.

"When you stop being mad, you'll admit you like it." He nuzzled the back of her neck. "Want to race?"

"What I want to do is—" She turned—another miscalculation. His hands slid up her wet skin to her breasts as he bent his lips to her throat.

"Me too," he murmured.

She lifted a hand to his shoulder where it skimmed over cool skin just beginning to heat. "Sam, I can't."

"That's okay. I can." He slid into her.

*　*　*

Johanna woke with a faint grumble and tried to roll over. It took her several confusing seconds to realize that Sam's arm had her pinned. Lying still, she turned her head cautiously to look at him.

He slept more on her pillow than on his own. No, they were both his pillows, Johanna reminded herself. His bed, his house. Would he think her a fool or a freak if she told him this was the first time she'd ever woken up in a man's bed? It didn't matter; she wouldn't tell him. How could she tell him he was the first man she'd cared for enough, trusted enough, to share that private vulnerability called sleep?

She still wasn't quite sure how he'd managed to nudge her into it. One minute she'd been standing, naked and dripping, by the side of the pool, and the next . . . They hadn't even made love there, but had simply fallen into bed much like two exhausted children.

He'd made her laugh, too, and he'd given her, all unknowing, the sweet daydream of her own making.

Now it was morning and she had to remind herself again that she was an adult. They had wanted each other, enjoyed each other. It was important not to add complications to that simple formula. There wouldn't be regret. Regret usually meant blame, and she didn't want that, either. Wisely or not, she'd made a decision. The decision had taken her into intimacy with Sam. She wouldn't use the word *affair*.

Now that it was done, she had to be realistic. This intensity, this flash of feeling, would fade, and when that happened, she'd be hurt. It couldn't be prevented, only prepared for.

Her emotions had already deepened beyond her control, but she still had her strength and her sense. No strings. He'd said it. She'd meant it.

Despite that, she lifted a fingertip to brush the hair from his forehead.

Oh, God, I'm in love with him, I'm so ridiculously in love with him, and I'm bound to make a fool of myself.

When he opened his eyes, those dark, heavy-lidded eyes, she didn't give a damn.

"Hi."

She lowered her hand, flustered because he'd caught her petting him. "Good morning."

It was there, even after their incredible night together. The trace of shyness he found so appealing. So exciting. Because he didn't want to give her time to layer it over with composure, he rolled on top of her.

"Sam—"

"It occurs to me," he began as he drew longer, lazier kisses from her, "that we never made love in bed." He ran his hand down her side, from shoulder to hip, from hip to thigh. "I'm feeling traditional this morning."

She didn't have time to analyze what she was feeling. Even

as she tried to say his name again, her breath caught. This morning he wasn't so patient—or perhaps she, knowing what could be, was more sensitive.

She curled around him and let herself go.

* * *

Time had gotten away from her. Everything had gotten away from her, Johanna corrected as she stepped out of the shower and began to towel off quickly. If she threw on her clothes, let her hair air-dry on the way to work and pushed the speed limit, she might just make it.

She grabbed a few basic cosmetics out of her purse. The effort would be sketchy, but it was all she could afford. In the bedroom she ripped the plastic off the first suit Sam had brought up from her car. Yesterday's blouse would have to work with it. Cursing herself for not having planned properly, she zipped the skirt and ran down the hall carrying her shoes.

"Where's the fire?" Sam asked her as she rested a hand against the wall and struggled into her shoes.

"I'm running late."

He lifted a brow. "Do you get demerits for being tardy?"

"I'm never late."

"Good, then you can afford to be. Have some coffee."

She took the cup he offered, grateful. "Thanks. I really have to run."

"You haven't eaten anything."

"I never eat breakfast."

"Today you do." He had her arm. To prevent the contents of the cup sloshing all over her freshly laundered suit, she kept up with him. "Five minutes, Johanna. Catch your breath, drink your coffee. If you argue, it'll take ten."

She swore, but downed more coffee as he pulled her into the kitchen. "Sam, you're the one who's on vacation, not me. I've got a full day scheduled that might, if I'm lucky, end before six."

"All the more reason you should have a decent breakfast." He couldn't remember ever having felt better in the morning, more alive or full of energy. Briefly he wished he was in the middle of filming so that he could pour some of that energy into a part. "Sit. I'll fix you some eggs."

Because her temper was beginning to fray, she drank more coffee. "I appreciate it, really I do, but I don't have time. We're shooting ads today for the home viewers' contest, and I'm the only one who can handle John Jay."

"A dubious talent." The English muffin he'd dropped in the toaster popped up. "You can at least eat this."

Annoyed, she snatched it from him, ignored the butter and jam on the table and bit into it. "There," she said, and swallowed. "Satisfied?"

Her hair was still dripping around her face, and she'd forgotten her lipstick. Eyes still shadowed from the long night glared at him. He grinned and flicked a crumb off her chin. "I love you, Johanna."

If he'd drawn back and planted his fist on her chin she would have been no less shocked. She stared at him as the muffin slipped out of her boneless fingers onto the table. Her step back was instinctive, defensive. Sam lifted his brow at it, but that was all.

"Don't say that to me," she managed at length. "I don't need to hear that. I don't want to hear it."

She needed to hear it all right, he thought. She might not have wanted to, but she needed to. He was going to see that she did, at regular intervals, but right now she'd gone pale again. "All right," he said slowly. "It doesn't change the facts one way or the other."

"I—I have to go." She ransacked her purse almost desperately for her keys. "I'm really running late." What was she supposed to say? What was supposed to be said on the morning after the night? With her keys clutched in her hand, she looked up. "Goodbye."

"I'll walk you out." His arm went around her shoulders. She tried not to tense. She tried not to lean against him. She could feel the tug-of-war as they walked. "There's something I'd like to tell you, Johanna."

"Please, it isn't necessary. We agreed even before—before last night—that there wouldn't be any promises."

"Did we?" Damned if he remembered that, but if he had agreed, that was one agreement that would have to be broken. He pushed the front door open and stepped onto the porch before turning her to him. "We'll have to talk about that."

"All right." She would have agreed to almost anything if it had meant he'd let her go. Because she wanted to stay. More than she'd ever wanted anything, she wanted to toss her keys over her shoulder, throw herself into his arms and stay as long as he'd have her.

"In the meantime, I want you to know that I've never had another woman in that bed." He saw the flash of doubt in her eyes before she was able to mask it. And before he could stop himself, he'd hauled her up by the lapels. "Damn it, a man gets tired of having everything he says dissected in that brain of yours. I didn't say there haven't been other women, Johanna, but there's never been another woman here. Because here's special to me. It's important. And so are you." He let her go. "Chew on that for a while."

* * *

Johanna thumbed another antacid tablet from the roll. She'd told Sam no less than the truth when she'd said she was the only one who could handle John Jay. It just so happened that today she wasn't doing a good job of it. The two-hour photo session had stretched into three, and tempers were fraying. If she didn't have the crew, equipment and two cars out of the studio in another forty-five minutes she was going to have the producer of *Noon with Nina* on her back.

Resigned, Johanna chewed the antacid and prayed it did its job better than she was doing hers. She signaled for a halt and hoped the five-minute break would keep the photographer from strangling her host.

"John Jay." She knew the game. Johanna pasted a smile on her face as she crossed to him. "Can I have a minute?" Her voice was calm, her touch light and friendly, as she took his arm to guide him to a corner. "Sessions like this are so annoying, aren't they?"

He literally pounced on the sympathy. "You have no idea, Johanna. You know I want what's best for the show, darling, but that man . . ." He glanced over at the photographer with loathing. "He has no conception of mood or image."

"That man" was one of the tops in his business and was being paid by the incredibly expensive hour. Johanna bit off an oath in time to have it slip out as a sigh. "I know, but unfortunately we have to work with him. We're running behind schedule, and the last thing I want is to have him take shots of the cars only." She let the threat hang until she was certain it had sunk in. "After all, there are three stars here. The cars, the show itself and, of course, you. The teasers went beautifully, by the way."

"I was fresh." He fussed with the knot of his tie.

"I understand perfectly. But I have to ask you to keep the energy up for just a few more minutes. That suit's very becoming, John Jay."

"It is, isn't it?" He held out an arm, turning it over to study the sleeve.

"These shots are going to make quite a statement." If she

didn't strangle him herself first. "All I want you to do is stand between those two cars and flash the smile America loves."

"For you, darling." He squeezed her hand, ready to sacrifice himself to the masses. "You know, you're looking a little dragged-out."

Her smile didn't fade, only froze. "It's lucky I'm not having my picture taken."

"It certainly is," he agreed, patting Johanna's head. He already knew his producer could grow fangs if he patted her elsewhere. "You have to try to relax more, Johanna, and take those vitamins I told you about. God knows I couldn't get through the day without them." He watched the photographer come back on the set. With a sniff, John Jay signaled for makeup. "Johanna, there's a rumor running rampant that you're seeing Sam Weaver."

"Is there?" Johanna ground her teeth as John Jay got a dusting of powder. "It's amazing how these things get started."

"What a town." Satisfied that he was perfect, John Jay strode over to do his duty.

It took only twenty minutes more. The moment she'd sent her host on his way, Johanna apologized to the photographer, offered him and his assistant lunch on her and handed out tickets to Monday night's taping.

By the time she drove from the studio in Burbank back to her offices in Century City, she was two hours behind schedule and had consumed almost half the roll of antacids in her pocket.

"You've got a half-dozen messages," Bethany told her the moment she walked in. "Only two of which require answers yesterday. I contacted Tom Bradley's agent. He's interested in doing the pilot."

"Good. Let's set it up." In her office, Johanna dropped her

briefcase, accepted the cup of coffee Beth was already offering and sat on the edge of her desk. "I've thought of twenty-seven ways to successfully murder John Jay Johnson."

"Would you like me to type them up?"

"Not yet. I want to wait until I have an even thirty." Johanna sipped her coffee and wished for five minutes, five full minutes to be completely alone, so that she could take her shoes off, put her feet up and close her eyes. "Bradley has a reputation as being very professional."

"A veteran. Did his first show in '72, when he was still wet behind the ears. It ran for five years, and he slid right into the old classic *Word Bingo*. That was on the air from '77 to '85. Pretty amazing. He retired as sort of the guru of game shows, but his face is still recognizable from occasional appearances on other daytime shows and grand-marshaling parades. Luring him back to the fold would be no small accomplishment."

She stopped because Johanna was drinking coffee and staring out the window. There were shadows under her eyes, Bethany noted, and a definite look of melancholy in them. "Johanna, you look terrible."

Taken aback, Johanna set her coffee aside. "So I've been told."

"Is everything all right?"

"Everything's fine." Except that Sam said he was in love with her and she was so terrified she wanted to get in her car and keep driving. She drew out her roll of tablets.

Frowning, Beth eyed it. "Was that a new roll this morning?"

"It was, before I spent most of it with John Jay."

"Have any lunch?"

"Don't ask."

"Johanna, why don't you take the rest of the day off, go home, take a nap, watch the soaps?"

With a small smile, Johanna rose to move behind her desk. "I've got to answer those questions yesterday. Beth, let's see if we can set that pilot up for the week after next. Be sure to notify Patterson Productions."

Bethany shrugged and stood. "You're the boss," she said, and set the stack of messages on Johanna's desk.

Absolutely true, Johanna thought as Bethany closed the door behind her. She was the boss. Johanna rubbed at the headache behind her temple and wondered why she felt as though someone else were pulling the strings.

*   *   *

He didn't know what he was doing there, sitting on her front steps like a lovesick teenager. Because he was lovesick, Sam told himself as he crossed his booted ankles.

He hadn't felt this stupid about a woman since he'd fallen like a ton of bricks for Mary Alice Reeder. She'd been an older woman, sophisticated, wise and like most sixteen-year-old girls, not very interested in a fourteen-year-old pest. But he'd loved pretty little Mary Alice with a kind of worshipful devotion that had lasted nearly nine months.

Calf love, his mother had called it, not unkindly.

Since then he'd fallen into the second stage, the care-for stage, with a number of women. But he hadn't loved anyone else since Mary Alice Reeder. Until Johanna.

He almost wished he could go back to that calf love. However painful it was, it passed, and it left a man with sweet and rather filmy memories. Hearts and initials carved surreptitiously in a tree trunk, daydreams that always ended with him saving his girl from some horrendous disaster that opened her eyes to his charm and bravery.

Sam laughed at himself and looked at a spiky blue flower

that was just beginning to bloom in Johanna's garden. Times changed. Mary Alice had slipped through his shaky fingers. But he wasn't fourteen anymore, and Johanna, like it or not, was going nowhere.

He wanted her. Just sitting there in front of her quiet, empty house, with a basket beside him and her flowers sleeping in the evening sun, he wanted her. For good. It wasn't a decision he'd made with a snap of his fingers, though she might think so. It was something that had happened to him, and not entirely in a way he liked. The only plans he'd counted on, the only pressure he'd expected, had been career-oriented.

If he'd had his choice, he would have cruised along for another few months, a year. Ten years. Time didn't have a damn thing to do with it. He'd looked at her, he'd touched her, and the decision had been made for him.

Hadn't he sat right here not so long before and told her they should get to know each other better? Companions, with no strings. He'd meant it, every bit as honestly as he'd meant it when he'd told her he loved her.

She'd accepted the first—warily, but she had accepted it. The second had been met with pure panic.

What was it that made Johanna so skittish? Another man? She'd never mentioned one, never even hinted at one. Unless he was completely obtuse, the woman he'd made love with the night before had been almost frighteningly innocent. If she'd been hurt, he felt it must be buried deep in the past, and it was time for her to let it go.

Time. He didn't have much of that, he thought as he lifted the lid of the basket to check on his gift. Any day he could get the call that would send him three thousand miles away. It would be weeks before he could be with her again. He could handle that. He thought he could handle that, but only if she gave him something to take with him.

When he heard the car he set the lid carefully back in place.

Lovesick, he thought as his stomach knotted and his nerves began to jangle. It was a very apt phrase.

Johanna pulled in behind his car and wondered what the hell she was going to do. She'd been so sure she would be able to come home, close herself in, maybe dive into bed and sleep for hours without thinking at all. But he was here, invading her privacy, stealing away her quiet hours. The worst of it was, she was glad, so glad to see him.

"You put in a long day." He rose but didn't cross to her.

"A lot of things are coming to a head at once."

He waited until she stood in front of him. "I know what you mean." He touched her then, just a light stroke down her cheek. "You look tired."

"So I've been informed, with annoying regularity."

"Are you going to let me come in?"

"All right." He hadn't kissed her. Johanna had expected it this time, had been prepared for it. As she turned toward the house she suspected that was exactly why he hadn't done it. She spotted the wicker basket and paused as he scooped it up. "What did you do, bring sandwiches in case I was late?"

"Not exactly." He followed her inside. It was precisely as it had been the last time, neat, homey, smelling faintly of potpourri and fresh flowers. They were peonies this time, fat red blooms in a dark blue jar.

Johanna started to slip out of her shoes, caught herself and set down her briefcase.

"Can I get you a drink?"

"Why don't you sit down and I'll fix you one?" He set the basket down next to the jar of flowers. "I'm the one on vacation, remember?"

"I usually just get some coffee, but—"

"Fine. I'll get it."

"But—"

"Relax, Johanna. It'll just take a minute."

He strode off as she stood where she was. As far as she could remember, no one had ever cut her off in the middle of so many sentences. Well, he'd invited himself, she decided. He could heat up the coffee as well as she. And she did want to sit down, for just a minute.

She chose the corner of the sofa and thought she might rest her eyes until she heard Sam coming back. Johanna stifled a yawn, shut her eyes and was asleep in seconds.

She awoke the same way, instantly. Somehow she'd snuggled down and had pulled an afghan up to her chin. Sitting up, Johanna dragged her hands through her hair just before she spotted Sam sitting across from her drinking coffee.

"I'm sorry." She cleared the huskiness out of her voice. "I must have dozed off."

She'd slept like a rock for half an hour. He'd tucked her up himself. "How do you feel?"

"Embarrassed."

He smiled and rose to go to the coffeepot he'd set on a warmer. "Want this now?"

"Yes, thanks."

"You didn't get much sleep last night."

"No." She took the coffee, studying the little painted cup as though it fascinated her. "Neither did you."

"I didn't put in a ten-hour day." He sat beside her. She was up like a spring.

"I'm starving," she said quickly. "There isn't much out in the kitchen, but I can put together a couple of sandwiches."

"I'll give you a hand."

Even as he rose, she was shrugging out of her jacket. "That's all right, it's no trouble." Nervous, she turned the jacket over, spilling out the contents of the pockets. Sam bent over and picked up loose change, a hairpin and what was left of the roll of antacids.

"What do you need these for?"

"Survival." Taking everything from him, she set them on the table.

"You put yourself under too much pressure. How many of these do you take?"

"For heaven's sake, Sam, they're more candy than medicine."

Her defensive tone had his eyes narrowing. Too many, he decided. "I'm entitled to worry about you." When she started to shake her head, he cupped her chin in his hand. "Yes, I am. I love you, Johanna, whether you can deal with it yet or not."

"You're pushing me too fast."

"I haven't even started to push yet."

With her face still caught in his hand, he kissed her. His lips demanded response, nothing timid, nothing cool. She could taste the trace of anger on them, the hint of frustration. Desire, kicked into high gear by other emotions, held sway. If it had been possible, she would have pulled back, ended it then and there. But it wasn't possible.

She touched a hand to his cheek, not even aware that she sought to soothe. As the kiss deepened, she slid her hand up into his hair. His name was like a sigh from her lips to his. Then she was locked close.

It was the whirlwind again, fast and furious. This time it was she who tugged at his shirt, wanting that contact, that intimate, secret feel of flesh against flesh. Her need was a springboard for his. Tangled, groping at buttons, they tumbled onto the couch.

Even last night, in that first burgeoning passion, she hadn't been like this. She trembled as she had trembled before, but now it was anticipation, even impatience, that shivered through her. To be swept away wasn't what she looked for now; to be taken wasn't enough. It had only taken one night for her to realize her own power. Now she was driven to test it again.

He struggled to keep his hands gentle as the insistence of

hers had desire clawing at him. Her mouth, open and hungry, sought the taste of him, chest, shoulders, throat, while she tugged at the snap of his jeans and sent his stomach muscles dancing.

"Johanna." As much for her preservation as his own, he tried to slow the pace. Then her mouth was back on his, silencing him, ripping the last shreds of control.

The last light of day streamed through the windows of a room scented by flowers in a house tucked almost secretly in the hills. As long as he lived he would think of her that way—in soft light, in fresh scents, alone.

She hadn't known she could be like this, so full of need, so desperate to be filled. Heedless, daring, reckless. She felt the teddy he'd slipped so carefully from her the night before tear as he yanked aside the barrier.

Then she captured him, drawing him in, arching high as pleasure arrowed into her. Fast, then faster still, she drove them both in a race for that final dazzling release.

He held on to her, even after her body went lax, after his own emptied. Her shyness had delighted him, lured him, but this Johanna, the one who could flash with white heat, could make him a slave. He wasn't certain what he'd done, he only remembered the grasping, titanic lunge into delirium.

"Did I hurt you?" he murmured.

"No." She was too stunned by her own behavior to notice any bruises. "Did I hurt you?"

He grinned against her throat. "I didn't feel a thing." He tried to shift her to a more comfortable position and spotted the remains of her teddy on the floor. "I owe you some lingerie," he murmured as he lifted it up.

Johanna studied the torn strap and rent seam. Abruptly she began to laugh. She felt like that, torn open, and God only knew what would pour through the holes. "I've never attacked a man before," she managed.

"You can practice on me anytime. Here." He picked up his shirt and slipped it over her shoulders. "I always seem to be lending you a shirt. Johanna, I want you to tell me how you feel. I need you to."

Slowly, hoping to gather up some of her scattered senses, she buttoned the shirt. "There are reasons . . . I can't talk about them, Sam, but there are reasons why I don't want things to get serious."

"Things already are serious."

He was right. She knew he was right even before she looked into his eyes and felt it. "How serious?"

"I think you know. But I'm willing to spell it out for you again."

She wasn't being fair. It was so important, and sometimes so impossible, to be fair. There was too much she couldn't tell him, she thought. Too much he'd never be able to understand even if she could. "I need time."

"I've got a couple of hours."

"Please."

"All right." It wasn't easy, but he promised himself he'd give her time, even though he felt it slipping away. He tugged on his jeans, then remembered the basket. "I almost forgot. I brought you a present." He plucked up the basket and set it in her lap.

He wasn't going to push. She shot him a quick look of gratitude, then added a smile. "What, a picnic?" She flipped back the lid, but instead of cold chicken she saw a small dozing kitten. Johanna drew her out and was instantly in love. "Oh, Sam! She's adorable." The kitten mewed sleepily as she rubbed its rust-colored fur against her cheek.

"Blanche had a litter last month." He tickled the kitten's ears.

"Blanche? As in Dubois?"

"Now you're catching on. She's sort of a faded Southern belle who likes to pit the toms against each other. This one's weaned, and there's enough cat food in the basket to get you through about a week."

The kitten climbed down the front of her skirt and began to fight with one of the buttons. "Thank you." Johanna turned to him as he stroked the kitten's head. For the first time, she threw her arms around Sam's neck and hugged him.

CHAPTER 9

He knew he shouldn't be nervous. It was an excellent production, with a quality script, top-notch casting and a talented director. He'd already seen the rushes, as well as a preview of the press screening. He knew he'd done a good job. But still he paced and watched the clock and wished like hell it was nine.

No, he wished it was eleven and the damn thing was over.

It was worse because Johanna was engrossed in the script Max Heddison had sent him. So Sam was left to worry, nurse the brandy he had no desire for and pace her living room. Even the redheaded kitten, which Johanna had christened Lucy, was too busy to bother with him. She was involved with wrestling a ball of yarn under Johanna's feet.

Sam made himself sit, poked at the Sunday paper, then was up again.

"You could take a walk outside for a change of scenery," Johanna suggested from across the room.

"She speaks! Johanna, why don't we go for a ride?"

"I have to finish this. Sam, Michael's a wonderful part for you, a really wonderful part."

He'd already decided that, but it was Luke, the character who would be exposed to millions of eyes in a matter of thirty minutes, who worried him. If he took on Michael, that would be another worry at another time. "Yeah. Johanna, it's lousy for your eyes to hold papers that close."

She moved them back automatically. In less than a minute she had her nose against them again. "This is wonderful, really wonderful. You're going to take it, aren't you?"

"For a chance to work with Max Heddison, I'd take it if it was garbage."

"Then you're lucky it shines. God, this scene here, the one on Christmas Eve, just leaves you limp."

He stopped pacing long enough to glance at her again. She was rereading it as avidly as she'd read it the first time. And the papers were an inch from her face.

"You keep that up, you're going to need glasses." He saw the frown come and go and was distracted enough to smile. "Unless you already do."

Without bothering to glance up, she turned a page. "Shut up, Sam, you're breaking my concentration."

Instead, he pulled the script away and held it at a reasonable distance. "Read me some dialogue."

"You already know what it says." She made a grab for the script, but he inched it away.

"You can't, can you? Where are your glasses, Johanna?"

"I don't need glasses."

"Then read me some dialogue."

She squinted, but the words ran together. "My eyes are just tired."

"Like hell." He set the script down to take her hands. "Don't tell me my sensible Johanna's too vain to wear reading glasses."

"I'm not vain, and I don't need glasses."

"You'd look cute in them." When she pulled her hands away, he made two circles out of his index fingers and thumbs and held them over her eyes. "Studiously sexy. Dark frames—yes, that would be best. Very conservative. I'd love to take you to bed while you were wearing them."

"I never wear them."

"Ah, but you do have them. Where?"

She made a grab for the script, but he blocked her. "You're just trying to distract yourself."

"You're right. Johanna, I'm dying in here."

She softened enough to touch his face. It was something she still did rarely. Automatically he lifted his hand to her wrist and held it there. "The reviews couldn't have been better, Sam. America waits for nine o'clock with bated breath."

"And America might be snoring by nine-fifteen."

"Not a chance." Reaching over, she picked up the remote to turn on the set. "Sit down. We'll watch something else until it starts."

He eased into the chair with her, shifting her until she stretched across his lap. "I'd rather nibble on your ear until it starts."

"Then we'll miss the first scene." Content, she rested her head against his shoulder.

It had been an odd weekend, she thought. He'd stayed with her. After her first unease, they'd fallen into a simple routine that was no routine at all. Lovemaking, sleep, walks, the little chores a house required, even a trip to the market to fuss over fresh vegetables.

She hadn't felt like a producer for forty-eight hours, nor had she thought of Sam as an actor. Or a celebrity. He'd been her lover—or, as he had once put it, her companion. How lovely life would be if it could be that simple. It had been difficult, even for these short two days, to pretend it could be. It had been much less difficult to wish.

She'd changed his life. He didn't know how to explain it,

or how to put it into words she might understand, but change it she had. He'd known that for certain when he'd gotten the script.

Max Heddison had been as good as his word. Sam had felt like a first-year drama student being offered the lead in a summer-stock production. It had come through Marv, of course, along with Marv's opinion about potential, the old school and the new, a million five plus percentages. Sam had taken it all in. It was never wise to forget that show business remained a business. Then he had devoured the script.

There was a part of him, a part he hoped would always be there, that could break out in a sweat at the chance to take on a new role. The character of Michael was complex, confused, desperately trying to unravel the mystery of his much-loved, much-detested father. He could already see Max Heddison in that role. Slowly, trying to see the script as a whole, as well as a vehicle, he'd read it again.

And he'd known he wanted to do it. Had to do it.

If Marv could get a million five, fine and dandy. If he could get peanuts and a keg of beer, that was all right, too. But rather than picking up the phone and calling his agent with a go-ahead, he'd bundled up the script and taken it to Johanna.

He'd needed her to read it. He'd needed her opinion, though throughout his career he'd always gone on his own gut instinct. Agent or not, the final decision had always been his. Now that had changed.

In a matter of weeks she'd become entwined with his life, his thoughts, his motives. Though he'd never thought of himself as a solitary person, he'd stopped being alone. She was there now, to share with—the big things, like the script, and the small things, like a new litter of kittens. It might have been true that she still held back from him, but in the last two days he'd seen her relax. Degree by degree, certainly, but he'd been able to see the change. That morning she'd seemed almost used to waking beside him.

He was giving her time, Sam thought as he brushed his lips over her hair. But he was also making his moves.

"Here come the teasers," Johanna murmured, and he was jerked back to the present. His stomach clenched. He swore at himself, but it tightened anyway, as it did whenever he prepared to watch himself on-screen. He flashed on, wearing only faded jeans, a battered panama and a grin, while the voice-over promised the sultry and the shocking.

"It is a nice chest." She smiled and kissed him on the cheek.

"They spent half the time spraying it so it'd have that nice jungle-fatigue shine. Do women really pant over a sweaty chest?"

"You bet," she told him, and settled down to watch the opening credits.

She was drawn in before the first five minutes were over. Luke drifted into town with two dollars in his pocket, a reputation on his back and an eye for the ladies. She knew it was Sam, pulling bits and pieces of his art together to meld with the writer's, but it rang true. You could almost smell the sweat and boredom of the sleepy little town in Georgia.

During the first commercial he slid down to the floor to give her the chair. He didn't want to ask her now, didn't want to break the rhythm. But he rested a hand on her calf.

For two hours they said nothing. She rose once and came back with cold drinks, but they didn't exchange words. On screen she watched the man she'd slept with, the man she'd loved, seduce another woman. She watched him talk himself out of one fight and raise his fists for another. He got drunk. He bled. He lied.

But she'd stopped thinking of him as Sam. The man she watched was Luke. She felt the slight pressure of Sam's fingers against her leg and kept her eyes on Luke.

He was irresistible. He was unforgivable.

When the segment ended, it left her hanging and Sarah's roses dying in the bowl.

Sam still said nothing. His instincts told him it was good. It was better than good. It was the best he'd ever done. Everything had fallen into place—the performances, the atmosphere, those lazy two-edged words that had first caught his imagination and his ambition. But he wanted to hear it from her.

Rising, he shifted to sit on the arm of her chair. Johanna, his Johanna, was still frowning at the screen. "How could he do that to her?" she demanded. "How could he use her that way?"

Sam waited a moment, still careful. "He's a user. It's all he knows."

"But she trusts him. She knows he's lied and cheated, but she still trusts him. And he's—"

"What?"

"He's a bastard, but— Damn, there's something compelling about him, something likable. You want to believe he could change, that she could change him." Unsettled, moved, she looked up at him. "What are you grinning at?"

"It worked." He hauled her up and kissed her. "It worked, Johanna."

She backed up enough to breathe. "I didn't tell you how good I thought you were."

"You just did." He kissed her again, then began tugging up her shirt.

"Sam—"

"I suddenly find myself with all this energy—incredible energy. Let me show you." He slid back into the chair, taking her with him.

"Wait a minute." She laughed, then moaned when his hands began to wander. "Sam, give me a minute."

"I've got hours for you. Hours and hours."

"Sam." With one laughing shove, she held him off. "I want to talk to you."

"Is it going to take long?" He tugged at the waistband of her slacks.

"No." To stop him, she framed his face with her hands. "I want to tell you how really exceptional you were. I pretended once that I didn't pay attention to your films, but I have. And you were never better than tonight."

"Thanks. It means a lot coming from you."

She took a deep breath, managing to push herself out of the chair. "You put a lot into that part."

She was leading somewhere. Though he wasn't sure he'd like the destination, he let her take the lead. "A part's not worth anything unless you do. Nothing is."

No, nothing was. "I, ah . . . I almost forget, when we're like this, who you are. These past few weeks, here, at the ranch, it hasn't been like being with Sam Weaver in capital letters."

Puzzled, he rose with her. "Johanna, you're not going to try to tell me you're intimidated by actors? You've been around the business all your life."

"All my life," she murmured. She didn't want to love him. She didn't want to love anyone, but most particularly not an actor, a movie star, a household name. The trouble was, she already did. "It's not a matter of being intimidated, it's just that it's been easy to forget you're not just an ordinary man who I ran into and grew fond of."

"Fond of," he repeated, drawing out the phrase. "Well, we're improving." He had her by the shoulders. That lazy drawl of a voice could fool you into forgetting how quick he was. "I don't know what the hell this is about, but we'll get to it in a minute. Right now, I want you to look at me. Really look at me, Johanna," he repeated, adding a little shake. "And tell me if you're in love with me."

"I never said—"

"No one knows better than I what you've never said." He drew her a little closer, insisting that her eyes stay on his. "I want to hear it now, and it has nothing to do with how I make my living, what the critics say or how much I'm worth at the box office. Do you love me?"

She started to shake her head but simply couldn't force it to move. How could she lie when he was looking at her, when he was touching her? She drew a deep breath to be certain her voice was calm. "Yes."

He wanted to take her then, just gather her close and hold on. But he knew that not only did he have to hear the words, she had to say them. "Yes, what?"

"Yes, I love you."

He looked at her for a long time. She was trembling a little, so he lowered his head and pressed his lips to her forehead. He didn't know why it was so difficult for her to say.

Not yet. But he was determined to find out.

"That should make things easier."

"But it doesn't," she murmured. "It doesn't change anything."

"We'll talk about it. Let's sit down."

She nodded. She didn't know what there was to say, but there had to be something. Trying to make it seem normal, she started to the front door to lock up for the night. Then she heard the quick report on the evening news.

"Sources report that Carl W. Patterson, respected producer, has suffered a heart attack this evening. Paramedics were summoned to his Beverly Hills estate, which he shares with his fiancée, Toni DuMonde. His condition at this hour remains critical."

"Johanna." Sam laid a hand on her arm. She hadn't gasped or cried out. There were no tears in her eyes. She had simply stopped in her tracks as though she'd run into a wall. "Get your purse. I'll take you to the hospital."

"What?"

"I'll drive you." He switched off the set and went to get her bag himself. "Come on."

She only nodded and let him lead her out.

*   *   *

No one had called her. The oddness of it struck Sam as they rode the elevator up to Cardiac Care. Her father had had a heart attack, and she hadn't been notified.

The year before, when his mother had broken her ankle in a nasty fall on the ice, he'd received three calls in a matter of hours. One from his sister, another from his father and the last from his mother, telling him that his sister and father were fuss-budgets.

Nonetheless the ankle had worried him enough to have him do some quick scheduling adjustments so that he could make the trip back East. He'd only had thirty-six hours to spare, but it had been time enough to see his mother for himself, sign her cast and put his mind at rest.

And a broken ankle was a far cry from a heart attack.

Johanna was Patterson's only child, yet she'd had to hear about her father's illness on the eleven-o'clock news. Even if they weren't close, as he'd already deduced, they were family. In Sam's experience, families stuck together in times of crisis.

She'd barely said a word since they'd left the house. He'd tried to comfort her, to offer both hope and support, but she hadn't responded. It seemed to him that she was just going through the motions, pale, a little dazed, but with the automatic control that had slipped effortlessly back into place. He watched her approach the nurse's station. Her hands were steady, her voice was calm and unwavering when she spoke.

"Carl Patterson was admitted this evening. They told me downstairs he's in CCU."

The nurse—sturdy, mid-forties and used to the night shift—barely glanced up. "I'm sorry, we're not permitted to give out patient information."

"He's my father," Johanna said flatly.

The nurse looked up. Reporters and the curious used all kinds of ploys to glean information on the famous. She'd already discouraged a few of them that evening. The woman on the other side of the counter didn't look like a reporter—the nurse prided herself on having a nose for them—but she hadn't been told to expect family, either. Recognizing doubt, Johanna drew out her wallet and identification.

"I'd like to see him, if that's possible, and speak with his doctor."

The nurse felt a stirring of sympathy. Her gaze shifted and locked on Sam. She recognized him, and though seeing him face-to-face would give her something to tell her husband when they passed over the breakfast table, she wasn't overly impressed. After twenty years of nursing in Beverly Hills she was accustomed to seeing celebrities, often naked, sick and vulnerable. But she did remember reading that Sam Weaver was having a fling with Carl Patterson's daughter.

"I'll be happy to page the doctor for you, Miss Patterson. There's a waiting room down the hall and to the left. Miss Du-Monde is already there."

"Thank you." She turned and started down, refusing to think past the moment, refusing to think past the action required to get beyond that moment. She heard a bell ding quietly, almost secretively, then the soft slap of crepe-soled shoes.

The panic was gone, that first thunder of panic that had filled her head when she'd heard the news report. Replacing it was the knowledge that she had to put one foot in front of the other and do whatever needed to be done. She was used to doing such things alone.

"Sam, I have no idea how long this might take. Why don't you go home? I can take a cab back when I'm ready."

"Don't be ridiculous," was all he said.

It was enough, more than enough to cause her breath to hitch. She wanted to turn to him, to press her face against his chest. She wanted to be held, to be passive, to let him handle whatever had to be done. Instead, she turned into the waiting room.

"Sam!" Toni's eyes, already damp, spilled over. She sprang out of her chair and launched herself into his arms. "Oh, Sam, I'm so glad you're here. I've been so frightened. It's a nightmare. I'm just sick with worry, Sam. I don't know what I'll do if Carl dies."

"Pull yourself together." Sam led her back to a chair, then lit one of the cigarettes she'd spilled from a pack onto the table. He stuck it between her fingers. "What did the doctor say?"

"I don't know. He was so technical and grim faced." She held out a hand to a blond man in a dinner jacket. "I never would have survived this without Jack. He's been a wall, an absolute wall. Hello, Johanna." She sniffled into a lacy handkerchief.

"Sam." Jack Vandear nodded as he patted Toni's hand. He'd directed two of Patterson's productions and had run into Sam at least a half-dozen times on the party circuit. "It's been a rough night."

"So we heard. This is Patterson's daughter."

"Oh." Jack rose and offered a hand.

"I'd like to know what happened."

"It was horrible." Toni looked up at Johanna through an attractive veil of tears. "Just horrible."

Jack sent her a look that was three parts impatient, one part sympathetic. He hadn't minded comforting her, but the truth was, he'd come for Carl. It went through his mind that with Sam here, the soggy-eyed Toni could be passed along.

"We were having a small dinner party. Carl looked a bit tired, but I took it to mean he'd been working too hard, as usual. Then it seemed he couldn't get his breath. He collapsed into a chair. He complained of pain in his chest and his arm. We called the paramedics." He started to skim over the rest, then decided Johanna looked strong enough to handle it. "They had to bring him back once." At that Toni put up a low, heartbreaking sob and was ignored. "The doctor said it was a massive coronary. They've been working to stabilize him."

Her legs were shaking. She could keep her hands steady and her face impassive, but she couldn't stop her legs from trembling. Massive coronary. Darlene, her father's wry and witty third wife, would have said that Carl W. Patterson never did anything halfway.

"Did they tell you his chances?"

"They haven't told us much of anything."

"We've been waiting forever." Toni dabbed at her eyes again, then drew on her cigarette. In her own way, she was fond of Carl. She wanted to marry him even though she knew that divorce would be at the end of the rainbow. Divorce was easy. Death was another matter. "The press was here five minutes after we were. I knew how much Carl would hate having them report this."

Johanna sat and for the first time looked, really looked, at her father's fiancée. Whatever she was, the woman obviously knew Carl. The heart attack was a weakness, and he would detest having it made public knowledge. "I'll handle the press," she said tonelessly. "It might be best if you, both of you," she said, including Jack, "told them as little as possible. Have you seen him?"

"Not since they took him in," Toni took another drag as she looked out into the corridor. "I hate hospitals." After crushing out the cigarette, she began to pleat the handkerchief. The silver sequins on her evening dress sparkled opulently in the dim waiting room. "We were supposed to go to Monaco next week. Carl had some business there, but for the most part it was to be a kind of prehoneymoon. He seemed so . . . well, so virile." The tears started again when the doctor came into the waiting room.

"Miss DuMonde."

She was up and clutching at both his hands, the picture of the distressed lover barely holding back hysteria. It surprised her to discover it was only half an act. "He's all right. Tell me Carl's all right."

"His condition's stabilized. We're running tests to determine the extent of the damage. He's a strong man, Miss DuMonde, and overall his health seems excellent."

He looked tired, Johanna thought as she studied the doctor. Unbearably tired, but she recognized the truth. She rose as he glanced her way.

"You're Mr. Patterson's daughter?"

"I'm Johanna Patterson. How serious is his condition?"

"I have to tell you it's very serious. However, he's getting the best care possible."

"I'd like to see him."

"For a few moments. Miss DuMonde?"

"He wouldn't want me to see him this way. He'd hate it."

Because Johanna could only agree, she ignored the little stab of resentment and followed the doctor out. "He's sedated," she was told. "And he's being monitored very closely. The next twenty-four hours will tell the tale, but your father's relatively young, Miss Patterson. An incident like this is often a warning, to slow down, to take a hard look at your own mortality."

It had to be said, just once out loud, though she knew she would get no absolutes. "Is he going to die?"

"Not if we can help it." The doctor pushed open a glass door. There was her father. She'd lived in his house, eaten his food, obeyed his rules. And she barely knew him. The machines that eased his breathing and monitored his vital signs hummed. His eyes were shut, his face pasty under his tan. He looked old. It occurred to her that she'd never thought of him as old, even when she'd been a child. He'd always been handsome, ageless, virile.

She remembered Toni using that word. Virile. That was so important to Carl. He'd often been described as a man's man— salty tongued, strong shouldered, reckless with women. He'd always been impatient with weaknesses, excuses, illnesses. Perhaps that was why, when he'd reached the middle of his life, the women he'd brought into it had become younger and younger.

He was a hard man, even a cold one, but he'd always been full of life. There was a genius in him, a genius she'd admired as much as she'd feared it. He was an honest man, a man of his word, but never one to give an inch more than he chose.

She touched him once, just a hand over his. It was a gesture she would never have considered making had he been awake.

"Will it happen again?"

"He has an excellent chance of full recovery, if he throws away the cigars, watches his alcohol intake and cuts back on his schedule. There's his diet, of course," the doctor went on, but Johanna was already shaking her head.

"I can't imagine him doing any of those things."

"People often do what others can't imagine after they end up in CCU. It'll be his choice, of course, but he's not a stupid man."

"No, he's not." She removed her hand. "We'll need a press release. I can take care of that. When will he be awake?"

"You should be able to talk to him in the morning."

"I'd appreciate a call if there's any change before then. I'll leave my number at the nurses' station."

"I should be able to tell you more in the morning." The doctor pushed open the door again. "You'd do well to get some rest yourself. A recovering cardiac patient can be wearing."

"Thank you." Alone, she started back down the hall. In self-defense, she blocked out the image of her father in the hospital bed. The moment she walked back in, Toni was up and grabbing both her hands.

"How is he, Johanna? Tell me the truth, tell me everything."

"He's resting. The doctor's very optimistic."

"Thank God."

"Carl will have to make some adjustments—diet, work load, that sort of thing. You'll be able to see him tomorrow."

"Oh, I must look a wreck." The need to check was so ingrained that Toni was already reaching for her compact. "I'll have to take care of that by tomorrow. I wouldn't want him to see me with my eyes all red and my hair a fright."

Again, because it was true, Johanna held back her sarcasm. "He won't wake up until tomorrow, according to the doctor. I'm going to handle the press—through a hospital spokesman, I think—and make certain his publicist has time to work up a statement. It might be a day or two before he's able to make those decisions for himself."

She wavered there a moment, trying to imagine her father unable to make any decision. "The important thing for you to do is to keep him calm. Go home and get some rest. They'll call if there's any change before morning."

"How about you?" Sam asked her when Jack had taken Toni down the corridor. "Are you all right?"

"Yes, I'm fine."

Wanting to judge for himself, he took her chin in his hand. There was something about the eyes, he thought. More than shock, certainly different than grief. Big secrets, he decided. Big fears. "Talk to me, Johanna."

"I've told you everything."

"About your father's condition." Though she tried to draw away, he held on. "I want to know about yours."

"I'm a little tired. I'd like to go home."

"Okay." Better, he thought, that they hash this, whatever it was, out at home. "We'll go back. But I'm staying with you."

"Sam, there's no need."

"There's every need. Let's go home."

CHAPTER 10

It was after one a.m. when they arrived at Johanna's house, but she went straight to the phone. With a pen in one hand, she began to flip through her address book. "It shouldn't take long for me to set this up," she told Sam, "but you don't have to wait up."

"I'll wait." There were things that had to be said, and he wanted them said before she had a chance to build the barricades again. Though she looked steady, perhaps too steady, he was coming to understand her. Still, he left her alone as she began to dial.

There was little enough she could do. She was certain her father would tolerate only the slightest interference from her, but he would want his people informed. Johanna fed information to his publicist, then hashed out a simple, straightforward press release.

While she was calming her father's assistant and making sure that the daily business of Patterson Productions would run as smoothly as possible, Sam handed her a mug. Grateful, Johanna sipped, expecting coffee. Instead she tasted the soothing herbal tea she'd bought on impulse and brewed occasionally after a particularly long day.

"I'll be able to tell you more tomorrow, Whitfield. No,

whatever can't be handled by you or another member of the staff will have to be canceled. That would appear to be your problem, wouldn't it?"

Across the room, Sam had no choice but to smile at her tone. As producers went, he'd never heard better.

"Where's Loman? Well, call him back." She made a quick notation on a pad. "Yes, that's right, but I'm sure he'll be giving you instructions himself in a couple of days. You'll have to check with the doctor on that, but I don't think you'll be able to discuss that or anything else with Carl for at least forty-eight hours." Her voice changed, went frigid. "That's not really the issue here, Whitfield. You'll have to consider Carl unavailable until further notice. No, I won't take the responsibility, you will. That's what you're paid for."

She hung up, incensed by the man's insensitivity. "Idiot," she muttered as she picked up her tea again. "His main concern is that Carl insisted on supervising the editing of *Fields of Fire*, and the heart attack is going to put the project behind schedule."

"Are you finished?"

Still frowning, she skimmed down her notes. "I don't think there's any more I can do."

"Come and sit down." He waited until she'd joined him on the sofa, then poured more tea into her cup from the pot he'd brewed. Sensing tension even before he touched her, Sam began to massage her shoulders. "It's hard, only being able to wait."

"Yes."

"You handle yourself well, Johanna."

She sipped tea and stared straight ahead. "I had a good teacher."

"Tell me about your father."

"I told you everything the doctor told me."

"I don't mean that." She was tensing up again, even as he

massaged the muscles. "Tell me about him, about you and him."

"There's really nothing to tell. We've never been particularly close."

"Because of your mother?"

She went stiff at that. "What does my mother have to do with it?"

"I don't know. You tell me." He'd been shooting in the dark, but he wasn't surprised that he'd hit the target. "Johanna, you don't have to be a gossip buff to know that your parents divorced when you were, what—four?"

"I'd just turned five." It still hurt. No matter how often she told herself it was foolish, even unhealthy, the child's pain and confusion leaked into the woman. "That's history, Sam."

He didn't think so. Instinct told him it was as much a part of the present as he was. "She went back to England," he prompted. "And your father retained custody of you."

"He didn't have much choice." The bitterness leaked out. She made a conscientious and difficult effort to bury it again. "It really isn't relevant."

"I'm not Whitfield, Johanna," he murmured. "Humor me."

She was silent for so long he decided to try another tactic. Then she sighed and began. "My mother went back to England to try to pick up the stage career she felt she'd sacrificed when she'd married. I didn't have a place there."

"You must have missed her."

"I got over it."

He didn't think so. "I don't suppose divorce is ever easy on a kid, but it's got to be worse when one of the parents ends up several thousand miles away."

"It was better that way, for everyone. They always fought terribly. Neither of them were happy with their marriage or . . ." She trailed off before she could say what was in her mind. *Me. Neither of them wanted me.* "With the situation," she finished.

"You'd have been pretty young to have known that." He'd begun to get a picture of five-year-old Johanna, dealing with the inexplicable ups and downs of a rocky marriage.

"You don't have to be very old to recognize turmoil. In any case, my mother explained it to me. She sent me a telegram from the airport." Her tea had gone cold, but she sipped automatically.

A telegram's just like a letter, the pretty young maid had told Johanna. If the maid hadn't been new, the telegram would have been handed over to Carl and disposed of. But the maid had been avid to know the contents, and more than willing to help Johanna struggle over the words.

> My darling girl. I'm devastated to leave you like this, but I have no choice. My situation, my life, has become desperate. Believe me, I have tried, but I've come to understand that divorce, and a complete separation from what was, is the only way I can survive. I despise myself for leaving you in your father's hands, but for now mine are too frail to hold on to you. One day you'll understand and forgive. Love. Mother.

She remembered it still, word for word, though at the time all she had understood was that her mother was leaving her because she wasn't happy.

Sam was staring at her, amazed that she could be so matter-of-fact. "She sent you a telegram?"

"Yes. I wasn't old enough to fully understand, but I caught the drift. She was miserably unhappy and desperate to find a way out."

Bitch. The word rose up in his throat, hotly, and he had to swallow it. He couldn't imagine anyone being so self-absorbed and selfish as to say goodbye to her only child by telegram. He tried to remember that Johanna had told him how her mother had taken her to feed the ducks, but he couldn't equate the two acts with the same woman.

"It must have been rough on you." He put his arm around her, as if he could find a way to protect her from what had already happened.

"Children are resilient." She rose, knowing that if he offered comfort she would break. She hadn't broken in over twenty years. "She did what she had to do, but I don't think she was ever happy. She died about ten years ago."

Suicide. He swore at himself for not remembering it before. Glenna Howard, Johanna's unhappy mother, had never quite achieved the sparkling comeback she'd sought. Disappointment had been eased by pills and alcohol until she'd taken a deliberate overdose of both.

"I'm sorry, Johanna. Losing her twice. It must have been hell for you."

"I never knew her that well." She reached for her tea again, for something to keep her hands busy. "And it was a long time ago."

He went to her, though she turned away. Patient but determined, he drew her back. "I don't think things like that ever stop hurting. Don't back off from me, Johanna."

"There's no use dredging all this up."

"I think there is." He took her shoulders, firmly enough to let her know he wasn't easing off. "I've wondered all along why you held off. I thought at first it was because you'd had a bad experience with another man. But it goes back farther than that, and deeper."

She looked at him then, her face set but her eyes desperate. She'd said too much, more than she'd ever said before. In saying it, the memories became all too clear. "I'm not my mother."

"No." He lifted a hand to brush at her hair. "No, you're not. And you're not your father either."

"I don't even know if he *is* my father."

The moment it was said, she went white. The hands she had fisted unballed and went limp. Not once in all of her life had she said it out loud. The knowledge had been there, locked tight but never completely silent. Now she heard her words echo back to her and was afraid, terribly afraid, she'd be ill.

"Johanna, what are you talking about?"

His voice was calm and quiet, but it shot like a bullet through her shock. "Nothing, nothing. I'm upset. I'm tired. Tomorrow's going to be a difficult day, Sam. I need to sleep."

"We both know you're too wired to sleep." He could feel the violent shudders begin as he held her there. "And you will be until you get the rest of it out. Tell me about your father, Johanna. About Carl."

"Will you leave me alone?" There were tears in her voice that only frightened her more. She could feel the walls cracking, the foundation giving way, but didn't have the strength to shore it up again. "For God's sake, can't you see I've had all I can manage? I don't want to talk about my mother. I don't want to talk about him. He could be dying." The tears spilled out, and she knew she'd lost. "He could be dying, and I should feel something. But I don't. I don't even know who he is. I don't know who I am."

She fought him, pushing away as he gathered her to him, swearing at him as he held her there. Then she collapsed in a storm of weeping.

He didn't offer comforting words. He hadn't a clue which ones to choose. Instead, he lifted her into his arms. With her sobs muffled against his throat, he sat down, cradling her to him. Sam stroked her hair and let her purge herself. He hadn't known it was possible to hold that many tears inside.

She felt ill. Her throat and eyes burned, her stomach heaved. Even when the tears were over, the raw, sick feeling remained.

Her strength had been sapped, as if someone had pulled a plug and let it drain away. She didn't object when Sam shifted her, nor when he rose. He was going away. It was something she accepted even as her own battered heart suffered another crack.

Then he was sitting beside her again, placing a snifter in her hands. "It might help some," he murmured. "Take it slow."

If there'd been any left, more tears would have fallen. She nodded, took a sip of brandy and let it coat the raw wounds.

"I was always in awe of him," Johanna began without looking up. "I don't know even now if I loved him as a child, but he was always the largest and most important figure in my life. After my mother left—" she paused to sip again "—after my mother left I was terrified that he'd leave, too, or send me away. I didn't understand then how important it was to him to keep his private affairs private. The public could accept and be entertained by his romances and marriages, but if he'd shipped off his only child without a blink, they'd have taken a different view. No one forgot that he'd been married to Glenna Howard and that she'd had his child. No one except him."

How could she explain how lost she had been? How confusing it had been to see her father entertain other women as though her mother had never existed.

"When he married again it was horrible. There was a big, splashy wedding, lots of photographers, microphones, strangers. They dressed me up and told me to smile. I hated it—the stares and innuendos about my mother. The whispers about her. He could ignore it. He'd always had that kind of presence, but all I could think was that my mother was being replaced with someone I didn't even know. And I had to smile."

Insensitive, selfish idiots. Even as he thought it, he tightened his arms around her. "Wasn't there anyone else . . . any family?"

"His parents had died years before. I remember hearing or

being told somewhere along the line that he'd been raised by his grandmother. By that time she was gone, too. I'd never met her. I had what you'd call a governess, who would have literally died for my father. Women react that way to him," she said wearily. "Nothing could have stopped it—my being in the wedding was important. Impressions, photo opportunities, that kind of thing. After it was over, I didn't see him again for three months. He was spending a lot of time in Italy."

"You stayed behind."

"I was in school." She pulled a hand through her hair, then clasped them in her lap. "It was perfectly legitimate for him to leave me behind with my tutors and instructors. In any case, his second wife had little tolerance for children. Few of his liaisons did."

Because she could feel his sympathy reaching out to her, she shook her head. "I was happier here. I spent a lot of time with the Heddisons. They were wonderful to me."

"I'm glad for that." He drew her hand into his. "Go on."

"It was after his second divorce, when he was involved with . . . it doesn't matter who. Anyway, I was out of school and feeling sorry for myself. I went up to his room. I don't even know why, except to be there, to see if I could solve the mystery of my father. I solved it.

"I'd always felt inadequate, awkward around him. There seemed to be something lacking in me that kept him from loving me the way that he should. He had this wonderful old desk in his room, one with all these fascinating cubbyholes and compartments. He was away again, so I didn't have to worry about him catching me poking around. I found letters. Some of them were from his women, and I was old enough to be embarrassed, so I put them away again. Then I found one from my mother. An old one, one she'd written right after she'd gone back to England. Holding it was like seeing her again.

Sometimes I hadn't been able to bring the picture of her into my head, but the minute I had that letter, I saw her exactly as she'd been. God, she was beautiful, so fragile and haunted. I could even hear her voice, that trained, extraordinary voice. I'd loved her so much."

He took the snifter from her and set it on the table. "You read the letter?"

"I wish to God I hadn't." She squeezed her eyes shut for a moment, but it was now, as it had been then, too late to turn back. "I was so hungry for anything she'd touched, any part of her, that I didn't even realize at first when I was reading. She must have been furious when she wrote it. It came across, the anger, the bitterness, the need to punish. I'd known, even as a child, that their marriage hadn't been smooth. But until I'd read the letter I'd had no idea how much hate had been built up between them."

"People say things they don't mean, or at least things that shouldn't be said under those kind of circumstances."

"Well, she's gone, has been gone, and there's no way of knowing if she meant what she'd said. No way for me to know, no way for my father—for Carl to know."

Her mouth was dry, but she no longer wanted the brandy. Johanna pressed her lips together and continued. "She brought up every hurt, every broken promise, every real or imagined infidelity. Then she brought out the big guns. Leaving me with him was the biggest payback she could think of. She was saddling him with a child who wasn't even his own. Not that he could ever prove it, or that she would ever tell him who had fathered the child he'd given a name to. There was, of course, the possibility that the child was his, but . . . She wished him a lifetime of hell wondering. And because I read the letter, she gave me the same."

Sam stared out the darkened window for a long time. The

rage was so keen, so close to the surface, he was afraid to speak. She'd been a child, innocent, helpless. And no one had given a damn.

"Did you ever speak to him about it?"

"No, there was no reason to. He didn't change toward me. I was well tended, well educated and allowed to pursue my own interests as long as I didn't embarrass him."

"They didn't deserve you. Either of them."

"It doesn't matter," she said wearily. "I'm not a child anymore." Nor had she been from the moment she'd read the letter.

"It matters to me." He cupped her face in his hands. "You matter to me, Johanna."

"I never meant to tell you, or anyone. But now that I have, you must understand why I can't let what's between us go too far."

"No."

"Sam—"

"What I understand is that you had a lousy childhood, and that things went on around you that no kid should ever be a part of. And I understand that there're bound to be scars."

"Scars?" She gave a quick, brittle laugh as she rose. "Don't you see, my mother was ill. Oh, it was kept quiet, out of the press, but I managed to dig it up. She was in and out of sanitariums the last few years of her life. Manic depression, instability, alcohol addiction. And the drugs . . ." Johanna pressed her fingers to her eyes and struggled to get a grip on herself. "She didn't raise me, and I can't be sure who my father is, but she was my mother. I can't forget that, or what I may have inherited from her."

He rose slowly. His first instinct was to tread carefully, but then he realized it was the wrong one. She needed to be brought up short, and quickly. "It's not like you to be melodramatic, Johanna."

His words had exactly the effect he'd hoped for. Anger flashed into her eyes and whipped color back into her cheeks. "How dare you say that to me?"

"How dare you stand there and make up insufficient excuses why you can't commit to me?"

"They're not excuses, they're facts."

"I don't give a damn who your mother was, or your father. I'm in love with you, Johanna. Sooner or later you're going to have to swallow it and take the next step."

"I've told you all along that it couldn't lead anywhere. Now I'm telling you why. And that's only half of it. My half."

"There's more?" He hooked his thumbs in his pockets and rocked back on his heels. "Okay, give me the rest."

"You're an actor."

"Right the first time, but you're not going to set any bells ringing with that answer."

"I've been around actors all of my life," she continued, searching for patience. "I understand the strain and demands of the job, the impossibility, especially for a talented actor, of maintaining a private life that keeps anything truly private. And I know that even with the best of intentions and effort relationships suffer. If I believed in marriage—which I don't—I still wouldn't believe in marriage to an actor."

"I see." It was difficult enough not to be angry with her, and it was impossible not to be furious with the people who had had the major hand in forming her beliefs. "Then you're saying that because I'm an actor—worse yet, a good one—I'm too big a risk."

"I'm saying that what there is between us can't go any further." She stopped, wanting to be strong. "And that if you don't want to see me again, I'll understand."

"Will you?" For a moment he studied her, as though he were considering it. A few steps away, Johanna prepared herself. She'd known it would hurt when it ended, but even her worst fears hadn't come close to this. When he crossed to her, she made herself look in his eyes. She could read nothing in them.

"You're an idiot, Johanna." He yanked her against him so hard that her breath whistled out in surprise. "Do you think I can turn my feelings for you on and off? Damn it, you do, don't you? I can see it in your face. Well, I'm not going to step neatly out of your life, and if you think you can push me out, you're going to be disappointed."

"I don't want you to go." Tears clouded her eyes, though she'd thought she was through with them. "I just don't think—"

"Then don't think." He swept her up into his arms. "You do too much thinking."

She didn't protest when he carried her upstairs. She was through with arguing, with excuses, with reasons. Perhaps it was a weakness to want to be taken care of, but she couldn't find the strength to stand on her own tonight. She didn't want to think. He was right about that. She didn't want to think at all for whatever hours of the night were left. For once, feelings took no effort and she could let them domi-nate.

She needed him. If she hadn't been so drained it would have frightened her to realize it.

The bedroom was dark, but he didn't turn on the light. The fragrances from her garden were carried up and through the windows on the night air. In silence he laid her on the bed and sat beside her.

There was too much to say to speak at all just yet. He'd once thought her cool, tough and self-sufficient. That woman had attracted and intrigued him. Intrigued him enough, Sam thought, to have caused him to dig deeper. The more he knew about her, the more layers he'd discovered.

She was tough, in the best sense of the word. She'd taken the blows, the disappointments, and had worked her way through them. Some people, he knew, would have buckled under, found a crutch or given up. But Johanna, his Johanna, had carved a place for herself and had made it work.

Underneath the toughness he'd found passion. He'd sensed and now was certain that it had gone untapped. Whether it was fate, blind luck or timing, he'd found the key that had released it. He wouldn't allow it to be locked again, or to be opened by anyone but himself.

Beneath the passion was a touching shyness. A sweetness that was a miracle in itself, considering her childhood and the disillusionments she'd faced so early in life.

Now, beneath all the rest, he'd found a core of fragility. He was determined to protect that vulnerability. And it was to the fragile Johanna that he would make love tonight.

In kindness as much as love. In compassion, as well as desire.

Softly, his touch barely a whisper, he brushed her hair away from her face. There were tears still drying on her cheeks. With his fingertips, he wiped them away. He wouldn't be able to prevent more from being shed, but he would do whatever he could to see that she didn't shed them alone.

He kissed her once, then twice, where the tears had lain. Then he kissed her again, tenderly. Night shadows shifted across her face, but he could see her eyes, half closed with fatigue but very aware, as she watched him.

"Do you want to sleep?" he asked her.

"No." She put her hand over his. "No, I don't want to sleep. And I don't want you to go."

"Then relax." He brought her hand to his lips. His eyes, so dark and intense, seemed to absorb everything she was. "And let me love you."

It was just that easy.

She hadn't known love could be soothing. He hadn't shown her that before. Tonight, when her emotions were raw and her self-esteem at its lowest ebb, he showed her another side of desire. A desire to please, and one to nurture. A desire to have, and one to heal. He touched her as though she alone mattered.

He drew off her shirt so that the material trailed over her skin before it was discarded, but he didn't take what she would have given. With his eyes on hers, he removed his own. When she reached for him, he took her hands, pressing them both to his lips.

He undressed her slowly, carefully, as though she were asleep and he didn't want to disturb her. The tenderness of it brought its own strange ache. Though she was naked and totally open to him, he contented himself with long, lazy kisses and the feel of her hair under his hands.

Her skin looked so white against the dark spread. He ran his hand down her arm, watching the movement. The moon had waned to a thin crescent, shedding little light, but he already knew her so well. Still, he traced her face with his fingertip, outlining her features for his own pleasure.

He'd never treated her like this before. Johanna closed her eyes as she began to drift into contentment. Even through passion and hunger, he'd always shown her an unexpected sweetness. But this . . . this was what it meant to be cherished. This was the way promises were given when they were meant to be kept. It made her eyes swim and her heart break, just a little, at the beauty of it.

He felt stronger somehow, being gentle. He'd never wanted her more than he did at this moment, and yet he had never felt less need to rush. The passion was there, and growing, but it was filled with a need to comfort.

Time passed unnoticed, unheeded. In the darkest hours of the morning, he led her gently higher.

The rhythm of her heart beat under his lips, fast, unsteady, but not yet desperate. Her arms were around him, holding him close, but there was no urgent press of fingers. She moved with him, willing to let him set the pace, grateful that he had understood, even if she hadn't, that she needed care.

Had she ever noticed how strong he was? How the muscles of his back and shoulders flexed and rippled with his movements? She'd touched him before, held him just like this, but each time she had she'd been driven close to the edge. Now the ride was quiet and unhurried, like floating on a raft on a still lake.

Inspired by love, she sought to give him the same gentleness he showed her. Her touch was easy, her demands few. She heard in the murmur of her name that he felt as she did. They might never come together so perfectly, so unselfishly, again.

Her sigh was quiet as she opened for him. They merged without heat but with much warmth.

Later, much later, she lay beside him, sleepless as the sky began to lighten.

CHAPTER 11

He could have strangled her. When Sam woke, he found himself alone in bed and the house empty. In the bath, her still-damp towel hung tidily over the rail. The room carried, very faintly, the scent of her. The clothes he'd removed from her the night before had been put away. Downstairs, he saw that her briefcase was gone and the flowers freshened. Her phone machine had been cleared of messages and reset.

In crisis or in control, Johanna was always organized.

He was sure he would strangle her.

In the kitchen he found the glasses they'd used the night before conscientiously rinsed and draining. Propped against the coffeepot was a note in Johanna's neat handwriting. *I didn't want to wake you. I needed to get to the hospital early, then to the studio. The coffee's fresh.*

She'd written something else, crossed it out, then signed the note simply *Johanna*.

His mother could have written it, Sam thought as he skimmed it a second time. Only she might have added, *Leave the kitchen the way you found it.* Damn it, Johanna.

He stood in the kitchen dressed only in jeans and tossed her note onto the counter. No one would ever accuse Johanna of not having her feet firmly on the ground. But there were times when it was better, even necessary, to keep them planted beside someone else's. She still needed to accept that he was that someone else. He'd been sure he'd gotten through, but he'd forgotten how incredibly stubborn she could be.

Absently he bent down and picked up the kitten, who was doing figure eights between his legs. She wasn't hungry. Johanna had left Lucy well taken care of, with a full dish in the corner. She only wanted some affection. Most creatures did, Sam mused as he stroked her fur. Apparently that wasn't enough to make Johanna purr and settle trustingly in his arms.

It looked as if he still had a fight on his hands. Sam gave the kitten's ears a last scratch before he set her down again. He could be hardheaded, as well.

* * *

She was thinking of him. Sam would have been amazed if he had known how hard and long she'd struggled over those few brief lines she'd left him. She'd wanted to thank him for being with her and to tell him how much it had meant to her that he'd been kind and understanding when she'd been down for the count. She'd wanted to tell him that she loved him in a way she had never before and would never again love. But the words had seemed so empty and inadequate on paper.

It was hard to need someone, really need him, when you'd spent your entire life making certain you could handle anything and everything on your own. How would he have felt if he'd known how close she'd come to waking him and asking him to come with her because she'd been dreading the thought of facing this day alone? She couldn't ask, any more than she could forget that she now had no secrets from him, physically or emotionally. Dealing with this day alone was imperative if she was ever to face another without him.

The nurse on duty this morning was younger and more

approachable than the one the night before. She told Johanna that her father was resting comfortably, then asked her to have a seat until Dr. Merritt could be located.

Johanna chose the waiting room because the corridors seemed so public. She'd managed to evade the reporters outside but didn't want to take any chances on having to deal with any who'd been clever enough to sneak in.

Inside, an elderly woman and a boy of about twenty sat half dozing on a sofa, hands linked. On the wall-mounted television a morning show flashed cheerfully, showing a demonstration of gourmet cooking. Johanna moved to a table where twin pots of coffee and hot water sat on warmers. She bypassed the tea bags, ignored the little bags of powdered cream and sugar and poured a cup black. As she took the first sip, she heard the break for local news.

Carl W. Patterson was the top story. Dispassionately she listened to the newscaster recite the press release she and the publicist had written over the phone the night before. It gave a great deal more information on Carl's career than it did on his illness, and she knew Carl would have given it his nod of approval. The report ended by saying that Toni DuMonde, Patterson's housemate and fiancée, could not be reached for comment.

At least the woman wasn't a fool, Johanna thought as she chose a seat. There were some, she knew, who would have spilled their guts to the press and enjoyed the melodrama. And if Toni had, Johanna imagined, Carl would have cut whatever strings tied them together as soon as he was able.

"Miss Patterson?"

Johanna rose automatically. The moment she saw the doctor, her calm fled. The nurse had said Carl was resting comfortably, but that was hospital talk. She fought back the touch of fear and offered her hand.

"Dr. Merritt, I hope I'm not too early." Or too late.

"No, as a matter of fact your father's awake and stable. As a matter of precaution we'll keep him in CCU for another twenty-four hours. If he continues to progress, he can be moved to a private room."

"The prognosis?"

"The prognosis is good, if he cooperates. A lighter work load is essential. How much influence do you have over him?"

Her smile was almost amused. "None at all."

"Well, then, he might find himself confined to the hospital a day or two longer than he's counting on." Merritt took off his glasses to polish the lenses on the hem of his coat. "As I explained to you last night, certain adjustments will have to be made. Mr. Patterson will have to realize that, like the rest of us, he has certain limitations."

"I understand. And I wish you the best of luck explaining the same to him."

"I've already spoken to him briefly." Merritt slid the glasses back on his nose. He gave Johanna a smile that was gone almost before it formed. "At the moment, it's more important to reassure him. We'll speak about future care soon enough. He's asked to see Miss DuMonde and someone named Whitfield. It may be good for him to see his fiancée, but—"

"Don't worry about Whitfield. I'll handle it."

Merritt only nodded. He'd already decided Patterson's daughter had a good head on her shoulders. "Your father's a fortunate man. If he's sensible, there isn't any reason why he shouldn't lead a full and productive life."

"Can I see him?"

"Fifteen minutes only. He needs calm and quiet."

She was both as she walked into the small curtained-off room in CCU. Her father was as he'd been the night before, eyes closed, wired to machines. But his color was better. She stood by the bed, studying him, until his eyes flickered open.

It took him a moment to focus. It occurred to Johanna that

this was certainly the longest their eyes had ever held. When she saw recognition in his, she bent to brush his cheek with hers.

"Good morning," she said, keeping her voice carefully neutral. "You gave us a scare."

"Johanna." He took her hand, surprising her. He'd never been quite so alone or quite so weak. "What have they told you?"

Why, he's frightened, she thought, and felt a stirring of sympathy. It had never occurred to her that he could be frightened. "That you're a fortunate man," she said briskly. "And that if you're sensible the world will still see quite a number of Carl W. Patterson productions."

It was exactly the right thing to say. She hadn't realized she'd known him so well. "Damned inconvenient time for my body to set booby traps for me." He glanced around the room, and the moment of closeness vanished.

"The hospital's contacting Toni," Johanna told him. "I'm sure she'll be here soon."

Satisfied, Carl looked back at his daughter. "They say they intend to keep me strapped down here another day."

"Yes. More if you make a fuss."

"I've work to do that can't be done from a hospital bed."

"Fine. I'll tell them to release you. You might be able to edit *Fields of Fire* before you keel over again."

His expression changed from impatience to astonishment, then to something she'd rarely seen directed at her—amusement. "I suppose I could spare a few days. But I don't want that ham-handed Whitfield to get his hands on it."

"I've sent for Loman." His expression tightened immediately, and he became the cool, disapproving man she'd lived with most of her life. "I'm sorry if I overstepped my bounds, but when I contacted Whitfield last night and saw how things were, I thought you'd prefer Loman."

"All right, all right." He waved away her apology. "I do prefer Loman. Whitfield has his place, but God knows it's not in an editing room. What about the press?"

He'd forgotten to be frightened. Johanna thought, and bit back a sigh. It was business as usual. "Under control. Your publicist issued a release this morning and will update it as becomes necessary."

"Good, good. I'll meet with Loman this afternoon. Set that up for me, Johanna."

"No."

The effort of making plans had already sapped his strength, and that only made him more furious. "No? What the hell do you mean, no?"

"It's out of the question." Her voice was calm, which pleased her. There had been a time he could have used that tone and made her quake. "It should be all right in a day or two, once you're in a private room and stronger."

"I run my own life."

"No one's more aware of that than I."

"If you've got some idea about taking over while I'm down—"

The fury leaped into her eyes and stopped him cold. He'd never seen that look before, or the power behind it. Or, if it had been there, he'd never bothered to look. "I don't want anything from you. I did once, but I learned to live without it. Now, if you'll excuse me, I've got a show of my own to produce."

"Johanna." She started to whip the curtain aside. It was the tremor in his voice that stopped her.

"Yes?"

"I apologize."

Another first, she thought, and made herself turn back. "All right. The doctor told me not to stay long, and I've probably already overtired you."

"I almost died."

He said it like an old man, an old, frightened man. "You're going to be fine."

"I almost died," he repeated. "And though I can't say my life flashed in front of my eyes, I did screen a few clips." He closed his eyes. It infuriated him that he had to stop just to gather the strength to speak. "I remember getting in the back of the limo—on my way to the airport, I think. You were standing on the steps with that dog Max forced on me. You looked as though you wanted to call me back."

Johanna didn't remember that particular incident because there'd been so many of them. "If I had, would you have stayed?"

"No." He sighed, not with regret but with acknowledgement. "Work has always come first. I've never been able to put a marriage together the way I could a film. Your mother—"

"I don't want to talk about my mother."

Carl opened his eyes again. "She could have loved you more if she'd hated me less."

It hurt. Even having known it all these years, it hurt to hear it said aloud. "And you?"

"Work has always come first," he repeated. He was tired, much too tired for regrets or apologies. "Will you come back?"

"Yes. I'll come back after the taping."

He was asleep before she drew the curtain aside.

*　*　*

Max Heddison's estate was as distinguished and well-tended as the man. Sam was ushered through the thirty-room house the actor had purchased a quarter of a century before. On the terrace were thickly padded chaises and half a dozen wicker chairs that invited company to spread out and be comfortable. An aging golden retriever was curled up in one, snoring.

In the sparkling L-shaped pool beyond the terrace, Max Heddison was doing laps. Across the sloping lawn, partially hidden by squared-off hedges, were tennis courts. To the east, identifiable only by a distant flag, was a putting green.

A houseboy in a spotless white jacket offered Sam his choice of chairs. Sun or shade. Sam chose the sun. As he watched, Sam counted ten laps, cleanly stroked and paced, and wondered idly how many Max had done before he'd arrived. The official bio said Max was seventy. It could have taken off fifteen years and still have been believable.

He accepted coffee and waited while Max hauled himself out of the pool.

"Good to see you again." Max dragged a towel over his hair before he shrugged into a robe.

"I appreciate you letting me drop by this way." Sam had risen automatically.

"Sit down, boy; you make me feel like a king about to be deposed. Had breakfast?"

"Yes, thanks."

The moment Max sat, the houseboy was back with a tray of fresh fruit and dry toast. "Thank you, Jose. Bring Mr. Weaver some juice. Straight from our own oranges," he told Sam. "I figure it only costs me about three dollars a glass." With a grin, he dug into his breakfast. "My wife's the health nut. No additives, no preservatives. Enough to drive a man to drink. She's at her morning class, which means I'll have time to sneak a cigarette before she gets back."

Sam's juice was served in cut crystal. He sipped, letting Max fall into a conversation about pruning and organic sprays.

"Well, I don't suppose you came here to discuss fertilizers." Max pushed his tray aside and reached in his pocket for a pack of unfiltered cigarettes. "What did you think of the script?"

"Who do I have to kill to get the part?"

Max chuckled and drew in smoke with great pleasure. "I'll

hold that in reserve. You know, I don't care too much for to-day's moviemakers—money-makers, I should say. In the old days, men like Mayer might have been despots, but they knew how to make films. Today they're a bunch of damn accountants running around with ledgers and red pencils—more interested in profit than entertainment. But my gut tells me we might be able to give them both with this one."

"It made my palms sweat," Sam said simply.

"I know the feeling." Max settled back, regretting only that his cigarette was nearly done. "I've been making movies since before you were born. Over eighty of them, and only a handful ever made me feel that way."

"I want to thank you for thinking of me."

"No need for that. Ten pages into the script and your name popped into my head. It was still there when I finished." He crushed out his cigarette, sighing. "And, of course, I went straight to my consultant with it—my wife." He grinned, drank more coffee and thought it a pity his wife had ordered decaf. "I've relied on her opinion for over forty years."

It made Sam remember how important it had been for him to hear Johanna's.

"She finished it, handed it back to me and said if I didn't do it I was crazy. Then she told me to get young Sam Weaver to play Michael. By the way, she admires your . . . build," Max said. "My sainted wife's an earthy woman."

The grin came quickly and lingered. "I'd love to meet her."

"We'll arrange it. Did I mention that Kincaid's been signed to direct?"

"No." Sam's interest was piqued again. "You don't get much better."

"Thought the same myself." Max watched Sam thoughtfully from under his bushy white brows. "Patterson's producing." He saw Sam's eyes sharpen and reached casually for more coffee. "Problem?"

"There might be." He wanted the part, more than he could remember wanting any other. But not at the cost of his still-too-tenuous relationship with Johanna.

"If you're concerned about Jo-Jo, I don't think it's necessary. The complete professional, our Jo-Jo. And she respects her father's work." He saw the dull anger in Sam's eyes and nodded. "So, it's gotten that far, has it? I wasn't sure Johanna would ever let anyone get that close."

"It wasn't so much a matter of choice as circumstance." He hadn't come just to talk about the script. When Sam had called to make the appointment, he'd already decided to dig for whatever Max might have buried. "I take it you haven't heard that Patterson had a heart attack last night."

"No." The concern came automatically. The friendship went back a quarter of a century. "I haven't so much as flicked the news on today. I go for days at a time without it. How bad?"

"Bad enough. As far as I know, he's stable. Johanna went back to the hospital this morning."

"He lives hard," Max mused. "Carl never seemed to be able to settle down long enough to enjoy what he was working for. I hope he still gets the chance." Max tipped back in his chair and looked out over the pool, the grounds. "You know, I have three children of my own. Five grandchildren now, and the first great-grandchild on the way. There were times I wasn't there for them, and I'll always regret it. Holding a family and a career together in this business is like juggling eggs. There's always some breakage."

"Some people juggle better than others."

"True enough. It takes a lot of effort and more than a few concessions to make it work."

"It seems to me that in Johanna's case she made all the concessions."

Max said nothing for a moment. He considered having another cigarette but decided his wife's sensitive nose would find him out. "I hate old men who poke into young people's business. Ought to be out playing checkers or feeding pigeons. But . . . just how serious are you about Jo-Jo?"

"We're going to get married," Sam heard himself say, to his own astonishment. "As soon as I talk her into it."

"Good luck. And that comes from the heart. I've always had a soft spot for that girl." Max poured another cup of coffee and knew he was a long way from ready to feed pigeons. "How much did she tell you?"

"Enough to make me understand I've got an uphill battle."

"And how much do you love her?"

"Enough to keep climbing."

Max decided to risk a second cigarette. If his wife came sniffing around, he could always blame it on Sam. He lit it slowly, savoring the taste. "I'm going to tell you things she wouldn't appreciate me saying. Whether it'll give you an edge or not I can't say. I can tell you I hope it does."

"I appreciate it."

With the smoke trailing lazily from between his fingers, Max looked back. A long way. "I knew her mother well. A beautiful woman. A glorious face. Bone structure always makes the difference. Johanna favors her physically, but it ends there. I can say I've never known anyone more completely her own woman than Johanna."

"Neither have I," Sam murmured. "It doesn't always make it easy."

"You're too young to want things easy," Max told him from the comfortable perspective of seven decades. "When something comes easy, you usually let it go the same way. That's my philosophy for the day. Now, Glenna was selfish, driven by her own demons. She married Carl after a brief and very torrid affair. Affairs were just as torrid thirty years ago, only a bit more discreet."

He drew in smoke and remembered a few of his own.

Though he'd let them go without regret upon his marriage, he could still be grateful for the experience.

"They were a golden couple, the photographers' darlings. Carl was dark, ruggedly handsome, broad shouldered. Glenna was almost waiflike, pale, fragile. They threw incredible parties and incredible tantrums. To be honest, I quite enjoyed both. You may have heard I was a hellion in my youth."

"I heard you were a hellion," Sam agreed. "But I didn't hear it was something in the past."

"We'll work well together," Max declared. He took one last drag before crushing the second cigarette out. "When Glenna was pregnant, she spent thousands decorating the nursery. Then she started to lose her figure and went on a rampage. She could sit for a photographer like a Madonna, then toss back a Scotch and curse like a sailor. Glenna had no middle ground."

"Johanna told me she was ill, a manic-depressive."

"Perhaps. I don't pretend to understand psychiatry. I will say she was weak—not weak-minded, but weak-spirited—and tormented by the fact that she was never as successful as she needed to be. There was talent in her, real talent, but she didn't have the drive or the grit to stay on top. It became easy for her to blame Carl for that, and the marriage. Then it became easier to blame the child. After Johanna was born, Glenna went through phases of being a devoted, loving mother. Then she'd be almost obscenely neglectful. The marriage was crumbling. Carl had affairs, she had affairs, and neither of them ever considered putting the child first. Not in their nature, Sam," he added when he saw the fury flare. "That's not an excuse, of course, but it is a reason. Carl wouldn't have cared if Glenna had had one child or thirty. He'd had no more than a passing interest. When the break finally came, Glenna used the child as a weapon. I don't mean to make Carl a hero, but at least he never used Johanna. Unfortunately, she was never that important to him."

"How could two people like that ever have someone like Johanna?"

"Another question for the ages."

"Is Patterson her father?"

Max lifted both brows. "Why do you ask?"

It was a confidence he felt he had to break. Not for himself. Sam had already decided her parentage meant less than nothing to him, but the truth would be important to Johanna.

"Because when she was still a child, Johanna found a letter her mother had written to Patterson right after she'd gone back to England. She told him she'd never been sure if he was Johanna's father."

"Good God." Max ran a hand over his face. "I had no idea about that. It's a wonder it didn't destroy Johanna."

"No, she wasn't destroyed, but it did plenty of damage."

"Poor little Jo-Jo," Max murmured. "She was always such a lonely little girl. Spent more time with the gardener than anyone else. It might not have mattered if Carl had been different. I wish she'd come to me with this."

"I don't think she's told anyone about it until last night."

"You'd better not let her down."

"I don't intend to."

Max fell silent for a time, thinking. Johanna's parents had been his friends. He'd been able to accept them for what they were and for what they weren't, all the while regretting it for the child's sake.

"For what it's worth, I'd say the letter was pure spite and total nonsense. If another man had fathered Johanna, Glenna would have blurted it out long before the separation. She could never keep a secret for more than two hours. Make that two minutes if you added a drink. Carl knew that." His face clouded as he hunched over the table. "I'm sorry to say that if Carl had suspected Johanna wasn't his flesh and blood he never would have kept her under his roof. He'd have put her on a plane to her mother without a backward glance."

"That doesn't make him a saint."

"No, but it does make him Johanna's father."

*   *   *

We have something special for our home audience," John Jay began, giving the camera a brilliant smile. "If you've been listening this week, you know that our Drive American contest is already underway. We at *Trivia Alert* are very excited about having the chance to show all of you at home how much we appreciate you. To win, all you have to do is watch and answer. Every day this week, sometime during the show, I'll be asking questions. Today it's time to tell you at home what you have a chance to win."

He paused, giving the announcer the time to describe the cars and eligibility requirements. As requested, the studio audience applauded and cheered.

"The week of Fourth of July," John Jay continued on cue, "one of you at home will win not one but both luxury cars. All you have to do is answer five questions in order. Send your answers to Trivia Alert, Drive American, Post Office Box 1776, Burbank, California 91501. Now for today's question."

There was a dramatic pause as he drew the sealed envelope from the slot. "Question number three. What is the name of Captain America's alter ego? Write down your answer and be sure to tune in tomorrow for the fourth question. All complete sets of correct answers will be part of a random drawing. Now, back to our game."

Johanna checked her watch and wondered how she could get through two more segments. They were already behind schedule due to a delay caused by an overenthusiastic member of the studio audience who had called out answers during the speed round. They'd had to stop, reset, calm the contestant and begin again with a new batch of questions. Usually she took that sort of thing in stride, but somewhere along the way her stride had broken. For the past few hours, Johanna had been struggling to find her pace again.

When the segment ended, she nearly groaned with relief. She had fifteen minutes before they would begin again. "Beth, I have to make a call. I'll be in the office if a crisis comes up."

Without waiting for a response, she hurried off the set. At the end of the corridor a small room was set up with the essentials. A phone, a desk and a chair. Making use of all three, Johanna called the hospital. She still had ten minutes left when she learned that Carl had been downgraded from critical to serious condition. She was rubbing her eyes and thinking about another cup of coffee when the door opened.

"Beth, if it isn't a matter of life and death, put it on hold."

"It might be."

She straightened immediately at the sound of Sam's voice. "Oh, hello. I didn't expect you."

"You don't expect me nearly often enough." He closed the door behind him. "How are you doing?"

"Not bad."

"Your father?"

"Better. They think he can be moved out of CCU tomorrow."

"That's good." He came over to the desk and sat on the edge before giving her a long, critical study. "You're dead on your feet, Johanna. Let me take you home."

"We haven't finished, and I promised to stop by the hospital after the taping."

"Okay, I'll go with you."

"No, please. It's not necessary, and I'd be lousy company tonight."

He looked down at her hands. They were linked together tightly. Deliberately he took them in his own and separated them. "Are you trying to pull back, Johanna?"

"No. I don't know." She took a long breath, and her hands relaxed in his. "Sam, I appreciate what you did for me last night more than I can ever tell you—the way you listened and didn't judge. You were there when I needed you, and I'll never forget it."

"Sounds like a kiss-off," he murmured.

"No, of course it isn't. But you should understand now why I feel so strongly about being involved with you. Why it won't work."

"I must be pretty stupid, because I don't. I do understand why you're scared. Johanna, we have to talk."

"I have to get back. There's only a few more minutes."

"Sit down," he told her as she started to rise. She might have ignored the order, but the look in his eyes had her sitting again. "I'll try to make it quick. Time's either a blessing or a curse now, anyway. I've got to fly east the day after tomorrow to start filming."

"Oh." She dug deep for a smile. "Well, that's good. I know you've been anxious to start."

"I'll be gone three weeks, probably more. It isn't possible for me to put this off."

"Of course not. I hope—well, I hope you let me know how it's going."

"Johanna, I want you to come with me."

"What?"

"I said I want you to come with me."

"I—I can't. How could I? I have my job, and—"

"I'm not asking you to make a choice between your job and us. Any more than I'd expect you to ask me to make one between mine and the way I feel about you."

"No, of course I wouldn't."

"I'd like to think you meant that." He paused a moment, searching her face. "The script that Max sent me—I want to do it."

"You should do it. It's perfect for you."

"Maybe, but I want to know if it's perfect for you. Your father's producing it, Johanna."

"Oh." She looked down at her hands a moment, hands that were still caught in his. "Well, then, you've got the best."

"I want to know how you feel about it, Johanna. How you really feel."

"It's more a matter of how you feel."

"Not this time. Don't make me use pliers."

"Sam, your professional choices have to be yours, but I'd say you'd be a fool not to grab a chance to work with Max and Patterson Productions. That script might have been written for you, and I'd be disappointed if I didn't see you in it."

"Always sensible."

"I hope so."

"Then be sensible about this. Take a few days off and come East with me." Before she could protest again, he was continuing. "You've got a tight crew, Johanna. I've seen them work firsthand. You know they could run things for a couple of weeks."

"I suppose, but not without any notice. Then there's my father . . ." She let her words trail off. There must have been dozens of reasons, but they seemed to slide away before she could get a grip on them.

"All right. Take a week to make sure your crew is on top of things and that your father's recovering. Then fly out and meet me."

"Why?"

"I wondered when you'd ask." He reached in his pocket to pull out a box. Through his life he'd done a great many things on impulse. This wasn't one of them. He'd thought it through carefully, and had kept coming up with one answer. He needed her. "Things like this usually speak for themselves." After opening the lid, he took her hand and set the box in her palm. "I want you to marry me."

She stared at the single flawless diamond. It was square-cut, very classic and simple. The kind of ring, Johanna thought, girls dreamed about when they thought of white chargers and castles in the sky.

"I can't."

"Can't what?"

"I can't marry you. You know I can't. I had no idea you'd started thinking like this."

"Neither had I, until today. When Marv called I knew I had two choices. I could go east and stew about it or I could take the step and let you stew about it." He touched her hair, just the tips. "I'm sure, Johanna."

"I'm sorry." She offered the box back to him. When he didn't take it, she set it on the desk. "I don't want to hurt you, you know I don't. That's why I can't."

"It's about time you unloaded some of the baggage you've been carrying around, Johanna." Rising, he drew her up with him. "We both know what we've got doesn't come along every day. You might think you're doing me a favor by turning me down, but you're wrong. Dead wrong."

His fingers tangled in her hair as he kissed her. Unable to deny him—or herself—she curled her arms up his back until she gripped his shoulders. She held on to him even while her mind whirled with dozens of questions.

"Do you believe me when I tell you I love you?" he demanded.

"Yes." She held him tighter, burying her face against his shoulder to absorb his scent. "Sam, I don't want you to go. I know you have to, and I know how much I'll miss you, but I can't give you what you want. If I could . . . if I could you're the only one I'd give it to."

He hadn't expected to hear even that much. Another man might have been discouraged, but he'd run into too many walls in his life to be put off by one more. Particularly since he had every intention of tearing this one down, brick by brick.

He pressed a kiss to her temple. "I already know what I need and what I want." He drew her away until their eyes met. "You'd better start thinking about yourself, Johanna. About what you want, what you need. Just you. I figure you're smart enough to come up with an answer before too long." He kissed her again until she was breathless. "Keep in touch."

She didn't have the strength to do anything but sink into the chair when he left her. The show was starting, but she continued to sit, staring at the ring he'd left behind.

CHAPTER 12

The man was playing games. Johanna knew it, and though she tried not to nibble at the bait, she was already being reeled in. He'd been gone two weeks, and she hadn't gotten a single phone call.

But there had been flowers.

They'd arrived every evening. Black-eyed Susans one day, white orchids another. She couldn't walk into any room of her house without thinking of him. After the first week they'd begun to arrive at her office—a small clutch of violets, a huge bouquet of tea roses. She couldn't even escape from him there.

The man was definitely playing, and he wasn't playing fair.

Of course, she wasn't going to marry him. That was absurd. She didn't believe people could love, honor and cherish for a lifetime. She'd told him so, and she'd been sorry, but she had no intention of changing her mind.

She might carry the ring with her—for safekeeping, that is—but she hadn't taken it out of its box. At least not more than two or three times.

She was grateful that her work load had intensified so that she was unceasingly busy. It didn't leave much time to mope around missing him. Unless you counted the long, solitary nights when she kept listening for the phone.

He'd told her to keep in touch, but he hadn't told her where he'd be staying. If she'd wanted to, she could have found out easily enough. It did happen that a few discreet inquiries had put the name and address of his hotel in her hands, but that didn't mean she would call him. If she called, he'd know she'd gone to some trouble—damn it, a great deal of trouble—to find out where he was.

Then he would know she'd not only nibbled at the bait but swallowed it whole.

By the end of the second week, she was furious with him. He'd pushed her into a corner where she didn't want to be, wedged her in and then strolled off, leaving her trapped. A man didn't ask a woman to marry him, drop a ring in her hand, then waltz off.

Once she'd considered putting the ring in the mail and shipping it off to him. That had been at three o'clock in the morning on the fifteenth day. Johanna had rolled over, slammed the pillow a few satisfactory times and vowed to do just that the minute the post office opened in the morning.

She would have, too, if she hadn't been running a few minutes late. Then she'd been tied up at lunchtime and unable to get five free minutes until after six. She decided against mailing it, thinking it would be more civil and courteous to throw it in his face when he got back into town.

It was just her bad luck he'd chosen to send forget-me-nots that day. They happened to be one of her particular favorites.

As the third week approached, she was a wreck. Johanna knew she deserved the wary glances of her staff. She pushed through Monday's taping, growling at every interruption. Her excuse was that she'd agreed to take duplicates to her father that evening.

He wasn't particularly interested in the show, she knew, but his recuperation wasn't sitting well with him. He wanted to live badly enough to follow his doctor's orders, but that didn't mean he couldn't review everything Patterson Productions had a part in. Johanna waited impatiently for the copies, pacing the set and toying with the ring box in her pocket.

"Here you go." Bethany put on an exaggerated smile. "Try not to gnaw on them on the way home."

Johanna dumped them in her bag. "I'll need you here by nine. We can work until it's time to set up for taping."

"Whatever you say."

Johanna narrowed her eyes at the overbright tone. "Have you got a problem?"

"Me?" All innocence, Bethany opened her eyes wide. "No, not me. Well, there is my back."

"Your back? What's wrong with it?"

"It's nothing really. It always aches a bit when I've been flogged."

Johanna opened her mouth, then shut it again on a puff of air. "I'm sorry. I guess I've been a little edgy."

"Just a tad. Funny, if someone had been sending me flowers every day for weeks I'd be a bit more cheerful."

"He thinks that's all it takes to twist me around his finger."

"There are worse positions to be in. Forget I said it," Bethany said immediately, holding up a hand. "There's nothing more diabolical than sending a basket of tiger lilies. The man's obviously slime."

For the first time in days, Johanna smiled. "He's wonderful."

The smile confirmed what Johanna's scowls had already told her. "You miss him?"

"Yes, I miss him. Just like he knew I would."

Bethany looked at romance in the most straightforward of terms. If you cared, you showed it, then put all your energy into making it work. Her solution for Johanna was just as simple.

"You know, Johanna, it's the same distance from the West to the East Coast as it is from East to West."

She'd already thought of going. Not that she'd *considered* it, but she had thought of it. "No, I can't." She fingered the box in her pocket. "It wouldn't be fair to him."

"Because?"

"Because I won't . . . can't . . ." On impulse she pulled the box out and opened it. "Because of this."

"Oh, my." Bethany couldn't help the long-drawn-out sigh. "My, oh, my," she managed, already smelling orange blossoms. "Congratulations, best wishes and bon voyage. Where's a bottle of champagne when you need it?"

"No, I didn't accept it. I'm not going to. I told him no."

"Then why do you still have it?"

Because the question was so reasonable, Johanna could only frown and stare at the diamond while it winked at her. "He just dropped it in my hand and walked off."

"Romantic devil, isn't he?"

"Well, it wasn't exactly— That's close enough," she decided. "It was more of an ultimatum than a proposal, but either way, I told him no."

It sounded wonderfully romantic to Bethany. She stuck her tongue in her cheek. "So you just decided to walk around with it in your pocket for a few days."

"No, I . . ." There had to be a reasonable excuse. "I wanted to have it handy so I could give it back to him."

Bethany thought that over, then tilted her head. "I think that's the first lie I've ever heard you tell."

"I don't know why I've still got it." Johanna closed the box with a snap, then pushed it into her pocket. "It's not important."

"No, I've never thought proposals of marriage or gorgeous engagement rings were anything to get excited about." She put a hand on Johanna's shoulder. "What you need is some fresh air."

"I don't believe in marriage."

"That's like not believing in Santa Claus." At Johanna's lifted brow, Bethany shook her head. "Johanna, don't tell me you don't believe in him, either? He might be something of a fantasy, but he's been around a while, and he's going to stay around."

It was hard to argue with that kind of logic. Johanna decided she was too tired to try. "We'll talk about the logic of that some other time. I have to drop off these tapes." With Bethany beside her, she started out. "I'd like you to keep this to yourself."

"It goes with me to the grave."

"You're good for me," Johanna said with a laugh. "I'm going to be sorry to lose you."

"Am I fired?"

"Sooner or later you're going to fire me. You won't be content to be anyone's assistant for long." Outside, Johanna took a deep breath. So much had changed since she'd walked with Bethany from the studio weeks before. "Leaving Santa Claus out of it, do you believe in marriage, Beth?"

"I'm just an old-fashioned girl with strong feminist underpinnings. Yeah, I believe in marriage as long as two people are willing to give it their best shot."

"You know what the odds are of a marriage making it in this town?"

"Lousy. But strikeout or home run, you've got to step up to bat. See you tomorrow."

"Good night, Beth."

She did a great deal of thinking as she drove to Beverly Hills. Not all of it was clear, but every thought circled back to Sam. Johanna was coming to realize that her thoughts would, whether she was with or without him.

The gates were locked, as they always were. Reaching out, she pressed the button on the intercom and waited for her father's housekeeper to ask her name. In moments the gates opened soundlessly.

The drive toward the house didn't stir any childish memories. She saw the estate as an adult. Perhaps she always had. It was stunning—the white columns, the terraces and balconies. The exterior had changed little from her earliest recollections.

Inside, it had gone through major overhauls, depending on its mistress. Her mother had preferred the feminine and delicate look of *Louis Quinze*. Darlene had chosen art nouveau, right down to the light fixtures. Its last mistress had gone for the opulently elegant. Johanna didn't think it would take Toni long to put her stamp on it.

The door was opened for her by the gray-uniformed maid before she'd reached the top of the wide, curved steps.

"Good evening, Miss Patterson."

"Good evening. Is Mr. Patterson expecting me?"

"He and Miss DuMonde are in the sitting room."

"Thank you."

Johanna crossed the glossy tiles, skirting the fish pond her father's last wife had installed. She found her father looking well, and impatient, in a dark blue smoking jacket. Toni sprawled lazily on the sofa across from him, sipping wine and flipping through a magazine. Johanna nearly smiled when she saw that it was one on home fashion and decoration.

"I expected you an hour ago," Carl said without preamble.

"We ran late." She took the tapes from her bag to set them on the table beside him. "You're looking well."

"There's nothing wrong with me."

"Carl's a bit bored." Toni stretched herself into a sitting position. She wore silk lounging pajamas the color of ripe peaches. The pout she wore went with them beautifully. "Perhaps you can entertain him better than I." Rising, she stalked gracefully out of the room.

Johanna lifted a brow. "Have I come at a bad time?"

"No." Carl pushed himself up and headed for the bar. Johanna bit back a protest and was relieved when he poured club soda. "Do you want anything?"

"No, thank you. I can't stay."

Carl halfheartedly added a twist of lime. "I assumed you'd stay until I'd previewed the tapes."

"You don't need me for that." He wanted company, she realized. Because she remembered how old and alone he'd looked in the hospital, she relented. "I could put them in for you, answer whatever questions you might have about the first segment or two."

"I've seen the show before, Johanna. I doubt I'd have any questions about my own show."

"No." She picked up the bag she'd just set down. "Then I'll leave you to it."

"Johanna." He cleared his throat and he turned back, then took his seat again. "You've done a good job with it."

This time both brows rose. "Thank you." She set her bag down again and checked her watch.

"If you've got some damn appointment, go on, then."

"No, actually, I was just marking the time. Since it's the first time in my life you've ever complimented me on anything, I want to remember when it happened."

"There's no need to be sarcastic."

"Maybe not." She crossed the room to sit but stayed on the edge of her chair. She'd never been comfortable in this house. "I'm glad you're doing so well. If you're interested, I can see that you get dupes of tomorrow's taping for the evening shows. We're giving away a trip for two to Puerto Vallarta during the speed round."

He only grunted at that. Johanna folded her hands and continued. "If a contestant reaches the winner's circle and can answer all of the questions himself, without deferring to his partner, he'll win a car. We're using a sedan this week. Four-door."

"I'm not interested in the prizes."

"I thought not, but you might prefer a different angle or see a flaw when you preview. I'm sure you know that you can accomplish as much here as most men can in an office."

"I won't be sitting here forever."

"There's no question of that." No, he would be back, full steam, very soon. Maybe this was the time, the only time. "Before I go, I'd like to ask you something."

"If it has to do with the new pilot, I've already seen it and approved it."

"No, it's personal."

He sat, cradling his glass. He didn't mind giving up liquor half so much as doing without his cigars. Rather than answer, he simply nodded for her to go on.

"Why do you want to marry Toni DuMonde?"

As far as Carl was concerned, the question had come out of left field. No one questioned his motives or his reasons. "I'd say that was between Toni and myself. If you're uncomfortable with the age difference—"

"It would hardly matter to me if there was twice as much difference as there already is," Johanna said. "I'm just curious."

"I'm marrying her because I want to."

Johanna sat for a minute, studying him. Maybe it was just that simple with Carl. I want, I do. I covet, I take. "Do you plan to stay married to her?"

"As long as it suits both of us."

She smiled a little and nodded. That, at least, was the unvarnished truth. "Why did you marry my mother?"

If her first question had surprised him, this one left him speechless. Staring at Johanna, he saw the resemblance he'd always ignored. But there was more character in this face. More courage. "Why are you bringing this up now? You never asked about her before."

"Maybe I should have. We began to talk about her when you were in the hospital, but I suppose I wasn't ready. Now I have a decision of my own to make, and I can't do it until I understand a little better. Did you love her?"

"Of course. She was beautiful, fascinating. We were both building our careers. There wasn't a man who met Glenna in those days who didn't love her."

She didn't find reasons for love and fidelity in those answers. "But you're the only one who married her. And the only one who divorced her."

"The marriage was a mistake," he said, abruptly uncomfortable. "We both realized it before the first year was out. Not that we weren't attracted to each other. As I said, she was beautiful, very delicate. You favor her." His glass paused halfway to his lips when he saw her expression. Perhaps he'd never been a loving father, but he'd always been an astute man. "If you're concerned about her health, don't be. Glenna was always erratic. Drinking made her more so, but I've never seen any part of that in you. Believe me, I've watched for it."

"Have you?" Johanna murmured.

"You've never been one for extremes," he went on. "Apparently you inherited enough from me to offset the rest."

"Did I?" This time her voice was firm and her eyes level. "I've always wondered what, if anything, I inherited from you."

His look was so blank that she couldn't believe he feigned it. "You're a producer, aren't you? And a good one. That should say something. The Pattersons have always been strong, practical people. Ambitious. I'd say, now that I think of it, that you take after my grandmother. She was strong minded, never one to sit around and let the world go by. Got the hair from her, too," he decided, looking thoroughly at his daughter for the first time in years.

A little dazed, Johanna reached up to touch her hair. "*Your* grandmother?"

"Didn't get it from your mother," he said with a sour laugh. "Got hers from her hairdresser. That was one of her most prized secrets. Hers was brown, mousy brown. God knows you didn't get your drive from her. That's the Patterson in you." He didn't say it with pride, just stated it as fact.

So this was her father after all. Johanna sat, waiting for a flood of feeling. When none came, she sighed. Nothing had really changed. Then her lips curved. Then again, maybe everything had.

"I'd like to hear about her sometime. Your grandmother." She rose, taking a look at her watch in earnest. "I really have to go. I'm going to be out of town. Everything should run smoothly enough without me for a few days."

"Out of town? When?"

"Tonight."

Johanna caught the last plane out. She'd had just enough time before final boarding to call Bethany and give her quick and not completely coherent instructions about the next day's business and the care and feeding of her cat. Bethany had been awakened out of a sound sleep, but she could be depended on.

Strapped in, Johanna watched L.A., and the resolutions she'd lived with all of her life, slip away. She'd taken a step, the largest one of her life, without even being sure she would land on solid ground.

Somewhere over Nevada she dozed, then woke over New Mexico in a kind of blind panic. What in God's name was she doing, traveling thousands of miles without so much as a toothbrush? It wasn't like her not to plan or make lists. They were taping the next day. Who would handle the details, check the staff? Who would deal with John Jay?

Someone else, she told herself. For once it would just have to be someone else.

She traveled from one coast to the other, sleeping in fits and starts and wondering if she'd lost her mind. In Houston she nearly lost her nerve, as well. But she changed planes and strapped in a second time, determined to see it through.

Perhaps she wasn't being smart or responsible, but everyone was entitled to do something on impulse once. Even if they lived to regret it.

Almost certain she would, she arrived in Baltimore just after dawn. The terminal was deserted except for a few napping passengers waiting for connections. The air was cool in Maryland, and she was grateful for her suit jacket. The same jacket, Johanna remembered, that she'd put on that morning when she'd still been sane. The sky, full of pewter clouds, promised rain as she climbed into a cab and gave the driver the name of Sam's hotel.

This was it, she told herself. It helped a little to close her eyes and ignore the unfamiliar landscape. If she didn't watch it, she wouldn't think too much about being on the other side of the country. In L.A. people were rolling over in bed, snuggling into pillows with morning still hours away. Here they were waking up, preparing to face the day.

So was she.

She paid off the driver and tried not to think. The rain began as she walked into the lobby.

Suite 621. At least she knew the number, so she'd be spared the embarrassment of going to the desk and convincing the clerk she wasn't a fan. Clutching the strap of her bag, she rode to the sixth floor. It was easy enough to step from the elevator. She even managed to walk down the hall to his door.

Then she stared at it.

What if he didn't want her there? What if he wasn't alone? After all, she had no claim on him, had made no promises. She'd refused to accept, even to listen to, his promises. He was free to . . . to do whatever he wanted, with whomever he wanted.

Certain she couldn't go through with it, she turned away and took two steps back from the door.

It was absurd, she told herself. She'd just spent hours in a plane, traveled thousands of miles, and now she couldn't even get up the nerve to knock on a door.

With her shoulders straight and her chin up, she knocked. When her stomach rolled, she reached in her pocket automatically for her antacids. Her fingers closed over the small velvet box. She drummed up her courage and knocked again.

He woke swearing. They'd worked until after two, and he'd barely had the energy to strip before tumbling into bed. Now the damn assistant director was banging on the door. Any idiot knew they couldn't film any of the scheduled outside shots in the rain.

Groggy and full of the desire for vengeance, Sam dragged the top sheet from the bed and wrapped it around him. He tripped over the hem, cursed again, then yanked open the door.

"Goddamn it—" His mouth dried up. He had to be dreaming. Johanna was a continent away, snuggled under the covers. Then he saw her lips curve before she began to stumble out an apology.

"I'm sorry I woke you. I should have . . . waited. Called." *Stayed away*, she thought desperately.

Then she didn't think at all, because he was dragging her inside. The door slammed and she was pressed back against it, her mouth captive.

"Don't say a word," he ordered when she sucked in her breath. "Not a word. Not yet."

It would have been impossible to speak. Even as he pulled her through the sitting room, he was peeling off her jacket, fighting the buttons on her blouse. With a throaty laugh, she tugged at the sheet. It was left behind in a stream of white as they worked their way to the bedroom.

Her skirt slid down to her hips, and he lifted her out of it. While his hands played over her, she stepped out of one shoe. They were nearly at the bedroom door before she managed to rid herself of the other.

He wasn't even awake. Sam clung to the drowsy fingers of sleep as they fell onto the bed.

She was here. Dream or reality, she was here. Her skin was just as soft under his hands, just as fragrant. Her lips as they parted for his had the same unique flavor he'd craved since he'd tasted them last. At her sigh, as her arms locked around him, he heard everything he needed to hear.

Delighted with each other, they rolled over the already rumpled bed as the rain grew heavy and streaked the windows.

She'd been right to come. Whatever had happened before, whatever happened after, she'd been right to take this moment. And to give this time to him. There would be no questions, no need for explanations or excuses, just gladness that was racing harder and faster toward dazzling pleasure.

In tune, body and mind, they came together, taking that pleasure to its pinnacle.

The thunder started as he gathered her against him again. Or perhaps it had been there all along but they hadn't heard it. Now, as the storm rattled over the city, they were together and alone and in love. Sometimes that really was all that mattered.

She kept her hand on his heart and her head on his shoulder as they floated down to solid ground. The gloom kept the room dim, but for Johanna there had never been a more beautiful morning.

"Were you just passing through?" Sam murmured.

She spread her fingers over his chest, watching the movement. "I had urgent and unexpected business on the East Coast."

"I see." He hoped he did, but he could afford to wait. "You on a contestant search?"

"Not exactly." The nerves began leaking back. "I take it you don't have an early call today."

"If the rain keeps up, please God, I won't have one at all." Slowly, like a man who had all the time in the world, he stretched. "We were scheduled to shoot down at the Inner Harbor. Terrific place. Best crab I've ever eaten." He was already imagining showing it to her himself. "Once that's wrapped, we'll be finished here."

A pout, something she never allowed herself, formed on her lips. "You've run a little over your three weeks."

He certainly hoped it was annoyance he detected in her voice. "A little."

"I guess you've been too busy to call and let me know how things were going."

"No."

"No?" She propped herself on her elbow to frown at him.

"No, I haven't been too busy to call. I didn't call."

"Oh, I see." She started to push herself up and found herself flat on her back again with Sam leaning over her.

"I hope you don't think you're getting out of this room."

"I told you I have business."

"So you did. Is it a coincidence that you have business in Baltimore and just happen to be staying at the same hotel—apparently in my room?"

"I'm not staying."

"Guess again." He nipped her gently on the jaw. "Why did you come, Johanna?"

"I'd rather not discuss it. I'd like my clothes," she said stiffly.

"Sure. Let me get them for you." He strolled out, leaving Johanna with the dubious cover of a pillow. She started to rise when he came back in with her suit bundled in his arms. Then she could only gape, openmouthed, as he opened the window and tossed them out.

"What in the hell are you doing?" She forgot the pillow as she leaped up and ran to the window. "You threw out my clothes." Dumbfounded, she could only stare at him. "You threw them out the window."

"Sure looks that way."

"Are you out of your mind? I flew out here with the shirt on my back, and now it's six floors down and soaked. I don't have anything to wear out of here but my shoes."

"I was counting on that. Seemed like the best way to guarantee your staying put."

"You *are* out of your mind." She started to crane out of the window, remembered she was naked, then dropped on the bed. "What am I supposed to do now?"

"Borrow another of my shirts, I guess. Help yourself." He gestured toward the closet. "You might toss me a pair of jeans while you're at it. It's hard for me to talk to you reasonably when we're not wearing anything but smiles."

"I'm not smiling," she told him between her teeth as she heaved jeans in his direction. "That was one of my best suits, and I—" Her fingers froze on the buttons of the shirt she'd pulled on. "Oh, God. Oh, my God, in the jacket. I had it in the jacket." With the shirt still half buttoned she jumped for the door. Sam was just quick enough to slam it closed before she ran out.

"I don't think you're dressed for a stroll, Johanna. Not that you don't look terrific. In fact, you look so terrific I think I'd like you to give me my shirt back."

"Will you stop being an idiot?" She tried to shove him aside but met with solid resistance. "You threw it out the window. I can't believe what a complete fool you are. You threw my ring out the window."

"Whose ring?"

"My ring, the one you gave me. Oh, for God's sake." She ducked under his arm to run to the window again. "Someone's going to take it."

"Your suit?"

"No, I don't care about the suit. The hell with the suit. I want my ring."

"All right. Here." Sam drew it off his pinky and offered it. "The box must have dropped out of your pocket when—when I said hello." Johanna had given a cry of relief and grabbed for it before she realized she'd been taken.

"Damn it, Sam, you had it all the time and you let me think it was gone."

"It was nice to know it was important to you." He held it between them. "Are you going to let me put it on you?"

"You can take it and—"

"I'm open to suggestions." Then he smiled at her in a way she found completely unfair. Even her temper failed her.

"I'd like to sit down a minute." She did, sinking into the bed. The relief was gone, and the anger. She'd come for a purpose. and it was time to see it through. "I came to see you."

"No? Really?"

"Don't make fun of me."

"All right." He sat beside her, draping an arm over her shoulders. "Then I guess I can tell you that if you hadn't come, or called within the next twenty-four hours, I was heading back, movie or no movie."

"You didn't call me."

"No, I didn't, because I think we both knew you had to make the next move. And I hope you suffered as much as I did." He pressed his lips to her hair. "So what's it going to be?"

"I want to tell you that I spoke with my father last night."

She tilted her head so that she could look at him. "He is my father."

Gently he brushed her hair back from her face. "Is everything all right?"

"It's not like a story where everything turns out beautifully at the end, but it's all right. I don't suppose we'll ever be close, and I can accept that now. I'm not like him, nor like my mother, either. It's taken me all this time to figure out that that's okay. I'm okay."

He kissed her hair again, enjoying the fragrance as much as the familiarity. "I could have told you that, if you'd listened."

"I can listen now, now that I've told myself." With a long breath, she took his hands in hers. "I need to ask you something, Sam. You could almost say it was the championship question."

"I work best under pressure."

But her eyes didn't smile. "Why do you want to marry me?"

"That's it?" His brows rose, and then he was laughing and holding her close. "I thought you were going to ask me a tough one. I want to marry you because I love you and I need you in my life. It changed when you walked into it."

"And tomorrow?"

"A two-part question," he murmured. "I could promise you anything." He drew her away to kiss her cheek, then her brow, then her lips. "I wish there were guarantees, but there aren't. I can only tell you that when I think about tomorrow, when I think about ten years from tomorrow, I think about you. I think about us."

He couldn't have said it better, she thought as she touched his face. No, there weren't any guarantees, but they had a chance. A good one.

"Can I ask you one more thing?"

"As long as I'm going to get an answer eventually."

"Do you believe in Santa Claus?"

What made it perfect, even more than perfect, was that he didn't even hesitate. "Sure. Doesn't everyone?"

Now she smiled, completely. "I love you, Sam."

"That's the answer I wanted."

"Looks like you win." She held out her hand so that he could slip the ring on her finger. It felt as though it belonged, and so did she. "Looks like we both do."

From #1 *New York Times* bestselling author
NORA ROBERTS
comes a suspenseful new novel "of nerve-jangling,
nail-biting suspense" (*Booklist*).

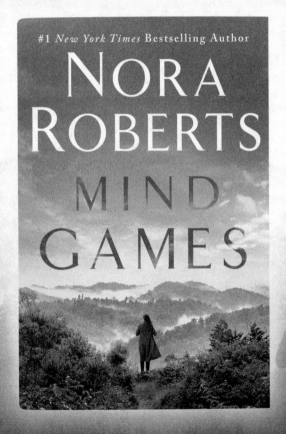

#1 *New York Times* Bestselling Author

NORA ROBERTS

MIND GAMES

She can read minds. So can the man who killed her parents.
Who controls the gift? Who controls the game?